THE MIGHT

THE RAVEN RINGS   SIRI PETTERSEN

THE MIGHT

Translated by Siân Mackie
and Paul Russell Garrett

Arctis

This is a work of fiction. Names, characters, places, and incidents
are from the author's imagination or are used fictitiously.

This translation has been published with the financial support of
NORLA, Norwegian Literature Abroad

W1-Media, Inc.
Arctis Books USA
Stamford, CT, USA

1 3 5 7 9 8 6 4 2

The Library of Congress Control Number:
2021944679

ISBN 978-1-64690-803-5
eBook ISBN 978-1-64690-602-4

Translation by Siân Mackie and Paul Russell Garrett
Jacket design by Siri Pettersen

Printed in Germany, European Union

To all those writing their first novels.

And to you. The one who has suffered loss. The one with so many scars that you feel ill when others say you're lucky. The one who has been broken into far too many pieces to believe you'll ever be whole again. The one who thinks you'll never rise again. This is your book.

BACK FROM SLOKNA

Rime bounded up the slope, confident that no one could see him in the dark. He reached the crest of the hill, pressed himself up against a crag, and looked out across the countryside. Where he should have seen a deserted landscape, there was instead a vast camp, with tents arranged in tidy rows. In patterns that were only found where discipline was the order of the day. Where someone was in charge.

An army.

It was too dark to see how far it stretched. A couple of thousand men, maybe, judging by the torches. He could see tracks in the snow—a black web connecting the tents. Men gathered around a fire below him. They moved with a spring in their step and laughed boisterously. Rime recognized the atmosphere. First or second night, if he were to guess. It wouldn't be long before they'd be hunched over in silence. Those who hadn't frozen to death or fallen ill.

The banners hung limply, but he knew they bore the sign of the Seer. Mannfalla's army, gathered outside the city. Why? What were they waiting for? What orders had they been given, and by whom?

She was right.

Damayanti had told him he'd find them here. She'd also told him it had to do with him. And with Ravnhov. But with Urd gone, she was no long privy to Council matters. The dancer's guesses were no better than his own.

It could be an exercise, of course. Troop movements. Or unrest in the wake of the war . . .

Tenuous explanations like those did little to settle the unease gnawing at his insides. A feeling that nothing was the way it should be.

Maybe it was the raven rings. Was it at all possible to move between worlds without the ground slipping out from under you? Some instability was to be expected.

But this was more than just a feeling. It was a certainty that stopped him from going straight home. He'd barely been gone twenty days, and in that time, someone had dragged the soldiers out of bed again. The watch on the city walls had been reinforced, and several of the guardsmen had been swapped out for men he didn't recognize.

Something was wrong.

He had to talk to Jarladin.

Rime ran back down toward the city. Packed snow creaked under his feet. He neared the city wall and proceeded with more caution, crouching down behind a cluster of junipers. Four guardsmen patrolled above the gate. Otherwise, long stretches of the stone wall, a gray-speckled serpent in the darkness, remained unguarded. He found his way back to where he'd climbed over. A part of the wall where he couldn't be seen from the gates.

Rime removed his gloves and shook the snow off them before stuffing them in the pocket of his bag. Then he bound the Might and started to climb. The rough stones gave him just enough purchase to reach the top of the wall. He pulled himself over the edge, crossed to the other side, and lowered himself onto the roof of a building. A tile came loose and skittered down toward the gutter. He threw himself after it, catching it just before it went over.

With the roof tile safely in hand, he sat and listened. A door slammed in the distance. There was a rustling in the alley below. A rat with its teeth sunk into a dead pigeon, trying to drag it across frozen leaves.

Rime wedged the tile back into place and continued across the rooftops toward the wall that separated Eisvaldr from the rest of Mannfalla. The buildings were close enough together that he could make it all the way there before he had to return to street level.

The wall itself wasn't much of an obstacle. People had always passed freely between Mannfalla and Eisvaldr. Even so, the watch had been increased here as well. Guardsmen flanked all the archways. A sign clearer than any road marking. Fear had taken over.

Rime slipped into an alley behind an inn. Singing reached him through an open window. Half-drunken verses, but even the notes were cleaner on this side of the city. He took off his bag and strapped his swords to the middle of it, so they wouldn't stick up over his shoulders like an open declaration of war. He pulled his hood all the way down and crossed the square. The guardsmen gave him a cursory glance but let him enter Eisvaldr unchallenged.

His city. The Council's city. The Seer's city.

The Seer he had killed.

The memories flooded back. Naiell, hissing in the corner like a cat. The resistance Rime's sword had met when it sliced through his body. The spatters of blood across Hirka's bare feet. The look in her eyes. Brimming with grief. With betrayal.

I am what I am.

Rime glanced up at the stone circle, where it stood feigning innocence, like the tip of an iceberg. The stones reached all the way down to a cave below Mannfalla. A cave he'd just come from, unbeknownst to anyone.

Here on the surface, the stones were just pale monoliths against the dark sky, at the top of the steps where the Rite Hall had once stood. Where he himself had stood. In the middle of the circle,

9

surrounded by everyone in the city. With Svarteld bleeding out on the ground in front of him. And for what?

Rime lowered his head and kept walking. He'd wasted enough time on loss and regret. More than he cared to think about. Now it was time to find out what had happened while he'd been gone.

Jarladin's house was at the top of the hill, one of many in a well-kept row of homes belonging to Council families. Rime slipped past some bare fruit trees, keeping to the paths to avoid leaving tracks in the snow. He had to remain unseen, at least until he knew for certain what was happening. He scaled the stone wall at the back of the house. It was late, but he could see light flickering in a window on the second floor.

It was a magnificent house in the Andrakar style, complete with columns and carvings in dark wood. Climbing it would be child's play.

Rime pulled himself up onto a pitched roof and crept along a ledge to the window. He pressed his hand against the glass, melting the frost so he could see inside.

Jarladin was alone in the room, seated on an upholstered stool, staring into the fireplace as though waiting for the flames to die out for the evening. He was turning an empty glass in his hands. His broad shoulders were hunched. Rime was painfully aware that he was part of what was weighing on the councillor. He'd disappeared. Without warning or explanation.

He fought off the urge to climb down again. To stay disappeared. A black shadow in the winter's night. When had he ever belonged inside in the warmth?

Do what has to be done.

Rime glanced back to make sure he was alone. Then he tapped the window three times. Jarladin gave a start. Dropped the glass on the floor, though it didn't break. He stared at the window. Then approached, squinting, with his shoulders hunched up by his ears.

Then came the recognition. Wide-eyed disbelief. He started to fumble with the hasps.

Rime shifted over so he was on the right side. Jarladin opened the window and grabbed Rime as if he were about to fall. Pulled him inside. Drew him close. Locked him in a bear hug. Drowning him in warmth.

The councillor pushed him back again, holding him at arm's length as he looked him up and down. He cradled Rime's head in his hand. Grabbed him by the hair, as if he was going to pull it. His eyes were shining. Rime braced himself, fully aware that the warmth would be short-lived. The change was already visible on Jarladin's face. Rueful joy gave way to confusion.

"Where have you been?" he murmured.

Rime pulled away without answering, going to shut the window.

"Where have you been?!" Jarladin's voice cracked, as if anticipating the pain to come.

Rime glanced at a chair by the fire. Wished he could sink into it. Rest. Slip into dreamless sleep. Instead, he had to answer for what he'd done. Try to explain the inexplicable.

"You wouldn't believe me if I told you," he said.

"Where have you been, Rime An-Elderin?" Smoldering anger now. A silent threat hanging between them. He needed an explanation, and it needed to be good. Jarladin had probably thought he was dead, but his reaction revealed a deeper desperation.

Rime forced himself to ask. "What's happened?"

"What's happened?" Jarladin repeated the words as if they were the epitome of stupidity. "What's happened?! You killed your own master in a duel, then disappeared! That's what happened! All of Mannfalla was there, and you haven't been seen since. I thought Slokna had taken you, Rime! That Darkdaggar had finally killed you. I thought . . ."

Rime looked away, trying to avoid Jarladin's gaze. But it was no use because the councillor was staring at him from the wall. Him and the rest of his family, framed in gold. No matter where Rime looked, there were eyes on him. He was a cold stranger in a warm room. A room that reminded him of Ravnhov, with a stone fireplace and wooden rafters. Cozy, but not for the likes of him.

"And the others? What did they think?"

Jarladin flung his arms out in exasperation. "What do you think they thought? The theories are getting wilder and wilder. Kolkagga killed you to avenge Svarteld, Ravnhov burned you alive, you drowned yourself in the Ora, or even better: the Council finished you off themselves. That was a popular one in the taverns, as if we didn't have enough problems! Rime An-Elderin vanishes following accusation of assassination and resulting duel. Your absence has poisoned us. What did you expect?! You were the Ravenbearer!"

Jarladin grabbed another glass from a tray on the table. He went to fill it, but the bottle was empty. Not a single drop came out. His knuckles grew white around the neck of the bottle.

"The dogs went for each other's throats. Each family grew suspicious of all the others, naturally. The corridors reek of past injustice. So now they're forming alliances. Hiring guardsmen. Building up their private forces, thinking they're doing it in secret, but any idiot can see that money is pouring out of Mannfalla. Out into the regions. All of Ym can see that the Council is falling apart. Before long we'll see kingdoms pitted against kingdoms. That's what happened, boy! Thanks for asking!"

Rime sat down on the stool. Dragged a hand over his face.

So that was why there were soldiers waiting outside the city gate. They were moving out into the regions. As gifts. To build alliances. Buy loyalty . . .

A bad sign, but nothing that couldn't be fixed. There was still hope. Still empty seats on the Council. Urd's. Darkdaggar's. Surely those could be used to bring stability.

12

"Has anyone laid claim to Darkdaggar's seat?"

Jarladin sputtered out a laugh. The truth cut like a scar across his face.

Rime got up, feeling a chill seep into his skin. "He still has it?"

The question hung in the air unanswered. Rime raised his voice. "He tried to have me killed, and he's still on the Council?"

"You weren't here!" Jarladin seethed. "You weren't here to sentence him. Darkdaggar claimed his confession was made under duress. He said you entered his family home. Uninvited. Threatened him. He had nothing to lose, Rime. Nothing. So he struck all the usual chords. Blamed Ravnhov. After all, that's where the assassination was attempted. And the Council believed him. Acted as if they believed him. Because they *wanted* to believe! Because they needed him. And because as far as they're concerned, you've been a walking disaster ever since you became Ravenbearer. If they'd held out any hope of success, most of the councillors would have done away with you personally. So yes, Darkdaggar still has his seat. Had you only let the assassin live, we'd have a witness, if nothing else."

Rime slumped back against the wall and shut his eyes. Laughed bitterly. "You sound like her. Live and let live, right? Do you really think Darkdaggar would have let him testify? The man was dead the moment he accepted the job!"

Anger is costly. Focus on what you can change.

For a moment he thought they were Svarteld's words, but it was something Ilume had said. His grandmother. A whisper from Slokna. A pointed reminder of his failure to master politics.

He looked at Jarladin. The bearded ox. The fire cast a red glow across half his face. The other half lay in shadow, as if he had one foot in Slokna.

"I'm here now," Rime said. "The damage can be undone. There are plenty of options. We could—"

"Rime . . . The Council had *one* wish, and that was to be rid of

13

you. You took care of that all on your own. It's over. They'll never take you back. Eir bears the staff again. I thought the augurs and the people would protest, but not so much as a stone has been thrown. They've heard that you promised a seat to Ravnhov. They've heard that the chieftain killed you for failing to honor your promise. Darkdaggar has done a great job of tarnishing your reputation. You lost your mind. You killed an innocent boy in Reikavik."

The words cut deep, opening a well of painful memories. The village by the river. They'd thought it was nábyrn. Deadborn. But all they'd found was a wounded bear in a cellar. The child . . . His frail body, resting against the wall. Red hair. Dead eyes. He remembered the man who'd killed the boy. Kneeling before him. And he remembered the taste of his own rage. Still he'd hesitated. Svarteld had had to finish what he had started. Svarteld, who had sacrificed his own life to teach him to finish what he started.

Rime took hold of Jarladin's arm. "You know what happened, Jarladin! I've never . . . I would never . . ."

Rime met his gaze and understood.

It didn't matter whether he'd killed the boy. Svarteld had been the only one in the house with him, and he wasn't around to testify anymore, either.

Rime sank back down onto the stool. He'd forgotten his words to Hirka, words spoken what seemed like an eternity ago. That unless it was useful to them, the Council had no interest in the truth.

Jarladin came over to him. Towered over him like the ox he was.

"So tell me, Rime . . . Where have you been?"

Rime felt leaden. Dragged down into a mire of death. Of injustice. His thoughts were murky. As if he'd been drinking. As if nothing was real anymore.

Somewhere deep down, he knew he'd accomplished something. Something important, something worth all of this. It would sound like madness, but it was a story that had to be told.

"I followed her," he started. "To the human world. I found dead-born brothers as old as the Might itself. Nábyrn who still remember the war. One of them is her father. She's half blindling, Jarladin. Half menskr, half deadborn. Daughter of an exiled warlord. And I found *him*. The Seer . . ."

Jarladin rubbed his chin. A telling gesture. Rime knew what he was thinking. That the Council was right. That Rime An-Elderin, grandson of Ilume, had lost his mind. Tipped over the edge. Gone mad.

Rime looked up at him. "He was real, Jarladin. The Seer was real."

Jarladin folded his arms across his chest. "So what did you do when you met him?"

Rime felt his body go numb. "I killed him."

"You found the Seer, and you killed him?"

Rime nodded. Stared into the fireplace. The flames had gone out. Red embers danced across the charred wood. He should feel something more than just emptiness.

"So you conquered your demon. You followed her to Seer-knows-where, and now you come back here thinking the world stood still. That your actions didn't have consequences. As if the rest of us don't have our own demons."

Rime stood up. "You think I'm imagining—"

Jarladin jabbed a finger at him. "I did everything in my power to protect you! EVERYTHING! You had *one* friend at the table, and you vanished! Without so much as a word! I defended you. I . . ." He stopped himself. Cocked his head. Stared with growing disbelief. His eyes searching for something Rime knew they wouldn't find. His tail.

Explanations were useless now. A chasm had opened up between them. The sides were too steep, and he wouldn't be able to surmount them. Not tonight.

DREYSÍL

From darkness to light.

Blinding white. Snow.

Flurries of white whipped past her. Sideways. Or was she falling?

Hirka leaned against the rock wall. Stone. Snow. She was through.

She fought back the nausea. Took a deep breath. It tore at her lungs. Cold. So cold. Something creaked.

She looked down at the metal box in her hands. Frost was spreading across its surface, forming roses around her fingers. She tucked the box under her arm and pulled her sleeves down over her hands.

Where am I?

The dizziness abated and she straightened up. What she'd thought was a rock wall was actually one of the stones in the ring she had just come through. The sheer size of it had been misleading. The stones towered over her. Reaching up toward . . . a ceiling?

Using her hand to shield her eyes from the light, Hirka peered up at the broken ceiling. Sharp sections jutted toward the clouds. She was in a hall. Or the ruins of what had once been a hall. Bigger than anything she'd ever seen before. Ice had forced its way inside and hung from archways on multiple levels. The wind blew through big gaps in the walls. And she was up to her knees in snow. Inside and outside at the same time.

A movement drew her eye. A man. He was running toward her. She could hear the sound of his shoes breaking through the frozen crust of the snow. Someone shouted after him. A voice that cut through the wind.

"Keskolail!"

The man kept running and didn't look back. He was close now. White eyes wild. A deadborn. Hirka dropped the box and groped for the knife on her hip, but it wasn't there. Fear gripped her.

Your boot! It's in your boot!

She wouldn't be able to draw it in time. But no sooner had the thought crossed her mind than she realized that the man hadn't even seen her. His eyes were locked on some point behind her. Between the stones. That was where he was headed.

A bowstring sang. Hirka opened her mouth to warn him, but it was already too late. The arrow thudded into his back. He stiffened. His legs gave out and he dropped to his knees in front of her. She reached out to him, wanting to help, but her feet were stuck in the snow. She couldn't get free.

He stared at her, white eyes mesmerizing. The wildness was gone. Death was a certainty that seemed to astonish him. He raised his hand and clawed at a teardrop-shaped mark on his forehead. His lips pulled into a grimace, revealing his canines. Then he toppled forward and lay with his face buried in the snow. A black arrow, short and sturdy, had pierced his shirt and was sticking out of his back. It seemed absurd that something so small could fell such a creature.

Death. In a world she'd never seen before. A world she doubted any ymling or human had seen. And death was the first thing she had encountered. What had he done wrong?

And me? Have I done anything wrong?

Was she a target as well? Hirka finally managed to free herself from the snow and looked behind her. The stones were dead. It was too late to turn back.

Four figures were approaching now. Three of them stopped a short distance away. The fourth headed straight for her. A woman. Was she the one who had shouted?

She walked with the utmost self-assuredness. As if no one would ever be able to touch her. A cloak fluttered behind her, so weightless that it seemed to be more for decoration than warmth. Leather straps were pulled tight around her waist. Her boots came up to her knees. But her thighs and arms were bare.

Hirka shivered. She pulled her own cloak tighter. What had she expected? That they'd dress like Graal did in the human world? Or walk around naked, like the ones she'd seen in Ym? She didn't know. Didn't know what she'd expected.

She picked up the box she'd dropped in the snow.

The woman stopped in front of her, hands on hips. Her lips were black. Her hair, too. A mass of long braids, in stark contrast with her pale face.

Hirka took an involuntary step back and looked up into milky white deadborn eyes, as difficult to read as those of all the other blindlings she had encountered.

Umpiri. They're Umpiri, and you're one of them.

The woman cocked her head, leaning toward Hirka like she was about to sink her teeth into her neck. Hirka didn't dare move. The deadborn breathed in through her nose as if scenting her. It was distinctly animalistic. Hirka held her breath. Glanced at the dead man in the snow. She couldn't help but feel like she was about to suffer the same fate. Like she was at the mercy of a wild animal. Naiell had been animalistic as well, but not like this. Maybe both he and Graal had been influenced by their time among ymlings and humans.

She's a friend! Graal promised I'd be met by a friend.

The woman straightened up again. Hirka thought she saw pain flash across her features, but she must have imagined it. Pain seemed too foreign to this creature.

"So it's true . . ." the woman said in broken ymish.

Remembering that the blind could smell their own, Hirka could only assume that she was referring to her being half blindling, but she didn't ask for clarification. She had the overwhelming impression that she wasn't welcome.

"I am Skerri of the House of Modrasme."

"Hirka."

"Hirka? That's how you introduce yourself?" Her displeasure was unmistakable.

Hirka nodded.

"Not anymore. Now you are Hirka, daughter of Graal, son of Raun of the House of Modrasme. And you have much to learn." Skerri nodded at the box. "Is that . . . ?"

Hirka nodded again. Finally she saw the shadow of a smile on Skerri's face. A quirk of her black lips. Naiell's heart in a box. Was that what it took to please her? Hirka shuddered.

Skerri glanced at the other three. "Keskolail!"

Hirka recognized the word from moments before. One of the three men came toward them, and Hirka realized it was probably his name. Meaning he'd been the one who'd loosed the arrow at Skerri's command. Why?

Keskolail was a large man and wore considerably more clothing—a black jacket with a shaggy sheepskin slung around his shoulders. He was carrying a bow. His hair was gray as steel, but he couldn't have been more than forty years old. That said, he was Umpiri. He could have been thousands of years old, for all Hirka knew.

He had the same mark on his forehead as the dead man. A gray teardrop. He turned his head and Hirka saw that it wasn't drawn on. It went deeper than that. Like a dull gemstone. He crouched down and pulled the arrow out of the man's back. There was a sound like something breaking. Blood dripped from the tip and into the snow.

19

Hirka stared at him, but he paid her no heed, not so much as glancing at her or Skerri.

He wiped the tip of the arrow in a fistful of snow before shoving it into a sleeve hanging from his belt. Then he gripped the dead man by the neck and dragged him outside, through one of the holes in the wall.

Hirka couldn't shake the feeling of powerlessness. What had she gotten herself into? She looked at Skerri. Her skin was pale as the sky above, making the black all the more stark and threatening. Her hair. Her lips. The leather. She was black and white. Nothing in between. She was the only deadborn woman that Hirka had ever seen, and the most terrifying of them all. Hirka clung to the certainty that Graal needed her. He wouldn't have sent her to her death.

"He wasn't after you," Skerri said, her eyes following the macabre trail left by the dead man.

"What was he after?"

"The Might," she replied, as if it were obvious. She turned suddenly, her black braids whipping across her back, weighed down by beads at the ends. She walked toward the two others, who stood waiting.

Hirka looked back, but Ym was gone. All she'd seen of it was a dark cave beneath Mannfalla, where the stones plunged through from above. And Damayanti. The merciless dancer had sent her onward without so much as a glimpse of the world above. She hadn't seen the city. Hadn't visited Lindri. She had a promise to keep, and she belonged here now.

Where is here?

Hirka followed Skerri, more out of necessity than desire. "Where are we?"

"This is Nifel, the broken city. We're not staying here."

Hirka resisted the temptation to ask what had felled it. "But . . . the world? What do you call—"

"Dreysíl. The first land."

"Oh . . ." Hirka shifted her bag into a better position. Snow had been blown into the hall and formed drifts. The walls had collapsed at one end. Broken columns stuck up like bones out of the snow. The two men were waiting by one of them. Skerri signaled something to them and they exited the hall before Hirka even had a chance to say hello. All she had time to notice was that one of them was as lightly dressed as Skerri. Undaunted by the elements.

"Where are we going?"

"Ginnungad," Skerri replied without turning.

"Is it far?" Hirka could feel the cold gnawing its way into her bones. She looked around, hoping to spot a cart and horses, but all she could see was snow. "Don't you have horses?"

"For what?"

Hirka almost got stuck in the snow again.

"For riding." Maybe it was a language thing? Skerri's ymish did seem a little shaky. It was as if she were speaking it against her will. But she stopped. Turned to look at Hirka and bared her canines. "Do I look like I need to be carried?"

Hirka shook her head. "I didn't mean—"

"Four days. Ginnungad is four days away." Skerri looked Hirka up and down. From top to toe. The disappointment was clear, even in her blindling eyes. "Let's say six days," she sneered, before walking on.

REFUGE

Rime crept across the rooftop until he reached the edge. There he stopped. Listened. The creaking of the ice along the riverbank. Someone emptying a washtub out a window a couple of houses along. He waited for a moment. Had to be careful. Coming here could put Lindri's life in danger.

The teahouse had become something of a refuge. A safe haven in no-man's-land. Lindri's door was always open, and Rime had nowhere else to go. Not without rumors spreading through Mannfalla, and he couldn't let that happen. Not until he had a plan.

The wind had picked up. Rime rubbed his hands together, trying to force some life into his frozen fingers. After twenty-four hours in this cold, even the Might had given up keeping him warm.

He grabbed hold of the edge, rolled forward, and dropped down onto the platform at the rear of the teahouse that served as a jetty of sorts. There was a rocking chair and an ice-covered lantern by the wall. A creeper had climbed as far as the eaves but then withered in the wintry cold.

He could see a sliver of light in the gap between the door and the frame. Rime knocked. It was quiet for a long time, then the door opened a crack and an eye peered out at him.

"It's me," Rime whispered.

Lindri recoiled as if he'd been burned. The door creaked open. A candle fell from his hand and went out as it rolled across the platform. Rime stopped it with his foot. The tea merchant let out a gasp and made the sign of the Seer, backing away.

Rime seized him by the arm. "No, no, I'm not dead, Lindri! Do you hear me? I'm not dead."

The look of terror faded, and he bundled Rime inside. He poked his head out and looked around before shutting the door. Like he was expecting others or simply couldn't fathom how Rime had gotten there.

The back room was cramped. Full of boxes and burlap sacks. The air was thick with hay dust, triggering a sudden memory. Rime had stood here with Svarteld the night Kolkagga had rowed out to Reikavik. They'd argued about things that now seemed trivial. What was it he'd said?

You can't govern the world from Slokna, boy.

Lindri ushered him farther into the teahouse. The tables and benches appeared gray in the darkness, the gleam of the wood stolen by the night.

"Sit, sit," Lindri said, pushing him firmly but gently onto a bench by the hearth. The fire had gone out, but some of its warmth remained. Just enough for Rime to realize how cold he was.

Lindri prodded the charred wood with the poker.

"Leave it, Lindri. No fire. Nobody can know I'm here."

Lindri rummaged through the wood pile. He tore off a strip of wood and started to build up the fire like he hadn't heard a word. Rime wanted to explain. Wanted to warn him that having him there was not without danger, but he knew Lindri wouldn't listen. The wrinkly old tea merchant had taken Hirka in without a thought for his own safety. Even after finding out she was menskr. Empty tables were the price he'd paid.

He'd taken Rime in before, too. When he was still the Raven-bearer. When Damayanti had given him the beak. And now, as a disgraced son of the Council. Presumed dead.

The fire crackled to life, casting a warm glow over Lindri as he crouched in front of the flames. Rime suddenly noticed he was in his nightshirt. And a cardigan that was fraying at the wrists.

Lindri clambered to his feet with obvious discomfort. He sat down across from Rime. His eyes were crinkled with age, making them small and round. He rested his hand on Rime's, warmth burning through a layer of loneliness.

Rime swallowed. "So you don't believe them? What they're saying about me?"

"Tell me what happened first and then I'll tell you what I believe," Lindri answered with a mesmerizing calm.

Rime chuckled, and then the floodgates opened. Words started pouring out of him, though he knew none of it would make any sense. He couldn't stop. For the first time in his life, he felt like he was sharing something real. He told Lindri about his visit to the human world. About the brothers, Graal and Naiell. About their thousand-year rivalry. One exiled, the other the Seer himself. The Seer that Rime had killed.

The lie he had been fed his entire life no longer existed. Instead he'd uncovered the story of the blindling who had betrayed his own people and conquered all of Ym.

He told Lindri about Hirka, about her blood. That she was one of them. Those who wanted to break through the gateways and enter Ym in order to reclaim what they had lost long ago. And there was nothing Rime could do to stop them. Not anymore. Not now that he'd thrown away what little power he'd had.

Words and strength failed him. He knotted his hands together and rested his chin on them. He looked at Lindri, waiting for a reaction to everything he'd said. But none came. Lindri sat nodding to himself, even though Rime had stopped talking. His eyelids were so heavy that for a moment Rime thought he'd nodded off. But then he straightened up and slapped his thighs.

"So the world is going to end? Is that what you're saying?"

"That about sums it up," Rime replied.

"Well, then there's only one thing to be done." Lindri rose slowly to his feet. The wrinkles on his face cut deeper, betraying the pain in his bones.

"What's that?" Rime asked.

"Make tea."

Lindri went over to the counter and lit a burner under one of the black cast-iron pots. They were all lined up with their spouts facing the same direction.

"Make tea? That's your answer to the world ending?"

"Do you have a better suggestion?"

Rime stared at the table. Its surface was rough as driftwood. Covered in nicks and scratches.

No, he didn't have a better suggestion. The storm would come no matter what he did.

Lindri set the pot down in front of him. A rich scent rose up. It smelled suspiciously strong for tea. He sat back down and pushed a full cup toward Rime.

"So you killed the Seer? Her father's brother?"

"He would have killed *her*, the moment he got the chance."

Rime felt the outline of the shell in his pocket. The pendant he'd given her when she'd left Ym. Now it was his again. Returned to him by Graal. With no explanation. Was it his way of saying that he should forget about her? That she was half blindling, destined for an altogether different fate than Rime?

He hoped so, because the alternative was far worse. That Hirka had asked Graal to give it to him. That it had been what she wanted.

His chest constricted. He grabbed the cup and downed it in one. It was blessedly strong, burning all the way down.

He hadn't realized how much he wanted her until they'd met in the room with the pounding music. Packed full of menskr. Children

25

of Odin everywhere he looked. But he might as well have been alone with her because everything and everyone around them was forgotten.

He would have taken her then and there if he'd had the chance. The feeling was that powerful, that all-consuming.

That destructive.

He'd done crazy things because of her. Things that had not only destroyed him, but now threatened to destroy the Council. Ravnhov. Ym.

He'd taken the beak. Made himself a slave. Something he'd neglected to tell Jarladin and Lindri. Nobody could know how powerless he actually was. That he was at the mercy of Graal's whims.

Graal was more dangerous than Hirka realized. He would pit them against each other if he had to. They could only hope that Graal loved her, too. Rime had seen a father's pride in his eyes. But also an absolute willingness to step over bodies.

That's what she says about me.

"I know what you are and what you're not, Ravenbearer." Lindri refilled his cup. It was as if he'd read his mind.

"I'm not the Ravenbearer anymore, Lindri. As far as anyone knows, I'm dead."

"If I may, Rime An-Elderin . . . You've told me what happened, and now I'm going to tell you what I think. I grew up in this city, and I remember the day you were born. It wasn't that long ago."

"It was almost twenty years ago, Lindri."

Lindri smiled, his crow's feet reaching his temples. "The child everyone waited for. The child the Seer said would live. I remember thinking it wouldn't be much of a life for a boy. Growing up under so much pressure. They were selling amulets with your likeness that same day. Did you know that?"

Rime was all too aware. He worried at a chip in the teacup with his fingernail. There was something familiar about it. He must have drunk from the same cup before. He took another sip. The smell stung his nostrils.

"The way I see it, Rime, you've grown up in a cage. A cage the rest of the world envies, but a cage nonetheless. Everything was set for you to become one of them. But they didn't count on you growing strong enough to choose your own path. I don't agree with everything you've done, but there's no denying your iron will."

The wind howled outside. Lindri started rubbing his wrists, as if the sound had reminded him how cold it was. He continued talking.

"They've been saying all sorts about you. Personally, I thought you were lost to us. Especially after you came here with that painted woman. The dancer. But that was about more than a young man's lust, wasn't it? I've lived through three quarters of a century, Rime. Do you think I've never heard of blindcraft? She did something to you, that much I know. You don't need to say what. I assume it's what you needed to follow Hirka. And yes, you killed Svarteld. Your own master. But that was his choice, not yours. You were deceived. What man wouldn't have done the same in your shoes?"

Rime looked away. Lindri's understanding was harder to bear than any judgement would have been.

"Rime . . . You're a young man. I wish I could tell you that distinguishing right from wrong gets easier with age, but it's not like that. Quite the opposite. The older you get, the more you see. And I've seen too many of people's flaws and shortcomings to think making the right choice is easy."

Rime snorted. "That's not what *she* says . . ."

"Hirka didn't grow up in Eisvaldr. You did. You're a son of the Council. You were never taught the right thing to do. You were taught that as long as you were the one doing it, it's right. The families are the law. The law is the families. But still you're fighting an internal battle, and that makes you a good man, Rime. A strong man. Only strong men can withstand losing everything."

27

"And strong women," Rime answered. He felt his shoulders sag. He clinked his cup against Lindri's, spilling a few drops that soaked into the wood before he could wipe them up.

"Do you know why she's doing it, Lindri? She thinks she's stopping a war. She thinks she can talk them out of their bloodlust. That's what she's doing. She thinks she can convince blindlings of the merits of peace. Stupid girl. She could annoy the moss off a rock, and she's going to rile them up more than ever."

Lindri tried to hide a smile.

Rime drank the rest of the tea. "What?"

"She brings out the best and the worst in you, Rime."

It was true. But it didn't matter anymore. She didn't belong to him. Never would. She'd chosen another world. Another life. If they met again, it would be on the battlefield. And he couldn't sit idly by, waiting for that to happen. He had to act.

But first a little rest. Here. At the table.

"Darkdaggar controls the Council, Lindri. Controls the army."

"Yes, so you keep saying."

"But not Kolkagga. They're far more dangerous than Mannfalla's army. Only they can stand against the blind. He mustn't gain control over them, too, Lindri."

Rime tried to give voice to his thoughts, but they had slipped away from him and were hopelessly out of reach. Like Kolkagga. The black shadows who were out of Darkdaggar's reach. But how loyal were they to the Council now? Who had taken over from Svarteld? And how would they receive Rime? The man who had killed his own master? Their master.

"Am I still Kolkagga? What do they think of me now?"

"There's no way of knowing, Rime."

"I have to find out. I have no choice."

"You can find out tomorrow."

Rime felt a blanket over his back and realized he was falling asleep.

A PROBLEM

The snow was so heavy that Hirka couldn't see where she was putting her feet. The wind had gotten colder, chilling her to the core. She'd put on every single item of clothing she had. The shirt from Stefan, the spare jumper, and the raincoat from Father Brody pulled over the cloak from Jarladin. All from people she might never see again. Maybe she would never see anyone again.

So far everything seemed to suggest that she would be lost to the snow in this frozen wasteland. The blind would get tired of waiting for her and simply leave her behind, and a hundred years from now they would dig up a cadaver not unlike Graal's dead raven. Skin and bones in a shirt emblazoned with English words that wouldn't mean anything to anyone.

Hirka forced a smile. She was surrounded by deadborn, in the kind of weather people went missing in, and she had no idea where she was going. She'd have to keep her spirits up if she were to survive.

They slogged their way up a steep slope that seemed to merge with the sky. A bluish-white expanse that dazzled her if she looked at it for too long. So far she hadn't seen a single tree or any other people. Just ice and snow.

Hirka tensed her jaw to stop her teeth from chattering. Her cheeks were so cold that it felt like they might split open. Beads of sweat had frozen in her hair. She had to heave her feet up out of the snow with every step. The staff helped. A hollow piece of wood that didn't weigh much but could withstand a lot. They all had one. They'd told her it was to breathe through if they got caught in an avalanche, and that it also helped people find you. As far as she could tell, they weren't joking.

Hirka knew she'd have to stop soon. She could taste blood.

She squinted ahead. Skerri was walking at a relentless pace, leaving a trail that made it easier for everyone walking behind. Hirka hadn't seen her pull her cloak around herself once. It was a wonder she hadn't frozen to death.

She was carrying a leather tube on her back. It looked like a quiver, but it was too big for arrows. Hirka didn't hold out much hope for it being a blanket.

Every time Skerri looked around to check on Hirka, the beads in her black braids beat against the quiver like hail. The sound had started to take on new meaning. An accusation that pushed Hirka onward.

"So who's Modrasme?" Hirka shouted, hoping conversation would slow her down.

"The eldest of our house," Skerri replied. She glanced at Hirka. "Of your house," she added. She made it sound more threatening than reassuring.

"So the houses are named after the eld—"

"We'll talk once we've arrived."

Hirka bit her lip. Maybe one of the others would be more forthcoming. She looked over her shoulder. The three men were following her in single file. The one bringing up the rear was called Hungl. A guardsman type with dark hair and a goatee. Grid walked ahead of him. He wasn't wearing much either, and he was the only one Skerri had exchanged words with. They seemed to know each other well. Had his hair not been as fair as Skerri's was dark, Hirka might have thought they were siblings. That said, it was rare for Umpiri to have more than one child, and that seemed to be what had given Graal and Naiell the standing they'd had before the war.

The man with the steely gray hair and the sheepskin around his shoulders walked just behind Hirka. Keskolail. The man who had fired the arrow. Hirka wavered for a moment, but then exhaustion won out over fear and she stopped to wait.

Skerri grabbed her arm and pulled her onward.

"Don't talk to the fallen," she said.

"Who are—"

"We'll discuss his punishment when we reach the camp."

Camp . . .

The word alone was like the warmth from a fire. Hirka suddenly felt reinvigorated. She put her head down and trudged onward.

But why would he be punished? Hirka stole a glance at the killer behind her. At the teardrop in his forehead. None of the others had one. He still hadn't looked at her. It was as if she didn't exist to him. And clearly he wasn't supposed to exist to her either.

The slope became so steep that Hirka had to use her hands to aid her progress. She avoided looking at her fingers. They were bound to be blue. At least the snow wasn't as heavy up here.

"Don't you have roads?" Hirka asked.

Skerri looked at her over her shoulder. "Roads? You think you're ready to be seen?"

It didn't sound like she was expecting a response, so Hirka held her tongue.

The ground leveled out as they emerged onto a snow-covered plateau. Windswept birches crept along the ground. The first trees that Hirka had seen. A raven screeched. She couldn't see it, but she was so relieved that a lump formed in her throat. There was life here. Life other than the blind.

A group of pointed tents jutted up from the other side of the plateau. They were weighed down by snow on one side, but the canvas

31

still yielded to the wind. Hirka looked around, spotting at least three places that would have provided better cover. It was as if no one had given it any thought.

Any hope of a cart and a hot meal was quashed. She wouldn't be getting any of that here. Realizing she was falling behind again, she hurried after Skerri.

"Is this the camp?" she asked. "You sleep here? In the open?"

"Yes."

"But . . . What about predators?"

Skerri looked at her. A frown line cut down toward her nose. "What are you trying to say?"

"That maybe we should . . . What if we're attacked?"

Skerri bared her teeth. Hirka took a step back, almost falling. Umpiri didn't need to fear predators. They *were* predators.

"Are you saying we wouldn't survive an attack?"

Hirka shook her head. "No. No, not at all. I was thinking more about . . . well, me, I suppose . . ." She trailed off, shrinking under Skerri's gaze. She felt like a hair in a bowl of soup.

Hot soup . . .

Skerri started walking again. Hirka followed, making a mental note of things she now knew not to ask about. Horses. Carts were probably out, too. As was anything that might suggest Umpiri couldn't rely on their own two feet. Or that they were tired. Or that they had anything whatsoever to fear.

Two deadborn came toward them. Both women, but very different. One was dark-haired and wore a long robe, like an augur or one of the learned. The other was blond and wore leather and fur like a hunter. Or a warrior, if her fierce expression was anything to go by. They spoke to Skerri in a language that Hirka didn't understand. The language of the blind.

The language of Umpiri.

It was strange yet somehow familiar. The words resonated with

32

her. It was like smelling something for the first time since you were a child. New, but just as much a part of you.

The two women looked at Hirka, both dipping one of their knees in some kind of greeting. Hirka had a feeling she ought to do the same. No sooner had she done so than a hand gripped her neck. Skerri had a hold of her and was steering her toward a tent. She pushed Hirka past the animal pelt serving as a tent flap. Hirka stumbled inside. She waited for Skerri to follow, but she stayed outside, barking orders at the others.

That suited Hirka just fine. She looked around. There was barely room for two. The tent was held up by a pole in the middle. The ground was uneven but dry, even though it was made of cloth. It was probably layered. Or greased underneath. Two woollen blankets lay rolled up on an animal skin. There was nothing else. Not even an oil lamp or anything to drink from.

Hirka dropped her staff and sank to her knees. She was thirsty, hungry, and tired, but she didn't know which was most pressing.

Thirst.

She took off her bag and untied the waterskin from the outside. She'd tried to drink along the way, but breaks had been few and far between, and the water had been too cold. She fumbled with the cork. It was frozen fast and she didn't have the strength to get it out. Her fingers were completely numb.

Her eyes started to sting. She was dangerously close to tears. What was wrong with her? Would she cry on the first day, in a place she'd chosen to come to? She had to remember that she was doing this for peace. So the deadborn wouldn't lay waste to Ym. She had to focus on that. Peace. That and obtaining the knowledge she needed to free Rime from the beak.

She closed her eyes. He had a beak in his throat. A raven's beak. Graal had power over him, just like he'd had over Urd. And Urd had rotted . . .

Hirka tossed the waterskin aside. Feeling an annoying lump of snow under the floor, she started bashing it with her fists.

What had she expected? What kind of people had she thought she'd find here? A family? Had she really been that naïve? Was she still nothing more than a girl who longed to feel at home somewhere?

The tent flap was torn aside. Skerri came in. Hirka leaped to her feet. She jumped every time she saw Skerri's face. Black hair and black lips against pale skin. Hirka would have guessed she was around twenty-five winters had she not been Umpiri. Young, almost girlish. An unnerving combination of beauty and danger.

"Sit," she snapped. Hirka did as she was told.

Skerri sat across from her. Her corset of leather straps creaked as it yielded to her lithe body.

"Kuro," she said, nodding at the box tied to the top of Hirka's bag.

"Kuro?" Hirka hadn't expected to hear that name here. That was hers. Something she'd come up with when Naiell was still a raven.

"Heart," Skerri said impatiently. "It means heart. Let me see him."

Hirka would have smiled at that revelation, had she had the energy. She removed the box from her bag and held it in her lap. It was unassuming, considering its contents. A boring metal box, tarnished as a worn knife blade. Cold against her fingers. Before she'd passed through the gateways, she'd been worried that the ice inside might melt. If only she'd known . . .

Hirka undid the catches on the sides and lifted the lid. Naiell's heart lay buried in crushed ice. Pale as a clenched fist. Hirka imagined she could still smell him. Graal's brother. Her father's brother. In Ym, he had been the Seer. Here in Dreysíl, he was something else entirely. A criminal. The enemy of the people.

Skerri snatched the box. Closed her eyes and took a deep breath, as if the smell could sustain her. Her lips twisted into a sneer.

"Naiell . . ."

34

It was a whisper so thick with hatred that Hirka realized she must have been very close to him. They must have known each other. Hirka stared at her. "You were there . . ."

Skerri opened her eyes. Milky. Distant. Fixed on something far beyond the small tent. "I swore an oath when the war ended. When I realized he'd betrayed us. When I saw him shackle and humiliate his brother. I swore I'd tear his heart out with my own claws. For a thousand years I've waited to smell him again. A thousand years. And now here he is. What more remains than to take back what is ours?"

Hirka didn't reply. She feared even one wrong word would make Skerri go for her throat. Her black lips twitched. The deadborn woman was grappling with a history that Hirka hadn't been part of. Was that why she was so angry? Because Hirka had brought them his heart? Had Rime done what Skerri would have preferred to do herself?

The air was thick with Skerri's disdain. Hirka nudged the lid with her finger and it clicked shut, snapping Skerri out of her trance. She moistened her lips. The color didn't fade. Was it an inking? Had she dyed them black?

She set the box aside.

"We have a problem, Hirka." She shook her head and her braids whipped back and forth, as if she were an animal shaking itself dry.

"What sort of problem?"

"You."

Hirka wanted to protest, but she was too nervous. And begrudgingly curious as to what was wrong with her.

Skerri cocked her head. A birdlike movement that made Hirka think of Graal and Naiell. She ventured to ask a question.

"Skerri, are we family?"

Skerri blinked as if thrown off guard, but she recovered quickly. "We are family, but not by blood. We belong to the same house. You'll meet your blood relatives once we reach Ginnungad, and therein lies the problem. I need to send the raven now. I need to tell them you're here. That you've arrived. But what am I to say?"

"What do you mean?"

Skerri lifted her chin, looking down her nose at Hirka as if she were an idiot. "You're like them! Look at yourself! You have eyes like them. You have no claws. No teeth. You're slow. Weak. Pathetic, like them. You're more menskr than Umpiri. And this so-called language is nothing short of primitive."

Hirka's features stiffened. Shame came creeping, as if she had been thrown back in time. She was in Elveroa again. With Father, who had always tried to hide her because he knew what she was. With Ilume, who'd dismissed her whenever she'd come looking for Rime. She was the monster. The tailless child of Odin. Even here.

She was little again. And it annoyed her. Hirka gritted her teeth.

"Sorry if I'm not what you expected."

Skerri snorted. "Apologizing won't help. You need to learn our ways before you can be presented, and time isn't on our side. To be honest, I knew we'd have this problem as soon as I heard about you. Graal was somewhat . . . evasive."

"So you're the one who talks to him?"

"Me. Nobody else."

The pride in her voice didn't escape Hirka's notice. Graal meant something, and that was probably the only reason she was still alive. But that didn't mean she would suffer through a lecture about everything that was wrong with her. She'd done that far too many times before.

"Just tell me what needs to be done, Skerri."

Skerri studied her for a moment. Then she stood abruptly. "I'll tell them you've arrived. That's all. Then we'll see what can be done. Language is our most pressing concern. Our house cannot be defiled by your language. Oni will instruct you on the way."

"Oni?"

"A servant. She works for the house. She is learned and can teach you to speak properly. And how to behave." Skerri looked her up and down. "We'll do something about your clothes later."

Language, behavior, clothes . . . Hirka couldn't have cared less. What she really needed was someone who understood the Might.

"What about . . ." Hirka almost said *blindcraft* but then caught herself. "What about the Might? I need to talk to someone who can teach me about the beaks." She raised a hand to her throat to illustrate what she meant.

Skerri gave her an empty stare.

Hirka had to find a different approach. Something that would force Skerri to help. Force her to answer. In other words, she would have to hit her where it hurt. Her pride.

"Are you telling me you have no one learned in the Might?"

Skerri's eyes narrowed to white slits. "Of course we do! The best! We have mightslingers and seers, but no one you need concern yourself with. They are not your priority."

Seers? The blind had seers?

Of course they do. Where else would he have gotten the idea?

Hirka couldn't help but laugh. Naiell hadn't been able to abandon his own world entirely.

Skerri turned to leave. "This is your tent," she said. "Stay here. Oni will come and get you once I've sent the raven. Then you'll meet the others."

She swept the tent flap aside. Light streamed in and across the floor. She looked at Hirka again. "And one more thing: if you ever bend the knee to anyone below your house again, I'll have your kneecaps."

Skerri stormed out, braids whipping after her.

Hirka closed her eyes.

Don't ask about horses. Don't question camp locations. Don't bend your knees.

37

JUDGEMENT

Hirka had been desperate for clarity. For information. But it was starting to dawn on her that too much information was worse than none.

Oni meant *tongue* in umoni, which was their language. It was also what everyone called the woman who was to be her teacher, and Hirka could understand why. Oni never stopped talking. And unlike Skerri, she seemed to have no qualms about speaking ymish, but then, she was too young to have fought in the war. It made her more curious than Skerri, and probably less prejudiced.

She'd been studying the language for two years, at Skerri's request. *Request* was Oni's word, but Hirka suspected *order* would be more accurate. It was only now that her would-be teacher had discovered why it was necessary. It was a well-guarded secret that the stone circles weren't all dead.

Oni took a keen interest in everything Hirka chose to share from other worlds, and kept having to rein herself in to do what she was actually supposed to be doing: teaching Hirka the ways of the blind. And explaining where she belonged in the hierarchy, of course. That seemed to be the most important thing here.

Of all the blindlings Hirka had met, Oni scared her least. Maybe it was her dimples. Or her brown hair, which gave an impression of warmth. Her loose tunic looked comfortable, in no way designed to draw attention to her physique. And then there was the fact that she actually talked. That certainly helped, since none of the others did.

Hirka felt like she'd been trapped in the tent with the woman for over an hour. She still hadn't been formally introduced to the others. Also at Skerri's request, she assumed.

Oni held the flap aside so Hirka could see out the tent as they talked. Four of the others stood a short distance away. Only Skerri was missing. Oni pointed at Grid, who stood a little way off, poking snow out of his hollow staff. He wore a tight, fur-lined vest. His bare arms were strong and sinewy.

"Grid isn't even three hundred yet, but he's won many . . . What are they called? Tournaments. He trains with Skerri. They're good friends. Skerri and Grid are the only ones here who are Dreyri. That means they have—"

"Blood of the first . . ." Hirka remembered all too well.

"Yes, that's right. Dreyri, of the old bloodlines. Only Dreyri have named houses. The rest of us are ordinary folk. Umpiri. We work for the houses. Hungl and Tyla over there, they're both servants for the House of Modrasme."

Hirka looked at them. Hungl with his goatee. Tyla with her fair hair. She hadn't been at the stone circle, instead waiting here in the camp with Oni.

"They don't look like servants. More like warriors," Hirka said.

Oni hid a smile with her hand. "We say servants. The houses don't have warriors. Or guards. That wouldn't do. Instead they have servants. Because—"

"Because they don't need help protecting themselves."

Oni nodded enthusiastically. "Hungl speaks a bit of ymish, but not very well, and . . ." She looked at Hirka, chewing nervously on her lip. "You need to speak umǫni well before you can be presented to the leading house."

Hirka pretended not to hear her. The thought of being shown off made her sweat despite the cold. It was already abundantly clear that she wouldn't meet the expectations they had of her.

"Are they building a fire?" she asked hopefully.

"Yes, I know you get cold quicker than us. Dreyri handle it best. They get cold too, but—"

"They're more worried about pretending they don't?"

"You learn quickly."

"What about him?" Hirka nodded at the man with the teardrop in his forehead. Steel gray hair and a stony face. He was headed for the fire with a bundle of twisted branches.

"He is kwessar. One of the fallen. There were two of them, but I understand the other died today. That's why you always have two. So one can kill the other if necessary. But you should never have more than that."

Hirka kept watching him as he slung the wood on the fire.

"Why not?"

"Well," Oni replied. "If you bring more than two men who have nothing to lose, then you've only yourself to blame if something goes wrong, you see?"

Questions were burning on Hirka's tongue, but Oni wasn't letting her get a word in edgeways. "The fallen don't belong to the houses. They're outside. You can tell by the drop, and by the name. His name was Kolail, but since he's fallen he is called Keskolail. Kes is a prefix that derives from kwessar, which means—"

Skerri suddenly stood in the tent opening. "You're wasting time, Oni. Have you taught her how to introduce herself? About the leading houses?"

Oni scrambled to her feet. Skerri dismissed her and crouched down in front of the tent. Hirka forced herself to stay seated by the opening, even though it was tempting to crawl farther inside. Skerri looked at her.

"Hungl and Keskolail fought in the war. That means they've seen the likes of you before. They know what to expect. But we can't afford to have rumors spreading that you're weak. We need to show them who you are. And we need to do it now. I'm going to ask you a question, and the only thing you're going to say is 'the ravens.' Even you can manage that. Do you understand what I'm saying?"

Hirka didn't understand, but she nodded nonetheless.

Skerri got up and motioned for her to follow. Hirka crawled out of the tent. She considered turning back for her cloak, but she didn't want to risk it. She followed Skerri to the fire. Hungl and Tyla had made themselves mounds of snow to sit on as they watched the fire grow. Oni ran over and sat down, too. Grid remained standing, of course. Sitting was probably too shameful for Dreyri.

The fallen sat a little way off from the others, breaking ice off his sheepskin.

Skerri pointed at Hirka as she addressed the others in umǫni. Hirka felt a little nauseous. She didn't know what was happening, only that she had some role to play. Had she only known what that was . . .

When Skerri was finished, she turned to Hirka.

"Keskolail fired an arrow in your direction. What is your judgement, Hirka, daughter of Graal, son of Raun of the House of Modrasme?"

Hirka frowned. Judgement? Was she being asked to punish him? The man with the teardrop? It sounded like it. But not for killing a man, something Skerri had ordered him to do. It seemed he was accused of having fired in Hirka's direction. But she had never been in any danger. A man who could hit a target at that distance, in this weather . . . He would not have missed.

Then why?

Skerri had told her to respond by saying "the ravens." What did ravens have to do with this?

Suddenly she understood. Her stomach dropped like a stone.

41

You give the dead to the ravens.

The Council families in Ym let the ravens eat their dead. Another custom Naiell had taken with him? Meaning she was now being asked to sentence this man to death. To be fed to the ravens. For doing what he'd been ordered to?

The silence around the fire was palpable. Insistent. The flames reached out in the wind, as if trying to grab her.

Hirka was chilled to the core. She'd been told what to say, but the words refused to pass her lips. She stared at the man she was meant to sentence, but he didn't look up. At her or at anyone else. He knew what was happening, but still he sat fiddling with his sheepskin, as if it had nothing to do with him. Steely gray hair. Steely gaze. Was he steel through and through?

Hirka had to say something. They were looking at her. Waiting for her. She didn't know why, but clearly Skerri needed her confirmation to get what she wanted. Hirka cleared her throat.

"I've been told Umpiri don't kill Umpiri."

Hungl, who had been taking a sip from his waterskin, spat most of it out. Tyla gave him a look and he composed himself. Oni looked like she was about to bite through her bottom lip.

Skerri lowered her head like an angry bull. Hirka could see her braids quivering.

"You're new here and don't know our ways," she said through clenched teeth. "We can make allowances for that. He is not Umpiri. He is kwessar. One of the fallen. But since no one else here can sentence him, we'll give you until we reach Ginnungad to make a decision. Think on it."

Skerri walked past her and disappeared inside her tent. Grid looked stunned for a moment. Then he nodded at Hirka and followed Skerri.

Hirka stood by the fire, uncertain what to do next. Her eyes lingered on claws curled around knees. Sharp canines. She was surrounded by strangers. Strangers who had expected her to sentence someone to death. Their clothes suddenly seemed ludicrous. A distraction from what they really were.

Hirka took a couple of shuddery breaths, then clapped her hands together in a futile attempt to shake it all off. "So, what does a girl have to do to get something to eat around here?"

Hungl chuckled. Oni got up. "I'll fetch the cakes."

Hirka looked at Keskolail.

Kolail. His name is Kolail.

Hirka knew that she was never going to call him anything other than Kolail, now that she knew that was his real name.

He finally looked up at her. His face was impassive. Then he looked down again and continued chipping the ice off the sheepskin.

KOLAIL

The snow had let up, giving way to a cold and dispiriting fog. But Hirka was prepared. After a freezing, sleepless night, she had gotten up and made a start on her survival project. Normal socks. Then the thick woolly ones. Trousers tied outside her boots so they wouldn't get stuck in the snow.

She had cut some strips off the woollen blanket and wound them around her hands and fingers. She'd also melted snow in her water-skin, but only a few drops remained, and they had frozen. Thinking about it only made her thirstier. And the tent she now carried atop her bag meant she was heavier than the day before.

But on she trudged, conscious that Tyla and Kolail were right behind her. She squinted up at the others. Shadows in the fog, making their way along the path ahead. Nobody seemed to have any plans to stop. Especially not Skerri and Grid. Always in front. Always first.

But Hirka had been the first to wake up. That had given her more time, and a sense of finally having one up on them. It wasn't much to brag about, but in that moment she didn't need much.

Naiell had also slept a lot. Pretty much wherever he could. In the greenhouse in York. In Stefan's car. On the plane. Hirka smiled, but then she remembered how everything had gone to Slokna. That she was carrying his heart in a box.

Hungl and Tyla had shared the tent closest to hers. She wasn't sure whether it was to stop her from escaping, or to stop anyone from hurting her. Neither reason made her feel much safer.

She'd defied Skerri the night before. Thwarted some sick plan she hadn't known the particulars of. The deadborn woman would probably snap her neck as soon as the opportunity presented itself.

Hirka had a dreadful feeling her life was balanced on the edge of a knife, one that she couldn't even see. Was she good enough, or wasn't she? And for what? And in whose eyes?

She feared she would find out sooner than she wanted to.

At least she'd found out that they had seers here. Umpiri who understood blindcraft. One of them had to know how they could get the Might back. Naiell had destroyed it, at the expense of countless lives, and in a moment of madness she had promised Graal that she would fix it. In exchange for peace. Had *she* even believed what she was saying? It was absurd. Heal the Might . . .

Heal Rime.

Hirka bowed her head and marched onward but walked straight into Hungl, who had stopped. He turned to her, frost in his goatee.

"The path . . . It's not there," he said in an awkward mix of ymish and umoni. He pointed at Skerri and Grid. They were standing next to a dark wound in the mountainside where the path ought to have been.

Oni came running over. "The path's gone. They're going to find another way. Wait here, Hirka," she said, gesturing for Hungl to follow her.

Tyla pushed past Hirka and followed them to see what had happened.

Hirka leaned against the rock face, grateful for a break. For a moment to be alone. But she wasn't entirely alone.

She glanced back. Kolail was standing nearby, claws buried in the snow. Using them to drink. Hirka had seen the others doing it as well. It seemed to make no difference whether they drank with their mouths or claws. It was so annoying. She had a frozen waterskin that would be put to better use as a rattle, while he could just plunge his fingers into the snow and enjoy a nice drink . . .

Hirka took off her bag and set it down. Then she scooped up a fistful of snow and shoved some into her mouth. It melted slowly. One drop. Two. Her tongue got cold and numb. She spat out the snow and then realized Kolail was watching her. What was that playing on his lips? Amazement? Or was he trying to hide his amusement?

His sheepskin was as gray as his hair. It was like dirty snow had settled around his broad shoulders. He had thick stubble and a strong jaw. Not unlike Father, she realized with surprise. A dead-born and slightly uglier version of Thorrald.

A pang of melancholy accompanied the memory of Father. It hadn't hit her so hard in a long time. She couldn't think about it. Had to focus on something else. Survival. Water. She needed water.

She walked over to Kolail and took his hand. He tore it back, staring at her like she'd tried to chop it off. Hirka pointed at her mouth. "Water . . ."

He frowned, causing the teardrop to move closer to the bridge of his nose. She took his hand again, and this time he let her. She lifted his fingers to her lips.

"Wait . . ."

It was the first word she'd heard him say. Ymish.

That's right. He fought in the war.

He shoved his claws into the snow again. Lifted them up and let her grab hold. Hirka put his fingers in her mouth and felt water trickle down her throat. Warmer than anything she'd drunk since coming here. It was incredible.

She gripped his wrist and sucked his fingers. His claws quivered against her tongue. Then he tore his hand back again.

Hirka suddenly felt like she'd done something terrible. Something she shouldn't have. A drop of water ran from her lips. She wiped it away with the back of her hand before it froze.

Kolail stared past her. Hirka turned.

Skerri was standing on the path ahead of her. Black lips pulled taut. She barked something incomprehensible at Kolail. He walked past Hirka, leaving her alone with Skerri. It felt like a betrayal.

Skerri stalked toward her. Pulled her arm back and swung. Hirka raised her own arm to protect herself, but she was too late. Her cheek burned.

"You do not touch the fallen! You do not abase your house!"

Hirka stumbled back. She could feel hot blood running down her jaw. Panic gripped her. Skerri's claws . . . How much damage had they done? She touched her cheek and then looked at her hand. Streaks of red stained the makeshift woollen glove. Small cuts. Nothing serious. Her hood had made sure of that.

Skerri stared at her. Her fury seemed to fade. Turn to confusion. Hirka's realization that she was waiting for the cuts to close was bittersweet.

"That's right. I don't heal like you."

Skerri closed her eyes and sighed in despair. "You couldn't even inherit *that* . . . It's like you're just not supposed to survive."

Skerri pulled the hood tighter around Hirka's face. "Don't let them see. They think little enough of you as it is," she said. Then she walked off.

Hirka pushed down her anger and followed.

Hirka couldn't sleep. They'd made camp next to an icy overhang that loomed over the tents like a huge canine. Threatening. Oppressive. Every time she closed her eyes, she heard it creak. As if at any moment it might snap and crush them all.

Skerri had chosen the site, undoubtedly as some sort of revenge for Hirka's comments about the location of the last camp.

Hungl was snoring like a snarling dog in the tent next to hers. The ice creaked again.

Hirka rolled back onto her other side, her tunic twisting around her body. She could smell fried fish, which could only mean that her brain had succumbed to the cold and was playing tricks on her. She hadn't seen proper food since she'd arrived here. The blind just stuck their claws into foul-tasting green cakes containing most of what they needed. Oni had said they were made from seaweed and a type of mushroom grown in caves.

Hirka had asked whether they ever ate in the usual way. The way she did. It turned out that they did a few times a year, during festivals, but always suffered for it the next day. It was as if they used to eat with their mouths, but then just stopped. That said, they drank a lot of strange things. Probably because sitting down seemed to be acceptable while drinking.

But she could have sworn she smelled fish. Greasy, fresh fish . . .

She crawled over to the tent flap. Pushed it aside and peeked out.

She could see red embers in the darkness a short distance away. Remnants of the campfire.

She pulled on her boots. They were cold, but dry. Then she wrapped the blanket around herself and went out, drawn to the heat and to the smell of food, like an animal. It was so dark that it was difficult to see much more than the snow beneath her feet. The nights were black here. Blacker than in Ym.

There was a figure sitting by the fire, poking the glowing embers with a stick. He was big and had a shaggy skin over his shoulders.

Kolail.

Hirka hesitated. Her cheek still stung from Skerri's claws. But she couldn't bring herself to feel ashamed of what she'd done, no matter what was expected of her. She was no longer the rot. She could

48

touch whoever she wanted. Sit with whoever she wanted. Eat with whoever she wanted.

She moved closer, sure that he had heard her coming. Her stomach tingled nervously, and not just out of hunger. She wanted to say something but didn't know what. They hadn't even been properly introduced.

"Kolail?"

He snorted. A sort of stunted laugh. "Not here."

It took her a moment to realize what he meant. That wasn't what he was called here.

She walked over to him. "But that is your name?"

He nodded. There was room on the stone next to him.

"Can I sit down?" she asked.

He looked like death wrought of steel. Gray hair, gray stubble. Cheeks slightly hollow. And with those deadborn eyes that always looked so impenetrable . . .

It had taken her a long time to get used to Naiell's eyes. You only had to look at them to understand where all the stories about the blind came from.

"I'd think you were free to do whatever your heart desired," he replied bitterly.

She loosened the blanket enough that she could sit down. A stick was planted in the snow, leaning over the fire. A trout the size of a forearm hung from the end. The smell of burnt fat made her stomach rumble. She was close to drooling.

"I didn't know you ate fish," she said.

"Go ahead."

She needed no more encouragement than that. She picked up the stick and sank her teeth into the fish. She'd swallowed three mouthfuls before it occurred to her to ask whether he wanted any. He shook his head.

Hirka couldn't remember the last time she'd eaten something so delicious. She devoured the fish, not stopping until only the bones and head remained. Kolail stuck his claws into that. In no time at all it was reduced to something that looked more like a ball of hair than anything else.

How could she possibly be one of them? Did she really share blood with a people so fundamentally different from herself? They were so perfect and so awful at the same time. And so . . . fearless. She'd been afraid her entire life.

"So how old—"

"Tell me . . ." he interrupted. "Who are you trying to get killed? Me or you?"

"Does talking kill?"

"Don't play dumb. You're not the type."

He was right. She knew exactly what he meant. He was one of the fallen. She didn't know what that entailed, but it had been made clear enough that he wasn't a friend. She decided it was time for a more straightforward approach.

"I could have killed you last night. You know that, right?"

"If you're waiting for me to thank you, you'll be sitting there a while."

"If you think I need thanks for not killing someone, you've been sitting in the cold too long yourself."

He met her gaze but said nothing.

She rubbed snow between her fingers, wiping away the fish grease. "Why didn't you say anything when she wanted to punish you?"

He snorted again and shook his head as if the question were idiotic. A moment passed before he answered.

"Because I was dead the moment Glimau started to run."

Glimau . . .

Hirka's stomach churned. The man he had killed was no longer a stranger in the snow. He had a name. The fire spat embers into the black sky.

"Why?" she asked.

Kolail glanced over at the tents and lowered his voice. "My options were refuse to shoot him and die, try to catch him and fail and die, or shoot him and maybe live. What would you have done?"

"Shot and missed?"

He looked at her. Yellow light from the fire danced in his eyes. She didn't look away. She knew she'd answered too quickly. Too self-assuredly. The truth was that she didn't know what she would have done. She wished she could take it back. Say something to make him realize that she understood. That she wasn't dumb.

"Look, where you fired is beside the point. I know that. It was all about getting the others to see me like they see *her*. That was what she wanted."

It was barbaric. Hirka bit her lip. Skerri had asked her to sentence a man to death for making the only choice he could have. All to instill fear. Because Hirka was what she was.

"But that will never happen," she continued. "I don't look like her. Like any of you. I'm—"

"Small." Kolail leaned forward with his elbows on his knees. He felt far too big and close. Strips of shabby fur were wrapped around his forearms. "You're small. Slow. Weak. You get cold easily. You need constant watering. No wonder they're already placing bets. Tyla's got two discs on you keeling over before we even get there, and truth be told, that would probably be for the best. Any idiot can see it's going to take some doing to make you Dreyri. To make you look like a member of the House of Modrasme."

Hirka stared at him. He didn't laugh, but a twitch of his lips revealed that he was enjoying himself. It warmed her more than the fire.

"Don't you think you're being a little too honest?" she asked. "Considering I've been asked to come up with an appropriate punishment for you before we arrive?"

He snorted again. His gray beard shook. "As if you've ever punished anyone."

Hirka felt her smile falter as she remembered Mickey. The knife she'd stabbed him with, in the alleyway by the church. Hot blood on her cold hands.

Kolail looked at her. "So you have? An accident, then?"

She shook her head, clutching the blanket to her chest. She'd taken a life, and not by accident. She'd been afraid. Desperate, even. But still . . . Deep down she knew that the knife hadn't found its way beneath his ribs by chance.

Kolail shrugged. "Then I'll just be another mark against your name. You've already sentenced me to death. If you think she'll let you get away with anything else, you're dumber than you look."

"And that doesn't bother you? That she wants to kill you for no reason?"

"She'd have found a reason, sooner or later. In any case, rabbits die."

Hirka turned to him, thinking she'd misheard. "Rabbits? What do rabbits have to do with this?"

"It's a . . . What do you call it? An expression?"

"*Rabbits die* is an expression?"

He nodded. Hirka got up. "That's the dumbest expression I've ever heard."

He shrugged again.

Hirka pulled the blanket higher so she wouldn't step on it. "Thanks for the fish," she said.

"It wasn't for you."

She knew he was lying. He could have eaten the fish raw if he'd wanted to. With his claws. There was no reason to cook it over the fire. No reason but her.

She turned to leave.

"Now that the world's about to be turned on its head," he said behind her. "Now that you're here, our great hope, our way to the Might. I have to ask . . . What's your plan?"

Hirka pretended not to hear him. She pulled the blanket tighter and stumbled away.

What's your plan?

It was such a simple question, yet of all the things she'd heard since she arrived, it scared her more than anything else.

CRACKS

Half a day had been lost following the path to nowhere, but according to Skerri, they were now only a day away from Ginnungad.

Hirka teetered between relief and panic. Relief because she was freezing cold and desperate for a warm bed. Panic because there was zero indication that she should look forward to meeting anyone in this city. Not even her own family.

Her conversation with Kolail had made her feel like a false seer. Like Naiell. What hope did they think she was bringing? What hope did *she* think she was bringing?

She leaned into the wind, keeping her eyes on the icy path. They'd been walking along the frozen river for some time, which twisted and turned like an enormous serpent at the bottom of the ravine. It had been terrifying at first, but now she was used to looking into the murky blue depths. Beneath her, cracks splintered off in every direction. Frozen bubbles looked like clouds. Some near the surface, others deep within the ice. It was like walking in the sky.

Sheer cliffs towered above them on both sides of the river. There was nowhere else to go other than straight ahead. But it seemed safe enough compared to everything else she'd seen. Impassable terrain. Cold and desolate. She'd started to understand why they always carried staffs.

Oni slowed down so Hirka could catch up to her again. She was rarely left in peace for long. Oni grew more tense with each passing day. And more demanding. Pushing Hirka to memorize. Repeat. Her unease was contagious. Hirka assumed she was under a lot of pressure from Skerri.

And from those waiting in Ginnungad.

"You understood that, right? The difference between the words for *I*? Anyone of a lower rank than you, you address as *oza*. Me, for example. But you use *oz* when you have the lower rank."

Hirka chortled. "Then I guess I'll manage just using *oz* . . ."

Oni's eyes widened. "No, no! Not at all. Haven't you been paying attention? You are Hirka, daughter of Graal, son of Raun of—"

"The House of Modrasme, I know."

It was a complex language, but it resonated with her. The sounds came naturally to her, and she could guess a lot of the words. It was like it had been lying dormant inside her since she was born.

Hirka looked up. It was starting to get dark. Soon the northern lights would appear, dancing green across the sky. The ice gave a ponderous creak up ahead. None of the others seemed to notice.

"Oni, why aren't we roped together?"

"Why would we do that?"

Hirka stamped on the ice to illustrate. She couldn't believe she had to explain something so simple. "In case something happens, you know? There are seven of us. If you fell through, we could pull you back up."

The dimples on Oni's cheeks were back, but she wasn't smiling. Hirka had noticed they also appeared when she was annoyed.

"Ropes would mean we were afraid of something happening. Ropes would mean we didn't believe we could manage on our own. That we needed others."

Hirka didn't say anything. She'd come to understand there were a lot of things Umpiri didn't need. Weapons, for instance. Kolail was the only one openly carrying a weapon. She suspected Hungl and Tyla had knives, though she couldn't be sure. They didn't use tools, either. If Umpiri ate like normal people, they probably wouldn't even use spoons. That would imply they were incapable of putting food in their own mouths.

"So how do you explain this?" Hirka raised her staff. "Doesn't this show I'm afraid of being buried alive by the snow?"

Oni hesitated, but only briefly. "That's different. It shows you know avalanches are possible, but you choose to walk there anyway."

Hirka gave an exasperated shake of her head. Oni was nearly four hundred years old. She couldn't begin to wrap her head around it. Was that what happened when you knew you might live for an eternity? You became incapable of fearing anything? Needing anyone?

Oni signaled with her hand to get her attention. In Ym it would have been a poke in the side. "Look . . ."

They were approaching a frozen waterfall. It cascaded down the rock wall in an avalanche of blue crystals. Skerri and Grid exchanged a few words up ahead. Set their bags down. It was time to make camp for the night. With the ice beneath them and the waterfall above.

Hirka cursed inwardly. She wished she'd never said anything about camp locations. She took off her bag and unstrapped the rolled-up tent. Found a barely suitable spot on the narrow lip of snow along the base of the cliff and unrolled it. The tent was her only refuge. A sheet of canvas between her and the others, that was it. But enough that she could be herself. Curl up without being scared of showing her feelings. She couldn't put it up quickly enough.

The others pitched their tents near hers. Hungl and Kolail brought bundles of kindling from the toe of a landslide farther up. Enough to start a small fire. Had she not known better, she'd have thought it was for her. But they probably just wanted a hot drink.

Hirka looked at the tent. She wanted to crawl inside straight away, but hunger won out.

She unsheathed her knife and walked out onto the ice. Got down on her knees and started chipping at it. Hungl and Tyla glanced up at her from the riverbank. They were sitting by the fire. Hirka turned her back on them and kept chipping away.

"What do you think you're doing?" Kolail's voice came from behind her.

"I'm fishing," she replied without turning.

"You do realize it's going to be light out by the time you're done?"

She scooped out a fistful of ice, then continued her chipping. She could still sense him looming over her. Then he kneeled down next to her, pulled out a knife that was considerably bigger than hers, and got to work. Hirka did her best not to smile.

Suddenly he stopped, mid-movement. Turned his head as if listening. Then he sprang to his feet. Hirka turned around. She'd heard something, too. A rumbling.

She got up. There was movement on the cliff, at the top of the waterfall. Animals? A mass of stone and ice came loose, breaking into smaller chunks as it fell, crashing down toward the tents.

Hirka screamed. Felt her lip split. She started running toward the tents, but then a hand yanked her back. Kolail pulled her close. Held her in his iron grip. He shouted to the others, so loud that it hurt her ears. Words she didn't understand.

She struggled to break free. "They're going to die! They're going to die!"

Hirka heard Skerri shouting. The echo bounced between the walls of the ravine.

The others came running toward them. The falling debris slammed into the ground, exploding in a flurry of snow and ice with incredible force. Hirka stood rooted to the spot, watching as two tents were consumed. The fire was sent flying in every direction.

Then the ice groaned, and a horrifying crack rent the air, continuing up the river. Hirka's knees threatened to give out on her.

"Run!" Kolail shoved her forward. Hirka ran. Toward the river-bank. Toward a blazing tent. Toward Hungl and Tyla.

Skerri raced toward her, her black braids flying out behind her. She reached out and grabbed Hirka, her claws digging into her arm. She was dragged forward, stumbling. There was more cracking beneath her. The world lurched as the ice gave way.

Kolail!

She spun around. He was behind her, but then a fissure appeared in the ice between them. Around them. The sheet he was standing on started to move, threatening to capsize. He was too heavy!

"Kolail!" Hirka tore herself free, dropping her knife in the process. She fell onto the ice. It teetered precariously beneath her.

"He's fallen!" Skerri shouted, grabbing Hirka by the foot.

Hirka kicked off her boot. Pulled herself away. Fallen . . . What did that even mean? She fumbled for the knife. Managed to grab it. Drove it into the ice and held on for dear life.

Where was Kolail? All she could see was bobbing ice, sheets of it colliding and rising up like mountains. The river flowed black and powerful around them.

A staff broke the surface of the water. Kolail! He was drowning!

Hirka held on to the knife with one hand and grabbed the staff with the other. His hand appeared. She grabbed it. His weight kept pulling her toward him. The sliver of ice she was lying on started to tip. Icy water rose around her.

She screamed. Someone grabbed her foot again. Dragged her backward. Her face scraped against the ice. Kolail was clinging to her. Or was it the other way around? She wasn't sure. Her hand was locked in his. She couldn't feel anything anymore. Someone had her by the feet, pulling her between fire and ice. The blazing tent flapped in the wind.

Kolail tore himself free and started crawling on all fours, like a half-drowned bear.

Hirka was lifted to her feet. She stared up into Skerri's face, into that terrifying rage. Her eyes were as black as her lips now. Skerri shook her, but Hirka only felt the movement. No pain. Everything was numb. "He is fallen! A murderer! You are Dreyri! The youngest of the House of Modrasme! You are Graal's blood, and you risk your life for *him*?! Do you have any idea how much more valuable your life is than that of a fallen? Answer me! Do you not understand who you are?!"

She pointed at the quiver that had slipped around to her chest. "I could have lost this! Don't you understand?!" Hirka stared at the worn leather holder. She suddenly realized what it contained. A raven cadaver. Of course. Identical to the one Graal had, and her only way of contacting him.

The cold was no longer so penetrating. It almost felt warm. But Hirka knew that was not a good sign.

She looked around at the icy chaos. She was an insect trapped in a bowl of salt. Hungl, Tyla, Oni, Grid . . . Alive. All of them.

Kolail rose unsteadily to his feet. His arms were wrapped so tightly around his chest that it looked like he was trying to tie himself into a knot. His legs gave out again and he dropped to his knees.

Hirka crawled closer to the burning tent. Heat . . .

She collapsed by the flames. If she'd had the strength, she would have walked straight into them. Let them consume her. Oni started to undress her. Hirka wanted to scream in protest, but she knew it had to be done. If she stayed in her wet clothes, she'd be dead in the blink of an eye. She could hear her teeth chattering. Oni was putting dry clothes on her, guiding her limp arms into the sleeves. A blanket was wrapped around her, and she was left lying with her back to the fire. Skerri was standing in front of her, shouting at Kolail. Her black lips opened and closed slowly, like in a dream.

"Iss ghené woykhail!"

Her braids swung across her back as she shook her fists. Did time stop when you were freezing to death? Hirka spotted the wooden staff. They'd been right. It helped people find you. And not just in an avalanche. She pulled it closer. Clamped it under her arm. If she survived, she'd never let go of it again.

Kolail didn't seem to notice Skerri's tirade. He stared at Hirka. His gray hair was frozen stiff. His skin was blue. Then his lips drew back into an awkward grimace. An attempt at a smile, she realized.

"What did I tell you?" he croaked. "Rabbits die."

BALANCING ACT

Garm Darkdaggar looked down at the road leading up to the house. It meandered in the flickering light from almost a hundred wind-swept torches. The carriages arrived in a steady stream, horseshoes clopping against the paving stones. Doors opening. Guests disembarking. Councillors. Nobles. Merchants. Bureaucrats. Friends. And the occasional enemy, if he were to be realistic, which he always was.

He tried not to concern himself with who was here. That didn't matter. What mattered was who *wasn't* here.

The laughter and conversation grew louder downstairs. He drained his wineglass and set it down on his desk. Let his hands slide across the gleaming wood. The desk hadn't been the same since the day Rime had burst into the room. Whereas before it had been an anchor, offering a sense of security, now it was just a painful reminder. Something he'd clung to, terrified as a pig going to slaughter.

He'd thought he was too old for that sort of thing. Too . . . practical. He was all about solutions. He was done with intimidation. Done with fear. But it was something else entirely to stand before Kolkagga. Before a young man full of rage. To feel steel against his skin.

It was so removed from the rest of his experience. So unfettered. Utter madness. He couldn't stop thinking about it. One simply didn't behave that way.

But he had. Rime An-Elderin had.

Darkdaggar looked up. The torchlight bounced off the frames on the wall. The maps. Lands, towns, and regions. Terrain was something he understood. There was nothing more beautiful than maps. They showed the world exactly as it was. As it always had been. Everything in its place. Lands shaped by the law. And if there was one thing he knew well, it was the law. So what was to be done when young men pretended it didn't exist? When they did whatever they liked, out of youthful arrogance? What was to be done when they challenged the way things were? When that which always had been was no longer good enough?

Darkdaggar had done what he'd had to. Accepted the duel. And he'd done it with the certainty that he would die. Say what you like about Rime An-Elderin, but the boy could fight. Svarteld's decision to fight for Darkdaggar had been nothing short of a gift. A lifeline. But the master hadn't been able to beat his own student. Had Rime not then disappeared without a trace, he wouldn't have been standing here today.

He'd been close to losing everything. His seat on the Council. His home. His family. His freedom. Reality was so fragile that it could be shattered by a single breath. Who would have thought?

He walked over to one of the maps of Mannfalla and tried to straighten it. It was no good. The frame was slightly crooked. He would have to have a new one made. Best to fix what he could. Seer knew there was plenty he couldn't.

He'd managed to keep his chair, but times were fraught. Nothing was certain. Nothing had fallen into place. What could be worse than that?

He needed this evening. He had friends to win. He needed to secure his own position and propagate the idea of Rime's madness. Whether he would be successful remained to be seen.

The door cracked open.

"Garm?" Elisa peered in, then walked over to him, fully aware of how good she looked. Her dress shimmered blue, bringing out the color of her eyes. What would he do without her? His rock. He'd married well.

She ran a hand over his close-cut hair. "Tyrme and Freid have arrived."

He put an arm around her waist and accompanied her downstairs to where their guests had gathered. Eyes were drawn to him as soon as they descended. Glasses clinked and silk rustled. He had friends. He had Elisa. He had daughters. Loyal servants. And if he played his cards right, he'd still have them once the evening was over.

Darkdaggar made his way to the end of the room and up onto a platform where the dancers would perform later. The most important moment of his life had arrived. It was here. Now.

"Friends!" The strength of his voice pleased him. The buzz of conversation died down.

"Friends, I must say a few words, though I don't really have any this evening. I'm speechless. I'm deeply and profoundly grateful for the support you have given me during this difficult time."

He was interrupted by a spontaneous round of applause. He let it simmer down before he continued. "I must be honest. I was close to losing everything. To the unbridled rage of youth. To madness. To Rime An-Elderin. My life, threatened by a family friend . . . Ilume's grandchild . . ."

There were murmurs of support from several quarters. He did his best to look mournful. "It comes as no surprise to me that Ravnhov tried to kill him. The fact that they might have finally succeeded comes as no surprise, either, no matter how it pains us. I will probably never know why he chose to believe that I was involved. Yes, I challenged him during the Council meetings. After all, that's what we're supposed to do. Challenge each other. But kill him? Never."

He paused for effect, letting his words sink in. "I have never tried to kill Rime An-Elderin. I told my darling Elisa the same. Do you know what she said? She said, 'I know.' I asked where this certainty came from. How she could know such a thing."

He looked at Elisa. "What was it you said, my dear?" Elisa gave a bashful shake of her head, as they had agreed she would. There were shouts of encouragement and she relented, answering quietly from the front row. "I said, 'Because you would have succeeded.'"

Darkdaggar repeated it louder. "Because you would have succeeded!"

Everyone burst out laughing and started to applaud. The sound of confidence. The sound of triumph.

He smiled. "She knows me well. Yes, had I tried to kill him, I would have succeeded."

He assumed a more solemn expression. Let the laughter die down. "Friends, all we can do is laugh. But we all know we're in the midst of a tragedy. Rime An-Elderin has disappeared. Every effort has been made to find him. To find answers. But the time has come to accept that he is no longer with us. His father's brother and family have moved on. Ilume's house stands empty. The sleeping dragon is dead. It is particularly tragic for those of us who served on the Council with Rime and saw him toward the end. Saw him sinking deeper and deeper into madness. Paranoia. The blind. Deadborn. Other worlds . . ."

Darkdaggar brought his fingers to the mark of the Council on his forehead and closed his eyes for a moment, as if in anguish. It wasn't difficult. It truly was a tragedy.

He straightened up again. "But we cannot harbor bitter thoughts about a madman. A dead man. We can only do our utmost to remedy the situation. That's why I've donated a year's funding to Mannfalla's foremost home for the mentally afflicted."

An appreciative murmur rippled around the room.

A lanky man over by the door craned his neck. Kunte. He shifted restlessly. Whatever he had to say, it was urgent.

Darkdaggar accepted a glass from Elisa and raised it.

"To family and friends!"

"Family and friends!" everyone repeated, clapping as he stepped down from the platform. A harp started to play in the next room. People drifted through. Darkdaggar excused himself and went over to Kunte.

"Can't it wait?"

Kunte shook his head. Darkdaggar led him upstairs and into his study. No sooner had he closed the door than Kunte exploded. "He's alive! I've seen him!"

He didn't need to say who.

Darkdaggar stared at his desk. The corner of one of his papers had curled. He smoothed it with his thumb, but it rolled straight back up again. He sighed. Kunte could have been mistaken.

"Where?"

"At the teahouse near the Catgut. In the alleyways by the river."

"Are you sure?"

Kunte didn't reply. Darkdaggar brushed his own question aside with a wave of his hand. "Of course you're sure. What more do we know?"

"We think he might have been to see Jarladin, but we can't be sure. Movement on a rooftop, but it might have been a trick of the light."

Darkdaggar smoothed the paper out again, only for it to spring back into place.

"So . . . He's back but not showing himself. And we can only assume he isn't planning to. Not without it being . . . dramatic. But this is a problem. A real problem."

"Do you want me to . . . do something about it?"

Darkdaggar looked at him. "What do you mean?"

Kunte ran a hand through his long, greasy hair. "Do you want me to take care of it? The problem?"

Darkdaggar assumed an expression of shock. "No, Seer preserve us, Kunte! We're not savages! Were I a killer, I'd have moved to Ravnhov a long time ago."

Kunte's shoulders sagged and he gave an awkward smile. Darkdaggar smothered a laugh. Kunte against Kolkagga? The fight would be over before it started. That was one of the reasons he hadn't used Kunte in Ravnhov. Maybe he should have. Instead he'd used an inept middleman who had the gall to tell the would-be assassin who had hired him! Was there no limit to incompetence these days?

Darkdaggar put an arm around Kunte's shoulders, being careful not to touch his hair.

"But thank you, Kunte. You're a good friend. A loyal friend. I really appreciate that. All I ask is that this stays between us."

"Always. We'll keep our eyes peeled. Find out where he's going."

"Oh, I'm pretty sure I know where he's going."

Darkdaggar opened the door.

"One more thing, Garm-fadri . . . I think there's something wrong with him."

"I could have told you that, but how do you mean?"

Kunte hesitated. "He doesn't have a . . . Well, he doesn't have a tail. Not anymore."

Darkdaggar frowned. "No tail?"

"None! Something must have happened. Maybe he lost it in battle?"

Realization struck, as beautiful as a pin in a map. Darkdaggar smiled.

He cut it off. He followed her.

"We might never know," he said, waving Kunte out of the room so he could think in peace.

Rime An-Elderin.

Where have you been, Rime?

And Jarladin . . . So he knew Rime was back. And he was keeping it from the Council. Which meant he didn't trust any of them. Or had he already allied himself with some of the others? Eir, perhaps?

Darkdaggar dragged a hand over his mouth. He hated being forced into action. He was a calm man. Patient. Organized. Mistakes were made when you were rushed. But now he had to act. Sooner than he would have liked.

He picked up the impossible sheet of paper and crumpled it into a ball. He couldn't let it get to him. This was *good* news. At least now he knew where he had him and could plan accordingly. Rime An-Elderin was letting people believe he was dead. A disgraced son of the Council. It had to stay that way.

Darkdaggar shoved the ball of paper in his pocket and went back downstairs to his guests. Their attention had been diverted. The evening's entertainment was the best money could buy. A dancer. Darkdaggar had asked for something tasteful. This was anything but. She was scantily dressed. The dance vulgar. Toeing the line between skillful and obscene. Between something to admire and something no one ought to feel comfortable doing in front of an audience.

She had two other dancers with her. A girl and a boy. Neither of them were old enough to have been through the Rite, but it was clear they'd done little other than dance for the entirety of their young lives.

Applause filled the room when they were done, persisting until they left.

When the evening was over and the guests had left, Darkdaggar found an orange scarf on a chair under the stairs. Shimmering, translucent fabric. And a small card inscribed with a single word.

Damayanti.

A NEW MASTER

The half-moon hung low, glowing red between the mountains.

Rime took the usual path into Blindból. He'd considered taking another route, but what was the point? He'd never get into the camp unseen. And though his body was telling him otherwise, he had nothing to fear. He wasn't an outlaw. He hadn't been declared dead. He hadn't even been formally relieved as Ravenbearer. He'd just been away.

The question was whether Kolkagga would see it that way. He hadn't been to Blindból since before Svarteld's death. Would they think him a murderer? A traitor? Maybe Darkdaggar had already won them over?

The trees were frosty white in the darkness. Trees he'd passed countless times before. Blindból was the only place he felt at home. Did he still have a home here?

He was desperately trying to work out what he would say, but it was a pointless exercise. Everything hinged on Kolkagga. How many of them believed Darkdaggar's lies? How many presumed he was dead? Or mad?

Maybe he was a madman. He'd traveled to another world. A world beyond his comprehension. He'd chopped off his own tail. Killed his own master. He'd resorted to blindcraft. Had a beak in his throat that made him a slave to a blindling. And only he could see the coming war.

All in all, a disturbing state of affairs.

A madman.

The loss of power was the least of his worries. He'd never wanted to sit on the Council in the first place. All he'd wanted was change. But what kind of change?

He came to the rope bridge and stopped. The moonlight bounced off the thin layer of snow, making it easier to see in the dark. A glimmering path in the night. He could still picture Launhug, bent double on the bridge. Close to dying, both from his injuries and from self-loathing after failing his mission in Ravnhov. How would the world have looked now if Launhug had succeeded? If Hirka hadn't been on the roof and Eirik had taken a knife to the back of the neck? How would the world have looked if Ravnhov were no longer a threat?

It would be a bloodbath . . .

Ravnhov was the only place with the strength to resist Mannfalla. Without Ravnhov, the kingdoms would have formed new alliances. Thrown themselves into battle. All against all. However you looked at it, two strong men were better than a tavern full of people who all thought they could win.

Rime started across the bridge. It swayed in time with his steps. He glimpsed movement in the darkness on the other side and knew he'd been spotted. There was no going back. He lowered his hood, wanting to be recognized. He had no intention of hiding.

He reached the other side and entered the woods, the trees forming a proper canopy over the path leading to the camp. Longing squeezed his chest when he saw the torches. Warm, flickering lights. One in front of each hut.

Home.

And they'd let him come. That was something. But the real test started now. Now, when the weight of everything that had happened and of everything that was to come was threatening to overwhelm him. It was time to stand before his own and show them he was in his right mind.

It was late. Teatime. The same as every night. Smoke rose from the rooftops scattered among the trees. Three fires burned in the yard. Kolkagga were squeezed together on long benches. Never had their name been more fitting. Black shadows.

Their usual lively conversations had died. The tea was forgotten. As was supper. Some of them sat holding bowls of soup. Others had gotten up. Quiet and expectant, they followed him with their eyes.

He approached the closest fire, where he recognized many of the faces. Men who had followed him before. He heard his name whispered, heard it ripple through the camp like wind through leaves. One of them got up and came to meet him. Dark eyes in a broad face.

Jeme.

Jeme had been with him at Bromfjell. Jeme knew. He was a friend. Had to be.

Jeme stopped in front of him. He looked Rime up and down like he was seeing a ghost.

"They said you were . . ." He wasn't able to finish.

Rime nodded. There was nothing more to say.

Jeme's hand cupped the back of his neck. Then he pulled Rime close until his warm cheek was pressed against Rime's cold skin.

"Rime . . . You're always late for supper. Always." He patted Rime on the back of the head. Rime felt a lump form in his throat. Home. He still had a home.

Jeme let go and stepped back. His eyes were shining. Rime had to blink back tears of his own.

A figure had appeared by Jeme's side. A woman.

"Rime An-Elderin . . ." she said with a wry smile. He offered her his hand. She took it in a firm grip.

"I'm Orja. Master Orja to you."

Rime did his best to hide his surprise. There were very few female Kolkagga, and even fewer who were masters.

"I've taken Svarteld's place, but fear not, I have no intention of letting you make a habit of killing your superiors." She returned to the fire. It was busier now. The entire camp had turned out. She looked back.

"You're alive. That's the good news. The bad news is that means a storm is coming."

He nodded. "Worse than anything we've seen before," he replied.

Black-clad warriors lingered around the fire. Some had already retired, well aware that a new day would soon be upon them and even Rime's return from Slokna wouldn't afford them any extra sleep. But most had stayed, refusing to pretend this was a night like any other.

The laughter was restrained at first, as they joked about how they might make use of the gateways. The raven rings.

Some claimed they would leave everything behind in the hope of finding a better world. Others said they'd use them as an escape route for an ingenious life of crime in which they plundered every world imaginable of riches. Torgar was keen on the prospect of having a woman in every world, until someone pointed out there wasn't a woman in *any* world who would say yes to Torgar.

Unsurprisingly, this led to speculation about how ymlings measured up to men in other worlds.

The laughter came more easily as the tea was passed around.

Rime was glad none of them knew what it took to leave. They asked, of course, but he said he didn't know. There were simply far too many things he couldn't tell them, which meant there were huge gaps in his stories. Judging by the long looks Orja was giving him, she'd noticed.

He could tell them about Graal, the deadborn who wouldn't rest until Ym belonged to nábyrn. And he could tell them about Hirka, who had traveled to their world in a futile attempt to stop them. But the beak in his throat? He could never tell anyone about that.

But there was no hiding the fact that he had chopped off his tail in order to survive in the human world. They mused on how it might affect his balance. Sveinn, who was always talking himself down, joked that even *he* could beat Rime now. The others laughed. Someone said *anyone* could beat Rime now. The laughing grew even louder.

But then they remembered the last person Rime had beaten. Remembered that the unassailable Svarteld wasn't with them by the fire, and never again would be. Their gazes faltered and they quickly found something else to talk about.

As soon as the opportunity presented itself, Rime slipped away. He'd barely spoken to Orja but had heard more than enough. She wouldn't support him.

He followed a narrow path to the peak of a forested mountain, to one of the training halls. The snow-covered roof also sheltered a narrow platform around the building. How many times had he walked around it on his hands? How many times had he been made to start over because he'd fallen?

Rime stepped up onto the platform and opened the folding doors. The wind rushed into the empty room as if to fill a void, bringing with it a fine dusting of snow that settled in the marks in the floor. Some of them hundreds of years old, others so recent they could have been his own. Marks from his sword. His and Svarteld's.

Rime closed his eyes. He could almost hear the clashing of steel. The clatter of staffs. Smell the sweat. Svarteld's voice came to him like an echo from Slokna.

The day I lose to you, it'll be out of love.

72

Rime felt his lips curl. He suppressed a grimace, and the grief he refused to let himself feel.

What should he have done? What was he supposed to have done? Let Darkdaggar get away with it? Not challenge him? And when he'd seen Svarteld standing across from him, should he have thrown down his sword? Let himself be killed?

Footsteps on the path. Someone was coming.

Orja.

She stopped in the doorway, hands on hips.

"You don't approve," she said.

Rime's mind had been elsewhere, but he didn't tell her that. She stepped closer. "We're Kolkagga, Rime. We can't choose who we listen to, or where our orders come from. Whether we agree with it or not, we're instruments of the Council. Regardless of who sits around that table."

Rime turned to face her. She was somewhere between thirty and forty winters. Her dark hair was tied at the nape of her neck. "I grew up in Eisvaldr," he answered. "I know how this works."

"Then why are you trying to do things differently?" Her voice was raised now. "What did you expect us to say?"

"You've made your choice," Rime responded.

She swept toward him. Pointed at him, as if he'd protested. "Rime An-Elderin, you have no idea what you've got. You're wanted, but not an outlaw. They're looking for you, but still just as a missing person. So you're free to stay here. No one will turn you in. A hundred men out there would give an arm to help you. Some of them their lives."

"The feeling's mutual." He turned away again.

She sighed. "Don't you think I'd help you if I could? I suspect you're right, Rime, I really do. From what I've heard, it's more than likely that Darkdaggar wanted you dead. Him and the others. But we can't act on suspicion alone. And if it turns out as you say, with

73

kingdom pitted against kingdom, with blindlings pouring into Ym . . . Well, we'll follow the Council's orders then, too."

He looked at her. He wasn't sure who she was talking to, but it certainly wasn't him. She leaned against the wall. Folded her arms over her chest. "I've heard about you, Rime. Heard a lot about you. You could get most of the men out there to turn on their leaders. Butcher Garm Darkdaggar in his sleep. You heard what they were saying. They'd follow you through the gateways to unknown worlds, if needed be."

"But not you?"

She sighed again. "Do you know why they chose me to succeed Svarteld as master? I wasn't next in line here. I was next in line in Haglefjell, but they moved me here. Why?"

Rime could think of many reasons, but he kept quiet. She continued. "Because they expected the men to protest. What does that tell you?"

Rime smiled. "That the Council doesn't know its own warriors."

She smiled back. "Exactly. They've never spent a day with Kolkagga. They don't understand that discipline is everything to us. Protest? That's not how we operate. To the Council, I was a means to an end. A way of regaining the trust of Kolkagga. The plan was simple: choose me, wait for protests, and when that happened, demonstrate their goodwill by replacing me. The Council's poor judgement is the only reason I'm still here. I know all of this, yet still I follow their orders. We live to serve. All we can do is wait and see."

"Until?"

The question seemed to take her by surprise. He made the most of it and continued. "Until they ask you to break the law? No, they're free to make that up as they go along. Until they attack innocent people? No, it's not up to us to determine guilt, that's their job. Until they ask you to fall on your own sword? That's your job, isn't it? If that's what the Council wants, then that's what you'll do."

Rime could hear the anger behind his words, but they had to be said. "When you say we'll wait and see, it means nothing. You've already put your heart in the hands of the Council. You've forfeited your right to an opinion. That's your choice, but don't insult me by pretending it has anything to do with your moral outlook, because you've long since entrusted your morals to others."

She went to leave. "Had that been true, Rime, a raven would already have been sent, bearing word of your return. For the time being, I'll respect the fact that you don't want to be found."

"So what will you do when the Council sends orders to attack Ravnhov because of an assassination attempt instigated by Darkdaggar? Ravnhov, our only capable ally in a fight against the deadborn?"

She left the hall, but he heard her answer as she walked away.

"We'll wait and see."

ONE OF THE FALLEN

Hirka knew it was Skerri just from the way the tent flap was yanked aside.

Skerri stopped in front of her, but Hirka didn't look up. She contented herself with staring at her boots. Black leather straps overlapping all the way up over her knees. Bare thighs. Pale and strong. It was as if every muscle had been carved from stone. So imposing. So otherworldly. So fearsome.

"We need to keep moving," she said.

Hirka quickly took stock of how she was feeling. She was warm again, thanks to the stones that Oni had taken from the fire and arranged around her.

She sat up. Reluctantly and somewhat stiffly. Skerri dumped something on the ground next to her. Her clothes. Dry now. She opened her mouth to ask how Kolail was feeling but then stopped herself. There was no point provoking her unnecessarily. Oni had already said that he was okay. That everyone had made it out alive.

"Grid found tracks," Skerri said. "They are almost certainly from the city."

"Whose tracks?" Hirka let the blanket fall from her shoulders and pulled her tunic on.

"Whose do you think?" Skerri snapped. Then she let out a long sigh and Hirka realized this was her trying to show some restraint.

76

"Listen, Hirka," she said, crouching down in front of her. "You should know that this is not our way. We are Umpiri. We do not hide. We do not ambush people. This was done by the lowest of the low. A reprehensible and spineless act committed by scum who won't even show their faces."

Hirka froze with her arm only halfway through its sleeve. "Someone did it on purpose?"

Skerri's white eyes narrowed. "Fallen. Or houseless. I'm sure of it."

"Why?"

"Because no one else would have done such a thing!"

"I mean why were we attacked?"

Skerri looked away. The beads in her braids clacked against each other, making a sound like hail. Her own personal storm. She drummed her claws against her knee. Finally she found the words.

"You should know that Dreysíl is not what it once was. The Might kept us together. After the war, things changed. You should have seen Ginnungad when it shone. We have more fallen now. More people lower down. And what was once easy has become—"

"Not easy?"

Skerri stared her down. "Everyone used to know their place. What you did out on the river will only make matters worse."

Hirka felt a prickling on the back of her neck. As if the words had rubbed her the wrong way. She pulled on her trousers. The knees were stiff and refused to sit properly.

She knew her place better than most. She had been a child of Odin. The rot. Menskr. Being the lowest of the low had been her life. Kolail might as well have been her. Drowning. Dying. Not worth saving. Anger smoldered in her chest, but she knew she would have to stamp it out.

"How do you become one of the fallen?"

"You kill," Skerri replied. "You spill the blood of your own. Do you understand?"

Hirka looked at her. "I understand. Then you become the weapon that others use to kill."

Skerri's gaze faltered. Then the meaning behind Hirka's words sank in and her eyes turned black. She stood up. "You will never be one of us. You are of the House of Modrasme, yet still you speak like an animal! You lower yourself to the level of the fallen without—"

Hirka stood up and snarled at the deadborn woman. *"Ozá kwo kwessere dósem!"*

I am also one of the fallen.

The words came from deep within. Words she hadn't realized she knew but that felt true to her. She knew they would cost her, but she hadn't been able to stop herself. And as if that weren't bad enough, she had used the superior form of the word *I*. As if she had been speaking to someone of a lower rank.

Skerri looked down at her. She was a good head taller. Something changed in her face. Anger was no longer all she was feeling. Hirka could have sworn she saw a hint of uncertainty. What would a woman like Skerri do if she were afraid?

Best not to find out. Hirka quickly changed the subject. "I've seen the Seer fall, Skerri. I know the cost of change. Things happen. Unforeseen things. People are people, no matter their kind, and fear is everywhere. Even among Umpiri. Would we have been attacked today if it weren't for fear?"

"We were attacked because Kolail has betrayed us," Skerri said. The tension had dissipated somewhat, much to Hirka's relief.

"I find that hard to believe," she replied.

"You think you know us? You think you understand Umpiri? He is the only fallen here."

Hirka was shaking, and she knew it wasn't just because she was cold. She took a breath, putting on a mask she knew was fragile. "How many know I'm coming?"

"Our house, and our closest friends in the top houses. Nobody else."

"Nobody else?" Hirka barked out a laugh. "If more than three people know, it's no secret."

For a moment she feared she'd affronted her again, but Skerri had looked up and into the middle distance. "You're right. A competing family. Someone who does not want to see us restored to our former glory."

For a moment Hirka felt for Skerri. Felt the weight of the reality that the blindling lived in. The levels. The rules. The constant pressure to be a force of nature. And she was to become part of this?

Skerri looked at her again. Her black lips thinned. "You had better be worth it," she said, before turning and disappearing through the tent flap.

As soon as she was alone, Hirka grabbed the tent pole to stop herself from falling.

GINNUNGAD

The distance to Ginnungad could be measured by the mood, which was becoming increasingly tense. Hungl, Tyla, and Kolail walked in silence. Skerri and Grid exchanged a few quiet words. Oni was the exception, of course. She was growing increasingly frantic.

". . . And remember not to cough, sigh, or yawn in the company of anyone of a higher rank. And don't point, obviously. And don't turn your back on anyone until you've been dismissed, and under no circumstances are you to bare your teeth."

"My teeth?" Hirka quirked an eyebrow.

"Oh . . ." The color rose in Oni's face. "Well, you do have just a touch of canine," she said, like she was trying to claw back her words.

Hirka ran her tongue over her teeth. They were no sharper than they'd ever been.

"What about food? I suppose I can't eat in front of people either?"

Oni clapped a hand over her mouth. "Heavens, no . . . May the First have mercy on you if you did! The one exception is during feasts. Where food is served and you're invited to eat."

Which happens twice a year. Great . . .

Hirka chewed her lip. She'd thought all the rules were made-up at first. Some kind of test. A joke. She'd probably still have thought that if Oni hadn't been so on edge.

They approached a bridge that was carved out of stone. It arched over a ravine that cut deep into the rock. But there was no railing. Nothing to hold on to.

Skerri and Grid crossed without hesitating. Oni, too. Hirka followed, forcing herself not to look down. She locked her eyes on a column on the other side. Once she'd made it across, she noticed the column was perfectly hexagonal, with small runes engraved all the way around. It came up to her shoulders but looked to have been taller once.

She caught up to Oni. "Is that a road marker?"

Oni glanced at the column. "In a way. This is the old road to Ginnungad, but it's no longer used. There was a statue here once. Of the ferryman. People used to leave coins in his boat when they crossed."

"For good luck and stuff?"

"Erm . . . Maybe more to avoid bad luck."

"What happened to him?"

"He was made of mightglass," Oni answered. "Before the Might disappeared. That sort of thing is extremely valuable now, so he was stolen. But I could show you drawings, if you'd like."

Hirka looked back at what remained of the stone column. "What's mightglass?"

Oni's cheeks dimpled again, as they did every time she realized how little Hirka knew. Every time a new topic came up that required more detailed explanation.

"Mightglass is stone that is shaped with the Might. By hand. Those who were most skilled could shape nature in their image. Become one with the Might and manipulate stone. Fire and water, too, some claim, but I don't know . . . Have you never seen stone braiding?"

Hirka shook her head, not wanting to interrupt. This was important. This was something she was desperate to learn more about. She couldn't care less about the names of the houses and who she

81

could and couldn't point at. But the Might, and how it could shape the world . . .

Like the Seer's tree. Naiell's destruction made manifest.

"Oh, Hirka! There are places in Ginnungad that will take your breath away. The oldest structures have entire walls dating back to the time before the war. Stone woven in patterns you wouldn't have thought possible. Nearly all of the House of Hod was built using the Might. And the old spires were built that way. But most of them are gone now. The rock was stretched so far that there was nothing to support it when the Might disappeared. The city collapsed. That was hundreds of years before my time."

"So you were born after the Might disappeared? You've never felt it? You've never been able to shape anything?"

Oni's gaze sank to the path as they walked. "You don't always need to have known something to know you miss it."

Hirka was worried she'd gotten too personal. That she'd struck a nerve. She tried to lighten the mood a little.

"So how did it work? You just pointed, and then ta-da! A tower?"

Oni laughed. "When has anything ever been that easy?" She held her hands together in front of her chest, then slowly began to move them apart. "You shaped things. Like out of clay, you know? There are skilled mightslingers you could ask. All I know is what I've read. But they made the most beautiful things!"

"When they didn't die," Kolail chimed in. Hirka turned to find that he'd snuck right up behind them without her noticing.

"They died?!"

He shrugged, as if it were so obvious that no explanation was needed. "In droves. Or they hurt themselves. Burned themselves getting too close. Cut themselves when they didn't have the edges under control. Some even managed to impale themselves. The Might offers many exciting ways to die."

Oni rolled her eyes. "He's exaggerating, most people—"

"Tell her about Felke," he interrupted.

Hirka looked at Oni. "Felke?"

Oni sighed. "That was at least twelve hundred years ago. Felke was one of the best. He was working on a bridge stretching between two houses in Nifel. The stone grew too hot and the air too cold, and the bridge shattered beneath his feet. Rained down on the houses below."

Kolail drew level with Hirka. "They found him on a roof," he said. "His body full of mightglass. He was more stone than man. Rabbits die. Didn't I tell you?" Kolail walked past them.

Hirka stared at his back. The sheepskin draped over shoulders broad enough that she could sit on just one of them. She felt ill. She remembered the Seer's tree. Glasslike stone, like tendrils of ink in water. The mere sight of it had driven Hlosnian mad. The old stone carver had never been able to make anything like it, which perhaps wasn't that surprising, considering it had been created by a force he would never be able to master. But the blind had.

Hirka had once stood with a blindling at the top of a waterfall near Ravnhov. She had seen the river turn to dust. Something only gods should be able to do. Sudden fear shot through her chest.

Gods . . . Dreysíl was populated by gods. What if the absence of the Might was the only thing restraining them? What would they be capable of if they got it back? Was that really something she wanted to help them with?

Oni touched her arm. She gave a start.

"Wait here," she said and continued toward Skerri and Grid, who had stopped a little way ahead of them.

Hirka walked over to Kolail. "What do they need to talk about? What's the problem?" Her fear had left her frustrated. She'd been dreading this since she'd arrived, and waiting was the worst part. Couldn't they just get it over with and get there already?

"They're discussing which route to take, and how to get you

83

through the city unseen." Kolail's voice reminded her of Naiell's. Rough as a raven's, from somewhere deep in his throat.

"Why can't we discuss it together?" She crossed her arms. Realized it wasn't so cold anymore.

"They're Dreyri. They don't include others in their discussions."

He was right. She had yet to see Skerri ask anyone for advice or involve anyone in a decision. Other than Grid, who was clearly worthy enough. But even he was treated like a whelp.

Kolail spoke quietly, knowing full well they shouldn't be talking at all. "First things first, they have to get you home. Then they have to teach you their ways. Dreyri ways. If they manage that, then I imagine they'll let you meet the House of Hod. Until then, you're a secret. Nobody can see or smell you. You'll be formally presented. With a lot of spectacle, if I had to guess."

He made it sound like he hated it but was nonetheless amused.

"Then we just sneak in! Hide."

"They're Dreyri. They—"

"Don't hide from anyone. Yeah, yeah, I'm beginning to understand how it works."

Kolail chuckled. "You'll outlive me yet."

Hirka poked at the snow with her staff. She knew exactly what he was getting at. His punishment. Which Skerri had asked her to consider.

Kolail spat in the snow. "She'll accept nothing less than me being raven fodder. And you'll end up going along with what she wants."

Hirka glared at him. She felt like slamming her fist into the teardrop in his forehead, just to really drive it home.

"Do I look like someone who goes along with what other people want?"

Kolail didn't reply.

Oni returned, the hem of her tunic wet with snow. "They're bringing you in from the south." She sounded almost apologetic.

Kolail snorted. "From the south? Really? That can't have been an easy decision. I doubt either of them have ever set foot there."

Oni pursed her lips. Pretended not to hear him. "Skerri would prefer not to run into Dreyri, particularly from the top houses. So we have to take an alternative route. Come."

They rounded a crag and the landscape opened up in every direction. A glacier stretched toward the horizon, so far that it seemed to merge with the sky. White with gray.

There were cracks in several places, which hopefully meant they wouldn't be trying to cross it.

"Ginnungad," Oni said, nodding at the glacier.

Hirka shielded her eyes, but there was no city to be seen. No semblance of a settlement.

"Where?"

"You'll see it soon enough," Oni replied.

They continued across the rocky ridge. Yellow heather poked through the snow. Hirka was starting to realize that the cracks in the glacier were much bigger than she'd first thought. There was a network of fissures running through the ice, like blood vessels. Smoke rose up in several places, and suddenly Hirka realized what she was looking at.

She stopped. Stunned by the scale of it. Each fissure made the Alldjup look like a scratch by comparison. These were great chasms cutting down through the ice and into black rock. Hirka could see openings in the walls. Homes. Smoke. Lanterns. Steps.

"The ice . . . The city is in the ice . . ."

"Not entirely," Oni replied, seemingly nonplussed. "It's rock with a thick layer of ice on top. A lot of roads and homes are inside the rock, so you can't see them from the surface, but you see where the ice is bluer . . ." She pointed into the distance. "That's pure ice. You can't see it from here, but the city stretches all the way to the sea."

Oni dragged her onward, and Hirka did her best not to stumble.

She couldn't take her eyes off it. There was a dark depression in the ice close to the horizon. Some kind of edge? A frozen waterfall?

The sky grew darker, and Hirka remembered how quickly night fell here. Soon it would be hard to see where she was walking.

Skerri stopped. The others did the same, like an echo. Like they always did. Oni took off her bag and pulled out a gray tunic, which she gave to Hirka. "Here. Put this on."

Hirka did as she was told. She didn't need to be asked twice to put more clothes on. Skerri came over and pulled the hood up over Hirka's head. "Keep it on until we're home. Make sure no one sees your face. Or your hands. And from now on, don't say a word, do you understand?"

Hirka nodded.

The hood hung down over her face. All she could see was the ground right in front of her. Skerri led them down to where two roads met. It was dark before they got there.

They continued along the road, keeping closer together than before.

A rock wall rose up ahead of them. Solid and black, reaching into the heavens. Hirka tilted her head back to take it in. It was so tall it looked like it was swaying.

The road disappeared into a tunnel. An oval opening in the rock. Hirka felt like an insect being swallowed by a big, dark nothingness. The walls were black and as smooth as glass. If anything was shaped with the Might, this had to be it. No living creature could make something like this.

Then came the sounds. Echoes of something on the other side. Another oval opening appeared at the end of the tunnel. It was like walking up a serpent's throat and getting spat out. Onto a street.

Hirka barely suppressed a gasp. The street was at the bottom of a ravine. Black cliffs loomed over them on either side, so tall that Hirka couldn't see the top from under her hood. Homes were carved directly into the rock. Doors, windows, balconies with no railings, stairs . . . Roads and small passages snaked around it at different heights, disappearing into the rock only to reappear elsewhere.

Even more astounding was the multitude of bridges. There were so many that it looked like someone had tried to stick the walls together. Covered them in tar and torn them apart so that countless sticky, gluey fibers had solidified between them. Thick and thin. High and low.

She didn't know what she'd expected. A snow-blown version of Ravnhov? Nothing like this, in any case.

And there were people here! Blindlings. Deadborn. Laughing. Talking. Shouting. Sitting at tables drinking. Pulling carts. Cages of small birds and buckets of fish. Piles of clothes and tools. At least *some* people here used tools.

Everyday activities, just like you might see in Mannfalla. Familiar sights in unfamiliar surroundings.

Kolail and Oni walked close to Hirka so that she wouldn't bump into anyone. She could smell food. Real food! That meant they had something to eat other than those disgusting cakes. Her hunger momentarily overshadowed her fatigue.

A low note from a flute drifted down from a window farther up. She could hear the sound of a winch nearby as ropes sent baskets from one side of the street to the other.

Hirka thought of all the things she'd seen since traveling through the gateways. York. London. Venice. She thought of the doors that opened themselves. Stefan's gun. The museum with the glass floor they'd shattered. Things she never would have thought possible.

But nothing had been as strange as this. Was it seeing all the faces with white eyes? Was it the claws? Or was it knowing they would all live thousands of years?

She felt utterly drained. Bone-tired. She was no longer capable of taking in all the things she saw. It was too much. Days slogging through frozen wastelands, and now this? They walked past stalls selling what looked like tea but turned out to be tobacco. Past dingy caves where bearded blindlings sat drinking in the dark. She saw Kolail nod at a man outside some sort of tavern. A man with a wolf on a leash. There was a red door behind him, tucked beneath the crumbling levels above.

The street branched off into other fissures in places. It suddenly felt warmer. Kolail grabbed hold of her. Pulled her back just in time to avoid a blast of steam from a crevice between two stalls.

"Look where you're going."

Hirka didn't have the energy to respond. How was she supposed to meet her family like this? The thought sent a shiver through her. She was here. In the same city as Graal's mother and father. Her grandparents. Family. Her legs wobbled. Kolail took her by the arm. Held her up. They stepped into a quieter street. People were more lightly dressed here.

Dreyri. The top houses.

The street opened up at the end. Onto a crater. No, the word *crater* didn't do it any justice. There were no words for this. This was the end of the world. A chasm leading to its very core. They emerged far down the wall of the crater, but she still couldn't see the bottom. It was too dark. Streets were carved into the walls here as well. Streets and homes. All the way around. Thousands of lanterns made the enormous hole look like the night sky. This was the heart of the city. The source of all the cracks. All the streets.

Hirka had never had a problem with heights, but now she felt dizzy. Empty. Exhausted. "Why?" she mumbled. "What is this?"

"Madness," Kolail answered.

She must have fallen, because he scooped her up and carried her onward. Skerri didn't stop him. Maybe the best hiding place was in the arms of one of the fallen. Too exhausted to think anymore, Hirka passed out.

BLOOD OF MY BLOOD

Waves raged outside. A sound she'd almost forgotten.

The sea.

Where am I?

Hirka opened her eyes. She was lying on her side, staring at a wall. Was she locked up?

Cold fear washed through her. She pressed her hands against the wall. It creaked but didn't give. Then the room started to rock. Was she in a boat?

She sat up. Not a cage. Not a boat. She was in a bed. What she'd thought was a wall was a high edge running all the way around. It was like sitting in a black wicker basket. It swayed back and forth, suspended from the ceiling by ropes.

Hirka dragged a hand over her face, feeling foolish.

She wriggled toward an opening at the bottom, swung her feet down onto a cold stone floor, and stood up. The gray tunic had twisted around her while she slept. Who had put her to bed?

The room was big. Black. Carved out of stone. The walls were rough and uneven, like in a cave, but both the ceiling and the floor were smooth. Clearly an intentional contrast. She looked down at her feet and saw her own reflection. It was like walking on a dark lake.

It ought to have been colder. Where was the heat coming from? There weren't any fireplaces. No lamps burning. The pale light was filtering in through a glass wall comprising many small panes that bulged slightly outward. They were darker at the corners, rendered murky by something that looked like ash. It gave her a sense of seeing through a bird's eyes.

Hirka walked over and rested a hand against the glass. Then she realized where she was. She was looking out over a crater. Big enough that it would have taken her the better part of a day to walk around. Its walls, which were riddled with homes, sloped down into the bedrock.

She was at the very top, at the edge. Just below the ice. Cracks cut through it and into the rock in several places. Fissures. Streets. Like the ones they'd walked along the night before.

Ginnungad. The first city. The blindling capital.

Wind threw snow from the glacier against the window before howling its way down into the crater. That was what had woken her. What she'd thought was the sea.

Someone knocked. Hirka jumped, suddenly conscious of two things. It was time to meet her family. And time to sentence someone to death.

She cleared her throat. "Yes?"

Oni came in through a sliding door that was almost indistinguishable from the wall. She seemed different now that she'd had a chance to wash up. Her brown hair curled around her face. She was carrying a bowl of soup that smelled like fish.

Her dimples deepened. "You must forgive us. We weren't aware of just how much food and warmth you needed." Hirka took the bowl and gulped down its contents. Oni looked uncomfortable, and that was when Hirka remembered. Don't eat in front of people. She blushed.

Oni pointed at some shelves by the door. "You'll find clothes over there. They used to belong to Skerri. We'll get you your own soon."

Hirka pictured Skerri in her tight leather with its straps and fastenings. She shook her head. "Thanks, but . . . I'll wear my own."

Oni pursed her lips slightly. "Strength and beauty must be displayed. You can choose from what's there." She pointed at a sliding door just across from the bed. "The bathroom's in there." She turned to leave.

"Oni, how was this formed? This hole?" Hirka nodded at the window.

"There was always a hole, but it got bigger when they mined for the Might," Oni replied. "You'd best hurry. They're all waiting. You're the youngest of the House of Modrasme and none of them have seen you yet."

Oni left the same way she'd come. Hirka slid open the bathroom door. Steps went straight down into the water. A sunken pit in the floor big enough for her to stretch out in. And the water was hot.

She tore off her tunic and sank into the water with a sigh of pleasure. If this was to be the last bath she ever took, then by the gods she would do it properly.

Hirka tugged at the tunic, but it was still too short, refusing to cover her navel. It was loosely knitted from a glimmering yarn that made it look like chainmail. What a pointless garment. But she needed to do her best to fit in.

She followed the sound of voices. The corridor had walls that curved inward, like an overturned ship. It led into a long hall with a ceiling that was open to the ice at one end, letting blue-green light shine down on a group of people. Too many people. Oni was standing by a wall, away from the others. Hirka's breath caught in her throat. She tugged at the tunic again. Ran her fingers through her hair, for all the difference it would make.

Family. Her family. Her blood.

They spotted her. The conversation died. It was so quiet Hirka could hear her footsteps on the stone floor. The wind sweeping across the windows. Row upon row of bulging glass panes. Maybe she could escape everyone's scrutiny by throwing herself through them and plunging into the crater. Though if the rough weather were anything to go by, the glass could withstand a lot.

Be proud. Fearless. Be Dreyri.

Hirka straightened up and lifted her chin. Oni came over and stood like a shadow behind her. Ready to help. Translate. Offer support. Or at least Hirka hoped so.

They were all so strange. She was suddenly struck by the enormity of being alone in a room full of deadborn. Strong and animalistic, with claws and milky white eyes. She took a deep, shaky breath.

A man approached her. A strong man. His tight black shirt made that very clear. He had a full beard that was clipped short and long hair that was heart-wrenchingly red. Red . . . Like hers. It tumbled down over his chest. Hirka pulled her lips taut to stop them from quivering.

He stopped in front of her. Broad-shouldered with a narrow waist. She looked up. The silence demanded action. She had to say something. No one else was. They were all waiting for him. For him to size her up. To reject her, or to accept her.

He turned to the others and flung his arms out. "Haaaaa!"

Hirka jumped. It was half laugh, half exclamation. He threw his head back and did it again. "Haaaaa!" He turned to her again and said something she didn't understand.

"Her umǫni is abysmal," Skerri said, folding her arms across her chest.

The man paid her no notice. "She has my hair!" he said in ymish. "My son's daughter!"

"And eyes like an animal," Skerri added.

Hirka wished she knew what she'd done to make Skerri mad at her. Apart from bringing a heart she'd probably dreamed of cutting out herself.

"My hair . . ." he whispered. He ran his claws through her hair. Hirka clamped her arms to her sides, suppressing the urge to return his touch.

"Look!" he said, choking up. "Look how young she is! Look at her!"

He threw his arms around her. Her face was pressed against a rock-hard chest. She felt his fingers curl around her head. His beard pricked her scalp. He inhaled the scent of her. "My son's daughter. Blood of my blood."

He pulled back again without letting go, studying her face.

"I am Raun," he said. The name burrowed into her heart and started to grow, making it difficult to breathe.

"I'm Hirka."

"Of course you are. Of course you are," he said, as if she'd just told him she was a goddess.

The moment was shattered by shrill laughter from one of the women. "This? This is what we are to present to the House of Hod?"

The House of Modrasme was a family of seven, not counting the servants. Red-haired Raun was friendly and handsome. His wife, Uhere, had short black hair and a slight underbite. It gave her an air of fury, like she was always clenching her teeth. Raun and Uhere. Graal's mother and father. Her grandparents. She repeated it to herself several times, but it was still unreal.

Uhere's father, Lug, also lived in the house. A thin man with lank hair that framed his face like dark curtains. He and his younger wife, Cirra, had a daughter, Vana, who at a mere two hundred and ninety-eight years old was the baby of the family. Until Hirka's arrival, of course.

Vana was draped across a chair covered in furs, twisting a necklace around her finger. She had brown curly hair and full lips that looked too big for her face.

Modrasme was the head of the family. She was more than three thousand seven hundred years old, but her face was completely devoid of wrinkles. Smooth as porcelain. She didn't spare anyone a glance, just sat motionless in a high-backed chair, staring into thin air. Her silver curls fell to her waist.

"Let me see her," she finally said. Raun led Hirka over to her chair. Hirka almost kneeled, but then caught herself. She leaned closer, toward Modrasme's raised hand. The woman for whom the house was named wore a weary expression. Not tired, but more like nothing would ever impress her. She cupped Hirka's cheek in a cool hand and studied her for a moment before sighing and waving as if to shoo them all away.

This seemed to amuse Skerri and Vana, who smirked at each other. Hirka still wasn't sure where Skerri fit into the family, but she spoke about it as if she were a cornerstone. Hirka struggled to keep up with their conversation, but she knew they were openly discussing her shortcomings. Her grasp of the language. Her eyes. Her scrawny arms. The claws she was starting to hate not having. They were talking about her like she wasn't there.

Oni translated for her. She whispered into Hirka's ear, seemingly oblivious to how much the words stung.

How had this happened? How had she ended up in a situation where she was some kind of savior to a deadborn family? They were strangers! With strange ways and strange customs. Their concerns meant nothing to her. Neither their houses nor their honor. She was only interested in one thing, and that was the Might. Their knowledge of it was the only way for her to understand the beak.

Hirka tilted her head toward Oni. "Tell them I need to see a seer. Tell them it's important."

Oni shook her head. "There are other matters that are much more important."

Hirka insisted. "Tell them."

Oni translated. The others looked at each other like they didn't understand. Vana laughed haughtily from the chair she still hadn't vacated. Considering she was Dreyri, this struck Hirka as odd.

It was Uhere who replied. Her grandmother, who looked like she had seen around thirty winters but had probably looked that way for an eternity. Her black fringe fell over her face. Concern crossed her features. She was wearing a neck ornament that looked uncomfortably tight. "No seer can help you with what you are to do now. Time is not on our side. The House of Hod knows you're here, and they'll demand to see you soon. If we're lucky, you'll be able to string together a sentence in umǫni by then. If we're luckier still, you'll be able to move and dress properly. Until then, there is no time for anything else."

Hirka lowered her gaze.

Raun lifted her chin with a claw. "Nothing to worry about. She'll be ready. She is our blood. Our youngest blood." Hirka saw Skerri and Vana glance at each other.

"You're the best news we've had since . . ." Raun didn't finish his sentence.

"He might disagree," Vana said flatly, nodding toward the other end of the room.

A bald-headed servant Hirka hadn't seen before came in with Kolail at his heels. The fallen stopped a short distance from them. He looked bored. Not like someone with only moments left to live.

Hirka felt a chill run down her spine. She'd had a plan of sorts. An idea that had seemed solid not that long ago. Now it was running away like fine sand.

"Keskolail! Come!" Raun waved him closer. Kolail obeyed. He didn't look at Hirka.

"Skerri says that you loosed an arrow and that it came close to hitting Dreyri. Is that true?"

Kolail nodded. Hirka gaped. Had she been standing closer, she would have kicked him. Couldn't he at least try to explain?

"And you did it in poor visibility, fully aware of the risk?"

Kolail nodded again. His steel-gray hair was sticking out in every direction, a testament to the weather outside. Hirka took a step toward Raun. "He had to. And he was doing what he was told."

"Well, I should very much hope so," Raun replied. Skerri smirked.

Hirka felt numb. Anger and despair warred within her, making it difficult to stay calm, but she had to. If she gave into her feelings, all would be lost.

Raun looked at her. "This is Dreysíl. He knows what he did. He knows the rules. But you are the one he wronged, so what is your judgement, Hirka?"

Hirka took a deep breath to steady her nerves. "His aim was true. In a snowstorm, and from a great distance," she said. "I was never in any danger. He is an exceptional archer, and where I come from, no one is punished for being good at what they do."

Raun nodded and ran his fingers over his beard, as if deliberating. Skerri gave an exasperated groan and opened her mouth to say something. Hirka continued so she wouldn't have the chance to ruin everything.

"But I know that rules are rules. So I thought . . ." She closed her eyes for a moment. Uncertainty wouldn't help her here. She needed to make herself clear. "His punishment is that he will serve me. He will teach me about life here, and the people. Things I need to know."

Raun folded his arms over his chest. "Oni is the best teacher you could hope for. You need no one else."

Hirka lifted her chin a touch higher. "Oni can teach me about life at the top. Ko—Keskolail can teach me about life at the bottom. Only a fool would ignore one of the two."

Raun raised an eyebrow. "One of the fallen put your life in danger, and you want to punish him by sparing his life?"

Hirka shrugged. "From what I've heard, it's not much of a life. Why not put it to good use?"

Raun threw his head back. "Haaaaa!" His laughter heralded victory. Hirka tried to hide her relief. She'd won.

"So, Keskolail," Raun said. "I assume we needn't go to the Council with this judgement. Do you accept?"

Kolail nodded again. That was all he'd done since he arrived.

"Good! You will come when you are needed, and do what she asks, until she sees fit to release you from your duties. You can still take on other work so long as she doesn't need you. You may leave us now."

Kolail glanced at Hirka. He shook his head, an almost imperceptible movement. She knew what he was trying to say. She was an idiot. She'd won, but she'd defied Skerri.

Only time would tell what it would cost her.

THE HOT SPRING

Rime had followed Kolkagga's network of paths and rope bridges as deep into Blindból as possible, but even they ended before he made it halfway to Ravnhov. From there he had to rely on instinct to get through the mountains towering above him, snow dusting their windward slopes. The terrain lived and died with the seasons. What had been a decent path one day could be a death trap the next. He had to be vigilant.

The cold was less biting than it had been only a day earlier. The spring equinox would soon be upon them, and much of the snow had melted. The terrain was negotiable at least.

Unlike Orja.

Kolkagga's new master was steadfast in her loyalty to the Council. He couldn't even put much pressure on her, since he was reliant on her goodwill to stay in the camp. He'd hoped to bring Ravnhov their salvation. An army of black shadows. Now he brought nothing but bad tidings. Troop mobilizations in Mannfalla. An impending war. Though he was sure Eirik had known about that for some time.

Regardless, the chieftain of Ravnhov was the one person in all of Ym who might actually be happy Rime was still alive. Together they would find a solution. Separate friend from foe and forge alliances that could crush Darkdaggar and Mannfalla's army before facing a greater enemy.

Eirik also had his own people behind him. He would be able to advise Rime on how he could win back Kolkagga. Change Orja's mind. Kolkagga were key. Without them there was no point trying.

The sky had started to turn gray. Rime slowed down. The familiar terrain evoked a memory, making his whole body tingle.

The hot spring.

It lay just ahead, in a hollow. The snow had melted around its edge. Steam rose from the green water, making the mountains in the background hazy.

He stopped. A murder of crows took flight and disappeared. He felt his strength disappear along with them. He was left alone, weakened, with the memories gnawing at his chest.

There by the rock, that's where she'd left her bag. And just over there, that's where he'd killed his own men, with Launhug bleeding out in the water. They had given their lives defending a seer he'd known didn't exist. Their remains had long since been collected by Kolkagga. The snow had covered all traces.

But his body remembered. A stabbing pain in his side, where steel had opened him up.

Rime stared at the water. He hadn't wanted to stop, but she'd insisted, as only she could. Said they needed to bathe. Threatened him with fleas and other critters.

His world had fallen apart. The Seer didn't exist, Urd had killed Ilume, and they'd had nowhere to go but Ravnhov. And she'd talked of fleas . . .

He smiled. His swords suddenly felt heavy across his back. Everything had seemed hopeless back then. But he couldn't have imagined things could get as hopeless as they were now.

He walked toward the spring and set his bag down. Rested his swords against the rock. He started to undress. Driven by a need to feel warmth. To go back in time. To a time before she'd turned her back on him. Before Darkdaggar. Before the beak.

He folded his clothes and set them on top of his bag. The snow melted beneath his bare feet. He slipped into the water. It burned against his skin. Loved him and punished him. Rime closed his eyes. Suspended between hot and cold. Between water and snow.

She'd been here too. In this same water. The girl who had put the world through the wringer. The girl he'd done so many stupid things for. The girl he had kissed.

His body quickened. Hardened. He remembered. Her lips against his. Her hand fumbling at his neck, seeking bare skin. She hated him now, but it hadn't always been that way.

Agony and ecstasy intertwined, becoming a need that demanded satisfaction. An expectation he had to meet. She had wanted him once. If they'd been able to, they would have made love there and then. He knew that.

Rime moved his hand lower. Felt his throat tingling.

His throat . . .

Graal!

The tingling turned to stinging. A very different kind of ache. A very different demand. His pulse quickened. He didn't know whether it was because he was hard or because he was scared. The conflicting sensations were making him feel ill. Rime twisted around in the water. Grabbed his clothes and found the small bottle Damayanti had given him. Blindling blood. Raven blood. And gods only knew what else.

What should I say?

Damayanti would already have told him about Darkdaggar, and that Rime had lost his seat on the Council. There was no point trying to hide that. How furious that had made him remained to be seen.

Rime clenched his teeth. Tried to resist the inevitable. Force himself to endure. Create an illusion of control. It was useless. The longer he waited, the more intense the pain.

He bound the Might. Opened his mouth. Let a couple of drops fall down his throat and felt the beak come to life, stirring like an animal. He forced down the nausea. Spat out some blood.

"Graal . . ."

He crawled out of the water. Rested on all fours in the snow. The words issued from his throat as if they were his own.

"When exactly were you planning on telling me?"

A laugh slipped out of Rime. "Tell you what? There's plenty to choose from."

"Rime, I like to think I don't take pleasure in being malicious, and truth be told, there is little pleasure to be had under the circumstances. But what did I tell you? Didn't I tell you that your influence lessened with every day you were gone? Didn't I tell you that you should never have come here?"

Rime forced out a deep cough, as if it might ease the throbbing pain. He knew all too well that he was at Graal's mercy. Naked and impotent in the snow. He was used to being able to fight. To hacking away at whatever threatened him. This couldn't be fought. It was a new feeling for him, and it enraged him.

"Difficult to say," he answered. "You're a chatty fellow. You've said so many things."

"This isn't a game!"

The beak gaped open. Rime clutched his throat. Coughed up more blood. Red rain in the snow. It was quiet for a moment.

"Rime . . . I wish I'd never met you. Things would be simpler then. But as things stand, I would like to spare you. Out of respect. For you and for her. This doesn't have to be difficult."

Rime fell forward into the snow. "Respect? Is that what you call it? You've sent her to Slokna out of respect?"

"I've sent her to her people, Rime. She belongs there. There she will have status. Elevate our house. She'll be better off there than anywhere else. And be happier than you could ever make her."

"Status?" Rime laughed. Tasted blood. "You think that's what will make her happy? You don't know her at all, do you?"

"I'm her father."

"You're a snake."

Rime waited for the pain to come, but it didn't. He rolled over onto his back and held his arm over his face. The cold seeped into his skin.

"Shall we try again when you're feeling more civil, Rime?"

Rime felt his lips twitch, but he didn't answer. His rage was smoldering with the Might. Growing with each beat of his heart.

Graal carried on as if he'd won. "You've lost power. You've made everything more difficult for me. What you need to concern yourself with now is ensuring Darkdaggar doesn't gain control of Kolkagga."

"Do you think I'm an idiot?" Rime swallowed blood. He wasn't surprised they shared the same aim. Neither of them wanted to face Kolkagga on the battlefield.

Graal sighed, soothing the pain like a cool breeze. "Without me, I have no doubt you would be. Be glad you took the beak. At least that way I can keep you alive."

Rime crawled back to the water.

Alive . . . But for how long? Until the war is over? Until I've done what you need me to do?

He was a tool. A weapon. A slave. But if Graal thought he was going to fight for the blind because he was afraid of a little pain, he was very much mistaken.

"You'll hear from me soon," Graal said. "And by then I expect you to have regained control of Kolkagga, and for them to be prepared to take on the Council."

Then Graal was gone. Rime was alone again. He lowered himself into the water. The warmth returned to his body. But he couldn't stop shaking.

AT THE BOTTOM

"The first families still live at the top, you see." Oni pointed up at the edge of the crater. "Those are the oldest structures in Ginnungad."

Hirka tipped her head back, trying to look up without revealing her face. That was a strict condition of her going out.

The houses Oni was referring to were situated in large caves in the north end of the crater wall. Tall and intricate, as if they'd grown out of the rock on their own.

Born of the Might.

They followed the road that wound its way down into the crater in a large spiral. Then Oni stopped. "There. Criers' Rock." She pointed at what looked like the start of a bridge sticking out from the crater wall a bit farther down. "All proclamations are made from there. The news about you will come from there, provided they accept you."

Hirka stared at the gray rock jutting out into nothing. It looked more like a place to plummet to your death than a place to make a proclamation. Though to her, both options held much the same appeal.

It was too far down to be part of the leading house at the top. "I thought it belonged to the House of Hod?"

"It does," Oni replied. "Everything from the top to Criers' Rock belongs to the House of Hod."

"Oh . . ."

Kolail cleared his throat like he wanted to say something, but he didn't. He followed them like a shadow, always close on their heels. He was the only one who could accompany them. Hungl and Tyla were known servants of the House of Modrasme and would attract unwelcome attention. Make people wonder about the girl under the robe. But no one looked at the fallen. Not even in disgust.

Two women approached them carrying a colorful carpet between them. Oni signaled discreetly and Hirka lowered her head again, keeping her eyes fixed on the ground as they passed.

"This is pointless," Hirka whispered. "I'm not a secret anymore."

The family had received a number of invitations and gifts over the past few days. It seemed that a rumor had spread. A rumor that something had happened. Something that would change the status of the House of Modrasme.

Oni gave a strained smile and waited until the women were far enough away before answering. "You're bound to the fate of the people. To the gateways and to the Might. Your coming is our biggest and most important news since the war!" She glanced around and lowered her voice again. "You're Graal's daughter. What do you think the House of Hod would say if others saw you before they did? It's unthinkable! You have to use your head, Hirka!"

Hirka had been told that more than a few times already. The meeting with the House of Hod was what they were waiting for. Everything she was preparing herself for. She would take them Naiell's heart as a gift and receive a gift in return. Something greater than she could imagine, she'd heard. She was supposed to be excited, but just thinking about it gave her goosebumps. Hirka was looking forward to the meeting and the gift about as much as she'd looked forward to going through the Rite.

"So let's go to the caves," she said. "There are no Dreyri there. No one who'll care."

Oni wrung her hands anxiously, caught between the urge to chide and the duty to serve. Between refusing and obeying. "I don't know why you want to go there. It's just roots and mushrooms. And the southern part of the city is no place for you. Surely you saw that when we arrived? Besides, I still haven't spoken to the tailors, or—"

"Oni, if I don't see something growing soon, I'm going to lose my mind."

Oni sighed. "Keskolail, are you familiar with these growing caves? Do you know the way?"

Hirka felt uneasy every time someone butchered his name. *Kes.* It was only one syllable, but it said so much. That he was one of the fallen. That he had killed. And that anything that followed was unimportant.

Kolail nodded, seemingly unperturbed by the same thing that made her blood boil.

He led them along a street, away from the crater, taking numerous shortcuts. Narrow staircases and rope lifts that went between levels.

Hirka was still struggling to wrap her head around their stance on tools in this world. Horses were out because that would be like saying your feet couldn't carry you. That you couldn't walk yourself. Rope lifts were another matter, because nobody could fly, so there was no shame in using those.

Some tools were more shameful than others. For example, using a knife was tantamount to saying your claws weren't sharp enough, whereas using a paintbrush was more acceptable. And so on. Basically, all weapons and tools could be ranked by how embarrassing it was to use them.

The same applied to clothes. Dressing in thick fur was like saying you couldn't survive in your own skin, but a thin cloak could be worn as decoration. You could lock your doors to protect irreplaceable things, but not because you feared an attack. Balconies had no railings, sticking out like lips from the rock because no one was scared of falling from them. Or at least they wouldn't let on that they were.

It was an endless balancing act between surviving and showing off. Ginnungad was a hotbed of arrogance.

Kolail continued into a narrow alleyway that led them into the street to the south. Hirka recognized a sloping bridge she'd seen the evening they'd arrived in the city. That was all she saw before Kolail led them into a tunnel. It grew wider and turned into another street. Not an open ravine, but one inside the rock. Lamplight shone from open windows. Not many had glass, and those that did became fewer and farther between as they walked. It started getting warmer even though she couldn't see any hearths. But she knew why that was now. The heat came through channels from hot springs located some distance away from the glacier. An unpredictable system. There were streets where ice clung to the rock walls, and others where it melted slowly from the top and dripped down.

There were more and more people the farther they walked, wearing more and more clothes. Fewer bare bellies and blue-tinged thighs. Maybe they'd stopped trying to prove anything here. Bowed out of the competition.

Oni slowed down and looked around. She clearly felt uncomfortable. "Are we safe here?" She looked at Kolail.

He didn't bat an eyelid. "Some of us live here and do just fine."

Hirka walked up beside him. "You live here? Can you show me?"

He didn't reply. Hirka looked around. Ramshackle houses made of stone and wood climbed the walls as if stacked there by a drunken giant. She could hear noise and shouts from the taverns. She'd expected beggars but saw none. Poverty had a different face in Ginnungad than in Ym.

"There," Kolail said eventually. It was more of a grunt. He nodded at a pile of shacks reaching almost all the way up to the ceiling.

"Which one?"

"The one with the shutters on the windows," he said. "The one you can't see inside because the guy who lives there doesn't like people sticking their noses where they don't belong."

She took the hint and didn't ask any more questions. His breath smelled of sweet smoke, so she could only assume he'd been out late the night before.

They made their way farther down. The air grew muggy and warm. The street ended in an open space with several smaller caves on each side. A group of what looked like foremen loitered outside the one closest to them. They spotted Oni and straightened up. She strode past them and inside. Hirka followed with Kolail on her heels. It was warm, like in a greenhouse. And there were beds. Beds filled with soil. Dark, wonderful soil. In long rows and steep terraces. A lump formed in Hirka's throat as she took in the smell. She had to suppress the urge to fall to her knees and start digging.

Umpiri walked between the beds, tending the plants. She recognized mushrooms, roots, onions . . . Some carried baskets over their shoulders for harvesting. The workers were thin, their backs stooped after years of work.

My people are starving.

Graal's words. She'd thought he meant for the Might, but maybe it was simpler than that.

"Seen what you wanted to see?" Kolail asked tersely.

Hirka looked at him. "What's wrong?"

"We shouldn't be here."

Hirka looked around and realized what he meant. Some of the workers had stopped what they were doing and were watching Oni walk between the beds like she owned them. Straight-backed, like

Dreyri. In a servant's robe that clearly belonged to one of the higher houses.

Hirka moved toward her. "Oni . . ."

As Oni turned, a wad of earth exploded in her face. She gasped. Soil trickled down her chest, collecting in the folds of her robe.

One of the foremen came running and grabbed a bald man by the neck, forcing his head back. The man didn't resist. His eyes were black. Empty. He started to choke. Hirka grabbed Oni's arm. "Stop him! Make him stop!"

Oni's eyes widened. "Stop?! Look at me! Look what he's done to our house!"

Hirka looked into her eyes. Strange. White. The dimples that had given her a warmth before suddenly seemed perverse. There was a chasm between her and Oni. Oni, the most ymling-like blindling she'd ever met. But they'd never be able to understand each other. And right now, she didn't have time to try.

"Oni, tell him to let go or I'll show my face. I mean it." Hirka brought a hand to her hood, ready to make good on her threat.

Oni snarled some words in umoni. Words Hirka was glad she hadn't learned yet. The foreman gave them an astonished look, but he let go. Oni stormed toward the exit, her robe flapping behind her.

Kolail steered Hirka ahead of him out of the cave, keeping right behind her, as if to protect her. She looked back. The bald man was gasping for breath and rubbing his throat as he watched them go. Then he stiffened, like he'd seen a ghost, and she realized her mistake.

She hadn't been thinking. She'd forgotten. In the midst of all the chaos, she'd done exactly what she'd threatened to do. She'd made eye contact.

They went back the same way they'd come. Oni didn't say a word. Her dimples were deep and angry. Hirka tried to quash her anxiety. She refused to apologize. Refused to let herself be manipulated into believing she'd done something wrong. No matter what Oni might think. No matter what every Umpiri in Ginnungad might think.

"Wait . . ." Hirka brushed soil from the back of Oni's robes.

The learned servant seemed momentarily conflicted, but then her shoulders sank. "You have much to learn. I know that. I understand. But how am I to teach you anything when you won't listen?"

"I'll never learn to punish innocent people, Oni."

"Innocent? He was anything but innocent! Don't you have eyes?"

Kolail stood nearby, throwing stolen glances at them.

Oni's gaze faltered. Almost imperceptibly so, as only the reflections in her white eyes gave her away. "Hirka, I'm not going to tell your family what happened today. I'm willing to chalk it up to ignorance. You just don't understand how things work here."

Hirka almost snorted. Oni was holding her tongue more for her own sake than for Hirka's. That much she was sure of.

"I don't understand how things work anywhere, Oni. Not here. Not in the human world. And not in Ym, even though I grew up there. The only thing I understand is this." She thumped a fist against her chest. Over her heart. "And I know you don't kill someone for throwing dirt!"

"This isn't about dirt!"

People were turning to look at them. Kolail put a hand on Hirka's back and steered both her and Oni between two stalls selling bags and staffs. Oni lowered her voice and repeated herself. "This isn't about dirt. This is about how they're presuming to do things that they never would have before."

"Who is? And why?"

Oni took a deep breath. "You have to understand that things have been changing for a long time. It started after the war, when we were mining for the Might. Many leading houses moved as close as possible, displacing the houseless. Suddenly it wasn't only the powerful who lived farther up. High and low lived side by side. Nothing has been the same since, even though some semblance of order has been restored."

Hirka could see Kolail listening out of the corner of her eye. Oni continued in a low voice. "And without the Might, trade suffered. Mightglass and art that was created before the war has been stolen and sold all over the world. The prices are ridiculous because everyone knows there will never be any more of it. Your bedroom windows alone could pay the salaries of an entire district, and the most wretched among them are well aware of that! Do you understand what I'm saying? It's only getting worse."

Hirka suspected she understood better than Oni, but she kept that to herself.

"Why's it getting worse?"

Oni glanced at Kolail.

He snorted. "You think I don't know?"

Hirka looked at them both. Tried to think like Umpiri. To see it the way they did. And then she understood.

"You might know, Kolail, but Oni doesn't want you to hear her say it."

Kolail stepped closer and snarled. "Then I'll say it for her! The wretched are doing things they've never done before because they *can*. Dreyri have been superior since the first. More fertile. Closer to the ravens. The highest houses superior to the lowest. And the lowest superior to the houseless. It's always been that way. But without the Might, they're no better than the rest of us. Neither stronger nor more powerful. Without the Might, we're the same."

The two blindlings stared at each other like feral cats. Neither of them were Dreyri, but they still saw them in completely different lights.

And me? What am I?

Oni rested a cautious hand on Hirka's back, as if to lead her away from him. "You're gambling with your life, Keskolail," she said without looking up.

Kolail didn't reply. Hirka had a feeling he cheated death on a regular basis. He looked at Hirka. "Can I go?" he asked. The bitterness was unmistakable. She nodded, ashamed that she had to give him permission. He turned and left.

An oppressive silence hung over them all the way home. Hirka had hoped it would lift when they got back, but there it was even worse. The House of Modrasme was silent as Slokna.

What's happened?

Skerri was standing with her arms crossed, looking out the window. She didn't spare them so much as a glance. Raun was leaning against the table, his red hair reflected in the black glass. He picked up a sort of disc and held it out to Hirka.

"Congratulations," he said, not sounding entirely convinced.

Hirka took it. It was a thin, round disc caught somewhere between glass and stone. Mightglass.

Letters she didn't understand had been carved into the surface.

She made herself ask. "What's this?"

Raun straightened up. "An invitation. It's time to meet the House of Hod."

"It's the first invitation we've received since the war," Skerri said from over by the window, the ashy glass casting long shadows behind her.

Hirka stared down at the symbols. Incomprehensible characters that seemed to swim together. Her hand trembled and she felt a sharp sting in her finger. A drop of blood welled forth. She'd cut herself on the edge.

LUCKY

The storm was raging. Snow from the glacier kept lashing at the window. Sleep was impossible.

Hirka stared up at the ceiling, at her reflection in the shiny stone. Everything was black. The ceiling. The blanket. The pillow. The hanging bed. The only thing that stood out was her skin. And her red hair, fanned out like she was drowning in a boundless sea of black.

At least if she drowned she wouldn't have to face the coming day. Face meeting the House of Hod.

Her temples were throbbing from days of memorizing words, names, and rules of conduct. All the things she could and couldn't do when standing before Hod and Tyr in the leading house. She hadn't met them, but already she hated them. Because they were all anyone talked about. Because she was losing sleep over them.

But the same was probably true of the tailor. He'd promised to have her dress ready by morning. A dress . . . Just thinking about it made her itch. She flipped over onto her side.

This meeting was so incredibly important to them all. A chance to elevate the house to its former glory. It was almost pitiful. But Hirka had promised Graal she would get them their honor back.

And the Might . . .

A promise she would likely never be able to keep. A promise made more complicated by Kolail's words. The Might was the cause of the differences in their society. The Might determined rank, and it favored Dreyri. It was probably just as well they no longer had it.

Her head was spinning. She was exhausted.

She knew Raun was the only one who believed her visit with the House of Hod would be a success. No one else. Skerri least of all. Hirka didn't know what was worse: the expectation that she would restore a family's honor, or the threat posed by those who thought she would fail.

The price of failure is worse.

If she failed, Graal would find another way. Buy his way to the top by sending Umpiri through the gateways. To the Might. But how many? Just the family, or all of Ginnungad? Would every deadborn in Dreysíl be sent to Ym?

And what would he do to Rime?

Hirka brought her hand to her throat. Imagined what it must be like to have a beak inside. Bones from a dead raven. She remembered how Urd had smelled, back on Bromfjell. The rotting hole in his throat . . . A knot tightened in her chest.

There had to be some way to save him. If only they would let her meet a seer. Someone who knew how. Maybe Graal was preventing it? He didn't want her to free Rime, that much was clear.

Hirka clutched her head in her hands. Too many expectations. No one to trust.

She sat up. The bed started to rock. She wriggled down to the end and climbed out. Went over to the window and rested her forehead against the cool glass. Born of the Might. Flecked with ash. Shaped by hand, from living stone, and worth more than she cared to think about.

She couldn't take another minute in here. She had to get out. The balcony was the closest she'd come to fresh air since the invitation. This was a prison. A luxurious one, but a prison nonetheless.

Hirka pulled on some clothes. Her own tunic and trousers. Then she put the robe on over top and pulled up the hood. Slid her knife into her sock.

There had been unrest in the city the last few nights. House-less had smashed windows, stolen anything of value, and burned everything else. There were watchmen patrolling the streets, but Ginnungad was a big city, so it hadn't helped much.

It's my fault.

Hirka knew she'd been seen. She was living proof that the gate-ways were open again. Something was afoot, and Umpiri could smell it.

She wouldn't be out long. Just a quick walk. To clear her head. She'd stay away from people. And dangerous areas.

She opened the sliding door a crack. Peeked out into the corridor. She could hear giggling from Vana's room. Then a low moan. Hirka hadn't met her boyfriend yet. Just heard him at night. Best to go a different way.

The balcony.

She pulled on her boots, found her staff, and opened the balcony door. It took some effort in the wind, but she was soon out on the slippery stone ledge. The road below was slick with slush, but it was plenty wide enough. She could manage it without rolling off and ending up at the bottom of the crater. Not that that would be such a bad thing. At least then she'd get out of meeting the accursed House of Hod.

Hirka hopped down onto the road and went down the steps to the level below. It was quieter there, even though she could still hear the wind howling across the glacier. She turned down the nearest crevice onto one of the main streets.

She had to be careful. Stick to safer areas. But the sense of free-dom was intoxicating. Banners fluttered from the bridges. Steam from the thermal vents was expelled from cracks in the walls that she'd learned to avoid. Even late at night, people were out and about. There were cantinas selling drinks and smokes. A glassblower was working late, doors wide open. And the farther she walked, the livelier it got. Dogs barking. People playing instruments and singing in taverns. She would have tucked the sounds away for later if she could, to enjoy the things that all the worlds had in common. Even in this world, where people lived for thousands of years and ate with their claws, they still drank like everyone else. Made music. Smoked. Loved. And shouted and screamed.

Screamed?

Hirka stopped. She heard the sound of glass shattering. People ran past, nearly knocking her over. The shouting subsided and she took cover in an alleyway that wasn't much wider than she was.

Trouble . . . And she'd wandered right into the middle of it. Fear gripped her. She'd walked farther than she'd planned. She had to find her way back!

She took a cautious step out into the street. Burning scraps of cloth rained down in front of her. She retreated back into the alleyway. Squeezed into the darkness. The sounds she'd been enjoying only moments earlier were gone. Replaced with sounds of fear. Rage. People running past. Some with teardrops in their foreheads, others without. Watchmen and rioters everywhere she looked. Who were the ones making trouble and who could help her? It was impossible to say.

It was hopeless. Tomorrow she'd be meeting the House of Hod, and still she didn't understand who was who in this city. Still she was an outsider. And stupid enough to die because of it.

No! Live, don't die.

Black smoke billowed through the street. It started to drift into the alleyway. Hirka held her hood over her mouth and ran farther along. Could she find a different way home? What choice did she have? She had nowhere else to go.

Kolail . . .

She wasn't far away. The main streets all branched off from the crater, meaning the alleyway she was in ought to lead to the south street. But that was an area that Oni had felt unsafe in. An area to avoid . . .

A bottle exploded right behind her. Someone opened a window and shouted down at her. To Slokna with how dangerous it was. Anything was better than standing here.

Hirka ran along the alleyway and came out on the south street. There was trouble here as well. She recognized the tunnel that led to the caves, crossed the street, and slipped inside. The noise was immediately muffled. It had been crowded here last time. Now there was virtually no one. The chairs outside the taverns were empty. A couple of lone souls hurried past, heading in the direction of the riots. To take part, she suspected.

Level upon level of lopsided homes were stacked on both sides. They practically hung over the street, so much so it was incredible they hadn't come crashing down a long time ago. Lamps were burning in the windows. The flames grew smaller and smaller higher up, revealing how cavernous the subterranean streets actually were.

The steps leading up to Kolail's were wedged between the structures. She could hear people arguing in a shack farther along. Judging by the smell, there was a communal outhouse close by.

A gawky man stood in the shadows beneath a balcony. His obvious effort to look casual bore the telltale signs of someone dealing drugs. She ought to know, she'd grown up with someone who'd done the same. She also knew that most weren't like Father, so she hurried up the steps and found what she hoped was Kolail's door.

She hesitated. A sudden barrage of thoughts stopped her from knocking. How well did she actually know Kolail? How much did she know about the fallen? Why had she gone out in the middle of the night? To get some air, or to run away? She shouldn't be here . . .

Hirka slumped down onto the steps. Steps so crooked it was clear they'd been carved without any aid whatsoever from the Might. She leaned her head against the wall. Listened to the sound of her heartbeat and the distant shouts from the streets.

Someone's coming!

Hirka leaped to her feet. Tightened her grip on her staff. Ready to strike, if she had to. A large man was climbing the steps. Unsteady on his feet. He grunted. Was he drunk? Hirka retreated farther up. Tried to hide against the wall, but it was hopeless.

The man stopped. He pulled down his hood and looked at her. *Kolail!*

They stared at each other in the dark. Why in Slokna was he out at this hour?

The answer was written all over his face. He closed his eyes for a moment. Pulled his lips taut. He was not happy to see her. Then he put the key in the door and turned it. Struggled to open it. Groaned. Hirka recognized the sound. He wasn't drunk, he was wounded. Or maybe both.

Hirka tore open the door and ducked under his arm so he wouldn't fall. His jacket smelled like the wolf she'd nestled up against in the human world. She eased him down onto a bed just inside and shut the door behind them.

The room was even smaller than the cabin in Elveroa. She groped her way around while her eyes adjusted to the dark. The stone walls were rough and uneven. The one small window was shuttered. Beneath it was a bench with grindstones, knives, feathers, and arrows on it. A wooden bowl. And what she needed—an oil lamp.

"Lighter?"

He grunted in response. She repeated herself, in case he hadn't understood. "Lighter. Fire. Light!"

"In the drawer," he puffed, pointing with a curved claw. His hand dropped to the bed again straight away. Hirka pulled open the drawer. Rooted through it until she found the only thing that could be a lighter. It was like nothing she'd seen before, but at least it made sparks. She managed to light the lamp, then put it on a stool by the bed. His bed was no rocking basket like hers, but a simple bench that occupied most of the room. Kolail leaned his head against the wall.

Sweat trickled down his forehead. His hair had clumped together into points, like little daggers. He tried to get more comfortable. Bared his canines in a grimace. Hirka spotted a red patch on his shirt, just below his ribs. She reached out to take a closer look, but he grabbed her hand.

"Don't touch me," he croaked.

"Don't be scared," she replied calculatedly. He let go, just like she knew he would. She braced herself for what she would see and hiked up his shirt.

Nothing. He was sticky with blood, but she couldn't see so much as a scratch. She pressed her fingers against his skin. Kolail screamed and swung his arm wildly. He was too weak and too drunk to land a blow.

She'd felt something. Under the skin.

Cold certainty washed over her. He was a blindling. Umpiri. She remembered seeing Naiell's wound close up before her very eyes.

The same thing had happened to Kolail, but there was something trapped inside. The thought made her feel ill. She dragged a hand across her mouth.

"Arrowhead?"

"Glass," Kolail answered. "Broken glass." His breath smelled of stale beer.

Hirka steadied herself. Broken glass. Pretty nasty, but nothing she hadn't seen before. The toughest part would be opening him up without the wound healing over again before she was done.

"At least we don't have to worry about stitches." She tried to laugh but ended up swallowing it. She pulled her knife out of her boot and warmed the blade over the flame from the lamp.

"What are you doing?" he asked through clenched teeth.

"What needs to be done," she answered. "Or would you rather find someone else? And maybe at the same time you can explain where you've been tonight?"

He snorted. "Someone else? There is no one else. Not here."

"You don't have any healers?"

"Why would we? If we needed healers, we wouldn't damn well deserve to survive. We stand until we fall. It's natural. Rabbits die."

Hirka shook her head. Turned the blade in the flame. "Idiot. Dropping like flies is natural? No wonder there are fewer and fewer of you."

She warmed her fingers over the flame, too. Holding them as close as she could. "Can you numb the pain? With your claws?" she asked, hoping it was something they could all do. Naiell had done it to her when she'd had to stitch herself up.

He shook his head weakly. "We're immune to our own poison. Besides—"

"You can handle pain. Yeah, yeah, I've been here long enough."

He smiled. His eyes looked even paler than normal. "It's not done. Maybe for your child. Someone you cared about. But not for anyone else."

Hirka looked at him. He lay there, unaware of the enormity of what he'd just revealed. Naiell had cared about her as if she were his own child. Naiell, the traitor. Her father's brother. And now she had his heart on ice, in a box.

Maybe he did care, but that was before he threatened me.

"You'd best grit your teeth then," she said and rested the blade of her knife on his skin. She held it there for a moment. Not cutting. Looking up at him. His face was twisted in pain and she hadn't even

119

done anything yet. Maybe his body was trying to heal itself. Around the shards of glass. A blessing had turned into an agonizing curse.

He opened his mouth to say something, but then he had to start over.

"Why are you so . . . so damn determined to save my skin?"

She attempted a smile. "That's what I do. That's all I know."

"Your first memory of this world is me killing a man . . ."

Hirka shook her head. "My first memory is someone shouting your name. And I assume from that point on you had no choice."

She pressed the blade against his skin. He tensed but managed to stay quiet. Until steel met glass. She gritted her teeth, then pushed the edges of the wound apart with her fingers. Blocked out his scream and did what she had to do. She pulled out a tiny beast of a shard. Thick. Probably from a bottle. Hopefully that meant it hadn't broken in his body. But she had to check . . .

She gently pressed her fingers to his skin, probing around the red opening. Nothing. He didn't shout either. Blood ran down his side, forming a dark stain on the carpet. She let go of the edges of the wound. Stared at them as they turned white. A kind of foam pulling them together. Had she not just witnessed the suffering it was capable of inflicting, she'd have wanted it for herself. Eternal life. They were invulnerable, like gods. What would be left of Ym if creatures like these were let loose upon it?

She wiped the sweat off his forehead. The teardrop felt like a pearl against her fingers. He looked at her from behind heavy eyelids.

"You're not like them. You'll never be like them."

"There is no *them*. There's only people, and people are all different."

"Yes, you would know, wouldn't you? You've been to three worlds." He said it almost as if in jest, but something else lay behind it. Envy? Admiration?

"No wonder you're important to them," he continued, riding high now that the glass was out of his body. Now that he was no longer in pain. "They think you'll unite them. Lead them to the Might. Which is great for them, but not for the rest of us."

Hirka wiped her knife on his shirt. "Is that why you've taken to the streets?"

He snorted. "What do you think will happen when we get a taste of the Might again? Dreyri will be strongest again. The power will stay where it has always been. That's why those of us at the bottom are pushing back."

"If it's that simple, then why do we keep trying to save each other's lives? You and I? Why am I still alive, when I'm the one who's supposed to lead them to the Might? You hide under a hood and throw bottles in the streets, but you don't do the one thing that could change the future. You don't kill me."

"It's not for your sake, if that's what you think."

"Then why?"

He sighed. His eyelids grew even heavier. "There's always hope, isn't there? Hope that change will lead to something better. And the false hope that saving you will give me my life back."

"What do you mean?"

He moved his claws to the teardrop in his forehead. "This. A false hope that they'll remove it. Pardon me. Make me Umpiri again, not one of the fallen. Isn't that what we're all fighting for? To be like them. Those who have everything."

His hand fell to the bed. Hirka felt drained of all strength. She had never been anyone important. She had been a child of Odin. The rot. Menskr. Lived in a red wagon along roadsides. In a cabin in Elveroa. Everything she owned fit in the bag on her back. She'd never had roots or riches. But now someone else was on the bottom. Now she was like Rime. Descended from a powerful family, with everything she could wish for. She was the lucky one, and it was like poison in her veins.

Kolail shut his eyes. "You could crush me with what you know now."

Hirka smiled. "Then I'd better give you something that could crush me, too." She got up and took off her robe. Then she took off her tunic and put the robe back on. She rolled the tunic up into a ball and put it on the bench under the window. "I need to talk to the Seer, Kolail. But they won't let me meet him. Find him and give him this. Tell him who I am. If he recognizes the smell, he'll believe you. Can you do that for me?"

Kolail nodded. "Hirka, you know what this means, right? People rioting in the streets?"

"Yes," she replied. "It means I'm out of time." She sat down on the edge of the bed again. Tired and drained.

He nodded sluggishly. "Once you've met the House of Hod, they'll present you to the city. To the world. I can almost hear them. I hope you're ready for this . . ."

She didn't answer.

"I'll take you home," he said listlessly. "But first . . . rest a little."

Hirka curled up at the end of his bed, resting her head on his legs. She was so tired that her eyes stung. She closed them.

"Kolail, how did you become one of the fallen?"

He turned his head, stubble scraping against the pillow. "I made the same mistake as you. I saved the wrong person."

THE TEA MERCHANT

Darkdaggar asked the coachman to stop the carriage a little way down the Catgut and paid him neither more nor less than he asked for. Anything else would have left a lasting impression, and on this particular evening, he didn't want to be remembered. He continued on foot with Kunte and Jarle close on his heels. Good men. Men he could rely on if anything went wrong.

The area was worse than he remembered. Or had it just been a while since he'd been here? Lamentably, most of the buildings were unpainted. Gray woodwork with crooked shutters. Haphazard extensions stuck out over the alleyways. A fire here would end in catastrophe. That was the problem with people down here. They never thought more than one day ahead, and that kept them living from hand to mouth. It wasn't a place he'd have chosen to open a teahouse.

Lindri's teahouse stuck out onto the Ora like a raft. Winter had started to loosen its grip elsewhere, but here by the river it was still hanging on. The glow from a fireplace played in the ice flowers on the window. Darkdaggar peered in between the glazing bars. It was just before closing time. No customers.

"Wait here. Make sure no one comes in."

Kunte and Jarle nodded and slipped into the shadows beneath the eaves. Darkdaggar gripped the door handle. Judging by how the door had frozen in its frame, the teahouse clearly wasn't the most popular place in Mannfalla. He had to yank it open. A wind chime tinkled mournfully in the draft. He went in.

A rich aroma of spices met him. Lindri was standing by the hearth, sweeping the floor. Probably to keep warm, more than anything else. He was wearing a cardigan and at least two tunics, one shorter than the other. He also wore a gray woollen hat that was too small to cover his ears. The tea merchant looked up.

Darkdaggar pulled his hood down and studied his reaction closely. Surprise. Fear. A slow bow, probably so he would have a moment to gather his wits. So as not to reveal more. But Lindri had already told him all he needed to know. Kunte had been right. There could be no doubting that Rime had been here.

"Garm-fadri . . . What can I do for you?" The tea merchant made the sign of the Seer.

Darkdaggar looked around. Sheepskins draped over benches. A long counter with a row of black cast-iron pots in a recess filled with sand. The wall behind the counter was lined with drawers, and shelves with cups on them.

"This is a teahouse, is it not?" Darkdaggar took off his gloves and put them on the table nearest the fire. A table that looked like it had been made using a less than exclusive selection of driftwood from the riverbank.

"That it is, councillor."

"Then one would hope a cup of tea might be possible." He smiled at the old man. Why use vinegar when honey would do the trick?

Lindri leaned the broom against the wall and went over to the counter. He used the tables to support himself along the way. Darkdaggar felt better already. He'd feared danger. An opponent, allied with Rime. An imminent revolt, even. This was just an arthritic old man with a teahouse no one visited anymore. It was reassuring.

"You're Lindri, right? You supply tea to us in Eisvaldr." Darkdaggar sat down on the bench. He put a gold coin on the table. Far too much, of course, but it was good to remind the man that he needn't live out his days in the gutter.

"Less so these days," Lindri replied.

"Well . . . We ought to do something about that. It's been a tough year, hasn't it?"

Lindri lit the burner under one of the pots on the counter. "I've seen worse and better."

Darkdaggar chuckled. "No doubt a healthy attitude, but it would take a lot for things to be worse. Almost everything is more difficult now. Since her."

He followed the old man with his gaze. A twitch in the corner of one eye indicated he knew who Darkdaggar was referring to. Lindri poured water into the pot. The stream betrayed the fact that he was trembling. Darkdaggar wondered whether the hunchbacked old man might be sitting on more information than he'd initially thought. He just had to get him talking.

"She found friends in the strangest places, that child of Odin. Before she died, that is."

"I heard she traveled to another world," Lindri replied.

The old man clearly couldn't help himself. He needed to deny that the girl was dead. That meant feelings were involved. The man cared about her. Meaning he probably cared about Rime, too.

"So you believe in these raven rings? That there are other worlds, like in the stories?"

"Don't you, Garm-fadri?"

Darkdaggar laced his fingers behind his neck. The question interested him more than he cared to admit. He stared into the flames. The charred logs were stacked in an almost perfect pyramid, but one of them had fallen annoyingly far away from the others. He looked at Lindri again.

"My wife is scared of the dark. She thinks things will appear out of nowhere as soon as she blows out the lamp. I keep telling her, if there's nothing there in the light, there's nothing there in the dark either. I'm a level-headed sort, Lindri. Worlds parallel to our own? Full of Seer-knows-what riches? There can be no doubting that such a thing would be . . . astounding. But I don't think there's any credence to it. Does that surprise you?"

The old man met his gaze. He was wrinkly as an old apple. "You threw her in the pits for coming from another world, so I assumed you were a believer."

Darkdaggar raised his eyebrows. The barb was unexpected, and all the more impressive for it. Maybe he had underestimated the tea merchant.

Lindri disappeared into a small room behind the counter and started rummaging around on the shelves. Darkdaggar leaned closer to the fire. He found the poker and prodded the runaway log. To little avail. It rolled straight back again.

"You're forgetting that the Council has many voices."

Lindri didn't reply. What was taking him so long? Darkdaggar abandoned the log and got up. He couldn't let the tea merchant out of his sight. Who was to say he wouldn't try to warn Rime? Maybe he had a raven back there.

Darkdaggar followed him into the room. It was small and dusty, little more than a cupboard. Lindri was standing on the bottom rung of a ladder, straining to reach something he clearly couldn't. His back was too hunched. He looked over his shoulder and almost fell when he spotted Darkdaggar.

"Something I can get for you, Lindri?"

Lindri climbed down from the ladder and rubbed his wrist. "My best tea," he replied. "I don't keep it behind the counter. It's under lock and key."

"Of course. Which one is it?"

Lindri pointed a knobbly finger at a red box. The only one with a lock.

Darkdaggar stepped up onto the ladder and plucked it off the shelf. He gave it to Lindri and went out to sit by the fire again. "As I was saying, the Council has many voices. But we're one short."

Unmoved, the tea merchant kept working. There was no point in mincing words anymore.

"Lindri, we're short Rime An-Elderin."

"They say he's dead," Lindri replied. He lifted the lid off the pot and dropped the tea inside. The steam made it difficult to read his expression. He carefully put the pot on a tray along with a cup, then shuffled back over to the table and set the tray down.

He turned to leave. Darkdaggar grabbed his wrist.

"Sit, Lindri. Keep me company."

The old man hesitated for a moment before sitting down across from him. Darkdaggar forced a smile.

"I don't think Rime An-Elderin is as dead as people would have him be. And with every day he's gone, the people suffer. We need him, Lindri. It's people like you this affects. Not us. Not Council families. We always manage. People in Eisvaldr have wealth to fall back on when times are tough. That's not the case down here. Had Rime cared about the people he's supposed to lead, he wouldn't have left. Is it fair that you're paying the price for his whims? For his madness?"

Lindri poured tea into the cup without answering. Without meeting his eyes. The man didn't know what was good for him.

Darkdaggar lifted the cup. "If you've heard anything, or seen anything . . . If you know where he is, Lindri . . ."

"I haven't seen Rime-fadri since he killed Svarteld."

Darkdaggar felt his smile falter. Lindri's words were saturated with meaning. Rime had killed Svarteld. Won the fight. Darkdaggar had lost and ought to have been rotting in the pits. But it hadn't turned out that way. The tea merchant knew that, and he wasn't afraid to say so.

What was it that motivated such people? What was it that stopped them from thinking clearly? What lunacy made them risk their lives, just to make a point? It was so meaningless. So self-destructive. As if life weren't . . .

His chain of thought came to an abrupt end. Darkdaggar froze with the cup to his lips, realizing the fatal error he had been about to make.

He had underestimated the tea merchant. Truly. Let himself be fooled by a slope-shouldered old man and his bad joints. But this was no old codger who was simply refusing to talk. This was a far worse foe.

Darkdaggar started to laugh. He couldn't help himself. It was too incredible. He put the cup down again. Pushed it toward Lindri. "Let's drink together. You first."

Lindri stared at him through narrow eyes. Defiant. Piercing.

Darkdaggar could feel his fury growing. Ripping through him like wildfire. It was most disagreeable. Like an animal that couldn't be contained. But if there was one thing he knew how to do, it was contain that animal. He was a practical man. A level-headed and meticulous man. Not an animal.

"Won't you drink with your councillor, Lindri?"

The tea merchant's hand started to shake. Darkdaggar slammed his fist down on the table. The cup tipped over, sending tea along the grooves in the wood and falling to the floor in a thin, yellow stream. Like piss.

"You let me get my own poison . . ." Darkdaggar got up. "You let me get my own poison!"

The emptiness in the old man's eyes was unmistakable. He knew he was going to die.

"Why, man? You must have known it would be the last thing you'd ever do! What do you think my men would have done had I not walked out of here? What do you think the Council would have done? Is my death worth so much that you would sacrifice your-self?"

Darkdaggar crouched down next to Lindri, eyes drawn to the sleeves of his cardigan. The fraying ends were trembling.

"Explain it to me, Lindri. I really want to understand. You don't know me. You have no reason to hate me. So why? What is it about me that's so appalling?"

Lindri stared into thin air. Silent to the last.

"No . . ." Darkdaggar stood up again. "It's not about me, is it? It's about him. Rime An-Elderin. A sick young man who has failed his people. Yet still you protect him?"

Darkdaggar walked around the table, trying to pinpoint the source of his rage. It was about so much more than the tea merchant's attempt to poison him. It was about this blind loyalty to someone who was completely unsuited to govern the eleven kingdoms. Where did it come from? What was it about Rime that made him so dangerous?

"You know . . . I was convinced that no Kolkagga would turn their back on Rime. But Svarteld agreed to fight for me. For *me*, Lindri! What a gift! It's probably the closest I've come to believing in gods. But do you know what I think now?" Darkdaggar leaned toward the hearth. "I don't think Svarteld ever had any intention of winning. And that niggling feeling has stolen into my dreams. The feeling that he said yes so that no one else would. That he did exactly what you're doing now: sacrificed his life for *him*." He massaged his temples. "Why? What has Rime ever done for you? What is it about him that is so beguiling? Can you tell me?"

Lindri pulled his hat off and dropped it in his lap. His lips moved as if in prayer, but no sound came out.

Darkdaggar set the cup down in front of him again and poured more tea.

"Let's not make this more difficult than it needs to be." He looked down at the man's gleaming crown. His wrinkled hands. A man driven to death by an emotional turmoil he would never understand. An infatuation of sorts.

The tea merchant lifted the cup to his lips. He took a small sip first. Then he downed the entire cup. He brought it back down onto the table so hard that it cracked. It seemed there was life in the old man yet.

He didn't look any worse for wear. Just pale and drawn.

"So what is it? What have you drunk?" Darkdaggar asked, not expecting an answer. Nor did he get one. He retrieved the red box from behind the counter. It would come in handy. He went back and sat across from the tea merchant again.

"I know he's alive, Lindri. And I have a pretty good idea who he'll seek refuge with."

Darkdaggar waited. Nothing happened. For a moment he worried he'd been wrong, but then the old man's head started to droop. He tried to suppress a groan, then slumped forward, face pressed against the table. His hunched back twitched as he breathed. Slower. More labored.

Darkdaggar picked the gray hat up off the floor and put it on the tea merchant's head. "Take comfort in knowing your death wasn't in vain. You've just solved my biggest problem."

Lindri turned his head. Still had enough strength to meet his gaze. Darkdaggar leaned closer. "Kolkagga, Lindri."

Lindri tried to move his lips, but his body had stopped cooperating. His eyes closed.

Darkdaggar checked his throat for a pulse. Dead. How sad and unnecessary. There was nothing more to say. Another death on Rime's conscience.

He picked up the coin glinting by Lindri's forehead. He'd never been greedy, but there was no point burning money. Was he to pay for an attempt on his life? How grotesque.

He picked up the poker again and pulled the annoying log out of the flames. He collected the oil lamps from under the teapots and smashed them on the floor. The fire immediately started devouring everything in its path, running along the benches, crackling across sheepskins, and catching on the tea merchant's tunic.

Darkdaggar tore open the door and went outside. Kunte and Jarle stared at him. He wiped his hands on his cloak.

"Well . . . *that* could have gone better," he said.

Behind him, the wind chime tinkled mournfully once more.

HOUSE OF HOD

Hirka stood naked and freshly bathed, a cloth over her eyes. Not to keep her from seeing anyone, but to keep anyone from seeing *her*. The green eyes that were proof she wasn't Umpiri. As if there were any hiding that. As if she weren't different from top to toe.

Hired servants whispered to one another as they dried her and rubbed oil into her skin.

She was blind. Standing in darkness, surrounded by strangers. Their hands were rough against her skin, and she had to fight back the urge to run. They had discussed every inch of her body as if she weren't there. Did they think she didn't understand the language? She understood more than she cared to. Which parts should be emphasized and which should be covered. A project that had taken all day so far.

Her hair was most important, since the color irrefutably identified her as Raun's grandchild. So she had spent the entire morning unable to see, with strangers washing and braiding her hair into a style she knew she wouldn't like.

But what *she* liked didn't matter. All that mattered was what the House of Hod thought, and how they would receive her. This meeting was so important they hadn't even discussed why she'd gone out in the middle of the night. That argument would have to wait until later. All anyone cared about now was getting through the evening.

Hands strayed across her back, across her tailbone and the scar Father had made when she was a child. Hirka flinched. They'd touched her breasts, too, but the scar somehow felt more intimate. More vulnerable. She clenched her fists. Stabbing her palms.

The claws . . .

It wasn't the first time she'd forgotten them. Imitation claws with intricate details. The result of a silversmith's tireless efforts over twelve days. They sat on each finger, open at the joints, so she could bend them. Finger jewelry. As beautiful as they were false.

One of the women strapped her breasts. Pushed them up as high as possible to make her look fertile. They were one of her strong points, she'd been told. She'd always thought of them as small, but in a world of lean, animal-like Umpiri, they were more than adequate. Hirka puffed out her chest, hopeful for a little breathing room when they were done.

They raised her arms. Pulled the dress over her head. It itched her skin. They laced it at the back and across her hips so that it fit snugly all the way down to her thighs.

"What is this?" Skerri's screeching voice. Someone immediately set to work adjusting the material under Hirka's arm, while the others sorted her shoes. Skerri's patience had clearly reached its limit, and she sent them all packing. Only Oni was allowed to stay.

Oni removed the cloth covering her eyes. Hirka blinked and went to rub them. Skerri grabbed her by the wrist. The make-up. She'd forgotten about that, too.

Skerri was a formidable sight. She seemed even taller than before, elongated by a sleeveless black leather dress. There were patterns stamped into the leather. Grooves like curved goat horns. Very dramatic when paired with her black lips and hair. She looked lethal.

"Do you remember what everyone is called?" she asked.

Hirka nodded.

"And you know what Jór looks like? He's the youngest. It's unlikely she'll mention him, but a great honor if she does. Do you understand? If you surpass yourself, she'll introduce him to you. I doubt that will happen."

"Then I'll have to find him and say hi on my own." Hirka had meant it as a joke, but Skerri was clearly not amused. She raked her claws through Hirka's braids.

"You think this is just about us, don't you?" she whispered, glaring at Hirka with her white eyes. "You think this doesn't concern you. You run amok in the streets at night, you talk about the Might and seers, wasting time that would be better spent preparing for this evening. For what is coming. What you have failed to realize is that if we fall, you fall with us."

Hirka met her gaze. "I'm sure you'd think falling was worth it if you got to see *me* fall with you."

Oni let out a barely audible gasp. Continued frantically winding white ribbons around Hirka's arm. A style they clearly thought was attractive here, but Hirka thought they looked more like bandages. As did the shoes.

Hirka bit her lip. Waited for Skerri's outburst. But it didn't come. Probably because she'd told the truth. Skerri looked her up and down. "It will have to do," she finally said. Then she turned on her heel and left the room.

Hirka went over to the mirror. For a moment she thought she was standing in front of an open door, looking at a stranger. A girl she'd never met before. Pale, with braids that coiled down her bare shoulders like red snakes. The dress was white as snow, but the very bottom of the skirt was an explosion of red.

It looked like she'd been wading in blood.

There were carriages waiting for them, the first Hirka had seen since arriving here. It seemed that as long as you were dressed impractically enough, you could get out of walking without losing face.

The carriages were drawn by men, much to Hirka's unease. She tried to avoid looking at them as much as possible. Hid under her hood. Which was easy enough to do, since it was designed to cover her face.

Her heart was pounding in her chest. She squeezed the box containing Naiell's heart, trying to keep her hands from shaking. She felt ridiculous. Like she hadn't belonged to herself all day. Like she never again would.

Raun sat right next to her. Dressed in black, with a shell pattern on his sleeves. Uhere and Skerri sat on his other side. The others were in the carriages behind them. Her family . . . She felt like she might suffocate.

Hirka stared out the window. It was snowing. They went along one of the roads that circled the crater, all the way to the House of Hod. The first. The leading house. She tried to run through all their names in her head but could only think of a few. It was as if everything Oni had taught her had been wiped out. Her brain wasn't functioning anymore.

Hod, the head of the family. Her husband, Tyr. Their son, Jór. Their daughter, Ganei, who was married to Skrim. Skrim's parents were called . . . No. They had a daughter named Meime. Married to . . .

Breathe! You have to breathe!

Skerri leaned forward. "Don't take off your hood until you're standing in front of them. Remember! And don't turn your back until they—"

"She knows, Skerri." Raun sounded convinced. Hirka wasn't.

The carriages slowed. Through the snow she could make out openings in the rock face. Apparently there was a small city through each of them. Firepits appeared along the roadside, their flames dancing in the wind.

The carriages came to a stop. Hirka had to force herself to get out. Raun placed a hand on her back and led her onward. Tongues of flame illuminated a wrought iron double door the height of ten men; it was covered in writhing serpents carved in such hideous detail that they looked alive. The doors opened and two women greeted them. They were smiling and pleasant, but Hirka didn't hear a word they said. Blood was rushing in her ears. She hugged the box closer. It was new. No longer a simple metal container, but a chest made of mica. Filled with ice. And burdened with the fate of an entire family. With the heart they hoped would elevate Graal's house.

Maybe if she succeeded that would be enough. Graal would find peace. Ym would be safe. Rime would be saved.

Rime.

The longing hit her so suddenly she had to gasp for air. She could almost hear him whispering her name. His low, husky voice in her ear. The kiss had made it deeper, as if she had broken through to a part of him that neither of them had seen before. It was dangerous, but it was hers. It was where she belonged.

So what was she doing here? This wasn't her home. This wasn't her family. By blood maybe, but she could never be like them. She couldn't survive here, in a society like this.

Rime grew up with this. He's an An-Elderin.

The thought made her stand taller. That's what Rime always did. He stood. Even when everything around him was falling. If he could put up with being a son of the council his whole life, surely she could manage a few months of this. Or one night at least, because there might not be any more.

But not even Rime had experienced grandeur like this. The house was bigger than any family could possibly need. They walked through corridors and halls with tall windows of colored glass. It reminded her of the Seer's tower. Naiell had taken a lot of this place with him. The Seer. Council families. What had Ym been like before he arrived?

Kingdoms. Ravnhov among the strongest.

They entered a hall that seemed unending. The vaulted ceiling was reflected in the floor. She felt like she was floating. There was a group chatting at the other end. They were dressed as Dreyri were wont to, revealing as much as possible without looking like they'd tried too hard.

One woman had little more than threads covering her upper body. A man wore a shirt that looked like it had been in a knife fight, but clearly that was the intention. Other women wore tops and dresses that exposed their navels, as if to scream that they were fertile. That they could multiply. That seemed to be their sole motivation in this world.

Hirka kept walking, not sure how her feet were managing it.

They approached a man and a woman on thrones that looked like boats turned on end. Cocoons of layered wood came together to form prows above them. They sat with an air of forbearance, as if they'd rather be standing but were forced to sit.

Hod. Hod and her husband, Tyr. Hod and Tyr. Remember their names.

The woman who'd led them in stopped. Hirka did the same. Kept her head bowed. Stared at Hod's black shoes. She heard Raun and Modrasme exchange the requisite pleasantries. She was glad she didn't have to take part.

Then Hod stood up. "Hirka?"

Hirka looked up and lowered her hood. "Hod, you honor me. I am Hirka, daughter of Graal, son of Raun of the House of Modrasme," she replied, without knowing whether the words had come out right.

Hod was like no woman Hirka had seen before. Her eyes angled dramatically upward in her narrow face. Beguiling and peculiar. There was something reminiscent of a squinting bird about her. But then, she was one of the oldest creatures in the world.

In all the worlds.

She was wearing a floaty robe with a close-fitting hood that Hirka had initially mistaken for hair. The yawning neckline extended all the way to her stomach. Hirka was sure that if she turned too quickly her breasts would pop out. But Hod made no sudden movements.

She approached Hirka, slowly and fluidly, drawing every eye in the hall. She leaned forward. Took in Hirka's scent with considerably more elegance than anyone had done before. She was so close that Hirka could hear her breathing.

Hod whispered in her ear. "Are you afraid, Hirka?"

Hirka tightened her grip on the box, hands clammy. Yes, she was afraid. Of everything, big and small. Afraid of making mistakes. Afraid of the consequences. Afraid of lowering her eyes and seeing far more of Hod than she cared to.

"I'd be a fool not to be afraid," she whispered back.

"Mmm . . . And you're no fool, are you?" It didn't sound like a question. Hod straightened up again.

Hirka held the box out to Hod. Tried to find her voice. "I am Hirka, daughter of Graal, son of Raun of the House of Modrasme, the thirty-third. I bring a gift for Hod and Tyr of the House of Hod, the first. This is all that remains of Naiell, who betrayed you all."

Hod already knew what was in the box. There was no doubting that. This was for the gallery. Hod accepted the box and lifted the lid with slender claws. She stared down at the heart. The rest of Hod's half-naked family crowded around them.

Hod inhaled deeply. Taking in the smell of the heart. She held her breath, as if she wanted to consume it. Become one with it.

"I remember you . . ." she whispered, her voice rasping with contempt.

She was talking about Naiell. Naiell, who had traveled with Hirka in the human world. Naiell, who liked to sleep in the rafters, who could make a chicken disappear in an instant, who had feared his brother to the very end. His death was all that drove these people. It was grotesque. A thirst for revenge in its most hideous form. A greed that made her skin crawl. The future would be built on the heart of an enemy.

Hirka was glad he was dead. Truly glad, for the very first time. Grateful that he didn't have to meet his people again and stand face-to-face with such hatred. Rime had killed him. But it was an offence that had spared Naiell a far worse fate. She had been extremely naïve to think otherwise.

Rime hadn't been his killer. Rime had been his savior.

And I let him leave, without a word.

Hod shut the box and looked at Hirka again. "You bring me the heart of the traitor. You've given us our enemy, and now I'll give you yours."

Hod motioned almost imperceptibly and a door opened behind the thrones. A woman emerged with a man in tow. He was struggling to keep up but had no choice. She had him on a leash. A golden chain, attached directly to his throat. No collar. They stopped in front of them. Hirka didn't understand what she was supposed to do.

Who was this? She stared at the man. He stood with his head bowed, wearing what could best be described as a sack. His hair was short and fair. The woman forced his chin up, and he looked into Hirka's eyes.

He had eyes like her. Like an ymling. Living, pale blue eyes. His cheeks were hollow. He had a scar on his forehead. Realization hit her like a punch to the gut. Hirka took a step back.

Urd. It was Urd.

Urd was almost unrecognizable, but she would never forget those eyes. Memories of their last encounter flashed through her mind. Her chopping off his tail. Him falling to his knees. Spitting blood. Coughing up the beak in his throat.

Bromfjell had been torn asunder. Erupted in red rivers of fire, and then the deadborn had dragged him between the stones.

What had they done to him? Somehow he seemed both younger and older. Younger because his beard was gone and his hair was clipped short. Older because his cheeks were even more hollow than before. His skin was sallow. The mark of the Council on his forehead was gone, replaced by an angry red scar.

He stood there, only a short distance from her. The man who had tried to sacrifice her to the blind. Had it not been for him, she might not have been here now. Without him, she might have still been in Ym. Living in peace. In Ravnhov. Or with Rime . . .

He recognized her. Took a step toward her but then seemed to remember the chain and stopped before it was pulled taut. The corner of his mouth was quivering. She thought he was going to say something, but then realized he was fighting back tears.

For the first time since coming here, she was looking into eyes like her own, and they had to be his? It was monstrous. The gods were toying with her.

Hod moved toward her. Hirka saw bare skin out of the corner of her eye but couldn't bring herself to look away from the councillor.

Think! Don't forget why you're here!

She had to be Dreyri now. Too much was at stake for her to be fazed. Even by this.

Hirka looked up at Hod. The woman smiled, visibly pleased. "We will look after your enemy until the evening is concluded. After that he is yours to do with as you wish. We would offer suggestions, but from what I've heard, you'll probably reward him by making him your servant."

Laughter rippled through the room. They were all looking at her. She was being tested. Forced to act. Raun's eyes were almost pleading. Skerri's jaw was set. The tendons in her neck sticking out like roots. Vana's lips were quivering. Modrasme looked away, as if she'd already lost. Hirka was a disappointment, as anticipated.

What was she to do? Refuse? Promise that Urd would suffer and die? Would that make her one of them? Would that win her the favor she needed to elevate the House of Modrasme?

No. She had to show them that she stood by her actions. Stood by her decision to spare Kolail. But she had to give them a reason they'd respect. And there was only one thing Dreyri would understand: unflinching superiority.

Hirka collected her thoughts. Went over what she wanted to say in her head so she wouldn't mess up the wording.

"Why wouldn't I make him a servant?" she asked, hoping to sound naïve.

"He is your enemy," Hod answered. More laughter.

Hirka dipped her knee slightly as a show of respect. "I fear *you*. And rightly so. But should I fear my enemies? Should I kill them so that I can sleep at night? No. I'm not scared of him. Neither him nor the fallen. I'm happy for both of them to sweep my floor."

Hod tilted her head and blinked, like a bird. It almost looked like she had eyelids on the top and the bottom, and when she blinked, they met in the middle.

Hirka held her breath. Then the most powerful woman in the world started to laugh. A throaty number that quickly spread through the room. Her husband, Tyr, nodded at Hirka with the hint of a smile. He relaxed in his chair, in a tunic trimmed with fur and feathers. A barely tamed savage.

"She *is* one of us!" Hod said and passed the box to her husband. "Hirka, daughter of Graal, son of Raun of the House of Modrasme, welcome to the House of Hod, and welcome to Ginnungad!"

The others started to beat their chests with their fists. A declaration of support, strange as it was. Hirka glanced over at her own family. Raun and Uhere were doing their best to look unmoved.

Hod waved over a man who looked younger than the others. He had flaxen hair of varying lengths, and a scaled serpent painted on his bare chest.

Jór. The youngest son of the house.

"Hirka, I hear you have a love for everything that grows," Hod said. "Herbs and teas and such. You'll find we have the finest collection in all of Dreysíl. My son, Jór, will show you what we have to offer. Won't you, Jór?"

"With greatest pleasure, Mother." Jór smiled at Hirka, a smile so dazzling she couldn't bring herself to be unsettled by his canines. He gestured in the direction of a row of arches. She realized she was expected to accompany him.

Hirka bowed to Hod and took a couple of steps back. Carefully, without turning her back on them. She shot Raun and Skerri a questioning glance. Raun gave a subtle nod. Skerri's black lips parted as if she were going to scream, but nothing came out. That was when Hirka realized she was gaping.

BLOOD MOON

The spring thaw in Blindból meant boggier marshes and collapsed paths. It had cost Rime an extra day from Ravnhov, but he was almost at the camp now. The final bridge hung a short distance before him, reaching toward a full moon bathed in deep orange.

Dense forest covered the mountaintops, but even the cliffs had knotty pines clinging to them. He could hear the meltwater trickling in the dark. A raven gave a deep *kraaaawk* just above him. Rime bound the Might, knowing that would placate it.

Blindból in the dark . . . There was nowhere more beautiful. Or was he just buoyed by Eirik's support?

Not that he'd expected anything else from their meeting, but even so it had been a balm for the soul. Good conversation and good food. Kolkagga or not, in Ravnhov you ate.

Sometimes Rime got the impression that Eirik understood the Council better than he did. The chieftain had set his fury aside a long time ago. He knew what he was dealing with. How truly despicable they were.

Eirik had been there the night Rime had dispatched Darkdaggar's assassin and had predicted that Mannfalla would try to pin it on Ravnhov. It came as no surprise to the chieftain. As for nábyrn, the people of Ravnhov had seen the blind with their own eyes.

So Eirik had let him ramble on about the blindling brothers, and about his visit to the human world. He'd listened until the ravens had come home, at no point intimating that Rime was in any way out of his mind. And once Rime had talked himself out, he'd patted him on the back and said that enough ale could solve most anything.

Rime smiled at the memory. Like him, Eirik could see the coming storm. War on two fronts, against deadborn and against Mannfalla. A war that couldn't be survived, much less won, without Kolkagga.

You don't need to win them over. They're already with you.

The chieftain's parting words. That was what was keeping him going now. Hope and faith in his fellow Kolkagga.

The gong sounded in the camp. Rime thought he could hear a faint echo from a camp farther away, too. Supper. He could still make it if he got a move on.

He crossed the bridge and ran through the forest. It smelled of damp earth. Death and new life. Rotting leaves covered the ground, and tomorrow's training was bound to involve some cunning and cumbersome method of clearing them.

The trees thinned out closer to the camp. Black-clad Kolkagga sat around several fires. Familiar faces that reminded him he would never be alone. Not after tonight.

He just needed to find Orja.

He spotted her next to the smallest fire with other Kolkagga higher-ups. People who in all fairness ought to have succeeded Svarteld before her. But they'd supported her, putting the Council's expectations to shame.

Rime smelled game stew and felt his stomach rumble, but it would have to wait. He went over to them. Orja got up as he approached.

"What did Ravnhov say?"

Rime smiled. "Hello to you, too."

She gave him a hesitant smile in return. "Good news?"

Rime had to think before answering. He couldn't share everything. Orja was teetering in the balance, but she was still loyal to the Council.

"Eirik has been busy, and Ravnhov isn't alone. But they stand against Mannfalla. And against Darkdaggar. They're strong. We can't afford to wait any longer, master. Kolkagga must choose a side."

A palpable silence descended around the fires. Everyone was suddenly very interested in their tea. Orja gestured for him to follow her. They walked a short distance away and stopped beneath the pine trees. Surrounded by black needles in the dark.

"Rime, I've already told you. Kolkagga can't choose. Others choose for us. That's been our lot since we were conceived. I know what you want, and I know it's difficult, but you have to understand—"

Rime gripped her arm. "Orja, you promised—"

"I promised I'd think about it! Until we knew more. But it's not like you think. You're wrong about Darkdaggar."

This conviction was new. Fresh as the buds in the trees. Rime struggled to hide his disgust. He let go of her. "What's happened?"

"What do you mean?"

"Don't give me that! You don't strike me as the type to be bought, so it must be something else. What's happened? Why can we suddenly not choose? Master?" The title suddenly had a bitter taste.

She sighed and scrubbed a hand across her forehead. "Not that it's any of your concern, but since you ask, the Council has demonstrated they're willing to listen to us. It's more than just talk, Rime. They've been here."

"Who's been here?"

"Garm Darkdaggar and Freid Vangard. With a handful of men. They told us about the problems the Council's been having. They were honest, Rime. Asked whether we had everything we needed. They want to give us more freedom, and more resources. And they're genuinely interested in how we operate."

She looked at him and answered his unasked question. "No, nobody's told him about you." She looked at the ground. Crushed a pine cone underfoot. "Rime, the Council knows they can't have an army they can't control—"

Rime gave a rueful laugh. "So that's all it takes? Two councillors come to visit and shake your hand, and now we can't choose anymore?"

Anger twisted Orja's lips. "Careful, Rime. Your name can't help you anymore."

She turned to leave. He grabbed her. "Don't you get it?! They know it all hinges on you! Why else do you think they'd come here?"

Orja looked at him. Anger turned to sadness, as if she pitied him. "That's just it. They didn't only come here. They went to every single camp in Blindból. You have to let this go, Rime."

"Every single camp? Why would they—"

He was struck by a sudden realization. His blood ran cold. He let go of Orja. "Every single camp?!"

Orja backed away from him as if he were a wild animal that might attack at any moment. A madman. Was he? Rime looked around. Men murmured happily around the flames. About Mannfalla. About training injuries. About the weather. But still . . . Every fiber of his being told him that something was wrong.

Then he saw the first sign. One of the men got up, saying he didn't feel well. He stumbled toward the huts, but only managed a few steps before falling and lying motionless on the ground. Three of the others hurried over to him.

The food!

Rime looked around frantically, but the soup bowls had already been collected. Someone by one of the fires groaned. Someone else tried to get up, but his legs fell out from under him. He ended up on his knees in the rotting leaves. His cup slipped out of his hand and rolled across the ground.

Rime started running. "IT'S THE TEA! DON'T DRINK THE TEA!"

146

He screamed until his lungs ached, but his warnings were drowned out by the noise. Screams of pain. Groans from men clutching their stomachs, and shouts from those trying in vain to help.

Rime ran into their midst. He knocked the cup out of Jeme's hands. The man looked at him, eyes dull, before slumping over the fire. Rime grabbed his limp body and heaved him out of the ashes.

"Jeme!" He shook him. Forced two fingers down his throat until he vomited. A pale soup poured out of his mouth, but Jeme's eyes were dead. His body was reacting without him.

Orja . . .

Rime looked around for her. She was behind him, leaning against a tree with both hands on her stomach. But at least she was still standing. She met his gaze. Understanding broke through her despair, and she nodded before pushing her fingers down her throat and throwing up.

Jeme grew heavier in his arms. A sign that he ought to do something. Had to do something. But what? What could he do?

Men lay on the ground. Dead, but still convulsing. Their bodies twitching as if they were dreaming. Slowly, as if time were grinding to a halt. He looked on as some of the men tried to drag friends to their feet. Others sat watching as if paralyzed. A chaos of black. A storm that could only be seen, not heard.

It was like his duel with Svarteld. A soundless nightmare. But this wasn't a sea of strangers. This was all he had. His home. His warriors. His life.

They can't have an army they can't control . . .

Rime pulled Jeme close. His body was heavy with death. He rested his forehead against his hair. Smelled the sweat of a hard day's work. Jeme, who had welcomed him back with open arms. His words were still crystal clear in his memory.

You're always late for supper.

Always late. Too late.

Rime felt cold. His hands clammy. His stomach churned, pressing something up and out. A blood-curdling scream. It took him a moment to realize it was his own. He smothered it in Jeme's hair. For a moment it was like he wasn't really there. Like he was on the outside, dreaming. So how could he smell Jeme? See the scratches in the cup on the ground?

Clear warning signs. He drew on the Might, binding as if his life depended on it. To numb the shock. But the Might ripped through him like a storm. Impossible to control. Hlosnian's words whispered in his memory.

Nothing feeds the Might like blood.

Rime let Jeme sink to the ground. He had no idea how much time had passed. A moment. An hour. A day.

He stumbled to his feet. Then he noticed he wasn't alone. Stiar was standing nearby, surrounded by bodies. Pale faces against black earth. More of them lay along the paths. And he knew that when he went into the huts, he'd find them there as well.

Rime went over to Stiar. His cheeks were stained with tears. He looked confused. "It . . . it keeps me awake," he said in raw shock. "I never drink it."

And I'm always late.

Rime looked around. The enormity of the scene before him settled around his neck like a weight. The weight of chance. Of horror. Injustice. A foul deed the likes of which no one had ever seen. Which should never have been able to happen. Now there were only two options: bow down or rise up.

Rime put a hand on Stiar's shoulder. Held his gaze until he was sure the man was with him and able to think clearly. "Stiar, search the camp. Find out whether any others are alive. Do you understand? I'm going to light the beacon."

Stiar snapped out of his daze. He nodded.

Rime snatched a burning log from the fire and started running toward the beacon. It had been built to the north, where it could be seen from other camps. How many, he didn't know. No one had threatened Kolkagga in his lifetime. Not in anyone's lifetime.

But he had to light the fire. Warn the others. Maybe he could still stop them. Stop them from finishing their supper. Draw them here. But Rime knew it was too late. Routine was in Kolkagga's blood, and routine had killed them all.

Rime smashed the pot of oil over the beacon and threw the log on it. The fire took straight away. The flames ate, but they ate alone, without any sign of an answer. He stared out into the darkness. Blindból had never been so dark. All that answered the fire was the moon. Round and red. A hole in the night.

They were dead. All dead. Every single one of them.

Rime felt numb. The fire warmed one side of him, but the other side was freezing. Darkdaggar had slaughtered his own men. His uncontrollable army. No sin in Slokna could compare to this. How could they? How could the Council support—

The Council!

A new certainty. A flash amid the grief. They hadn't supported it. The Council would never have supported this. Never. Darkdaggar had known he wouldn't be able to hide his complicity, but he'd done it anyway. That could only mean one thing.

He's going to overthrow the Council!

Rime took off along the cliff's edge. Branches whipped across his face. He ran. He could taste blood but didn't stop. He had to warn Jarladin. The rest of the Council. Anyone who wasn't in Darkdaggar's pocket.

Their lives are in danger!

Rime ground to a halt on the other side of the mountain. Something pulsed red on the horizon. Eisvaldr was burning.

HOWL

The waiting was unbearable. Hirka clasped her hands together and leaned forward. Sat staring at her thighs. She felt naked. Cold. And they hadn't even left the house yet.

Even through the stone walls she could hear the sound of thousands of Umpiri crowding into the streets, making their way to the crater, to Criers' Rock. It would be hours before all the space was filled. Laughing and shouting mixed with all the other sounds in a buzzing chaos. All of Ginnungad brought together. For her.

What none of them knew yet was how she would be introduced. Yes, she was Hirka of the House of Modrasme, but would they still be the thirty-third house? Would they be promoted? Or . . . Could they even be demoted? Had Hirka's conduct sent them farther down the rankings than even Naiell had managed in his time?

No one would know until the carriages from the House of Hod arrived. And with them, the family's future.

Skerri paced back and forth, biting her claws. Uhere was fussing with her hair. Putting it up, letting it fall, then putting it up again, with Raun stroking her back the whole time. Even Vana had set her arrogance aside, in a rare moment when she didn't have her boyfriend glued to her side. This was a time for family, not for lovers.

Modrasme stared out the window, silver hair hanging in her lap. She was nearly four thousand years old. Whatever temperament she'd once had had long since faded. Her stony features were locked in their usual expression, devoid of any expectation. Nothing was good enough for Modrasme. Everything and everyone was doomed to be a disappointment. Raun had called his mother a *sekhþainari*. An untranslatable word. The best Hirka could come up with was "woe-wallower," someone who liked to shroud themselves in their own suffering. Nurture it. But not even Modrasme had been able to hide a certain cheerfulness after the meeting with the House of Hod.

It had gone well. At least Hirka thought so. In good moments. At other times, she was certain she'd unwittingly committed some outrage. Maybe she'd tossed her braids and offended the ancestors or something equally horrific.

There was no knowing. Everything was out of her hands. And soon they would have their answer. A number. Nothing more than a number. Meaningless to her. The world to everyone else in the room. But she knew that if she'd been successful, Graal's honor would be restored. Maybe then he'd let go of her? Let her return to Ym to live in peace?

Stupid girl . . .

The bald servant, Skilborr, scuttled into the room. "The carriages are on their way!"

Everyone leaped to their feet. Brushed non-existent dust off their clothes and lifted their chins. Hirka got up, leather creaking. The dress was gone. Now she was a warrior, descended from a long line of warriors who were clearly obsessed with demonstrating how little protection they needed. All she had on were leather straps and belts pulled tight around her chest. And a short skirt, held in place by metal rings at the side, like a halter. That was what she was. A horse. A beast of burden.

The sound of the door echoed in the corridors. Skilborr and Oni left the room again, returning with red cheeks, along with who they'd thought would be a messenger. Instead, it was Jór. The youngest son of the House of Hod. Nobody had expected him.

Uhere clutched her chest as if her lungs had failed her. Modrasme stood up, her hair tumbling to her waist.

Jór gestured disarmingly. "The formalities can wait," he said with a wide smile. He handed a black disc to Modrasme, identical to the invitation they'd received.

"I wanted to deliver it personally, and to be the first to congratulate you. Take all the time you need. I'll be waiting with the carriages. But the crater is starting to fill up, so we shouldn't wait too long." He winked at Hirka and took a couple of steps back before he turned and left. A courtesy he was under no obligation to show them.

Modrasme raised the disc and read in silence.

Then she sat down again and handed the disc to Raun.

"What does it say?" Skerri leaned over him.

Raun looked at her. "We're the seventh house . . ." His voice was small. Full of doubt.

Skerri's eyes widened. She snatched the disc from him, scanning the words to make sure he hadn't read it wrong.

Raun gripped Modrasme's hand. Wrapped it in his. "Mother, we're the seventh house. The seventh. Do you hear me? We're back on the Council." His voice cracked on the last words.

He didn't wait for a response. He walked over to Hirka and crouched down. Cradled her face in his hands. "The seventh, Hirka . . ."

Hirka nodded. Tears began to roll down her cheeks. Why? What did this mean to her? This had never been a part of her life. But a family was rejoicing around her. Deadborn who had shown about as much emotion as stone ever since her arrival. Now they lived. Now they felt.

Raun clenched his fist and pressed it to his mouth. As if it could hide his tears. Skerri stood with her eyes shut. Modrasme had rested a hand on her shoulder in the only show of physical contact Hirka had seen between them. Uhere embraced her wiry father and his wife. Vana was the first to laugh. To start the discussion. How many men and women would they get? How big would their household be? Would they have to move, and how soon?

Raun shook his head. "A thousand years . . . A thousand years as the traitor's father. And now . . ." His hand was warm against Hirka's cheek. "Blood of my blood."

"We'd best get a move on," Skerri said from behind him.

Hirka flung her cloak on and went out to the carriages. She didn't want anyone looking at her now. They were so happy. So wild. So strange.

But none of them had to stand before every deadborn in Ginnungad.

The House of Hod had multiple levels. Hall upon hall set into the rock face. Hirka stood alone in one of them. Surrounded by black stone walls that looked like a viper's nest. Woven by the Might, long before the war. They slithered over and under each other, brought to life by a long row of torches. Windows of mightglass rose up before her, painting the crowd outside an ashen gray.

There were so many people. Unbelievably many. It had started to get dark. Lanterns burned high and low, all the way around the crater.

Hirka brought her fingers to her mouth to bite a nail. Forgetting that she had claws. Silver claws. She was like them. Was supposed to be like them.

In another time, she had awaited her Rite day with dread. In hindsight it was ridiculous. What had she had to dread back then? The Council in Eisvaldr? A bunch of wrinkly old men and women who had thrown her in the pits. Nothing compared to what thousands of Umpiri could do.

One point to you if you pull me up.

Rime . . . Would she ever see him again? Was this the step that would take her away from him for good? Hirka gripped the window ledge. Reminded herself to breathe.

It's a dream. It's just a dream. You'll wake up soon.

"Come . . ." A serving boy motioned to her. She took a breath. Followed him into the corridor. It was narrow, but just as lofty as the hall. The walls here had also been formed by the Might. The rock stretched upward until its color changed from black to a pale pink. It made her feel like she was inside a woman, walking through a birth canal. With a bloodred curtain at the end. The opening.

The servant pulled the curtain aside, and she stepped out onto Crier's Rock. There were already a lot of people on the ledge. Her own family. Hod's family. Jór was standing right next to her. He smiled with conviction. She fought off the urge to grab his hand.

Stay on your feet. It'll be over soon.

Hod stood at the very end. She raised a hand and the crowd fell silent. Hirka's gaze swept the walls of the crater. People stood the whole way around. In the streets below, and in the streets above. The distance to the other side was too great for her to see, but she assumed there were people there, too.

All this, just to tell them that she was here? That Graal had had a daughter?

And that the gateways are open. The way to the Might.

Hod started to shout, voice loud and clear. Echoing between the walls. Hirka had to concentrate to hear over the sound of the blood rushing in her ears. Her heart thundering in her chest. Hod spoke of a long wait. Of living without the Might. Of treachery. Of Graal's fate. Hirka understood a lot, and it was easy enough to get the sense of the words she didn't recognize. She understood she'd been a rumor that Hod was now confirming. And that this was the beginning of the end.

The end? What end?

Hirka looked at the others, but none of them would help her. They stood tall, like warriors, hands behind their backs.

"So powerful is our blood," Hod proclaimed, "that even in exile, even without his manhood and without the Might, he begot a daughter. Graal's blood has returned. His heir. His wrath. And she brings with her the traitor's heart. Through the gateways she has carried it. Through the gateways she will carry it again."

Hirka was shaking. She tensed her jaw to keep her teeth from chattering. Hod's words sank into her like claws.

"We have waited a thousand years. But this is the year we journey to the Might. Mannfalla's days are numbered. Hear me, Umpiri: I, Hod, of the House of Hod, the first, give you Hirka, daughter of Graal, son of Raun of the House of Modrasme, the seventh."

Hirka had been told what to do. It wasn't much. It wasn't difficult. But right now she remembered nothing. She struggled to get her feet under control, and they reluctantly advanced toward Hod. Their jubilation washed over her like a wave. Hod opened the lid of the box. Hirka felt like she was standing outside her body. Like this wasn't really happening.

She plunged her hands into the ice. Wrapped her fingers around cold flesh. Naiell's heart. The man who had cost these people everything they held dear. Her father's brother. He had betrayed her, too, but she had never wished him dead. She'd loved him.

Memories flashed through her mind as she lifted his heart. Kuro, the raven who had found her by the Alldjup. Naiell on the floor of the greenhouse. Stefan's constant moaning about the blindling's refusal to wear clothes. Naiell, crawling before Graal on the floor of the church. And the worst memory of all: when he'd crumpled to the floor. Executed by the man she loved. Still.

Hirka fought back tears. She knew what she had to do. She raised Naiell's heart high above her head. The jubilation became a wall of sound. A chaos of howls that assaulted her ears. It was like being in a ravenry full of frenzied birds.

She suddenly felt dizzy. Her vision was blurred by tears. The lanterns bled fire and she understood. For the first time, she understood what war meant.

There was no force that could stop this howl of rage. It couldn't be calmed or reasoned with. It was animalistic. Primal and all-consuming.

Kolkagga. Kolkagga can stop them! Rime and Svarteld.

She realized she was clinging to a hope involving the thing she hated most. Killers. Warriors. Who better than warriors to stop a war? But this wouldn't be a war. This would be an annihilation.

STONESONG

Rime lifted his sword and squinted along the edge. His effort was starting to pay off. He shifted position, held the blade to the whetstone, and continued with a steady hand. Out and in. Out and in. Like breathing. An accompaniment to the distinctive sound from the stone. A song that soared higher and higher as he switched to finer stones.

He wet the stone again. The water had turned to gray milk, colored by the process. There was muck all over the floor. Dirty footprints crossing the boards. He'd have to clean up after he was done. This was Svarteld's hut. Svarteld would never have tolerated such a mess. It was just as well he was sleeping in Slokna. That way he didn't have to see it. Nor did he have to see the end of everything he'd lived for. The death of his men.

The folding doors stood open. Beyond them was the path, with the dead laid out on both sides, lined up as far as Rime could see in the darkness. Their masks had been pulled over their faces. They looked like a black, rolling landscape. Rain drummed against their bodies.

Rime tightened the cloth protecting his hand from the blade, winding it around white knuckles. Continued honing the edge. Out and in. Out and in.

He could hear someone coming. The footfall told him it was Stiar. He paused in the doorway, saying nothing until Rime looked up.

"Ketill's back, master. He's got another three with him. I know one of them. Sveinn."

Rime squinted along the edge again. "Which camp?"

"Breifjell, master."

Three from Breifjell. Sixteen survivors. So far.

"Good. And the swords?"

Stiar stepped into the hut to get out of the rain. "Erlendr is still counting them, master."

Rime brought steel to stone again. The singing resumed.

"What about Orja and the others?"

"They . . . They're still vomiting. We've tried everything, but . . ."

"Thanks, Stiar. And the provisions?"

"We did as you said. Everything's been burned. Food. Tea. Raknar and Od came back with a deer not long ago. A couple of the others have relieved them and gone out looking for more."

Stiar shifted nervously. He was a couple of years older than Rime. A good man. Obedient, but perpetually anxious. "Marrow's on his way back from Mannfalla, master. He'll bring word soon."

Rime nodded. It wouldn't be much. Just confirmation of what he already knew. He set aside his sword and found a finer whetstone. Wrapped it in a cloth and brought it to the steel. Stiar was still standing there. Rime didn't look up.

"Was there something else, Stiar?"

"You haven't eaten anything since—"

"I'm fine."

Stiar took a step closer. His sandy hair was plastered to his forehead. "Erlendr is worried. He says you haven't—"

Rime looked up. Stiar fell silent again. Withdrew and disappeared along the path between the dead men. Men who would still be with them had Rime stayed in Ym. The camp would have been alive with the sound of cursing. With sweaty and exhausted bodies. And Darkdaggar would have been rotting in the pits.

Finer details were starting to emerge. The blood groove was more pronounced. The steel harder along the edges. Rime held the sword steady and drew the stone along the blade. Out and in. Another song.

Perfection took time. But time was something he was sorely lacking. Sooner or later the beak would take its toll. Graal would call on him and Rime would have to answer. He had lost the Council. Lost Kolkagga. He was a broken sword. He was no longer valuable to Graal. Probably not even as leverage against Hirka.

Hirka . . .

She hated him for what he had done. She would hate him even more for what he was going to do.

"Master?"

Marrow was approaching the door, shoes squelching. He was drenched. Rime waved him inside. Marrow bowed, sat down on the floor, and pulled off his hood. Then he frowned, assuming the same concerned expression as Stiar.

"Have you been here since I left?"

"Mannfalla, Marrow?"

Marrow scratched his forehead. "It's as you say. People are talking about it, but no one knows for sure what's happened. Or who's alive. Darkdaggar and his family have moved behind the walls of Eisvaldr, and Tyrme, Saulhe, and Freid have likely done the same. Most are saying Eir is dead, though I've heard as many versions of what happened as there are people in Mannfalla. Jarladin's house is empty, so he's either betrayed us and joined Darkdaggar, or . . ." He dragged a hand through his wet hair. "They could be on the run," he continued, not sounding hopeful.

Rime wetted the edge and kept honing. "What about Lindri? The tea merchant?"

Marrow shook his head. "Fire."

Grief tore at Rime's chest, trying to penetrate the cold he'd been living with for the past few days. He barred its way, letting it freeze for the time being. It would find an outlet in due course.

Marrow got up. "But that doesn't mean the tea merchant's dead. He might have—"

"He's dead."

"Or maybe he's staying with others?"

"Look around!" Rime threw the whetstone aside. It bounced off the wall. "Kolkagga are dead! Everyone who was ever loyal to me is dead! Those who supported me on the Council. Lindri. Jarladin. My own family fled the city weeks ago, even though I've barely seen them in years. The servants? Probably dead. There's no use thinking otherwise!"

Marrow stared at the floor.

Rime took a moment to compose himself. Closed his eyes. Embraced the cold. "Go and help Stiar with the preparations. We don't have enough wood, so we're burning them in their huts."

"Can we burn that many? It'll . . . They'll be able to see the smoke from Mannfalla, master. He'll know we've survived."

Rime looked up at him and smiled. Marrow swallowed and took a step back. "You *want* him to know?"

Rime didn't reply. He picked up another whetstone and held it between his thumb and the steel. Out and in. Out and in.

The song chased Marrow out of the hut. He disappeared into the darkness.

Rime looked down at the sword. The cloth he'd wrapped around the edge was red and wet under his hand.

CAPTIVE

The House of Modrasme was no longer a home. It was an exhibition. The hall that Hirka begrudgingly called the hearth room was completely packed. Guests came and went in a seemingly endless stream. The outer doors were constantly open, making it impossible for her to keep warm. And she couldn't just sneak off, because she was the one they'd come to see.

They brought colored ribbons with symbols on them. Motifs of the various houses. Alliance ribbons. Decorative oaths of loyalty that were making her increasingly uneasy. But she accepted them with a smile. A mask so stiff that it took everything in her power to keep it from slipping. Every ribbon she was presented with she placed over the arm of Modrasme's chair. There were so many it looked like someone had given her their laundry.

Each house presented itself as if it were the one and only house she'd met, but their names and faces mashed together in her head. And for every new face, Modrasme would rest a cold hand on Hirka's arm. A matriarch staking her claim. It made Hirka's hair stand on end.

Many had come with gifts. Everything from tobacco and tea to precious sculptures made of pre-war glass, all depending on the wealth and ambitions of the family. The table behind her overflowed with things she'd never asked for.

A couple pushed their way forward and introduced themselves as the House of Semre. The woman was dressed in pale blue, presumably to match the gift she'd brought. Three caged birds. Gray, with blue breasts. They flapped their wings frantically. Hirka accepted the gift and looked at them in amazement.

"They're glowing . . ."

The woman raised her eyebrows smugly, as if she'd made the creatures with her own two hands. "We call them living lamps. Aren't they beautiful?"

Hirka clicked her tongue, which seemed to calm them. "They're magnificent," she said.

The woman shook the cage and the silvery glow intensified. "Whatever you do, don't put them in a bigger cage. They need to be in a confined space. They only shine when they're stressed."

Hirka felt her smile fade. The birds cheeped. The cage grew heavy in her arms. The woman stood there like some charlatan waiting for affirmation. Hirka had to force the word out.

"Thanks."

She turned and put the cage down. Braced herself on the table. She just wanted to slide down onto the floor and sleep. Forget. But she couldn't. She couldn't even sit. Modrasme was the only one sitting, though she made it look like she wasn't happy about it.

Hirka heard Raun's monotone laugh and scanned the hall for him. He and Uhere were mingling in the middle of the crowd. They were talking to a couple wearing strained smiles. There was an air of resentment about them. Hirka couldn't help thinking that her family's victory was another family's loss. That the House of Modrasme now being seventh could only mean someone else had lost their position.

Were they here tonight? Were they just as pleased about Hirka's arrival? Had they willingly relinquished their status in the hope of being able to conquer Ym and feel the Might again?

The howling in the crater echoed in her memory.

Yes. All indications were that they were willing. All too willing.

New faces appeared in front of her. They came and went. They gave her ribbons and gifts. Talked, though none of the words succeeded in penetrating her thoughts.

War . . . She had never understood how deep the urge to kill could be. Not a superficial desire, but a powerful motivation. With an undercurrent of greed. An entire people's sense of justice.

You could stop *one*. Ten, maybe. But how could you stop hundreds of thousands?

Graal had known. He'd known she'd never be able to stop them, and he had used her. And there was nothing she could do. The blind had her. He had all the power.

And he has Rime.

The thought made her stomach turn. Bile rose in her throat.

The guests were talking about a new era. About the Might. About the land on the other side. But that couldn't happen. She had to talk to Graal, and she had to talk to him now.

Hirka looked down at the ribbons she'd just been given. She'd wrapped them so tightly around her hand that her skin was white. She unwound them and added them to the pile with the rest.

The guests were standing so close together she had to squeeze between them to reach Skerri by the serving table. Her black leather dress had started to bunch up around her hips. The only sign of a long day. Skerri herself still looked immaculate.

Even clothes tire before Umpiri.

Grid stood next to her. He whispered something into her ear that made her smile crookedly. He tossed his head, leaving the strap tied into his hair hanging against his collarbone. It was weighed down by five metal beads. One for each victory in the arena, she'd heard. All the same, she knew Skerri regularly beat him senseless during sparring sessions. Perhaps unsurprising given Raun was the best trainer in the city.

Skerri picked up an egg from a bowl on the table, poked a hole in the top with her claw, and stuck her finger inside. It wasn't impolite to eat that way, Hirka had realized, as long as you ate through your claws and the food was considered liquid. Yet another rule Hirka would never understand or have any use for. She wasn't like them. She'd never be like them.

She went over to Skerri. Tried to veil her desperation. "We have to talk."

Skerri wrapped the eggshell in a napkin and crushed it in her hand. "So talk."

"To Graal. We have to talk to Graal."

Grid appeared to prick up his ears. A bearded man spotted Hirka and saw his chance to cut in line. He approached them and offered his congratulations to the house. Skerri thanked him. Hirka tapped her feet until she could wait no longer. She put her hand on Skerri's arm. "Skerri, it's important."

Skerri growled. She dragged Hirka into the corridor and pinned her against the wall. "We've just been elevated to seventh house. Seventh! People have traveled a long way to see us. To see *you*. The wonder who never should have been born. Yet you feel you have time to spare?"

"It won't take long, and I have to!"

Hirka tried to move, but Skerri pressed her against the wall again. "You need to shut up, and you need to stand tall. That's what you have to do. You have to conduct yourself like Dreyri!"

Three guests approached, their servants close behind. Skerri released Hirka and thanked them for coming. Hirka tried to smile, without much luck. They disappeared outside, and Skerri leaned toward her. "We'll talk to Graal when *I* say so," she snarled before bundling Hirka back into the hall.

Hirka clutched her hand to her chest. She couldn't stand any more of this. She had to get away.

Skerri was making her way over to Grid, her back turned to Hirka. Hirka slipped into the corridor again and snuck toward her bedroom. She rested her hand on the door. Gave a start when she heard scraping. Her claws. The false silver claws that fit over her fingertips. She tore them off, opened the door, and threw them on the floor.

Something stopped her from going in. A breath of cold air from an unknown source.

Behind her was a wide staircase leading to the floor below. It was carved directly into the rock, like most everything here. Downstairs there were a number of rooms. Skilborr's and Oni's rooms. Guest rooms. And the raven room—currently serving as a prison.

The word rubbed her the wrong way, but what else could she call it? She'd refused to let the family kill Urd, so there had been no other option but to lock him up. The room where the carrier raven lived was the most practical. The window was small, and the door could be bolted from the outside.

She'd passed the staircase several times over the past few days but hadn't ventured down.

Hirka glanced back toward the hall. Heard Raun's laughter above the chatter. Uhere's excessive clapping. Her mind flashed back to the day Rime had returned to Elveroa. He'd said he was accompanying Ilume to Mannfalla. Hirka had told him that if she had a grandmother, she'd just call her *Grandmother*. What had Rime replied?

Not if she were Ilume . . .

He'd been right. Raun and Uhere were Graal's parents. Her grandparents. But she couldn't bring herself to call them that. Or think of them like that. They were deadborn. Dreyri. They ate with their claws and had milky-white eyes. And today they'd all howled for her, marking the differences between them as one voice.

She went down the stairs.

The sound of the guests faded to a muted hum. She followed the corridor toward the faint light at the opposite end. It came from the raven room. From Urd's room. From a small window by the door, inset with mightslung glass that looked like a spiderweb.

A grate. A cage.

The raven gave a deep *krooo*. A warning she already knew she'd ignore. The draw was too strong.

She looked inside.

The raven was perched on a crossbeam under the ceiling. Above a hole in the floor where its droppings seemed to be concentrated. Its sleepy eyes were mere slits, squinting at a glowing storm lamp in the corner. Urd was puttering about at the back of the room. The wall behind him was covered in black symbols. Ymish and umǫni letters. Occasionally he stopped to write something on the wall with a piece of charcoal she assumed he'd found on the shelves. Then he continued walking in circles.

Once again she was struck by how young he looked without a beard and with short hair. He was barely older than Father had been when he died.

Urd frowned. His lips moved as he thought, as if he were trying to teach himself something. Did he deserve to learn? Did he deserve anything? The man who had tried to sacrifice her at Bromfjell? Who had stabbed Ilume?

They should have killed him straight away. Not given him to me.

She was ashamed at the thought. And angry. Seeing him had made her feel like she was someone else. As if he suddenly had the power to determine who she was.

He stopped mid-step. Stood with his back to her, waiting. He cocked his head as if to listen.

He knows. He knows I'm here.

Urd turned. The thin chain attached to his throat was wound around his hand. As if he were walking himself, holding his own leash.

He was sallow. Blue under the eyes. It looked like he hadn't slept in days. Hollow cheeks made it seem like his cheekbones cut all the way down to his mouth. She wished she could call him hideous.

He came closer. Hesitantly, like an animal. Skittish and exhausted. But too desperate for help to resist. She worried she looked the same.

He stopped in front of her. All that separated them was the mightglass spiderweb. She searched for her fear. For her rage. But she couldn't find the strength for either. She was too tired of pretending to be someone else.

She just had to see him. See something familiar. It didn't matter that he was an enemy.

Hirka held her hand up to the grate. Heard him drop the chain on the floor. The weight made the loop tug at his throat. He rested his fingers against hers. Skin against skin through the glass spiderweb. His fingertips were like hers. Rounded, like hers. No claws.

The scar on his forehead was nasty. Red and puckered. Someone had removed the mark of the Council and stitched up the wound. Poorly. Either half-heartedly or heedlessly.

Her heart clenched. Sympathy warred with anger. Longing with disdain. What was like her with what was unlike her.

Her gaze fell to a sickle-shaped scar in his throat. Left by the raven beak. She'd seen it exit his body. He was proof that anything was possible, that there was life after the beak.

Urd was her enemy, but he was also the closest thing she had to a hope.

Someone shouted her name upstairs. The raven shook itself, plucking at some feathers under its wing. Hirka took a step back. Urd wrapped his fingers around the grate. Tightened his grip until his knuckles were white. A silent plea for her to stay. She neither could nor wanted to. Even though she had so much to say. But right now, she couldn't for the life of her remember any of it.

Urd lowered his head and pressed his forehead against the grate. The light from the lamp made his hair glow. Like the birds she'd been given. Frightened creatures in a cage.

"I've asked them to arrange a room for you," she said. Her voice was thick, as if she hadn't used it in a long time. "It'll be ready tomorrow."

Urd nodded so imperceptibly that she might have imagined it.

Hirka retreated into the darkness, not turning until she was sure he could no longer see her.

BLACK AND WHITE

The morning light was barely able to penetrate the bathroom's pre-war windows. Hirka looked in the mirror. The black glass drained all color from her, making her look gray, like one of Hlosnian's sculptures. Halfway between human and deadborn. Daughter of Graal. A man she wasn't even allowed to talk to.

He must have known it would be like this.

The water trickled down the wall and collected in a hollow in front of her. She splashed her face before pulling on some clothes and slipping out of the bedroom.

None of the others were awake yet. Umpiri slept a lot. Even Vana's room was quiet. No laughter. No groans of passion and desire. Not that it was about desire, according to Uhere. It was about getting pregnant. Winning back the attention that Hirka had stolen. "Relax, it will never happen," Uhere had added, as if Hirka had been worried.

They're mad. The lot of them.

The party had left the hall an ungodly mess. Modrasme's chair was bathed in blue light from the ice above, the armrests buried under loyalty ribbons from countless families. The gift table by the wall was still overflowing. Hirka picked up a figure made of ashy mightglass and turned it in her hands. A woman and a man intertwined. The woman had her arms around the man's neck. It looked like she was whispering something in his ear. A secret.

Hirka put it down again. This house didn't need any more secrets. There were too many of them already. Embedded in ancient walls. Entombed in stone, under a lid of ice.

Someone had put the birdcage under the table. She lifted it as carefully as she could. A pale light surrounded the birds. A silver glow that seemed to come from within.

She opened the door and went out onto the balcony. The cold seeped through her socks. It was so early that the streets around the crater were deserted. In a few hours they would ring with hammer blows. Fallen and houseless had been put to work. Kolail, too. The new arrivals needed places to stay, and they had come in droves. From towns all over. Modrasme had called it the sound of defeat. Hammers. Brute force to shape stone. That was how low they'd sunk.

Hirka pushed the thought away. It was still quiet, and she didn't want to feel the weight of what she represented. The hope. That was why they were coming from so far away. To become strong in the Might once more. To invade.

To annihilate.

She opened the cage. The living lamps took flight and disappeared. She couldn't care less what they'd cost, or whether she was offending anyone. If light meant others had to suffer, she'd rather live in darkness. People could say what they wanted.

The ravens were awake. They swooped in and out of the mist hanging over the crater, giving playful cries she chose to interpret as support. Hirka took a moment to bask in her small act of rebellion, finally feeling like she'd done something right.

She went back inside and stashed the cage behind Modrasme's chair. Then she took the wrought iron stairs up to a chilly storeroom just beneath the ice. It creaked above her. A sign of spring, she'd realized. And it would only get worse. The ice was due to crack in a few weeks. She cut slivers of meat from a deer thigh that was hanging from the ceiling. Filled a bowl and climbed back down.

She scattered the food across the balcony before going back in and closing the door. The ravens descended straight away. She chewed on a chunk of salted meat as she listened to the beating of their wings. The enticing, silky sound of an impossible dream—being able to fly away from here.

But she was wingless. Mightless. And her only way to freedom was through Graal. Had he been planning a war all along? Had he betrayed her?

She looked out into the corridor. Skerri's door was ajar. One of her leather boots was lying in the opening. Apparently it had been quite the night. The kind that made you sleep like the dead.

Hirka crept closer and peered inside. A bed identical to her own hung at the back of the room. The leather straps that could barely be called clothes lay in a heap on the floor.

At the other end of the room was a table and benches. Wooden boards on slender iron legs, easy to move when Skerri wanted to relieve some stress with her combat staffs. She had several, all propped up against the wall, some short and some long. Hirka chewed her lip. The staffs were part of both Skerri and Raun's everyday lives. She knew she'd get a taste of them sooner or later.

The round container sat on the table. The leather was green. Weather-beaten and faded. The black strap was secured with nails.

The raven . . .

Hirka realized she'd taken a step into the room. She looked over at the bed. She couldn't see into it, but it wasn't moving. Skerri was asleep.

The raven quiver caught the light from a narrow window. A morning light that belied any danger, lulling her into what she knew was a false sense of security. But the raven was the way to Graal, and she had to talk to him. Before everything went to Slokna.

Besides, she'd started her day by breaking the rules, so why not continue?

Hirka padded over to the table and gripped the container with-out knowing when she'd decided to take it. What if it was empty? Should she check?

She glanced over at the bed again. Skerri was breathing through her nose. The rhythm of sleep.

Hirka held her breath as she eased open the clasps, lifted the lid, and looked inside. Empty eyes stared back. The beak pointed up at her. The bones that had been wings were clamped to its sides. It seemed simultaneously dead and alive. A cadaver that could be awakened. She'd seen Graal do it. With blood.

Blindcraft. Mightcraft. Old as sin. She was powerless to resist. She reached inside to touch it.

But then she was torn back. Suddenly. Violently. Her tunic cut into her throat. For a moment she thought it was the raven. The will of a dead bird. But then she was thrown at the wall and caught a glimpse of Skerri. Hirka's back slammed into stone and pain ripped through her. She sank to the floor, heart pounding in her throat. Fast as a bird's. Like an injured sparrow's.

Skerri stood over her. Naked. Pale and terrible. Braids swinging in her face, beads clacking against each other. The sound of hail. Of a storm.

Hirka stared into the black triangle between her thighs. As black as her lips. Surrounded by scars. A wing of old wounds stretching across her hips. Up toward her waist. Burns.

Hirka scrambled back but hit the wall again.

"*Gweni!*" Skerri snarled.

Hirka knew the word. *She-beast.* A female animal who wasn't Umpiri. She wanted to say something. To explain. But nothing she could say would make a difference.

"The raven is mine!" Skerri pounded her chest with her fists. "Mine! Understand? It was mine when it was alive, and it obeys only me! *I* alone talk to Graal!"

Her fury was laced with something else. Some sort of hysteria. Fear.

The realization helped Hirka to her feet. She looked at Skerri. It was like seeing her for the first time. "That's why you're here . . ." she whispered. "We're not related. Not by blood. You're here because you have the raven . . ."

Hirka knew it was true as soon as the words were out of her mouth. The raven gave Skerri her position. The power to talk to Graal. Contact between worlds. Who would she be without it?

Skerri's reaction confirmed it. She narrowed her eyes. Bared her teeth. Her canines. Her shoulders lifted as if she were about to strike.

Hirka knew all too well how strong she was. There was no point defending herself. Or running. But she could say something. The one thing that might have power over this creature. The one thing that would either save her or leave her with a broken neck.

"What am I supposed to say when my father wants to talk to me?"

The words stopped Skerri in her tracks. Hirka continued before she had time to change her mind. "Sooner or later, Graal will want to talk to me. What am I supposed to say then? That you refused to let me?"

Skerri grabbed her by the tunic and pulled her close. So close that Hirka could tell which wine she'd been drinking.

"You would play with me?" Her eyes blackened. "You think you're better at this game? Prepare to lose, *gweni*."

She pushed Hirka away. "The raven is mine."

Hirka backed toward the door. The numbness was starting to ebb. Pain shot through her hips. Her shoulders. She turned and left the room.

"We'll talk to Graal tomorrow evening," she heard Skerri say behind her.

If she hadn't been in so much pain, she'd have smiled.

OH . . .

The pot was burning hot. Hirka barely got it off the fire before she had to let go. It teetered on the edge of the hearth. She nudged it back into place. Cursed and cooled her fingers against the wall. She was nervous. Impatient. And she didn't have much to work with.

Umpiri rarely prepared food, so it would have been an exaggeration to call the room she was in a kitchen. It was a place to fill their glasses. Sink their claws into meat. They took what they needed and discarded the rest. They aged food, not because it made it better, but because it changed it. Developed other nutrients they needed. There was no need for boiling or baking. Or tasting.

She would have survived better in the wilderness.

At least space wasn't an issue. A palace beneath the ice, where even the larders were bigger than the room Kolail called home. She was surrounded by beautiful windows made of mightglass. Ceilings sloped at various angles. It was a peculiar mix of grandeur and simplicity. Created to show mastery. Power. Not for comfort.

Yet another place she didn't belong.

Hirka fiddled with the lid of the tea box without opening it. The box wasn't the problem. Nor was the pot or the hearth. It was the knowledge that the others were sitting in the next room talking to Graal.

She heard Skerri's screeching voice again. Interrupting, as always.

Soon she'd come out to fetch her. Soon Hirka would get to talk to Graal, too.

Hirka snapped open the lid, painfully aware that she was pinning far too much hope on this conversation. Graal knew what he was doing. He'd known all along. So what good would come of this, other than perhaps getting a chance to vent her anger? She probably wouldn't even get to do that. She couldn't say half of what she thought and felt. Not in front of the rest of the family. Refuse to lead an invasion to Ym? Refuse to be the successor to a warlord?

Skerri would sink her claws into her if she tried. Drain the life from her.

Hirka sat down on the floor in front of the hearth and poured hot water over the tea leaves. A gift from Jór. A touching gesture from the House of Hod that had the rest of the family speculating wildly. Jór was still to choose a partner. Was this some kind of signal? Did they want to form closer ties to the House of Modrasme? Did they have plans for the houses after the war?

After the war . . .

Hirka closed her eyes over the teacup. The steam warmed her face. It smelled like the moss near the Alldjup after a rainy day. It smelled like everything used to be. So familiar that it hurt.

There was no after the war. Not that she could see. It was an unbearable thought. So what could she do? Tear down the raven ring so no one could leave?

She remembered the size of the stones she'd come through. It would take an eternity to tear them down, even with the help of every houseless in Ginnungad. And even if it were possible, would she do it? Would she destroy the only chance to restore the Might? The only way to travel between worlds?

Naiell had done it. Perhaps without understanding the consequences, but still. He had condemned worlds to an infinitely slow death, just so he could live like a god. Until he grew tired of it.

Hirka clutched the cup in her hands. Knew she was lying to herself. She pretended it was about the greater good. A nobler fight. Save the Might. Save the pathways between worlds. The truth was so simple in comparison. So selfish and so small. The truth was she was terrified of being here. Of being trapped here for the rest of her life. She was terrified of seeing so many die, but mostly those she cared for. Lindri, Svarteld, Rime . . .

Rime and Kolkagga. They can stop this. They can stop anything.

The ache in her heart laid bare the true reason she would never be able to destroy the gateways. She'd left Rime before. He'd come after her. Found her. And trapped her. At least that was how it felt. As if he'd given her a part of his soul with that kiss. It lived inside her. Grew inside her. Woke her up at night . . .

The doors to the counsel room slammed open, crashing into the walls. Skerri emerged. Hirka felt her cheeks blazing. She leaped to her feet, dropping the teacup. It shattered on the floor. The tea spilled out and ran between the stone tiles. There was something about the sight that made her shudder. As if it meant something.

"He wants to talk to you. Alone." Skerri's expression left no doubt as to how she felt about it. The others came out behind her. Hirka stood still, her gaze shifting between Skerri and the broken teacup.

"Get in there! Skilborr will see to that." Skerri tossed her head in the direction of the door.

Hirka did as she was told. She went into the counsel room and closed the doors behind her.

The room was shaped like a boat. Figures were carved into the walls. Members of the family, dead and alive. Modrasme's was a stunning likeness. Head raised, gaze averted. A *sekhpainari*. A woe-wallower. Someone who loved receiving confirmation that nothing was good enough. Hirka, for example.

Raun didn't look much like his usual self without his red hair. The stone was colorless and sucked the life out of him. Modrasme and Uhere were better suited to stone. Graal she recognized from his somewhat mournful eyes. She'd only seen him in a suit, but here he was depicted in some kind of armor that covered his chest and one shoulder—a reminder of who he was. The plinth next to him was empty.

Naiell.

There was a row of lamps along the other wall, and colored linen stretched over a skeletal frame, like black cocoons. The light flickered behind them, making it look like they were about to birth something horrible.

Hirka went over to the raven. It was standing on an oval table in the middle of the room. She'd decided to keep calm. Ask for time. Ask for help. Whatever it took. But she hadn't expected the maps on the table. They were old, and pressed into rigid wooden frames. Ym. Mannfalla. Foggard. Ravnhov . . .

Disgust welled up inside her. A sickening despair that made her hands tremble. She rested them on the table and leaned over the raven bones.

"You lied!" she seethed. "It wasn't supposed to be like this! It wasn't supposed to go like this! I said I'd find a way, but not this! We agreed! Not like this!"

"How have they received you, Hirka?" The raven moved its beak, but the voice was Graal's. Just as she remembered it. Deep. Treacherously warm. And completely indifferent to her accusations.

"How do you think?! Don't pretend you don't know! I stood on Crier's Rock with his heart in my hand, and they told everyone what I am. That I'm yours. That they're going to conquer Ym. They're coming from all over this frozen rock to join an invasion that will never happen! Do you hear me?!"

"What about Skerri? How is she treating you?"

"She—It's not—" Hirka struggled to find the words. He was trying to throw her off balance. He wouldn't hear any of it.

"Blood of my blood . . ." He said it so gently that the words burrowed inside her. Cradled her heart as if he wanted to rock it to sleep.

"Hirka, you're alive. You're alive because you're useful to them. Be useful and stay alive. I want you alive."

"Useful?" Hirka felt faint. She stared down at the map of Mannfalla. Black lines on gray paper. "I've elevated you to the seventh house. I've done almost everything you asked. You're loved again. A leader again. What more do you want?" She tried to lace her words with scorn, but instead they sounded hollow.

"Whatever happens. They know the raven rings are open. The way to the Might. Had you thought they would simply starve to death when sustenance is within their reach?"

"There are other ways! If you would all just let me meet the Seer! You said I should learn about life and death. About the Might."

"And you shall. When we have it, Hirka. There will come a time after this. In Ym. You will be surrounded by the Might and people who can teach you to use it. But you have to be patient."

Hirka shook the table, but it barely moved. "No! This isn't the way! Let me talk to Rime. To the Council. There are places where Umpiri can live. Far to the north, where the ice is—we can—your people can . . ." The howling from Crier's Rock echoed in her head. She knew what she was saying didn't make any sense. Umpiri and ymlings? Together, in the same world?

She laughed joylessly at her own words. Dragged her hands across her face.

The raven lifted its head. "Rime is powerless, Hirka. I warned him against leaving Ym, but he did it regardless. He came for you. And so, he's no longer ravenbearer. He's lost his place on the Council."

Lost his place . . .

No one lost their place on the Council. No one. A myriad of scenarios played out in her head. None of them pretty. She gritted her teeth. "To who? Who has his place?"

"It's complicated."

"Tell me! I want to know!"

The raven shifted the bones that had once been wings. "I'd hoped to control the Council through him, but that wasn't to be. But all is not lost. The Council is reeling, and that serves us well. Darkdaggar tried to assassinate Rime and that was a fatal error. He ended up in the pits but was pardoned in Rime's absence. Even though Rime won the duel."

Hirka let out a snort. "Try again, Graal. Do you think I'm an idiot? Rime in a duel with Darkdaggar? An ordinary councillor? If that were true, he'd be raven fodder now."

"Darkdaggar didn't fight him. Svarteld did, and he died for him. Or had you forgotten?"

Hirka's breath caught in her throat. What? What nonsense was this?

But she'd heard it before. That Rime had killed Svarteld.

She slumped down onto the bench. "That was a lie! Allegra was lying. You said so yourself it wasn't true."

"What did I say wasn't true?"

There was genuine uncertainty in his voice. She thought back to the conversation they'd had when he'd met her at the zoo. "You lied about Rime and Sylja getting married. About him killing Svarteld! And about Lindri being . . ."

"Svarteld was no lie."

"But you said . . ." She was on the verge of tears.

"Hirka, listen to me," said the dead bird in front of her. Light from the lamps played over the bones. "I remember you asking about Lindri. I told you that was a lie. But you never asked about Svarteld. I thought you knew."

Hirka stared at the skeleton. What in Slokna kind of blindcraft let a pile of bones tell her Svarteld was dead?

"Hirka?"

She remembered to breathe again. Forced out the words. "Why? Why would Svarteld fight—"

"Who knows. It was his own choice."

Svarteld.

She could picture him so clearly he might as well have been standing right in front of her. Black as jet. Bald with piercing eyes. The man who had been there after the nightmare in the Rite Hall, when she'd woken up in Blindból. The man who had taught her to kick. And the man who had loved Rime like a son, despite his obvious difficulties in showing it.

"You're wrong," she whispered. "Svarteld didn't die for Darkdaggar. He died for Rime."

Hirka squeezed her eyes shut. What had it cost him, to face his own master? To kill him?

But wasn't that what Rime did? Killed? And wasn't that what she now hoped would save them all?

Hirka looked at the raven again. Felt a cold smile cross her lips. "He's going to assemble Kolkagga."

He's going to kill you all.

"I believe so," Graal answered.

Fragments of memories surfaced in her mind. The cracks in Stefan's phone, like a glass spiderweb. Not unlike the grate that had separated her from Urd. An enemy she had more in common with than her own family. Spiderwebs. Threads.

Graal. Her father. A spider.

Rime had taken the beak of his own free will, he'd said. A choice that couldn't be undone. But it gave Graal power. He knew that. She knew that. Both she and Rime were slaves. Pieces in a game that would end in war.

For revenge. For the Might. For all the right reasons, and all the wrong ones. But right and wrong no longer existed. Everything blurred together. There was no one to trust.

The doors opened. Hirka sat up. Hurried to wipe away the tears.

Raun came in, features drawn and eyes hollow, like he'd seen a ghost. "Graal . . . He's here. He's come to see her."

The raven twisted around. "Who?"

Raun didn't reply. A heavy silence had descended on the room. Then the bones creaked again. The beak cracked open. "Oh . . ."

That was the most loaded little word Hirka had ever heard.

He knows who has come.

A figure entered the room, swathed in black. Black robe. Gloves. With a hood drawn over his head. So long that it covered his face like a veil, hanging all the way down to his middle. He was like darkness in motion. Like Kolkagga. But even Kolkagga had a slit for their eyes. And Kolkagga didn't walk hunched over.

Hirka realized that the creature in the doorway was the only Umpiri she'd seen that bore signs of age. Or illness. Despite the robe, she could see that his shoulders were sloped. His head seemed strangely elongated. It was like something from a dream, one that made you wake up with a scream lodged in your throat.

No one made any move to stop him. That was the most terrifying part. Even Skerri stood quietly by the door.

The figure limped closer. He leaned on the table, thumb bent back at an impossible angle. Hirka could tell from his breathing that he was struggling. She slid a little farther up the bench.

"Graal's . . . blood." He sounded like a hissing cat. As if the words were being expelled directly from his lungs. She stared at him as he pulled a bundle out from under his robe and threw it on the table. It was her tunic. The old green tunic she'd given Kolail.

It was the Seer. He'd come.

Hirka got up so quickly she almost tripped over the bench. Raun moved toward her as he talked to the raven. "Graal, I've explained that we have other priorities. Hirka needs to understand how the houses and the Council work. She needs to learn about leadership.

Culture. Combat. She still has much to learn of our language, and we haven't even started with the staffs . . ."

Raun's obstinacy was pervaded by doubt. Hirka heard the Seer coughing and wheezing under the robe and realized he was laughing. He walked past Raun. She got the impression he used sound to guide him. Then he leaned forward so his hood grazed the raven. "At the head of ten thousss . . . sand men she will walk. A daughter of Dreyri. Of ravenbinders. Without understanding the Might?"

His voice cracked at times, but he seemed to take no notice. "The girl will come to me as sss . . . soon as the ice breaks." He turned his back on the raven, as if there were nothing more to discuss.

"Seer?" The raven craned its neck, vertebrae creaking.

The Seer stopped but didn't turn. Listened.

"Teach her what she needs to know. No more. Do we understand each other?"

"Don't we always, Graal . . ."

The Seer limped back out. Step by agonizing step. Hirka could smell it. Feel it. She'd seen enough people trying to conceal pain to recognize it.

Suddenly she realized they were looking at her. All of them.

Modrasme. Raun. Uhere. Her own bloodline. Uhere's parents, Lug and Cirra, were outside peering in. Vana stood gaping, as if waiting for some explanation. Skerri came toward her. Reached for the tunic on the table. Hirka grabbed it and clutched it to her chest.

She knew there was no explaining this, but it didn't matter. She'd gotten what she wanted. The Seer had recognized her smell. He had come.

She would learn everything she needed to know. She'd won. So why didn't it feel like it?

VILLAINY

Far too many dead. Hundreds. Stacked in the huts. Poisoned by those they were meant to serve. It was an act that would have made the gods weep. An act of villainy. A sin so heinous that even the flames renounced it. They swirled skyward, flickering in every direction as if trying to flee.

The fire feared Kolkagga. Even in death.

Rime pulled his mask up over his nose to lessen the stench. They could have stood farther away, but he wanted to be close. He had to watch them burn.

He wasn't alone.

Forty-seven men had survived. Forty-seven heartbroken men. They stood grief-stricken around him. Friends and strangers, from all over Blindból. Some from camps he hadn't even known existed.

Rime nudged Stiar. He looked at him and understood. Pulled his own mask up, too.

The heat washed over them like a wave. The fire ate. The fire crackled. Smoke and ash poured out of the huts, taking to the skies. The roof nearest them collapsed. Crashed down in a flurry of sparks. The walls blackened and disintegrated, and the bodies came into view. Ravenous flames tore at them, giving the false and terrible impression that they were moving. Trying to escape from the fire.

Rime forced himself to stay where he was. Forced himself to watch. Watch everything, so he'd remember what he was avenging.

He heard the others withdraw. One by one. In the end Stiar went, too.

Marrow came up behind him. "Sure, let's stand here a while longer," he mumbled behind his mask. "What can it hurt . . ."

Rime was glad Marrow was one of the survivors. He was the sort of man you could rely on, even when everything fell apart. He had a dark sense of humor that lifted the mood if it got too bleak. If the rumors were true, he'd been called Marrow ever since he'd suffered a nasty break of his arm and taken the opportunity to taste his own bone marrow.

"I need you to do something for me, Marrow."

"No."

Rime looked at him.

"No, master."

Marrow pulled his mask down. "I'm not going to look after anyone while you're gone. I'm not going to drag that lot to Ravnhov while you go to Mannfalla to die."

Rime stared into the flames. "So you want to come with me? Is that what you're saying?"

Marrow moved to stand in front of him. Blocking his view of the fires. "Rime, I was there. Eisvaldr is impregnable. They're fortifying the old complex, behind the walls. They have more men than we've lost, and they have control of the city. Do you think they don't have the sense to protect themselves?"

Rime knew he was right. He'd snuck into Eisvaldr before, but that time he'd had Hirka. Without her, the Might was a shadow of what it could be. Without her, he'd die in the attempt.

The final hut collapsed. A charred body rolled away from it. The fire puffed like bellows. Rime turned and started to walk toward the camp.

"It'll still be worth it."

Marrow caught up to him. "Isn't it enough that they've lost everything? Would you also take from them the one person who can lead them? The one person who can talk to Eirik and win this war?"

Rime didn't reply. Marrow grabbed hold of him. "I get it, Rime! I know how it feels. You're not alone here. But you're the best chance we have at making this right. We can't lose you. Not now. Not like this."

Rime heard himself laugh. They would lose him either way. Perhaps as soon as Graal next contacted him.

Marrow meant well, and he was no idiot. But neither Marrow nor the others knew how pressed for time he was. None of them knew what was in his throat. That he was a slave.

He had to get to Darkdaggar before Graal found out that there had been a coup and that Kolkagga were lost.

Marrow gave him a warm and inquiring look. A silent plea. Rime felt a sudden urge to tell him everything. To lessen the unbearable burden that was his alone to bear.

Stiar came running, saving him from sharing what would have changed everything.

"People, master! Sveinn says they're entering Blindból through the mountains in the east. Maybe they saw the fires."

Rime followed him. "Councillors? Soldiers?"

"Sveinn says they have kids with them. Ordinary folk. No more than twenty. But he says two of them have ravens on their foreheads!"

Refugees!

"Marrow and Torgar, come with me." Rime looked at Stiar. "Are they wounded?"

"Not from what I've heard."

"Bring supplies, just in case." Rime tightened the straps of his Kolkagga blacks. "Stiar, lead the way."

Rime ran with his heart in his mouth. Councillors. Fleeing Mannfalla. He hated himself for hoping Jarladin was one of them. Hated preferring someone else was dead, but it was what it was. If it were up to him, Jarladin and Eir would be the two survivors.

He drew on the Might and sped between the trees. He could hear the others behind him. Quiet as raven wings.

Stiar gestured. They were close.

They climbed up onto a rock. Sveinn was crouched close to the edge, barely distinguishable from the boulders around him. Rime crawled up next to him and spotted them.

They were struggling their way toward the mountain pass with far too much in tow. Heavy bags, a cart that would never survive Blindból, kids . . .

Rime squinted into the darkness and found him. Jarladin. They were fairly bundled up, but the ox with the full white beard was unmistakable. He carried a sword on his hip, but none of them had bows—meaning none of them could loose an arrow by mistake.

Rime signaled to the others, and they jumped down from the rock. Gathered in the mountain pass and waited.

The exhausted group came closer. They spotted Kolkagga and stopped. For a few seconds they stood silent. At a loss. As if they weren't sure what to do. Run. Scream. Or celebrate. One of them decided to run. Jarladin grabbed him, and that triggered a panic.

Rime went down to meet them. "Jarladin!" He shouted to make himself known.

Jarladin squinted at him. "Rime?"

Rime heard his name ripple through the group. He went to meet the councillor. The escape had taken its toll. He had bags under his eyes and wasn't dressed for travel. He brought a hand to Rime's chest, as if to confirm what his eyes were seeing. Eyes that were threatening tears.

Rime was glad Jarladin was alive, but he couldn't let himself feel the councillor's grief. He was done grieving. Tears wouldn't help anyone. He just needed to know who was alive and who was dead.

"I heard there were two of you." Rime scanned the faces. A broad and angular woman elbowed her way through. Sigra Kleiv.

Rime was unable to hide his surprise. Sigra. The Council's stone woman. The most belligerent of them all, and probably the one who'd gotten on his nerves the most. She thought bloodshed solved everything. And she couldn't even *say* Ravnhov without spitting.

What was she doing here? He'd have expected her to be the first person to side with Darkdaggar.

The mannish woman lifted her chin and glared at him. "You thought I'd have stayed," she said bitterly.

Rime shrugged. "The Council or nothing. That's how it's always been for you. And I assumed you'd stick with whoever intended to destroy me."

Shame passed over her features before she could stop it. "Think what you like, boy. You could irritate blood from stone, but you were on the Council. And the Council I'm on doesn't kill each other."

Rime looked at the others. Most of them were members of Sigra's family. If he remembered correctly, she had twelve children of various ages. Some of Jarladin's family were there too. Then he recognized a girl. Sylja. Sylja from Elveroa. She smiled at him like he'd asked her to dance. Not like they were fleeing into Blindból in the middle of the night. And not like she was surprised to see him. Jarladin must have told them that he was alive.

Rime looked back at Jarladin. "Who?"

Jarladin pulled his granddaughter close and put his hands over her ears. "Noldhe was the first. She died peacefully in her sleep, they say. Miane Fell has been thrown into the pits for . . . treason." The word seemed to bite into his tongue.

"Eir?"

Jarladin shook his head. "Fire . . ."

Rime looked away. He'd known Eir his entire life. The Raven-bearer had been one of Ilume's closest friends. A steady presence during his childhood. Nothing was as it was supposed to be any-more.

"And the rest are with him? With Darkdaggar?"

"We don't know. We know about Tyrme, Saulhe, Leivlugn . . ."

Sigra cut in. "The man's almost a hundred. I doubt he under-stands what's going on."

Jarladin nodded. "But Freid Vangard is with him. And Telja Vanfarinn."

Rime closed his eyes. Pinched the bridge of his nose. Telja . . . Urd's distant relative. The spectacle that had swept into the Council Chamber in a black mourning gown, desperate for Urd's chair. So she'd finally gotten the place she'd longed for.

He sighed. "Any sign of Ramoja?"

Jarladin shook his head. Rime hoped she'd taken Vetle to Ravn-hov.

Rime gestured for them to follow. "You've not picked the easiest route."

"We were trying to avoid Blindból at first," Jarladin said behind him. He was trying to sound chipper, as if attempting to gloss over how their last encounter had ended. "But the terrain was too open, and we thought someone was following us, so we had to make our way into the mountains. Even though we couldn't be sure wheth-er . . . We weren't sure how things stood with Kolkagga."

The words were probing. Jarladin was perceptive enough to real-ize that something had happened.

"I can tell you how things stand with Kolkagga," Rime said. "We're dead. Almost to a man."

He heard Jarladin stop. Rime looked over his shoulder at him as he kept walking. "But so is Darkdaggar, if that's any consolation."

Jarladin hurried to catch up. "Rime, you can't! He's positioned his men with the army. He has Eisvaldr. Trying would be suicide."

Marrow approached them. "That's what I told him."

Rime let them continue the discussion without him. He heard Sylja call out to him, but he couldn't face her. Not now. Jarladin and Marrow tried to keep pace as they talked about what had happened. About how crucial Rime was. How he would have to bring the rest of Ym together. How he was their protector.

Him. A slave to one of the deadborn.

If only they'd known . . .

Jarladin caught up with him again. Grabbed his arm. "Rime, you need to listen—"

Rime tore himself free and turned toward him. "No! *You* need to listen! Darkdaggar is a dead man. Tomorrow might not be the day he dies, but I promise you, tomorrow will be the day he finds out how close he is to Slokna."

SIGN OF THE SEER

Darkdaggar was torn from a dream. Had he heard thunder? He sat up in bed. Someone was pounding on the bedroom door.

Kunte shouted his name outside, over and over again. Guardsmen were running along the corridors. It was a spectacle that could have raised the dead.

Elisa grabbed hold of him. "Garm? What's happening?" Her voice was feeble and rough with sleep. She hadn't been herself since they'd moved behind the walls. She slept and ate too little. In moments of weakness, he thought she could sense all the things he hadn't told her. That she knew.

Darkdaggar got up and tightened the belt of his robe. "Sleep, my dear. It's probably just another runaway."

There had been a couple since he'd seized power, but that was to be expected. An inevitable cost, under the circumstances.

Elisa sat up and stared at the door. She brought a hand to her mouth. He walked around the bed and pushed her back down onto her pillow. Stroked her hair away from her face.

"I'll be right back. Stay here."

Her eyes were wide. He was gripped by an urge to force them shut. As if she were a corpse. He was ashamed at the thought. None of this was her fault. The last few days had been chaos. A time of change. A time of upheaval. But they'd won. The Council had endured. His people, under his leadership.

But it worried him that she wouldn't sleep. He'd purged the Council. Purged the army. But he'd also made a mess of what they had. Maybe when victory was assured, and the kingdoms were at peace . . .

He tore open the door. Kunte knocked in mid-air before realizing. Darkdaggar stepped out and closed the door behind him.

"You're scaring people to death, Kunte!"

"I know, Garm-fadri, but someone's been in."

Darkdaggar cursed. He'd forgotten his slippers. "In where? Who's missing?"

"No, it's nothing like that. Everyone's on high alert. Two teams are out looking, but . . . No one's seen anyone."

"You're not making sense, Kunte. What's happened? Is someone dead?"

"No, but . . ."

A door cracked open farther along the corridor. Freid Vangard leaned out with a lamp in her hand. Darkdaggar gave her a disarming wave.

"Nothing to worry about. Go back to bed, Freid." The councillor muttered to herself and disappeared back into her room. Living on top of each other was by no means ideal, but unfortunately it was necessary. At least until their control was more established. For the time being, Eisvaldr had shrunk to the oldest part of the city. The core that had once been reserved for the Seer, inside the white walls.

Darkdaggar sighed. "Kunte, you've woken all of Slokna. No one's missing. No one's dead. And you're looking for someone no one's seen. Would you kindly explain?"

"I have to show you," Kunte replied, gesturing for him to follow.

"Wait." Darkdaggar opened the door and stepped back into his room. It was almost impossible to see anything in the dark, but his slippers were in their usual place. At least *something* was as it was supposed to be. He pulled them on as he whispered to Elisa. "It's nothing, just as I thought. I'll be right back."

He didn't wait for an answer. Just went back out and followed Kunte.

The corridors were narrow in this part of Eisvaldr. The doors lower and the rooms more cramped, as if people used to be smaller. The only light came through the narrow windows overlooking the courtyard. He could hear the rattling of armor. Kunte opened a door and hurried down the steps toward the open square.

Darkdaggar looked around. The work wasn't as far along as he'd hoped. The well was in use again, after several hundred years. But the vegetable gardens needed time. The aim was to live self-sufficiently within the walls, as in days gone by. But it often felt like flogging a dead horse. Eisvaldr had lived in luxury, secure in its own superiority, for almost a thousand years. The arrow slits had grown into windows. The portcullises had rusted open or been removed long ago. He had men working day and night to close off alleyways and tear down bridges and flights of steps. After little more than a week, Eisvaldr was almost unrecognizable. It was starting to look like something that could be defended.

Kunte crossed the courtyard. There was something unsettling about his haste. It made Darkdaggar's hands sweat, even though the night air was frigid.

They continued up onto the wall on the other side. From here he could see what remained of the Rite Hall. An open area between the two parts of the city. The stone circle stuck up in the middle, like a garden ornament. It made him feel uneasy, like it was taunting him with an unspoken question.

What if . . .?

Kunte went into one of the towers in the wall. Darkdaggar was starting to lose his patience, but when they came out on the other

side, Kunte stopped. Men with torches ran past below, flames trail-ing behind them.

Kunte didn't need to point. Darkdaggar gazed out across Blindból. The sight sent a surge of cold through him. Like his lungs were shrinking. His tail drooped between his legs. He gripped the railing.

Swords stood planted in the ground. Hundreds of them.

Close together, in the sign of the Seer. A steel raven, so ripe with meaning that he could almost hear it screaming. And so enormous that he understood why Kunte had brought him so high up.

Kunte took off his cloak and draped it around Darkdaggar's shoulders. "So some survived," he said. "That's all it means. So what? There can't be many of them. And this . . . It might not be Rime."

Darkdaggar forced a smile. "Oh, I promise you—it's Rime."

The wind blew between the blades, making them sing. A chorus of dead men's swords that chilled him to his very core.

BREAKING POINT

Hirka kept a safe distance from the fighting. She looked around for a bench, with no luck. Anywhere else she might have had a hope, but of course looking for something to sit on where the ring fighters trained was pointless. If Umpiri were proud, this lot were something else entirely.

Benches would have been difficult in any case, as the cave was bowl-shaped. Perhaps carved out of a subterranean lake that had long since dried up. There was a whole chain of them not far beneath the street running east toward the sea.

Maybe she could sit on the ground.

She looked over at Skerri and decided to stay standing. She'd pushed the woman to breaking point already. Kolail, the raven, the Seer . . . It was only a matter of time before she cracked.

Skerri spun her staff around as if it weighed nothing. The end slammed into Grid's chest. The sound made Hirka flinch. He groaned, stumbled back, and fell out of the circle for the third time in a row. Being Skerri's friend clearly afforded him no advantage. On the contrary, she seemed to take more pleasure from beating him than any of the others. It was as if she wanted to punish him for caring.

I wonder how she treats her enemies . . .

There were five rings in the room, painted in flaming yellow on the stone floor. No mats. No sand. Nothing to break their falls.

It probably hadn't even occurred to them. That wasn't how their minds worked.

To Hirka, this was a room where needless and nasty accidents were inevitable. For one thing, the rings were too close together. How many skulls had been cracked by errant staffs? There were also far too few lamps to provide adequate lighting. Had they not seen so well in the dark, they'd all have been killed. And at the end of the room there was a drop down into the next cave. How many had tumbled over that? Had their ridiculously long lives cut short by stupidity and pride?

A drawn-out groan echoed around the room. An immense rumble from the ice, as if the walls were about to rupture. It had been creaking more and more over the past few days. It was only a matter of time before it lost the fight and cracked.

The girl will come to me as soon as the ice breaks . . .

She was going to meet the Seer. The thought filled her with so many conflicting feelings, she worried she might rupture, too.

Grid was on his feet. He held his staff out in front of him with both hands, as if he knew he needed all the protection he could get. Hirka was glad she was only watching. A small comfort, though, considering she'd have to participate soon enough. Skerri was pushing to get her in the ring at the earliest opportunity. Her excuse was Hirka's obvious weediness. She was small. Weak. More menskr than Dreyri. She would never be a warrior, but the family still agreed that they had to do their best to make her look like one.

But first she was to observe. That was what Raun had decided.

Hirka turned her attention to him. His red hair, so much like her own, had been pulled back into a bun. He was fighting a woman right by the drop. One wearing wide steel cuffs around her arms. Weights, Hirka had realized. They were using shorter staffs than Skerri and Grid, one in each hand. It had taken Hirka a while to understand why staffs were fine while other weapons weren't. Weapons were for weaklings. Cowards. The low houses, or the houseless. But a staff was just a staff. Something you happened to have to hand.

Hirka tugged at her skirt in an attempt to cover her thighs, but it was no use. She was more naked than clothed. Clothes here weren't made to keep you warm or protect you. They were made to intimidate. Show off muscles. Superiority. On her they were a joke. Svarteld would have laughed.

Svarteld . . .

The thought cracked open the door to a grief she didn't want to face. She started walking around the edge of the cave as she observed the warriors. They were fast. Strong. With impressive control. It was clear they'd been doing what they were doing for generations. Kolkagga might have stood a chance here. Few others would.

The ice groaned again. Louder. More drawn-out. It felt like the very foundations of the city were shaking. The fighting stopped. The blindlings looked around. Grinned at each other. Even Skerri joined in. She thumped Grid on the arm, and he grinned back. Hirka almost felt sorry for him. How many beatings had he taken just to be close to Skerri?

Hollow laughter came from one of the tunnels sloping down from the street. Another group entered. Men and women walking shoulder to shoulder and guffawing. A close-knit bunch. The others straightened up and Hirka realized the newcomers had to be from a higher house.

Hirka assumed the session was over. She picked up her cloak from the floor.

"Hirka?"

She recognized the voice straight away. Jór from the House of Hod.

Don't turn your back on him, don't leave without permission, don't interrupt him, don't . . .

Hirka took a deep breath and plastered on a smile before turning. "Jór."

His fair hair looked so haphazard that she knew a lot of work had to have gone into it. Even his fringe was different lengths. He put a hand on her arm. Ordinarily, that alone would probably have been enough to elevate her from the seventh to the sixth house. The bitter thought made her feel ashamed. Jór didn't seem that bad. Unless he'd just learned to hide it better than other Umpiri.

"Did you get the tea? What do you think?" He lowered his chin and eyed her with genuine interest, as if he in no way expected her to sing its praises.

"It was lovely, Jór. Thank you. I look forward to the day you get to try tea from Himli—" The word stuck in her throat. Tea from Himlifall. When would Jór get to try that? When Ym was invaded and the ymlings were wiped out?

"I look forward to that, Hirka." He didn't seem to notice her discomfort, instead flashing her a dazzling smile.

The red serpent slithered across his chest. An inking stretching over his shoulder and around one arm. It struck Hirka that she hadn't seen many inkings in Ginnungad. Was it because any marking of the skin suggested you weren't good enough as you were? If so, it was something Jór had decided to ignore. But that was probably easier to do when you belonged to the leading house.

He lifted a bag from his shoulder and gave it to one of the others without taking his eyes off her. Several people had gathered nearby, their curiosity poorly concealed.

He pulled her farther away from them. "It's lucky we ran into each other, Hirka. You know . . . There are a lot of old maps of Mannfalla, but my mother says that the war cabinet disagrees on what has changed since they were last there. No point arguing when we've got you, right? But they're too old to admit they've anything still to learn. I, on the other hand, am apparently too young and careless." He winked at her. "Do you think you could help them?"

Hirka stiffened. His unguarded face was a stark contrast to what he was asking for. Maps. Maps of Mannfalla. Would she help them destroy her own capital? Her own people?

You've never been an ymling. You're menskr. You're Dreyri.

Jór smiled as if all he'd asked her to do was point at the sky. She opened her mouth to answer, but nothing came out.

"Of course, she would be honored, Jór." Skerri appeared next to them.

Jór glanced at her. "Then let us honor her in return by letting her speak for herself," he said, looking at Hirka again. She wanted to scream. His words were far from helpful. Quite the opposite. Her discomfort grew, caught between Jór's expectations and Skerri's hatred. All Hirka could do was nod.

"Good! Then I'll send an invitation." He reached out and caught a staff thrown to him by one of his fellows. Then he nodded as well and entered the rings with the others. Their staffs started crashing together in an erratic rhythm. Like her heart.

"You've got to give him points for effort," Skerri snarked behind her.

"What?"

"Trying to treat you like one of us."

Skerri moved in front of Hirka, forcing her closer to the curved wall. Her black lips twitched. Her canines flashed as she spoke. "But you're not one of us, are you? You came here as a demonstration of Graal's power. To front the war. But you don't want that. You're not loyal to your house. To your blood. You're loyal to *them*. The dogs you grew up with."

She leaned closer, fresh sweat beading on her skin. Her braids brushed against Hirka's chest. "Half of Dreysíl would kill for Jór's attention. To get a foot in the door of the House of Hod. But not you. So who is it, Hirka? Who are you loyal to? Is it that black shadow who couldn't even keep his seat on the Council?"

Hirka made a futile attempt to hide her reaction. Skerri slithered around her. So close Hirka could feel the heat emanating from her. She felt claws scrape against her neck. Lips against her ear. "Rime? Was that his name? Is he the one you're loyal to? Is he the one you're going to betray us for? It's no use, Hirka. If he wants to save himself, he has to stop fighting."

Hirka wrenched herself away from Skerri's claws. "Clearly you don't know him very well."

Skerri snorted. "All I said was his name, Hirka." Her voice was hoarse. Strained, like all she really wanted to do was scream. "All I said was his name, and now I can smell him on you. You think you can hide your desire, but it burns within you. Pushes its way out through your pores. You can't lie to me. Your loyalty reeks. I can taste it on your skin."

Hirka clenched her teeth. She felt exposed. Furious. Skerri had forced her way in where she wasn't allowed. Into the place that held the truest thing Hirka had. The only thing that felt real.

"Oh, so you were young once?" Hirka regretted it the moment the words were out of her mouth.

Skerri swung her staff at Hirka's legs and her knees gave out. Skerri slipped behind her and clamped her thighs around her sides. Pain tore through her ribs. Hirka was trapped. Skerri was like a bear on her back. Then she felt the staff pressed against her throat. Her pulse hammered against hard wood. Was this how it would end? All it would take was a simple twist and Hirka's neck would snap.

Skerri leaned forward and hissed into her ear. "I'll kill you before I let you betray us!"

"Skerri!" Raun was coming toward them.

Suddenly the walls gave a deep rumble, as if from the depths of the world.

The ice!

The thwacking of staffs died. Skerri let go of Hirka. There was another rumble. The ice was far above them but sounded much closer. There was a crash like lightning. Followed by a series of creaks, each fainter than the last. The room suddenly exploded. The warriors waved their staffs and bumped chests with a childlike glee that likely heralded a night of heavy drinking. A party in Ginnungad.

Hirka raised a hand to her throat. Clambered to her feet. She gave Skerri a cold smile. She couldn't help herself.

"Seems you'll have to kill me some other day. Right now, I have an appointment to keep."

THE SEER

An unfortunate consequence of being Hirka of the House of Modrasme, the seventh, was that she rarely got to go anywhere alone. Not even to the Seer.

A few warriors accompanied her through the streets, clad in servants' robes. Hirka was sure everyone knew exactly why they were there, but obviously Dreyri feared no one and didn't need protectors. An escort with staffs, however, that was fine. The staffs were for digging yourself out of the snow, not for fending off an attack and knocking someone's block off. That would be preposterous.

Kolail was the only one not pretending to be anything other than he was. The teardrop in his forehead said it all.

He kept behind her, off to one side. The others were clearly uncomfortable with his presence, keeping a constant eye on him, as if he were up to something. The truth was he felt like a shield between her and the rest of them. Protection from the ones who were meant to keep her safe.

The streets were bustling. The ice had cracked and thawed something in the people as well. They crowded around the stalls to trade. Animal carcasses and other wares. Talked to strangers. Thumped acquaintances on the back. They hung from windows and raised bottles and drinking horns when people passed below. Hirka hoped their high spirits wouldn't lead to trouble flaring up again. The nights had been quieter since Hod's speech.

It was a relief to reach the narrower alleyways. They were little more than deep cracks in the rock, only big enough for two people to walk abreast, but there were fewer people staring at her. People minded their own business.

She took a deep breath. The family's reaction to the Seer had made her nervous. She had no idea how to treat him. No one had taught her any rules for seers. The staff she was holding was a gift for him. She'd made it shorter and lashed a crosspiece to the top. A crutch. But Umpiri were Umpiri, so she had to find something else to call it. Or simply refrain from giving it to him. She'd have to wait and see.

Based on the maps she'd seen, she knew they were approaching the sea. What the maps hadn't revealed was how the road sloped downward. Steeper and steeper. She glanced at Kolail. He nodded. They were on the right path. She remembered the stooping figure who had limped into the room. It seemed unlikely that the Seer would walk here. Not without it taking half the day. Maybe he didn't go out that often?

The alleyway opened onto a street where water pooled in holes in the uneven ground. It wasn't meltwater, like she'd first thought. It was seawater. Farther ahead, the street continued straight into the sea. The sea crashed rhythmically against the cliff, sending spray raining over them.

The smell hit them in waves. Wonderfully familiar. Hirka licked the saltwater off her lips.

Kolail grunted, which she interpreted to mean they'd reached their destination. Not that they could go any farther. Steps angled upward, carved directly into the rock, ending at a landing by a door, halfway up the cliff.

Hirka turned to her escort. "Wait here."

Much to her surprise, they obeyed without protest. It was very disconcerting.

She went up the steps and paused in front of the door. It was made of iron, but so rusty that she'd thought it was old wood at first. She knocked, but there was no answer, so she knocked a little harder. Red flakes broke off and sailed past her on the wind. She glanced down at her entourage. Just standing there was embarrassing, so she tried the door handle. The door was heavier than she'd expected, but it opened. For the first time in a while, judging by the screeching of its hinges. She entered a dark corridor and closed the door behind her.

"I'm coming in," she said, feeling she ought to say something. There was no indication that anyone had heard or cared.

Her eyes adjusted to the dark as she followed the corridor slanting away from the door. She could hear water dripping from the ceiling. Close by and far away. A sure sign that this place was bigger than it appeared.

The corridor opened onto a cave. There was a warmth to it that made her think of Lindri's teahouse. Half the room had a wooden floor, the first she'd seen since coming to Dreysíl. It was old and worn, with dust in the cracks. There was a table and benches at one end. Animal skins to sit on. Light flickered from an open hearth in the section of the room that had a stone floor.

Drying herbs hung from the ceiling, next to an opening that wound its way farther up into the rock. The walls were lined with cabinets of shelves, drawers, and boxes filled with things she couldn't quite understand the purpose of. Jars of dead seahorses. Feathers, snail shells, teeth, rocks, skulls belonging to birds and small rodents. And one that must have belonged to an infant. It was grotesquely small, and it struck her that it had to be an even more shocking sight for Umpiri, immortal and virtually childless as they were.

Hirka felt a sudden urge to clean.

An old nest containing three crushed eggshells lay on a bench. Near that was a bowl with a bird fetus floating in a yellowish liquid. Something that looked like a millipede hung from a hook. She stepped closer and realized that it was the spine of some unrecognizable animal. Dead creatures that looked like maggots were squeezed together in dark jars, their pale flesh pressed against the glass. Two white crabs were fighting in a wooden bucket on the floor. Hirka got the sickening impression that edible and poisonous stood indiscriminately side by side.

The room smelled of sea and mushrooms. A faint odor of rot that was verging on unpleasant. She looked back the way she'd come. It wasn't too late to turn . . .

But she knew she couldn't. The macabre clutter around her was a reminder of all that was at stake. War. Death. Survival. The bird skulls pointed with their beaks as if to torment her. Reminding her that there was one in Rime's throat.

She jabbed the staff into the bucket and separated the crabs. They retreated to opposite sides. Made the most of the unexpected reprieve.

A door opened by the hearth. The draft tugged at the flames and made herbs sprinkle down from the ceiling. Hirka took the staff out of the bucket and stepped back. The black-clad Seer entered. The roar of the sea grew louder, but then he shut the door.

He looked at her, though she wasn't sure how she knew. The veil-like hood covered his entire face. Hirka looked around to avoid staring at him.

"I thought it would be . . . bigger," she said, immediately hoping she hadn't offended him. He was the Seer. She'd imagined a palace along the lines of Eisvaldr. Something closer to what Naiell had built.

"It *isss* . . . bigger." His voice made her hair stand on end. She hadn't been able to get it out of her head since he'd paid them a visit. There was an animal-like quality to it. Especially when he got stuck on his esses.

He picked up a bowl from the edge of the hearth and went over to the table. His robe swept the floor, but it couldn't conceal his crooked gait. He bobbed with each step, as if one leg were too short.

"Can I . . ." Hirka bit her lip. She'd almost asked if she could help, which would most likely have ruined any chance of getting the answers she needed. "Can I sit down?" she asked instead.

"If you are tired."

She *was* tired. And she was sick of maintaining a mask of infallibility. "You know, I am actually. It's been a tough year, to be honest." She leaned the staff against the table and plopped down on the bench. He didn't reply. She took that to mean it was fine.

He pushed aside a box of speckled eggs and put the bowl on the table. He was wearing black gloves that didn't do much to hide his claws. Or the contorted angle of his thumbs.

"You thought I didn't know," he said. "You thought I had to smell you to know you were here."

Hirka looked down at her tunic. Realized what he was talking about. "I had no idea what you knew and didn't know. I thought it was best to be sure," she answered with far more confidence than she felt.

She craned her neck to see inside the bowl without being too obvious. She'd hoped for tea, but it looked like thick milk. Still a relief, considering her surroundings.

He stood next to the bench, making no move to sit down. "That does not change the fact that you are sss . . . seeking counsel from someone who you thought ignorant. Either you know the answer yourself, or you have no one else to ask."

"Well, I'm not exactly drowning in friends here . . ." She smiled bitterly.

He pushed the bowl toward her. There was something demonstrative about the movement. An indulgence that signaled an expectation of failure. It reminded her of Modrasme.

A test . . .

The milk smelled fermented. And of something else she couldn't place. It didn't look particularly tempting. She looked up at him. "Why did I have to wait until the ice cracked?"

He cocked his head, making its peculiar shape even more distinct under the hood. He held his shoulder at an odd angle, as if he'd snapped his collarbone and never had it put back in place.

"Because the ice is all the ravens sss . . . speak of, until it cracks. You have to wait till then to get a sss . . . sensible word out of them."

"And did you? Get a sensible word?"

He didn't reply. She knew he was waiting for her to drink, so she brought the warm bowl to her lips and took a small sip. The milk was sour and tasted of goat. It trickled through a skin on the top. Then came the taste of blood. She choked down a mouthful. Put the bowl back on the table.

"They say you don't belong here," he said at last.

Hirka had a feeling that deprived her of the right to help. "Then ask other ravens," she said, staring down at the bleeding milk. The congealed layer on the top had split. Red intermixed with white. Spread across the surface like blood vessels.

He went on as if she hadn't said anything. "They sss . . . say you belong to all. Child of Odin. Menskr. Umpiri. You have mixed blood. But you are living proof of Graal's potency. His ability to preside across worlds. Sss . . . so no matter how odiously weak your blood is, you are still a lodestar."

An odiously weak lodestar.

Hirka suddenly felt the need to drink something, no matter how disgusting. She took another sip from the bowl. Warm blood. Warm milk. Sour and metallic. She tried to conceal a grimace.

"Why this obsession with blood?" she asked. "It's all you think about. Who has whose blood. Who has blood of the first. As if there were any first!"

Spite helped her stifle her nausea and empty the bowl.

"Come with me," he said and limped toward the door he'd entered through. Hirka followed him into a room that was wide open to the sea. The wall must have collapsed ages ago. Dripstones hung down from the ceiling like a forest of needles. The floor was the only level surface. Fragments of patterned tiles still decorated the walls.

The Seer waved her closer to the edge.

The sea churned beneath her. Waves as big as houses crashed against the cliff. Everything was gray as far as the eye could see. Sky and seething sea as one. The Seer's robe fluttered in the wind, revealing his shape. Hunched shoulder blades and an impossible curve in his spine. A face so deformed that it looked like he was wearing a mask under his hood.

In the daylight, she could see that his robe was made of a discolored and wrinkled material. His entire appearance gave the impression of a crumpled and withered leaf.

"Look at thisss," he said, his voice barely audible above the roar of the sea.

She leaned forward and saw how the cliffs plunged down. Sheer and stubborn, riddled with what had once been homes. A lot of homes.

"The sss . . . sea eats away at us," he said. "My father's house has crumbled to nothing. Can you look at this and claim there are no higher powers? That everything and everyone is equal? Wake up! Our blood is the strongest. No one can use the stone doors without it. The children of Ym and Embla have offered blood to stone for generations, without undersss . . . standing. They drink it, ingest it, yearn for it, because it makes them better. Our blood wants to destroy other blood. Our blood wants to rule. Devour and transform. That isss the truth."

The Seer turned toward her. "Whether you like it or not changes nothing. Dreyri have pure blood. Someone came first, and we are closer to the first than any other creature, in any other world. You are a fool to cling to any other reality."

His words tore at her. Tried to wear her down, like the sea against the cliffs. Shame and anger fought for space. Like the milk and blood in her belly.

For all she knew, this seer was older than sin. But how many worlds had he been to? How could he know that he belonged to a race that was closer to the gods than any other? How could he know that the gods even existed?

A wave crashed into the cliff face just beneath her. She stepped back to avoid getting soaked. Three ravens plunged off the roof and soared across the sea, screeching all the while.

The Seer hobbled back toward the door. "But before the first came raven, of course. Raven created the world. The Might was raven's breath. And from the Might, he created the first."

Hirka followed him back into the hearth room. She sat down on the edge of the bench, close to the fire.

"And without the Might?" she asked.

He shook his head. Hirka felt a sudden sense of urgency. That the answers she needed were slipping away from her. She grabbed his arm. It felt knobbly under his robe. He tore it away from her as if she'd stabbed him. Desperation grew inside her. He didn't understand how important this was.

"That's why I'm here," she said. "You have to help me. We have to . . ." She searched for the right word in umǫni. "We have to get the Might through the gateways again! We have to mend the flow of the Might!"

"No."

"No? How can you say no? Nothing can live without the Might. You know that. I know that. It has to be put right!"

He turned his hunched back to her. "It can't be done."

Hirka felt paralyzed. All this talk of power and superiority, and there was nothing they could do? "Why? Why can't it be done?"

"What the Might has desss . . . stroyed cannot be mended. Trust me."

Hirka got up. "There must be a way! Naiell did it! And I know I can! I've felt the Might, I . . ." She hesitated, not wanting to tell him about Rime. About the strength they had between them. That would expose them both.

He turned toward her again. "Naiell had three things you will never have. He had the flow of the Might. It was sss . . . stronger than ever before. Than ever after. And I've watched it ebb for a thousand years. Like blood in a corpse. He also had menskr to channel it through. Emblings, drunk on his blood. Empty shells that could contain the Might for him. And most importantly, he could *use* it. In all your arrogance, you've failed to mention that you cannot bind. What do you hope to do when you can't even sss . . . sling the Might? Even if you could, it would break those pathetic arms of yours."

Hirka felt the tears coming. "Why bring me here if I'll never learn to bind the Might? If the flow of the Might can't be mended?"

"Learn to bind?" He laughed hoarsely. "Child, it's in the blood. The Might finds you when you are born. But you were born in a world without the Might. And your birth, I am afraid, is an event that you cannot change."

"But you can, can't you? *You* can fix the Might?"

He laughed again. "Truly you are not one of us," the Seer said. "You do not want war, do you?"

Hirka leaned against the table. She couldn't answer. It felt like a trap. "You said so yourself, I belong to no one. I belong to everyone."

"Yes, I sss . . . said so." He hobbled around the table until he was right next to her. "Hirka, daughter of Graal, let me borrow a drop

209

or two of your blood, and I will sss . . . summon you if there is any power in it."

Hirka straightened up again and did her best not to glare at him. "I don't need your pity. I need to learn how to control the Might. And how to get a damned beak out of a throat."

"Oh . . ."

She looked at him. "Let me guess . . . That can't be done, either?"

He shrugged his stooped shoulders. "The beaks belonged to the first ravens. They had names in life, and they have names in death. That is what binds them. If you know their names, you can summon them. But they cannot be persuaded. They cannot be removed. A beak is for life. As brief as that may be."

He stated it as an observation, not a death sentence.

"You can't know that!"

"I ought to know. I've made a couple in my time."

Hirka felt so incredibly tired. Nauseous. She had to get home. The staff she'd brought with her rested against the table. She pointed at it. "That's for you."

His head twitched under the hood. "You're giving me a cane? A crutch?!"

Hirka moved closer to him. "I used it to get the crabs to stop fighting, so what I'm giving you is a crab staff. What you call it is up to you."

He gripped her wrist. His claws stung, even through his glove. She thought he was going to say something, but he stayed quiet. He let go of her again.

She felt unwell. Nausea forced her out. Along the corridor and through the door. Going down the steps to the street made her feel worse. Her throat constricted. Her face started to tingle. She couldn't hold it back. Milk and blood poured out of her in a violent spasm. All at once. She supported herself on the rock. Sour milk trickled from the corner of her mouth. Dripped from her chin and formed pale rings in a puddle.

Someone shouted her name. She felt Kolail's arm around her, and she buried her face in the sheepskin he wore over his shoulders. Painful certainties pounded inside her head.

It's over. The Might can't be healed. War will come. Rime will die.

Farther up the street, she heard people hollering and making merry. The celebration of the ice had started. She was an odious lodestar. She was a black maelstrom in a sea of exultation.

URD

Hirka drew the bolt and pushed the door aside. Urd sprang up from the windowsill and stared at her. She wanted to elbow him in the face and break his nose. Lay into him.

She couldn't lay into the Might for not finding her. Or the Seer for saying it couldn't be healed. She couldn't lay into Graal, either. He was a world away, on the other side of the raven rings. She couldn't even lay into Umpiri for planning a war.

She was powerless, just like the Seer had said. With a foul mix of mightless blood. Urd was the only enemy in her reach. The only justice she had in sight.

She clenched her fists. Her hands were clammy. "Can I come in?"

His lips twisted into a grimace, as if she had touched a sore spot. Then he pulled himself together again. "It's been a long time since anyone bothered to ask."

His voice gave her a start. It was rougher than she remembered. Damaged.

The beak.

He sat back down on the windowsill, as if to make himself appear less threatening. Or perhaps to lure her inside. Not because he was planning to do anything to her—that much she was sure of. Perhaps more to stop her from leaving him again.

The room they'd moved him to was smaller than hers. The ceiling was sloped. A candle burned in a niche. The light reflected off the thin chain hanging from his neck down into his lap.

Hirka stepped inside. "You killed Ilume."

She said it to keep her anger burning. To remember who he was. The memory came back for the first time in a long time. The Seer's tower. Ilume's lifeless body on the floor. The shattered tree that had rained black shards down on them.

Urd didn't answer. She walked over to him. Pointed, as if there were any doubt who she was talking to. "You killed her! While we watched! You used blindcraft to open the gateways on Bromfjell. Destroyed them. Forever. And you tried to sacrifice me to the deadborn! You attacked Ravnhov. People died because of you. You started a war. A fucking war!"

He looked up at her. His eyes were so tired that they were rimmed in red. "From what I understand, you're about to do the same."

Her body suddenly grew heavier. She sank down next to him on the windowsill. Drained by everything that had happened. Everything that would happen.

The mightglass cast shadows over his face. Like streaks of ash. He closed his eyes. "Reel off my sins like I've been brought before the assembly," he said slowly. "There are certainly enough of them. You could even make some up. Atrocities that would make the blood run cold. Use your imagination, it won't change anything. Whatever you come up with, I've paid for it."

"You're still alive," she said dryly.

He looked at her again. "Yes, because they kept healing me."

The scar in his forehead puckered. What had they done to him? Things hadn't been easy for her since she'd arrived, and she was Graal's daughter. What was Urd to them, other than an ymling? An animal?

The light was waning outside. She could hear people in the streets below. There would probably be a lively mixture of festivities and

213

riots that night as well. She pulled her feet up onto the windowsill, hugging her knees.

"I'm so tired of them," she whispered. "They think they're gods. That their blood is the first. That their world is the first. But what have they done? What have they created that's so amazing?"

She looked at the former councillor. "You're just like them," she said. "You step on everyone around you. Crush. Destroy. Kill. Because what you want is far more important than everyone else." She felt a tear run down her cheek, but she didn't care. It was anger. Not sadness. "You're pompous, like them. Inconsiderate, like them. You're—"

He folded his hands around the chain in his lap. "Blind, like them?"

She didn't reply.

"How old are you now? Seventeen?"

She didn't have the energy to reply to that, either. It dawned on her that all she really wanted was for him to keep talking so she could hear ymish again. It didn't matter that it came from him.

"I was younger than you when I met Damayanti," he said. "She was a dancer. An exceptional dancer. There's not a man in Ym who would have said no to her, and I was only a boy. I know what you're thinking, but she never offered herself to me. She had other things to give."

Hirka made no effort to hide her disgust. "A beak in your throat and the delusion that you could control the gateways? And you think you're smarter than others . . . You haven't a clue, have you?"

Urd tried to laugh. It sounded more like a growl. "I didn't even know the Seer was a lie. That the Almighty didn't exist. I thought he would forgive me. Heal me and give me peace."

"Peace?" Her face felt numb. As if it had frozen into a grimace. "No one can give you peace. You've doomed yourself to an eternity of nightmares in Slokna. For Ilume. For Ramoja. For Vetle.

214

There are no words for what you've done, Urd. No words, and no forgiveness."

He pulled his feet up onto the windowsill and hugged his knees, just like her. Mirroring her as best he could in his sack-like robe.

"You're right, of course. And yet you saved my life. You could have let me die or rot in the House of Hod, but you showed mercy. I have to say, it was quite the performance. Perhaps you remembered the pits in Eisvaldr. You had some savage on you with his trousers down, remember that? I stopped him. I got you out of there."

Remember that?

The question was an insult to the vividness of the memory. Urd's act of violence had stopped another, and it pained her that it made it more difficult to hate him. That she had to remind herself that what he'd saved her from was exactly what he'd done to Ramoja.

His eyes burned into hers. The first spark of life she'd seen.

"Got me out? You dragged me out so you could sacrifice me to the deadborn!"

"Sacrifice? I wanted to give you to them. You were a gift they were supposed to have had all along." He raised his hands. "And here you are! It just took a bit longer."

She snorted. "You wanted to sacrifice me. To save your own skin."

"True. But need I remind you I was a slave to the beak back then? I was drinking blindling blood. There wasn't much ymling left in me. I know what I did is indefensible, but you have to understand, it was never . . ."

He didn't need to finish his sentence. "Personal?" Hirka said. "Then it wasn't personal when I saved your life, either. It had nothing to do with you. It had to do with *me*. I'm not like you."

He swallowed. Not without difficulty, it seemed. "No. If you were, we'd actually stand a chance."

"What are you trying to say?"

"I'm saying you need to use people to survive in a place like this."

Hirka looked at his haphazardly shorn hair. Yellow, like Vetle's. The son he'd ruined using the Might, either to kill him or to hide the fact that the boy was his. So that was how he wanted it? People using each other?

She reached over and gripped the chain. Unease flashed across his features, but he let her do it. She coiled the end until it was taut. The chain was thin as a necklace. Almost delicate.

"Is that how you want it?" she asked. "You want me to use you to get the answers I want? The way you do? With threats? With coercion?"

He tried to hide a smile. She tugged at the chain. Carefully, but hard enough that his smile vanished. "What did you do to the guardsmen in the pits? You killed them with the Might. How?"

He tilted his head forward to give the chain some slack. "It's no big secret," he replied. "The body is weak. It can't take much. If you draw enough of the Might through it—"

"Then why hasn't anyone else done it? What made you so special?"

"Do you need to ask?"

"Blindling blood. You drank blindling blood. So how did you get the beak?"

"Damayanti." No sooner had she asked than he answered. Not out of fear, but because he wanted to. Was this the first proper conversation he'd had since coming here?

"And how did you get rid of it? I saw it crawl out of your throat. You threw it up on Bromfjell, and you're still alive! How did you get rid of it?"

He looked at her. Blue under the eyes. She could see that he was starting to have doubts. That he wasn't sure where he had her. Who she was. It suddenly occurred to her that she wasn't sure herself. She dropped the chain and it fell into his lap.

He sighed. "I don't know, Hirka. I don't know how I got rid of it." His eyes fell to her throat. Curious, and slightly anxious.

216

She shook her head. "Not me."

He came to a realization and nodded. "Ah . . . Rime?"

She didn't reply, just stared out of the window at the crater reaching down like a hole to Slokna.

"How long did it take?" She sounded hoarse. "How long before it started to rot?"

Urd let slip a joyless laugh. "Not as long as you're hoping."

Tears pricked her eyes again. Hirka forced them back. This was a pain she refused to let Urd see. She scowled at him. "He's not like you."

"Not like you, either."

It was true. Hirka got up to leave. Her heart skipped a beat when she saw Skerri staring at them from the doorway. No words were needed. It was all in her eyes. Accusation. Fury. Disgust at Hirka for sitting and talking with an enemy.

Hirka got up and brushed past her. "I'm ready to start," she said.

"Start what?" Skerri shouted after her.

"With the staffs."

GRAAL'S POWER

They were tired and spent. They were in a bad way. Injured. And despondent. Twenty adults and seven children. The children were actually coping better with the situation than the adults. Had these been ordinary people, things would have been easier, but these were Council folk. Ymlings who had been brought together by circumstances during the coup. They weren't used to torn trousers or wet shoes. And they certainly weren't used to fearing persecution.

Rime stayed up front, carrying Sigra Kleiv's granddaughter on his shoulders. A dark-haired six-year-old who was on the verge of sleep, her grip on his neck becoming looser and looser. Rime grabbed her small hands to make sure she didn't fall. The girl had sprained her ankle but hadn't made so much as a peep. A stark contrast to Sylja, who'd done nothing but complain.

Marrow sidled up next to Rime in the dark. "Can I throttle her?" he whispered.

Rime smiled crookedly. "If anyone can resist the urge, it's you. In any case, we'll be at the camp soon."

Marrow grumbled. Had Rime not shut out his feelings, he might have sympathized. With Sylja, too. Her life had been turned upside down without warning. She'd been with Ve, Jarladin's grandson. Her current favorite, apparently. They'd been enjoying some wine in the warmth of the Snake Mirror when his father had come to get him. She'd faced a difficult choice. Flee with them or remain in Mannfalla?

Rime had no doubt she'd made the right choice. Her ties to Jarladin and to himself were too strong. There was no place for her in Eisvaldr—other than the pits.

The ascent to the camp was difficult for them. Rime had two men stay back with the eldest so they could take all the time they needed.

Sylja came up behind him. She huffed. "Look at the state of these shoes! I shouldn't even be here!"

"None of us should be here," he replied.

"You lot belong here! You have everything you need. I don't even have a change of clothes!" She lifted up her cloak. From the look of it, she'd been dragging it behind her the entire way.

Rime lowered his voice, hoping she would do the same. "You've more on you than most people here own."

"I never asked to—" She stopped and scrunched up her nose. "What is that smell?"

"The pyres. We burned the dead today."

Sylja recoiled like he'd just struck her. She looked around the camp in disbelief. Black-clad Kolkagga sat around the fire, staring at her. She wrapped her arms around herself. "Then where are we supposed to sleep?"

Rime eased the young girl down from his shoulders and handed her to Od. The man cradled her against his chest, then gathered the rest of the children to put them to bed.

"You'll stay in the huts until first light, then you're all off to Ravnhov," he answered.

"Ravnhov?!" Sigra's outburst came as no surprise to Rime. He heard her start up a discussion with Jarladin, for all the good it would do. They had nowhere else to turn.

Marrow turned to Rime. "What do you mean 'all'?"

Rime pulled him aside. "You have to lead them, Marrow. Take them to Ravnhov. Eirik is expecting us. He knows what's happened."

Marrow's jaw tensed. He looked around, as if he were afraid someone might hear. "None of us are leaving without you! None of us. I know what you're thinking, Rime, but there's no chance in Slokna of us letting you face him alone. You need us! Darkdaggar doesn't just have men, he has an army!"

Rime dragged a hand over his face. "That's not what I had in mind, Marrow."

Marrow folded his arms across his chest and raised an eyebrow. Rime wished he could tell him the truth. Say it as it was. That he had a beak in his throat. That he didn't know how much time he had. And that he posed a danger to everyone close to him. Only Damayanti could know how much of a danger, and she was the one he had to talk to.

Jarladin and Sigra came over. Sensing the mood, Marrow left them alone.

Jarladin looked pained. Exhausted. But he didn't say anything. Neither did Rime. There was nothing to say. They stood watching the red glow between the trees. The remains of the funeral pyres. Black-clad men went in and out of huts behind them. Carrying blankets and heating food for the Council folk. Some of them had started to pack away what little they owned. Kolkagga were leaving Blindból.

Stiar approached but stood a short distance away. "The ravens, master? What do we do with them? Arn is dead, and he was the one who—"

"Find the cages, Stiar. They're going with us to Ravnhov."

"Yes, master." Stiar disappeared between the huts.

Sigra watched him go. "Master of Kolkagga . . ." she whispered. She looked at Rime. "How many?"

"There are fewer than fifty of us left," Rime croaked.

"This is . . ." Sigra slumped down onto a stump. "This has to be the blackest period in our history. Never has . . ." She looked from Rime to Jarladin. She didn't finish. Rime couldn't blame her. There were no words.

"But still . . . Ravnhov?" She looked up at him. "That's no place for us."

"Right now, that's the only place for you, Sigra."

"But we've . . . We can't . . ."

Rime stared at her. She looked like a man. Broad and angular. And fierce. Always ready to do battle. Whenever an opportunity to speak out or act against Ravnhov arose, she took it. Now she had nowhere else to go. She was a refugee. Reliant on the mercy of a place she'd done her best to raze to the ground.

"We can and we will," Rime answered. "Eirik knows what's happened. He knows we're coming. You'll just have to hope he receives you better than you'd receive him."

Sigra opened her mouth to answer. Out of habit, Rime assumed, because she was at a loss for words. Jarladin seemed equally speechless. There was nothing of the Council left in them. No leadership. No power. Rime could see the wrinkles on their faces. Age had crept up on the most powerful people in Ym. People he'd learned to respect from the day he was born. Now they were barely able to survive.

"Listen . . ." Rime put his hand on Jarladin's shoulder. "He will pay for this. That's the one thing I'm certain of. Everything else, we'll just have to take as it comes. Ravnhov is willing to take us in. With Eirik, we'll have a better foothold in the north, and we can forge new alliances. From a position of strength. We can—"

Suddenly he felt an intense itching in his throat. The blood sank in his body.

Graal . . .

"Rime?" Jarladin gave him an inquisitive look.

Rime excused himself and raced off through the camp. Toward his hut. He knew what was coming, and he had to get away. As far away as he could. Farther than a scream could carry.

The beak writhed in his throat. Demanding. Impatient. His feet pounded the path. Itching turned to stinging. The hut appeared at the edge of the cliff, and he flung the door open. Stumbled inside. He fumbled in his pockets for the bottle from Damayanti. He had to have it. Had to drink. Blindling blood was the only thing that could open the way for Graal, and the only thing that could ease the pain.

He found the bottle. Stared at it. Knowing what power it had over him was worse than the pain at times.

He drank and bound the Might. Sensed he was no longer alone. The beak opened in his throat. Tore at his insides.

"Anything you'd like to tell me, Rime?"

Graal's voice was strained. He knew. He wouldn't have asked if he knew everything, but he knew something. How much had Damayanti learned, and what had she revealed?

Rime considered trying to buy time. Pretend everything was fine. But it would catch up to him sooner or later.

"Darkdaggar has seized control of the Council," he replied.

Graal sighed. A sound of impatience. Rime grabbed his throat. It swelled up around the beak. Tightened until he had trouble breathing. It was no use. Graal knew.

"They're dead," Rime whispered. "Kolkagga are dead."

"How many?"

"How many do you think?! All of them!" Grief and rage swam together. "There aren't even fifty of us!"

The beak went still. Testament to the shock. A cold smile spread across Rime's lips. "You'd hoped we would wipe each other out," he gasped. "Kolkagga and Mannfalla. Clear the way before the dead-born arrive. Think again, Graal."

Rime leaned against the folding door. Looked out over Blindból. He steeled himself for the pain he knew would come. The moment seemed to last an eternity. Soon he would know who Graal was. Who he really was. Man or monster.

The pain struck him like lightning. A furious attack. His throat tore inside. Rime dropped to his knees. Screamed. Blood sprayed over the folding door. Collected in the carvings. Dripped from dragons and serpents. He collapsed onto his side. Dragged himself toward the door. His elbows were shaking. He gritted his teeth. The taste of blood made him nauseous.

Then a calm came over him. The Might tingled under his skin. He was Kolkagga. He endured.

Rime exhaled. Spat red.

"Forgive me," Graal said. His words made a mockery of the ebbing pain. "Forgive me. But you lost them, Rime. You lost Kolkagga. I have to do whatever it takes to make you listen. You have to gather the troops in Ravnhov, and you have to do it now. Understand? Build a new army to face Mannfalla."

Rime didn't reply. He could hear someone approaching through the woods outside. He whispered. "I'm not alone . . ."

All at once, Graal was gone. Rime dug his nails into the wooden floor. He had to pull himself together. Quickly. He made it as far as his knees. His body simply wouldn't obey.

"Rime?"

Sylja . . .

Sylja of Glimmeråsen. Memories of Elveroa pushed to the fore. From another life, another time. So removed from everything he was. Everything that had happened.

She stood in the doorway. It was dark, and he hoped she couldn't see the blood. But she must have been able to smell it . . . It filled him. Filled the room. Blood. That was all he was. All he ever would be.

"Rime? I can't stay out there. We don't know what's happening, and I refuse to sleep surrounded by those . . . those . . ." She entered the room. "Will you protect me tonight? Can I sleep here?"

Rime started to laugh. Their two realities collided in a stark contrast. Her world and his. Flirtation and pain.

She kneeled in front of him. Her fair hair tickled his face. "Heavens, Rime, you're bleeding! Are you wounded?"

Rime gasped, caught between laughter and tears. *Wounded* . . .

He wasn't wounded. He was what he'd always been. He was already dead.

INJURED

Raun walked ahead of Hirka along the rows of staffs. Every now and then he lifted one from the hooks on the wall, tested its weight, and put it back. He chose one of the shorter staffs. Spun it in his hand with depressing ease. "This is better suited to your height. Why don't you try it?"

Hirka tightened her grip on her own staff. "I've got an agreement with this one. We like each other, and it's served me well thus far."

Raun threw his head back. "Haaaaa!" he laughed. "That is important, but who's to say it'll look after you in the future?"

Hirka hoped he was joking.

She'd said she was ready, but she wasn't. Not in the least. All she wanted was to hit back. Hit something or someone, whether it was with a staff or with her bare hands. But now that the opportunity had presented itself, she just felt like she'd landed herself in even deeper water. Found something else she couldn't do or protect herself from.

Fate seemed to be chasing her like a tidal wave. With an all-consuming wildness and fury. Every time she looked back, it was closer. It seemed ridiculous that she'd once thought she could reason with such a force of nature. Her, the girl who couldn't even bind. Whose blood was impure. Who was too weak to make a difference.

All she could do was learn to protect herself and hope she lived long enough to see Rime and thousands of Kolkagga end the war she'd been stupid enough to think she could prevent.

Hirka hesitantly lifted the staff, then looked at the others swinging away at each other in the rings. They constantly changed grip, moving their center of gravity from attack to defense. The staffs were like living extensions of their arms. Sometimes so quick she couldn't see the movement, merely sense it. It seemed as natural to them as flying was to birds.

Raun took her hand and measured it against a thick leather strap. Once again her eyes landed on the mark over her artery, where the Seer had grabbed her. The thought made her shudder. Brought back the taste of milk and blood.

Raun started securing the strap. It covered almost her entire forearm. Protection, she thought, until he let go of her hand and it dropped like a stone. It was probably filled with sand.

"Start with these," Raun said, wrapping her other arm as well. "They're the lightest."

Raun was more easily amused than any other Umpiri she'd met, but he didn't seem to be joking now. Hirka glanced at the other arm cuffs on the wall, some of them made of iron.

"Aren't you wearing any?"

"Haaaaa!" He thumped her on the back. "I wore them for seventy years. It's your turn now."

Seventy years . . . a fraction of his lifetime.

Nothing about the man in front of her suggested he'd lived that long. He had the body of a young warrior. Compact and strong. His veins wound around sharply defined muscles. Her father's father. She could see pale scars on his shoulder. How bad did a wound have to be to leave Umpiri with scars?

Hirka trotted over to the far ring. The one mostly in the shadow of the curved walls. Raun followed her, humming to himself. His optimism was irreproachable.

She stopped in the center of the ring and lifted the staff so she was holding it across her body with both hands. Raun loosened the grip of one, turned it palm up, then closed it around the staff again.

It was going to be a long day.

Hirka was beginning to understand what it might be like to live forever. It meant unrivalled patience when it came to certain things. Umpiri always had time to immerse themselves in what they were doing. To repeat things endlessly, knowing that perfection was only a couple of hundred years away.

Raun was so patient that she felt stupid for dreading this. He laughed so often that his red hair threatened to come undone. He was clearly enjoying teaching her even the most basic things. Exercises he hadn't needed to do in who knew how many years.

He lifted her spirits. Took the edge off her grief for Svarteld. Eased her frustration and fear. She knew it didn't matter to him how she performed. The most important thing was that he had an heir. A grandchild to pass his knowledge on to. Raun had lost two sons. Naiell and Graal. One a traitor and the other an exile, unable to escape his banishment due to his scorched blood.

The insight made her feel ashamed. She wasn't the only one in a situation she'd never expected to end up in.

Raun drilled her in different ways of standing, and in finding the right center of gravity. Let her practice landing basic blows from above, followed by blows from both sides. Hirka did them one after the other, over and over again, until she found a kind of peace. A stillness amid everything that hurt.

She could almost hear the echo of Svarteld's laughter. How he'd shaken his head. Asked her to try again. And again. She'd done as he asked. Kicked and kicked, in the middle of Blindból. Between lush green mountains on the cusp of autumn.

But Svarteld was dead. And here she stood, in the hollow left by a dried-up subterranean lake, surrounded by the thwacking of staff against staff.

"Put your hips into it," Raun said. "Rotate when you swing." She did as he said. "Good! Keep doing that."

"How many times?"

Raun blinked in confusion. "What do you mean?"

"How many times should I hit?"

"Haaaaa!" His laughter bounced around the room. "You are funny," he said, though she wasn't sure what he meant. "I'm going to go a round with Grid, but Skerri will take over here."

No! Not Skerri!

She opened her mouth to protest, but he had already gone. He exchanged a few words with Skerri, who met her gaze. Hirka felt her hands start to tingle, like she might lose all feeling in them at any moment. The staff grew heavier in her arms. It had already given up.

Skerri came over, swinging her staff as she neared. It crashed into Hirka's before she could react. She lost her grip and it clattered to the floor.

Skerri gave her a resigned look. "Just as I suspected."

Hirka picked up the staff without comment. No good would come of it. She didn't have time to get up before Skerri brought her staff down from over her head. Hirka thrust out her staff in both hands to block the blow. Skerri swung again. Hirka blocked it again. She'd feared a fight, but what she was getting was an endurance test.

They repeated the exercise until Hirka's hands were shaking. She could do this. After all, it was better than a beating.

"So what did the animal say?" Skerri asked, mid-blow.

"What animal?" Hirka almost lost her balance.

"The one you spend more time with than your own family." She struck again. Harder this time. Hirka took a step back as she defended herself. Her elbows gave out and she only just managed to protect her head.

Urd. She's talking about Urd.

Skerri continued, not letting her answer. "He's an animal. An ymling. An enemy who tried to kill you, and what do you do? Show him mercy, give him a room, food to eat, books to read. Maybe he's not an enemy at all." Her staff spun into the attack, coming in sideways. Hirka lowered her arms but was no match for Skerri's speed. The staff hit her in the side, crashing into her ribs and knocking her to the ground. Pain radiated out into her arm. She tried to push herself up onto her elbow. Skerri grabbed the straps around her chest and pulled her to her feet.

It didn't feel like help.

Hirka gasped for breath. "What . . . What else would he be?"

"An ally?" Skerri lashed out again. Hirka jumped back and out of the ring. She was pulled in again straight away. Skerri leaned toward her. "One of your own. That's what he is. You'll never be like us. We don't forgive those who want to destroy us. We don't make pets of our enemies."

She spun around. Hirka lifted her staff, but the blow came in low, hitting her leg so hard that she dropped to her knees. Blood seeped from a gash in her calf. For a moment it was numb, then it started to throb. Hirka tried to pull herself out of the ring with her arms.

"Skerri!"

The booming of Raun's voice was enough to make everyone stop what they were doing. He came over to them. "She doesn't heal like us!" His jaw was tense. His voice rough with feigned calm.

Skerri lowered her staff. "I forgot," she said with the hint of a smile, before going back to Grid in the next ring.

Raun ran a thumb over Hirka's calf. She flinched. He stared in amazement at the bleeding cut.

Hirka clenched her fists and fumbled for her staff. The blood roared in her ears. "What have I ever done to her?" she asked through clenched teeth, not expecting an answer. Raun gave her one anyway.

"You were born."

Hirka used her staff to pull herself up onto one leg. "I thought that was the whole point! She wanted a higher house, and that's what she got. She wants a war, and that's what she'll get. Because I was born. So why? Why does she hate me?"

Raun gazed at Skerri as if trying to see her for the first time. "So many years have passed since Graal," he said quietly. "They were made for each other. They were as one as two can be, and she hasn't touched anyone else since."

He looked at Hirka. "But Graal has, and you're living proof of that."

Hirka closed her eyes and pressed her face against the staff.

They were lovers . . .

The mystery that was Skerri became clearer in her mind. That was why she was part of the family without being a blood relation. Skerri and Graal. They had been meant for each other. Perhaps they'd even intended to have children together. Instead he'd had Hirka. With an embling. An unknown woman. A human.

Skerri had no ties to the House of Modrasme apart from a broken dream. She was all that remained of Graal.

Hirka wiped the blood off her leg. She remembered her smile when she'd seen Naiell's heart for the first time and realized that Skerri wasn't waiting for war.

Skerri had been at war for a thousand years.

SHADOWS IN SLOKNA

Hirka was careful to keep her weight on her right leg. The one that was still working properly. She lifted the staff a little off the ground and waited for the next gust. The wind took hold of her. She picked up speed as it pushed her backward across the ice. It was so slippery that she didn't have to do anything. Just slide around on the glassy surface and stop when she got too close to the edge.

The ravens drifted lazily in the sky above her, weighed down by the food she'd given them.

She heard steps on the ladder and turned. At first all she saw was claws digging into the ice. Then Kolail appeared. She steered herself toward him with the staff until the ground was easier to walk on. She did her best to hide her injury from him.

"Honey biscuits?" he asked, handing her a linen bundle that had been fastened to his belt. "Any other humiliating tasks for me?" He glanced at her leg. "Maybe I could get down on all fours and carry you around until you're back on your feet?"

"I *am* on my feet," she replied, her voice strangely high. She opened the bundle. It was still warm, and so full of biscuits that one of them fell out. She managed to swoop it up before it hit the ice. "Did he follow the recipe? No fish, no seaweed?"

"Dragging one leg behind you like a tail isn't the same as being on your feet."

Hirka handed him a biscuit to shut him up before remembering that he ate with his claws.

She stuffed the biscuit in her mouth and chewed, crumbs sprinkling everywhere. Kolail raised an eyebrow, but she ignored it. She put the bundle down on the ground. Held the staff in the air and circled Kolail a few times to demonstrate.

"I can walk without my staff."

"You're limping."

"But I—"

"They're not going to let you out until that limp is gone."

He was right. They'd taken her home from the training halls in the dark. And even then they'd formed a tight ring around her and pulled her hood down low. No one was to be seen injured.

Hirka put the staff down. "They're like dogs," she muttered.

"Dogs hunt. That's what they do." His cheerfulness was gone. He stared at her leg as he pulled a brass bottle out of his pocket and drank. His hands were rough. Rock dust clung to his jacket, probably from his day labor carving new dwellings. It reminded her of the other thing she'd asked him for.

"Did you bring the nippers?"

He wiped his mouth on his sleeve, tucked the bottle away, and pulled a small tool out of his side pocket. One of the few tools she'd seen here. He didn't ask what it was for.

"So what happened?" he asked instead.

She was pretty sure he wasn't expecting an answer, which was just as well, because she wasn't going to give him one. The simple answer would have been "Skerri," but that would have required too much explanation. And she didn't want to talk about Skerri. It felt dangerous.

Hirka snagged another biscuit and turned the question back on him. "What happened to you the night I pulled that piece of glass out of you?"

232

Kolail grimaced. Probably an attempt at a smile. "Fine, we won't talk about it then."

Hirka nodded. "Who let you in?"

"Skerri."

Hirka stopped chewing and raised her eyebrows. Kolail snorted. "I'm kidding. Raun let me in. So what are you doing up here?"

Hirka flapped a hand in the direction of the ladder. "I opened the hatch in the larder and found a . . ." She searched for the word, but nothing came. In any case, calling a handful of rusted metal rungs in the rock a ladder was a bit of a stretch. "I'm feeding the ravens," she said instead.

"Feeding the ravens? They come to you?"

She nodded. The teardrop in his forehead shot up with his eyebrows.

"Impressive, isn't it?" she said.

"Yes, there aren't many who can call ravens."

Hirka laughed. "I mean *that*." She pointed across the ice.

Kolail looked around, as if it were his first time here, too. But she was pretty sure it wasn't. She'd seen steps leading up to the glacier in other places. The ice stretched out before them like a frozen lake. Shimmering blue against the gray sky. With a labyrinth of cracks that went straight down into the streets below, where people walked around like ants between stalls and bridges. But up here, on the roof of Ginnungad, there was nothing but calm. Ice. Wind. And a dark horizon where cloud met sea.

Hirka pointed at him with the staff. "Come on. Grab hold."

He gave her a skeptical look but took hold of the other end of the staff. She tried to pull him out onto the glassy surface, but he was too heavy. Instead he ended up pushing her, slowly gathering speed before sliding along with her. They spun around, each holding on to an end of the staff. Hirka shrieked with laughter. Spun in circles with her injured leg lifted up off the ice. Kolail pushed off to make them go faster. Her stomach fluttered. She squealed. Kolail grinned, baring his canines and a little too much gum. His gray hair whipped across his face. His sheepskin flapped in the wind. He looked like a giant dog.

Then his smile faltered. He used his heel to bring them to a stop. Skerri stood at the edge, staring at them. Disgust pulling at her black lips.

Kolail headed for the ladder. He hesitated when he neared Skerri. Stared, as if he wanted to say something.

Skerri narrowed her eyes. "Make sure no one sees you on your way out, Kes." The rest of his name was left off.

Hirka felt a sharp pain in her calf. Defying Skerri came at a price, but in that moment, keeping quiet felt like it would cost her more.

"Thanks for the biscuits, Kolail!" she shouted after him, preparing to defend herself on the icy surface. But there was no reprimand. Not even a scathing insult. Skerri smiled. A scary sight, even under normal circumstances. Now it was outright terrifying. It could only mean she had something far worse in store.

"He wants to talk to you."

Graal . . .

Skerri climbed down. Hirka scooped up the biscuits and followed her, a knot growing in her stomach. Something had happened. Something to make Skerri smile.

Hirka looked up as she descended the ladder. The ravens gathered on the edge above her. There were more of them now. They were clustered together, staring at her like she was their next meal. A fallen soldier on the battlefield.

"He's waiting!" Skerri barked. Hirka climbed down through the hatch, following her through the larder and down into the hearth room. Raun was rubbing oil into some leather armor. Uhere sat across from him writing in a book. Keeping an eye on the money,

Hirka supposed. It was an unexpected picture. Almost harmonious. They looked like a normal family. Though they were anything but.

Skerri opened the lid of the raven quiver.

"Alone," a hollow voice said from inside.

"I'm not leaving *her* alone with the raven!" Skerri crossed her arms. Hirka had been alone with the bird before. Had she become less trustworthy, or did Skerri just want to gloat about listening in? Both, probably.

"Skerri . . ." Graal didn't raise his voice. He didn't have to. Hirka knew that all too well.

Skerri grumbled but gave the quiver to Hirka. Then she spun away, braids whipping around. "Bring it straight to me when you're done," she said.

Hirka took the quiver into her bedroom. Climbed into the swinging bed and sat down.

"Graal?"

"Hirka . . ." As ever, his voice was all it took to start a war within her. She loved and hated the way he said her name. It always hinted at a longing. A father's love. That said, she knew he was using her, and she was probably no more than a tool to him. He continued, voice treacherously warm.

"Damayanti says you knew the tea merchant in Mannfalla? The one by the river?"

Knew . . .

The word stung like a needle. A warning of worse to come. She didn't say anything. Didn't ask. Didn't want to hear more. But her silence was in vain. Graal continued anyway.

"He died in a fire. Arson, Damayanti says. It seems Darkdaggar was there looking for Rime, or looking for information about him. We're not entirely sure."

Hirka squeezed the round container in her hands. Stared down into the empty eye sockets of a bird that had died long ago. She'd

235

heard this lie before. In London, on the run with Stefan. A cruel attempt to draw her out. She didn't need to remind Graal of that. He said it for her. Said he understood it was hard to believe. That he'd never wanted it to be that way. That he was sorry.

The pain grew. The certainty that it was true.

Lindri . . .

Graal kept talking, as if she were in any fit state to listen. Fire. The teahouse was gone. His words were just noise. A hollow sound between her hands. Darkdaggar? Why? Why Lindri? It didn't make sense. Lindri had never hurt anyone. He was old. Full of peace. Full of arthritis. He owned nothing more than the teahouse and wanted nothing more than that. He was harmless!

Hirka remembered Darkdaggar. One of the three councillors who'd visited her in Blindból. One of the councillors who'd asked her to leave Ym after Rime became Ravenbearer. Hirka had said things that had rubbed him the wrong way, and he'd gotten up and left. She'd almost laughed at him back then. A cold man. Small. He'd wanted her gone but hadn't been able to force her. A powerful man rendered powerless.

Hirka caught a few more of Graal's words. The ones that broke through the grief and confusion. He was talking about a coup. About a changed Eisvaldr. And he was talking about how Kolkagga were no longer a threat.

She shook her head. Tried to clear her thoughts. "Wait . . . What are you saying? What do you mean?"

"I'm saying he wiped out Kolkagga. Single-handedly. Poisoned every last one of them. Primitive, but effective. I admit it changes things, but in many ways, it makes everything much simpler." She could hear thumping. Her heart, she realized. "Rime's fine," he added, as if he were doing her a favor.

The words bore into her.

Wiped out Kolkagga.

"No! It's not true! No man in any world can wipe out the black shadows. No one!"

"I didn't believe it either, but at least he's saved us the bother."

Us.

A horrible little word. As if she were a part of this. As if she were on anyone's side anymore. Hirka pulled herself up onto all fours. The bed started to rock. She grabbed hold of the edge, but that just made it worse.

"Hirka?" She could hear uncertainty in his voice. He had no idea what he'd said, or what it meant to her. "We have to consider this *good* news," he said. "For you, too. You want a war with less blood-shed, and you'll get that without Kolkagga."

Hirka crawled to the end of the swinging bed. A ship in a storm. She fell over onto her side. It felt like knives were shooting up her leg from where Skerri had hit her. Up to her hip. Cutting into her heart. Cold, cold pain.

"Hirka . . .? Did you know any of them?"

Hirka clenched her teeth. Got up on one knee. Swayed along with the bed, keeping her eyes shut. "No," she said gruffly.

The lie made her throat grow tight. Forced out tears. But Graal couldn't see them. And he wouldn't hear them, either. The grief was hers alone. She'd lived in Blindból, with Svarteld, Jeme, and all the others. It was where she'd found her way back to herself after the Rite Hall fell.

Kolkagga. What was it Rime used to call them?

Already dead.

The only ones who could have saved Ym were dead. Shadows sleeping in Slokna. Bloodweed haunting their dreams. Like Father.

All she wanted to do was curl up in her boat of a bed. Stay there until it saw fit to drown her. But she had to get back on dry land. She could just about make out a crossroads ahead, where everything depended on her.

She wiped away the tears. Quietly, so he wouldn't hear. She got out of the bed. It still felt like everything was rocking. Like she wasn't on solid ground. She put the lid back on the container. Squeezed it. Harder. Harder. She wanted to crush the raven. Squeeze its bones until they were no more than dust. Then Graal would never again be able to talk to his own people. No more plans with Skerri and Raun. No opening the gateways. Perhaps even no war.

No. He could still talk to Damayanti. And he was smart enough to already have blindlings in Ym in case something were to happen to the dancer. The war would come regardless. And what would Graal do if she destroyed the raven?

Destroy Rime.

Her whole body was shaking. She loosened her grip on the quiver. Graal had the power. All the power. As long as he controlled Rime, he also controlled her.

Hirka picked up her staff from the floor. Limped into the hearth room and left the raven quiver on the table without looking at anyone. Without meeting Skerri's gaze. She continued past them and into the corridor on the other side of the room. She banged on Urd's door, bursting in before he had a chance to answer.

"How did you get rid of the beak?"

Urd got up from the windowsill and gave her a questioning look. She closed the door behind her and hobbled closer. "Answer me! What did you do? What did you say?"

He took a couple of steps sideways. Along the wall, like she was a wild animal. A wolf. "I've told you all I know. You know as much as I do."

She pointed the staff at him. "I saw it crawl out of you! Why? You must have done something!"

He held his hands in the air. "I don't know! If I knew, I'd have told you."

"Liar. You're a liar, just like the rest of them. A monster. A brute. Killer. Enemy." She lifted the staff over her shoulder. The urge to strike him was all-consuming, like a hunger. "Tell me what you did!"

"I don't know!" He retreated toward the window again. Stared at her. Uncertainty flickered in his eyes. "Do you want me to make something up? So you won't take my head off? Is that how it works now? Do you want me to lie?"

Hirka lowered the staff to the floor. "You think the worst I can do is hit you? Tell me what you did or you're a free man, Urd Vanfarinn."

Naked fear spread over his face. She could see it sinking in. The realization of what she was threatening him with. A free man. Out on the streets. An ymling in Ginnungad. How long would he survive?

"I didn't do anything! I didn't say anything!"

"You must have said *something*?!" Her voice screeched like Skerri's. Distorted by grief.

Urd was trapped in a corner. "Said something?! What would I have said? I was crawling around on all fours, or have you forgotten?!"

"Then what were you *thinking*?"

He gripped his head in his hands. Clearly distressed. Angry. Scared. "What do you think I was thinking?! I'd lost everything! I was surrounded by Kolkagga, by blindlings! I wasn't thinking anything! All I knew was that I was going to die!"

He stumbled against the window and collapsed onto the sill. Hirka closed her eyes. He wasn't lying. He'd lost the beak because he thought he was going to die. A conviction so strong that it had driven the blindcraft out of his throat. As if its will to survive were stronger than his own.

Hirka slid down next to him onto the windowsill. Her staff fell to the floor. It rolled under his bed and came to a rest.

"You thought you were going to die . . ."

Hirka felt a grimace pull at her features. She pressed her palms to her eyes and groaned. It didn't help. Nothing helped.

She felt a hesitant hand on her shoulder. "What have they done to you?" Urd whispered. She wanted to answer, but where would she start? What had they *not* done?

She looked up at him. He pulled his hand back, as if he'd done something wrong. Hirka picked up his chain. Wound it around her hand until it pulled taut. She tugged on it, forcing him closer, until they were almost cheek-to-cheek. He held his breath.

Hirka tested the ring piercing his throat. He'd been clever. Moved it regularly so it wouldn't get stuck. His pulse raced against her thumb. A bead of sweat ran from his hairline down into the hollow of his neck. Hirka pulled out the nippers Kolail had found for her. Positioned them around the ring and squeezed. It snapped clean through. She coaxed the ring loose from his skin and let go of the chain. It clinked to the floor.

Urd retreated farther along the windowsill. Brought his hand to his throat. She could see the toll it was taking on him. Could see herself in his eyes. It was taking a toll on both of them.

She put the nippers back in her pocket and asked him to tell her everything he knew about Garm Darkdaggar.

FROZEN

Hirka could tell she'd put too much weight on her leg. She'd sent for Kolail in the hope that he could accompany her, but he wasn't home. The distant sound of mayhem and drunken shouts made it easy to guess what he was up to: hiding under a hood and throwing bottles in the streets. Drinking until he could fool himself into thinking he was making a difference. Unless he had a new job. Or maybe he'd come to his senses since she'd dug the glass out of him, though she doubted it. He was wasting time.

Time she didn't have. So she'd snuck out alone, expecting too much of her injured leg when she'd jumped down from the balcony.

She limped onward in the darkness, through the wet street stretching east from the crater down toward the sea. The rain drummed against her hood. She'd pulled it down over her face so no one would see who she was. But they looked at her anyway. Because Umpiri didn't limp. Umpiri didn't show weakness. They could rot for all she cared. Spend eternity in Slokna dreaming of being old, hurt, and helpless.

Like Lindri . . .

He was so alive in her memory. His hands, wrapped around the teapot to gauge the heat. His wrinkles, which deepened when he smiled. His hat, which was too small for him. If there were gods, she hoped they'd let him pass before the flames took him.

Hirka suppressed a sob.

Why? What was the point? Kolkagga were warriors, but Lindri . . .

More will die. Innocent people. People who've never wanted war.

She used her staff to support herself on the steep slopes down toward the sea. Toward the Seer. The accursed creature who refused to help her. Who had nothing more to tell her than how hopeless she was.

She pulled herself up the steps, one at a time, and opened the rusty door without knocking. She knew it was late, but she went in anyway, closing the door behind her and cutting off the sound of the rain.

"Seer!" Her shout was swallowed by the darkness. She stubbed her toe on the wall and swore. Why weren't there any straight walls in this place? She continued into the hearth room. He was sitting on a stool in front of the fire. He looked like he'd been carved from stone. Part of the rock. He stood up. The flames flickered and threw sparks at the ceiling.

"Why haven't you sent for me?" She was breaking all the rules of etiquette but couldn't bring herself to care. Rules were trivial. Trivial things had lost all meaning. She was raw with loss.

"You said you'd send for me, and now it's too late. The war hasn't even started and people are dying. You were going to help. I know you took my blood. You stuck your claw in me!" She held out her hand in accusation.

The Seer hobbled toward her. The staff she'd given him was leaning against the wall. Her despair grew at the sight of him. Had she really expected someone with a limp worse than hers to be able to help? Someone who wouldn't even show his face?

He didn't look like he wanted to argue, but she shouted all the same. "I'm not weak! There's a lot I can do! I can sense the Might when others use it. I can make them stronger. I have blood that can cure the rot. I could learn, if anyone was brave enough to teach me! But you don't teach emblings, do you? You share nothing with those you consider weak. Lesser. Fallen."

He sat on the bench and put his hands on the table between a box of broken eggs and a tray with a dead crow on it. It was on its back, feet in the air, and its chest was open, gaping red. The smell of blood mixed with the sweet odor of decay.

"You're not one of them," he said.

"So what am I? Why haven't you sent for me?"

"I have not been sss . . . silent because you're weak. I've been silent because you are strong," he wheezed.

Hirka pulled her hood down. Rain dripped from it onto the wooden floor. His words drew her closer.

"Sss . . . say you found a man in the snow," he continued slowly. "Almost frozen to death. You'd help him. Hold him, while he told you how far he'd walked. But as he drew his last breath, would you sss . . . say food and warmth were around the next bend? Knowing he'd never make it?"

Hirka thumped her staff against the floor. "I don't have time for this, Seer! I've found men in the snow, and I can't help them anymore, so stop speaking in riddles."

His head twitched. Some sort of involuntary spasm. "You're the one lying in the snow, child. In your blood you have the power to transform, just like Dreyri. And the power to contain, like menskr. You are no one, and you are both. You're the only one of your kind. You could have been strong, but you can't bind. Would you have had me summon you to tell you what could have been? A futile deed. The Might was never yours because you were born without it. And no one can be reborn."

"I don't need to have been born with it. We can do it together! Or I can do it with Rime. I know we can. I've felt the Might through him. I know it's possible!"

"Feel it, yes, but what use is that? You want more than that. You want to do the impossible. And even if you could bind, you'd never be able to fix what Naiell desss . . . stroyed. The flow of the Might

243

was cut off. If you were to tear the veins out of a man, do you really think you could undo that damage? Shove them back in place and get his blood to flow through them again? It's as I say: even the Might cannot heal what the Might has destroyed."

Hirka put her staff on the table and leaned forward. "You're wrong, Seer! I saw Rime shatter Naiell's tree. If one man can destroy what the Might has built, it can also be repaired."

The Seer stood up again, turning his back on her as if *she* were the one who didn't understand. She looked down at the dead bird. Disgust welled up inside her.

"You don't care . . ." she said. "Umpiri live for thousands of years, but you don't care at all. Where do you think you'll live when the Might dies for good? When worlds crumble and turn to dust. Deserts. Sand in broken hourglasses. What do you think will become of the ravens if you don't help me fix what was destroyed?!"

He leaned against a cabinet, back hunched, shoulder blades sharp under his robe. "You haven't even seen twenty winters and you speak of eternity? You sss . . . sail into a storm that has been brewing for a thousand years and claim you can heal? What do you think you've figured out that I still don't know?"

Hirka had a bitter taste in her mouth. "That there's no harm in hoping!"

He turned toward her so quickly that she jumped. His veil brushed against her as he moved. Light as a feather across her chest. "Hope? You think you understand hope? You don't know me. You don't know your own family. They've been wallowing in hope and secrets for an eternity, and if you had any sense, you'd listen to those who know better than you. And I'm sss . . . saying it as it is. No one can heal what the Might has destroyed!"

Hirka stared at him. How had she ever thought he'd help? "You're old," she whispered. "You're trapped in a reality you'll never find your way out of. You've given up. And you call *me* weak?"

The Seer reached up and tore off his hood, revealing his face.

Hirka forgot how to breathe. She backed away, almost falling over the bench. This was no deadborn standing before her. This was a monster.

He stared at her. *It* stared at her. No mouth. No nose. Just a red hole beneath a half-formed beak. His tongue writhed inside. Black and sharp. The skin of his throat was puckered. He was neither man nor raven. He was something in-between. A fever dream. A nightmare.

He blinked at her with beady, misaligned eyes.

"I was here when he took the Might," he hissed. "When he drew it out of the earth. Out of the air. I was here when he created the tree. Halfway between man and raven. This is how the Might left me when it died. And now here you come, saying everything can be healed. That everything can be changed. You think you can teach me anything at all about healing? About the Might? About hope?"

Hirka was speechless. She knew she was gaping at him. She knew the shock had to be written all over her face, but she couldn't help it. If this was his face, what was under his robe? Nothing was where it was supposed to be on his body. Eternal life as an abomination. Frozen in suffering. Frozen in a transformation that would never be completed.

No one can heal what the Might has destroyed.

She'd come here thinking nothing was worse than death . . .

The fury in his raven eyes squeezed her heart. Squeezed until tears ran down her cheeks. She raised a hand to his face. He grabbed her wrist, his claws digging into her skin. "Pity? Is *that* what you'd give me?"

He let go of her. Shoved her back. "Go. Now!"

Hirka fumbled for her staff on the table, found it, and backed away. Into the corridor, into a blessed darkness, and out into the rain.

ONE LAST ENCOUNTER

Rime bounded from roof to roof across the alleyways along the river, heading toward Damayanti's place. He kept to the shadows, his hood pulled low over his face. But people were more vigilant than before, even at night. Instability in the Council, rumors of war and blindlings . . . It made them nervous. Mannfalla had become a more difficult place to hide.

But they still drank.

It was late. Damayanti's was emptying. Rime stole across the roof to an extension where the window was open a crack. He listened to the sounds from the street, the winding down of a drunken evening. It was too risky for him to go in the front door; people were still lingering outside.

Rime opened the window and slipped inside. Eased himself down into a loft space and followed a rafter along the corridor. Noises from rooms and booths told him that not everyone had retired for the night.

At least people paid less attention when they were lost in the pleasures of the flesh.

He dropped down onto the floor and found the door to Damayanti's room. Knew it would be locked. He pulled out his picklock. Glanced behind him. Still alone. The lock yielded with a click, and he went inside. He left the door unlocked so he wouldn't scare her needlessly.

He'd forgotten how simple her room was. A quiet corner in a building otherwise abounding with colorful silk and clattering beads. The only piece of furniture was a bed big enough for three. Extravagance, he'd thought the first time he saw it. An endless stream of partners. For all he knew, that was true, but there were other reasons for having a bed so big it could barely be moved. It concealed the trapdoor leading down into the old city walls. To the part of the stone circle that was underground.

He sat down on the edge of the bed by a couple of goatskin cushions. There were niches in the wall decorated with animal bones and skulls with spiral-shaped horns.

Rime waited. The bed called out to him. Promised to let him sleep and forget everything he'd seen that night. Jarladin's burned-out home. Eisvaldr under close guard. The charred ruin of Lindri's teahouse. He'd been drawn to them. Had to see them with his own two eyes.

Footsteps . . . She was coming.

He heard her stop outside the door. Hesitate for a moment. Then she came in. She looked almost relieved to see him. Who had she been expecting? She closed the door and locked it behind her.

"Rime . . ."

She went over to one of the niches and lit an oil lamp. Her snake-like movements were accompanied by the rattle of the bone beads on the hem of her see-through skirt. The lamp flared to life, the flame licking at the animal skulls and casting macabre shadows across the ceiling.

She sat down next to him. Closer than strictly necessary.

"I need blood," he said.

Her closeness unnerved him. She was Graal's servant. She'd given Rime the beak. Her being in love with him didn't make it any less twisted.

"Ravnhov?" she asked. He didn't know whether she'd anticipated his leaving or whether Graal had told her. It made no difference either way. He nodded.

"I'll need enough to last a while. Until the world goes to the dogs or thereabouts."

"Then this is the last time we'll see each other? Until . . . until the end?" The back of her hand brushed his thigh. He swatted it away. Rougher than he'd intended. She looked up at him. Her eyes were rimmed with kohl. Paint the color of mica had been applied to her temples, twisting down into a spiral on her chin. Her gaze was more serious than usual.

"He hurt you . . ."

Rime looked away. Sympathy from the woman who'd made it possible for Graal to hurt him was more than he could swallow.

"Rime, you have to believe me when I say he doesn't mean to harm you. I know him. He would never harm you unless it was necessary. I don't know what you've been doing, but . . . but you have to stop. It's much simpler to just do as he says. He cares about you, Rime. I know he does."

Rime would have laughed had it not been so unbelievably tragic. "Cares? You think he cares? That he does it out of love? If you think *that's* love, you know less about it than I thought."

She didn't respond.

"How much has he hurt *you*?" he asked, looking at her throat. It was slim and unblemished. No scars. No sign of the beak.

Damayanti put her hand under his chin and tilted it up. "You're looking in the wrong place," she whispered. "I've taken the beak, too, but not there."

He opened his mouth to ask, but then he understood.

Her full lips narrowed into a smile, as if his realization pleased her. "A beak is a beak, Rime. It needs only flesh and blood. I chose to have it somewhere else. That way, he can give me as much pleasure as pain."

Rime couldn't stop himself from glancing at her crotch. He felt ill. He didn't know whether his queasiness was because of what she'd done or what she was saying.

"And that makes it worth it?" he rasped. "Is that what you're saying? That you've betrayed Ym and your own people for pleasure? Their coming will end us! Do you think this is a game?"

She lay down on the bed, propping herself up on her elbow. "I think one's as bad as the other," she replied. "Nábyrn or ymling, there's good and bad in all of us. Do you truly think the world will be worse under them than under Darkdaggar? The blind are no more savage than you."

Rime got up. "Do you have the blood or not?"

Damayanti slunk off the bed and went over to one of the skulls. She lifted it ever so slightly and pulled a bottle out from inside.

"Not too much, remember."

Rime took the bottle. He stuck it in his pocket and turned to leave. "You forget that I've met him, Damayanti."

"What do you mean?"

"I'm saying you've picked the wrong side. You've given yourself to someone who talks like a savior but who would sacrifice you without a moment's thought. He's merciless. Stone-cold. What you see as passion only makes him more deadly."

She smiled lazily. "I know . . . I tend to fall for that type."

Her words felt like a slap.

"Try Darkdaggar, then," he answered bitterly.

"I have. It won't work."

He stared at her. Not sure he'd heard right. She shrugged. "Graal thought it was worth a try. So yes, I spoke to him. But I could read him well enough to know I was wasting my time."

Rime saw unease flash across her features and suspected the encounter had cost her more than she was letting on. What, though? How much had she shared with the enemy?

Damayanti slipped between him and the door. "You're talking like I don't recognize passion, Rime. I live off it. I know fire when I see it. Fire can be used. Shaped. Fire wants something. Darkdaggar doesn't have it. He's never burned for anything in his life. A true councillor. There's no point trying to set a fire under men who won't burn. So I'm afraid you'll have to bring him down yourself."

Rime didn't know how to respond. Was there no one she wasn't willing to seduce? Was no enemy too brutish to bargain with? His lips twitched. He wanted to say something, but the words wouldn't come.

He opened the door. Damayanti latched onto his arm. "Rime . . . I mean it. He's a . . . practical man. He's not like Urd. He won't burn out. It makes him more dangerous than you think."

Rime almost snarled at her. "I'm touched by your concern."

He pulled himself up on the door and jumped onto the rafter. It wasn't until he was back out on the roof that he heard her shut the door.

BORN OF EARTH

Hirka pulled herself up onto the balcony and lay there with her cheek against the cold stone. The rain had given way to snow. White flakes danced around her. Melted on her lips. If she stayed there long enough, they would cover her. Erase her without a care, as if she'd never existed.

You're the one lying in the snow, child.

She pushed herself up onto her arms. Skerri was right. They were weak. Useless. A silky sound approached. The beating of wings. She looked up and stared into the eyes of a raven. It leaned forward and cocked its head, as if trying to see her better under the wet clumps of hair hanging in her face.

I'm not dead yet . . .

But the raven wasn't looking for a meal. It opened its beak and dropped something in front of her before taking flight again.

A stone. It had left her a stone. Hirka picked it up. It was spiral-shaped, like a snail shell. Just like the one she'd gotten from Hlosnian.

Hlosnian . . .

What had become of him now that everything had changed in Eisvaldr? Was he dead, too?

Hirka looked for the raven, but it was gone. As was the call she'd learned back in Ym. She was just too tired to remember.

She put the rock in her pocket, stumbled to her feet, opened the balcony door, and went inside. The door on the other side of the room stood ajar. Someone had been in. Realized she was gone. Luckily it was nighttime, so the confrontation could wait until morning. Talking to anyone now would be impossible. She wouldn't be able to string together a single coherent sentence. She wasn't whole enough. Her body felt like a broken husk. Her thoughts turned to dust.

She spread her cloak out over the bench in front of the window, where it could drip onto the floor. The bed was only a few steps away, but it still seemed too far. She sat on the bench and stared out through ash-flecked mightglass, a reminder of everything that was no longer possible.

She dragged a hand over her face. Her skin felt tight where her tears had dried. Had she seen what she thought she'd seen at the Seer's? Had that been real? Or had she breathed in something strange? Gods knew what he had amid all those herbs, beasts, and bird embryos.

What the Might has destroyed cannot be healed.

"Where have you been?" The voice cut through the air behind her. Hirka whirled around. Skerri was standing in the doorway, fists clenched. Had she been waiting up for her?

Not now . . .

Hirka closed her eyes. It was a simple question, but so full of accusations that she didn't know which one to respond to first. Should she apologize for going out alone, without an escort? Or should she apologize for letting people see her limp? She might just as well have apologized for being born.

Skerri strode into the room. "We were out this evening, Grid and I. To keep an eye on the houseless. Keep the rioters in check. I ran into one who works in the growing caves." Her voice was hoarse with anger. Hirka knew why. Knew what was coming.

"He had a strange tale to tell . . ." Skerri stopped in front of her,

252

hands on her hips. "An incident he wanted to offer his sincerest apologies for. Need I go on?"

Even if she'd had the energy, Hirka wouldn't have had a chance to answer. "A worker threw dirt at one of our servants, and you refused to let them reprimand him?! You defended one of the houseless? Someone who insulted us?!"

She looked up at Skerri. Her gaze was inky black. Furious. But none of what she was saying was important. Servants. Houses. Reprimands. Snowflakes melting on stone.

"He was no man. He was . . ." Hirka tried to remember his awful face. The gaping red hole that almost split him in two. No teeth. Just a sharp black tongue. She moved her palm down in front of her face, as if that would explain what she'd seen. "He had no nose. Just a sort of . . . beak . . ."

For a moment, confusion replaced the fury on Skerri's face. Her coldly beautiful face. With its black lips and sharp canines. She was a monster. They were all monsters. In a world full of monsters.

"You've seen him?!" Skerri loomed over her. "Of course you have . . . What is it about you that makes everyone open up? What is it that wins you everyone's favor?" The words collided with Hirka's reality.

Favor? What favor? All she'd known was pain. Everything she cared about was being torn apart, and there was nothing she could do to stop it.

Skerri stroked her wet hair. A gesture Hirka never would have imagined could feel threatening. "It's nothing you've done, that's for certain. Or anything you have. They probably still think you're going to save them. They don't realize you've already betrayed us."

"It doesn't matter anymore," Hirka replied. "I was born in the wrong place. I'm unearthed. I always will be. The earth won't have me."

Skerri barked out a laugh. "This is what I mean! We're marching on Ym in the autumn, and what have you contributed? Indignity. Absence. Lectures about the earth. And now you're grieving Kolkagga! You're lamenting the fact that the only people who might have posed a challenge for us have been wiped out."

She straightened up again. "You were supposed to be something we could be proud of. Something we'd want to stand behind. But you're nothing. You're nothing at all, are you?"

Hirka got up. Looked at the monster before her. But Skerri was far from the only one. Hirka herself was a monster. Always had been.

"I can tell you what I am, Skerri. I'm Graal's daughter. I belong to him and who knows what beautiful woman. I'm his. I'm hers. But what I'll never be is *yours*."

Skerri's mask cracked. For a moment she was grief personified. An open wound. Hirka looked at her and saw a reflection of herself. The words she'd just said made her feel sick. She put a hand on Skerri's arm.

"I didn't mean—Skerri, there are ways! He'll never be able to use the gateways, but you can get to him! Go to him. You can be with him in the human world. You can . . ."

Skerri's face contorted with fury, revealing a truth Hirka realized nobody else knew. She looked at the deadborn woman. Heard herself whisper what Skerri would never have said herself.

"He doesn't want you there . . ."

Skerri was laid bare before her. Graal was what tied her to the family, but it was a tie that had long since been severed.

Suddenly Skerri gripped her by the throat. Hirka gasped, the air escaping her lungs. Fear threatened to paralyze her. She twisted to get free. Felt claws dig into her neck. The pain radiated down into her chest.

"Your compassion will be the end of you," Skerri hissed in her ear. "The earth won't have you, huh? Then you've not tried hard enough!"

Hirka tore herself free, but she had lost all feeling in her arm. She felt numb. Poisoned. Foggy. Her body grew colder. Collapsed.

Rime . . .

He was the last thing she saw. Before everything went black.

Wolf eyes.

Hirka fought to wake up, knowing she had no other choice. She had to.

She clawed her way back to consciousness but still felt like she was floating. On her back. She was being carried. Carried! The word signaled danger. Sent jolts of fear through her.

Where am I?

Her body was numb. Heavy. She blinked, just about able to make out shadows in the darkness.

Skerri!

Hirka tried to move her arms, but they refused to cooperate. It was like she couldn't even find them. Someone tightened their grip on her. Voices. People talking in hushed tones. The sound was hollow. Contained.

Where?

She kicked. Or at least she thought she did. Her feet weren't listening, either. She felt like she'd been asleep for a hundred years.

Earth. She could smell earth. Then she was falling. She landed hard but felt no pain. She was a living corpse.

A weight dropped onto her stomach. Then more. Heavier and heavier. Dirt trickled over her face. Panic ripped through her like lightning. She tried to scream, but all that came out was a wheeze. The silent scream from a nightmare.

She was being buried alive. And there was nothing she could do about it.

Hirka tried to concentrate on her arm.

Up! You hear me?!

It moved. Bumped into something. She grabbed it. Felt its shape with her fingers. A staff. Her staff. Right next to her face. It was getting darker. Her arm was being weighed down. Her face smothered by the earth. A smell she loved, and now it was suffocating her. She gasped for breath. Dirt filled her mouth. She tried to spit it out but didn't have the strength.

She was going to die. Fear was going to kill her.

Calm. She needed to find calm. To regain control. One step at a time. Calm. Calm.

The staff pressed against her cheek. It was planted next to her. Like a grave marker.

Here . . . here she lies. The dead girl.

No! It had some other significance. It was important. Air!

She held her breath and wrenched her head to the side, keeping her eyes closed. She couldn't have opened them if she'd wanted to. She was pinned by the weight of the earth. It listened to her. Heard and mimicked her heartbeat. Like an echo.

Don't think.

She felt air coming from the end of the staff. Far too little. She tried to suck down more and ended up with grit in her throat. She coughed. There was nowhere to turn, nowhere to spit. She choked on a sob.

She tried to pull one of her knees up. Nothing happened, but she could feel her foot now. Pain and terror combined, enveloping her in a new and heavier fog. She could move her fingers. Her hand.

I'm alive!

Hirka dug her fingers into the earth, pushing herself up. Something yielded. She wasn't sure whether it was her or the earth. She forced her head upward. Like a plant. Her neck was screaming.

Was this how she would die? Stray thoughts broke through her panic. She was a seed. A fetus in the earth. Germinating. She was submerged. Ripe. New.

She was like Naiell. Naiell pushing his way out of the raven. In a greenhouse in York. Raven. First came raven. Raven was the first. The Might was raven's breath.

Hirka screamed. Heard her own voice, muffled by the earth. She grabbed the end of the staff. Drew in air. The pressure in her lungs lessened.

Voices. Hands.

Help. Someone was helping her!

Her heart was in her mouth. Her blood was roaring. She was going to live.

Her head broke the surface. One arm. Then the other. She clawed her way out. Pulled herself up. A germinating seed.

She crouched on all fours. Whoever was holding her let go. She used her staff to push herself up onto her knees, looked up into a face she'd seen before, and realized where she was. The man worked here. In the growing caves. He had thrown soil at Oni.

Her stomach clenched. She threw up mud. Spat out dirt. She was sticky. Her clothes were wet.

Her body was alive. But was *she*?

Hirka smiled. Grit crunched between her teeth. The man backed away. He wasn't alone. More workers had come over and were standing between rows of plants, staring at her. She crawled out of the bed and got up.

None of them dared say anything. No one asked.

She walked past them all and out of the cave.

She knew where she was going, and what she had to do.

RAVEN ESCORT

Hirka followed the alleyway that sloped down toward the Seer's house. It was still dark, but dawn wouldn't be long in coming. A sliver of sky was visible between the clifftops, far above her. Millions of stars strewn like dust. More stars than people. More stars than Umpiri, humans, and ymlings combined. The world was infinitely bigger than the creatures it contained.

The roar of the sea drowned out the rush of wings, but she could see them. Black shapes that swallowed the stars where they flew. The ravens kept close to her. Always just ahead of her on the road, the way Kuro had once done. They were shadows of him. Shadows of everything she'd lost.

Part of her had died that night. Along with Lindri. Kolkagga. Svarteld. Along with Father. She had one foot in Slokna, and she always would. Between worlds. Between life and death. And now, between right and wrong.

The rusty door screeched open. She went inside. Heard the ravens settle down on the steps outside. The cave was quiet as the night. The ceiling dripped like it was crying in the pitch-blackness. She rested her staff against the wall and felt her way to the hearth. Got the fire going. Dead things kept her company. Stared down at her from the shelves.

After a while she heard him come. His robe whispering against the steps behind her.

"No need to get worked up," Hirka said, shifting a log so it would catch. "I'm not here to offer pity. I'm done with that."

She turned to look at him. He hadn't covered himself. His hood was draped around his shoulders. His face an impossibility. Half man, half raven. But it seemed less frightening now. Perhaps it had just been the shock. Either that or she was no longer the same.

"You lied to me," she said.

He tightened the belt of his robe. Studied her with a look that swung between anger and concern. He could land on whichever side he wanted. She was done pussyfooting around. Done believing help would come if she just did her best to please everyone.

Her clothes were dirty and damp, but she knew he wouldn't ask why. She pulled off her shoes and set them down by the fire. "You said I was already born. That there was nothing I could do about it. But that's not true, is it? It's possible to be reborn. I've seen it with my own eyes. Naiell was born from the body of a raven. In another world. I can do the same. I *will* do the same. And you will help me."

He stood there for a moment, not answering. Then he limped over to a bucket, filled a pot with water, and set it down on the edge of the hearth next to her shoes.

"You knew," she said. "You knew it was possible. You should have told me."

He shook off a tic. His forehead sloped straight back from his brow to the top of his head. The skull of a bird.

"Whatever they've done to you, what you're asking for is worse. Ravenborn? You? You don't even have pure blood. At best, it would kill you. At worsss . . . st, you'd end up like me."

"Enough!" Hirka moved toward him. "Enough lies. You'd have me believe you were sparing me? I'm nothing to you! You kept quiet for your own sake. You said so yourself: I have everything I need, apart from the Might. I can shape it. I can channel it. You being too scared to hope won't stop me. I will be reborn."

He dropped some tea leaves in the pot and carried it over to the table. Sat down on the bench. "So you think you can be ravenborn in Ym? Be born again with the Might, so you can bind?"

Hirka sat down across from him. "I don't think so. I know so."

It was a truth with many reservations. But the part of her that was certain had overpowered the other. She'd chased the Might for as long as she could remember. Through Rime she'd felt it. Felt what it could do. Raw power had torn down the walls of the Rite Hall. It had been part of her. Just as much as the blood in her veins. Always there. Always meant to be there.

He poured tea into a cup. "I thought I knew, too. Doesss it look like I was right?"

Hirka leaned back. "Really? Self-pity? Is that all you've got to give me?"

He stared at her. One eye half-closed and a little lower than the other. A half-formed creation. He made a creaking sound, like an old door. "Why do you think Dreyri hold the power in Dreysíl? What makes us a ruling minority in a world where no one wants to be ruled? Yes, a lot is said about our superiority. Sss . . . strength, power, and ferocity. But do you think that's a difference that resides in the body?" He pointed at the shelf behind her. Dead things in jars. "If you cut open Dreyri and Umpiri, would they look different? No. We're made of the same sss . . . stuff. Power is all in the head. Dreyri were brought up to be superior and continue to be superior."

"What about the cold? You can endure more. I've seen Skerri walk through a storm half naked!"

"Perhaps . . ." He looked at her. "Or perhaps she's been told she can endure more since the day she was born."

He pushed the tea toward her with rough black hands. They looked almost charred. Unnaturally long fingers curled around the cup. "The only true difference is the blessing from the first. Dreyri can forge bonds with ravens and take the form of a raven. A gift more costly than you know. Something even the best of us do only once in our long lives. And that's what you're asking for. Because you think you can undo an act that led to our ruin. Or is it because you think it will make you strong enough to protect your home?"

Hirka didn't answer.

He waved his hand as though it didn't matter. "Even if it were possible, with your mixed blood, you would still need the blessing of one of the first ravens. And you have no raven to ask."

"Would a beak do?"

His beak-like upper lip curled toward his ear in what was probably supposed to be a smile. "Do you have a spare?"

"I will. But I'll have to kill for it."

"You wouldn't be the first."

He'd misunderstood her, but she didn't say anything. Some may have killed for the beaks, but she doubted they'd killed someone they loved. Like she'd have to. At the very least she'd have to make him think he was going to die.

"Aren't you going to drink your tea?"

She shook her head. He shrugged and took the cup back. Poured the tea into his gaping red mouth.

"So what will it be, Seer?"

He got up. "What do you think your family would say if I helped you do something that could cost you your life? Without you having any reason to believe you'll succeed? You don't have a raven, you don't have pure blood, you don't have—"

Hirka stood up. Couldn't listen to him anymore. She'd had enough of doubt. Of fear. She went into the corridor and opened the outside door.

"Hedra!" she shouted out into the street. And they came. The ravens flew past her. Wings brushed through her hair. She followed them through to the Seer. There were many of them, but they were quiet. No screeching. No commotion. They flew in circles. Settled down under the ceiling. On the table. On the shelves. Talons scraped against wood and stone.

"I don't have *one* raven. I have many. Ask them," she said.

He looked at her and, much to her surprise, made the sign of the Seer. Not even that had belonged to Naiell. It was older than him. It was the sign of the raven.

For a moment the Seer just stood there, eyes closed. As if hesitating. Or listening. Then he pried open a drawer in one of the cabinets. Handed her a sealed bottle, smaller than her hand.

"Drink half today and the rest in eight days. It's a start."

"What is it? Raven blood?"

"No. That comes later." He lowered his gaze. "Now that I'm helping you, can I ask you for something in return? You had his heart with you. May I see it?"

Hirka nodded. "The House of Hod has it, but I'll see what I can do."

She put the bottle in her pocket. He rested a knotted hand on her arm. "Hirka . . . You must see that you've already lost? Even if you can get to Ym and be ravenborn. Even if you find the Might and can contain as much of it as you think . . . you still won't be able to fix what he destroyed. You'll never find a strong enough flow of the Might."

Flow of the Might . . .

He was wrong. She remembered Graal's words. About the tree Naiell had created, built on the blood of thousands. His words had been an echo from Ym. A whisper from the Seer halls. The sad truth about where the strength of the Might had come from. The power to fight the blind. Written in black and white in the Book of the Seer.

And the tree grew straight up into the heavens, blackened and vigorous from the blood of all those who had sacrificed their lives.

She felt the coldness of her own smile. "You're forgetting one thing, Seer. Nothing feeds the Might like blood. And we have a war knocking at our door. We're going to see more blood than anyone has in a thousand years."

ALIVE

Hirka could hear the ravens following her all the way back. When she reached the house, they settled down atop the ice. She opened the door and went in. A chorus of voices died instantly, giving way to an intent silence. She knew they'd woken up and been unable to find her. And now they could hear her coming.

The corridor seemed more oppressive than before. The grooves in the walls that had once reminded her of an overturned ship now seemed more like segments of a worm.

Oni and Skilborr came to meet her. Neither of them managed to hide their reaction. Oni was the first to regain her composure. She took Hirka's cloak. Asked whether she was hurt. Whether she'd fallen. Why she had sand in her hair. Why her clothes were so dirty.

Hirka didn't answer. She continued along the corridor and into the hearth room. A cavernous hall, bathed in blue light from the ice. Had she really thought she'd find warmth here?

Raun and Skerri were sitting on either side of a long table with a board game between them. Like they'd needed a distraction. She knew Skerri liked to play, but no one liked to play with Skerri.

Both of them got up when they saw her.

Raun came toward her, but something made him hesitate. Only the day before she would have searched for signs of worry in his gaze. For concern. But that had been before, when she'd needed it.

"You're bleeding . . ." Raun brought his fingers to his lips.

"It's not my blood."

Hirka looked at Skerri. The deadborn woman was tense as a bowstring. Waiting for a move. An accusation. Hirka guessed she'd had her defense all planned out for some time. Had she known she would survive? Given her even half a chance? Or had she been a slave to her own temper in the moment? Maybe she'd only intended to humiliate her.

Either way it didn't matter.

"Where have you been?" Raun looked tired. His red hair was tied back, ready for the training halls.

"Raun, I want to talk to Skerri alone," Hirka replied, not taking her eyes off her.

He lifted a hand, as if to put it on her shoulder, but then thought better of it. He moistened his lips, as if he wanted to say something, but didn't do that, either. He nodded, then left.

If anyone in this family cared about her, it was Raun. Her father's father. Hirka had seen it in his eyes. She'd given him something. Something more than status. He'd be furious if he found out what Skerri had done. But furious enough to cast her out? The woman who controlled the dead raven and their only means of talking to Graal?

Unlikely. In any case, Raun wouldn't be finding out.

Hirka ignored the jolts of pain in her calf and walked toward Skerri. Clearly surprised, Skerri took a step back and stumbled against the bench, falling and sitting with her back to the table. Game pieces toppled over on the board. Hirka leaned forward and put her hands on the edge of the table, one on either side of Skerri, trapping her between her arms.

"I've told people what you did," Hirka said, not recognizing her own voice. "And if anything happens to me or anyone I care about, the next heart I give as a gift will be yours. Do you understand what I'm saying?"

Skerri's eyes narrowed into white slits. "You've got nothing on me. You deserved it. No one will believe you."

Hirka leaned so close that Skerri's cheek touched hers. There was something exhilarating about being so close to an enemy. So close to someone who wished her ill. The effect was intoxicating. "You can't smell any fear, can you, Skerri?" she whispered.

Skerri didn't reply. Hirka stared into her white eyes. "But do you know what? *I* can…"

Skerri's eyes flooded black. The only confirmation she needed.

Hirka let go of the table and straightened up again. "They don't need to believe me, Skerri. There'll be plenty of others to tell them. Some willing to lie through their teeth for me, if necessary. That's the difference between you and me. You think I'm weak, but I'm not alone. And you'd better believe I'll destroy you if I have to."

Hirka could taste the force of her own words. The power. It elevated her. Made her stronger, angrier, wonderfully whole.

"Just give me a reason. Give me the slightest reason, and I'll tell Graal you tried to put an end to his line. I don't think he'll care about the details, do you?"

Skerri swallowed. "You can't tell Graal anything without me. Without my raven."

Hirka cocked her head and looked at Skerri. "Do you think I need that? Do you really think it's more important for me to talk to Graal than it is for you? He can rot, for all I care. *You* are the one who needs him. Without him you have nothing. But whatever, I can start by telling Raun. I'm sure he'd want to know."

Hirka turned to leave.

"Wait!"

She stopped, waiting for submission.

Skerri got up. "What is it that you want?"

Hirka picked up one of the toppled game pieces and put it back on the board. "You'll find out soon enough."

Skerri tossed her black braids back. "If you think I was trying to kill you, you're stupider than I thought. You had your staff, didn't you? I knew you'd be fine, And I knew people would come if—"

"Did you know humans don't burn their dead?" Hirka interrupted. "They don't give them to the birds, either. They do something far worse. They bury them. Let them lie rotting in the earth, as if they were victims of some heinous act. You might have thought that grave was for me, but really, you dug your own grave, Skerri. When the war is over, and we become the second house, where will that leave you? When I, Hirka, daughter of Graal, son of Raun of the House of Modrasme, have given the Might back to Umpiri, who will decide whether there's room for you then?"

Skerri sized her up. No answer seemed to be forthcoming, but Hirka wanted one. She banged her staff against the floor. "Who, Skerri?"

Skerri's lips quivered furiously. "You."

Hirka gave her a lopsided smile before once again turning to leave.

"I didn't think you wanted this war," Skerri said behind her.

"On the contrary, I *need* this war."

Hirka went out into the corridor and stopped, waiting for the sound she knew would come. And come it did. The delightful cacophony of game pieces raining down on the floor.

A STRONG HEART

Hirka spread out her cloak on the ice and sat down. There was a raven over by the edge, pecking at something. Otherwise, she was alone, on the roof of Ginnungad. The city around the crater. The city of ice and stone.

She'd always felt there were only two sides in Ym. The haves and the have-nots. In Dreysíl, there were a thousand stages in between. Perhaps it was best that way. Perhaps it gave people more hope. An illusion of something better being within reach. Or perhaps it was the very idea of something better that drove people to war.

She'd looked at the war as a wave. A wall of death that was hurtling toward her. Everything had been about stopping it. She'd tried her best to find a solution that would make the war unnecessary. Searched for a way to share the Might. Heal it so that everyone could live in peace. As if there were any way of getting people who had tasted blood to live in peace.

No. The wave was unstoppable. It would hurtle onward. It had to. She needed it. They had to strike Ym at the same time, she and the war. Death wasn't coming for her; it was hurtling alongside her. A companion. They had to accept each other.

But what she would never accept was annihilation. Kolkagga were no longer. They couldn't save Ym from the deadborn. But she would create her own force. Umpiri would not sweep through the eleven kingdoms unchallenged. They'd meet resistance. She'd make sure of that.

The box was cool and heavy in her lap. Its mica lid glittered. She opened it and looked down at Naiell's heart, half buried in crushed ice. She had to make sure it didn't melt before she returned the box to the House of Hod. Not that there was much danger of that in a place like this. Practically nothing melted here.

Every time she opened the lid, she saw something new. Felt something new.

The first time, she'd reacted the way she knew she ought to. With disgust. Despair. Sorrow. The only way that was natural. The only way that was right. Gradually she'd become more numb, as if it no longer upset her.

The heart hadn't changed. She had.

It unsettled her, but now she understood everyone's need to see the heart. She understood their fury. She understood their thirst for revenge. In that moment, she'd gladly have exchanged this heart for another. Skerri's, for burying her alive. Darkdaggar's, for killing Lindri and wiping out Kolkagga. Damayanti's, and maybe even Graal's, for making Rime a slave.

What did this anger mean? This willingness to accept death? Had she finally become one of them? Dreyri? Enough to be ravenborn? Enough to find the Might?

The raven glanced over at her, continuing to tear at the carcass of a less fortunate bird.

Hirka ran her fingers over the heart. "See what you've done. Did you know what it would destroy? Did you know you were sentencing worlds to slow deaths? It wasn't just your brother you were condemning, but so, so many more."

An act of war. A thousand-year-old injustice, and now she was holding the consequences of that in her hands. Her, the girl who'd always been afraid of people, and who had now stood before tens of thousands. The girl who'd always fought against death, and who now depended on it. In horrific numbers. To perhaps save everyone. To put right a single act: a brother's treachery.

It wasn't fair.

She'd felt too much. The weight of the world had always pulled her down, but it wasn't like that anymore. She'd crawled up out of the earth, but she'd left so much behind. So much that her heart could now endure what she had to do. The way Naiell's had done.

How far was she willing to go? Could she sacrifice Rime so that everyone else could live? So that entire worlds could live?

No!

She had to get that beak out of his throat. Free him from Graal. Only then would she be able to do what she wanted. Only then would no one have power over her. And if she managed that, she'd have the beak of one of the first ravens. One that could give her a new birth. A ravenbirth. If she had what it took.

If . . . then . . . maybe . . .

Far too many maybes.

But she couldn't let all the uncertainty dissuade her. If she started to think of everything that could go wrong, she'd lose the ability to act.

She took the bottle from the Seer out of her pocket and drank the rest of its contents. Blindling blood mixed into a sweet, spiced liquid. Something good to prepare her for something bad. For what would come later.

Hirka curled her fingers around the heart. Felt the weight of it. "I'm going to be like you," she said. "A traitor. Pitting blindling against blindling. Those who have nothing against those who have everything."

The fallen and the houseless would be her Kolkagga.

She put the heart back and closed the box. Got up, grabbed her cloak, and shook it off. The ice stretched out around her like a frozen lake. Seemingly endless. Covered in scars and wounds. With a gaping chasm leading straight to Slokna.

She walked over to the edge to climb down. The raven hopped away from its meal. Something caught Hirka's eye, and she crouched down to have a look. A gray bird with a blue breast. One of the living lamps. She'd freed it herself.

She got up again.

That was just the way it was. Some would die. Others would live. And she would be the cause of both, whether she liked it or not.

BLOODBORN

Hirka pushed the staff away from her chest, but Skerri's volley of blows forced her back. Their staffs crashed against each other, the impact jarring her knuckles. It was enough to distract her from the pain in her lower leg, which was a good sign. That meant it had gotten better—or at least that it had stopped failing her at inconvenient moments.

It would have been a stretch to say Skerri was being cautious, but still, something had changed. It was like she was no longer looking for a reason to destroy her. Hirka was under no illusion that it was out of concern. Nor out of fear, even though Hirka had threatened her. No, it was something else. A feeling she'd been accepted by Skerri, albeit begrudgingly.

The deadborn woman observed more than she attacked. Focused on repeating rather than outdoing. Twice Hirka had almost hit her, and both times Skerri had nodded in involuntary recognition.

Had the same thing happened during the last full moon, Hirka would have struggled to hold back tears. Now it was nothing more than proof that behaving like them worked. She hadn't really been accepted. Skerri had just seen something in Hirka that she could recognize. The part that was Dreyri.

Not that the incident had been mentioned since. Not the grave and not Hirka's ensuing outburst. Rage. Threats. Even blackmail. Far from her proudest moment, but it was clearly what they wanted.

And that's what they'll get.

Hirka crouched down and swung her staff at Skerri's knee. It buckled slightly, but she stayed on her feet.

"What the—?" Skerri yelped. She looked confused, like she hadn't quite realized she'd been hit.

Hirka ignored her. Attacked while she had the chance. The arm cuffs slowed her down, but she pushed herself to make short, quick jabs that drove the as yet unbeatable woman backward out of the ring. Hirka gasped for breath, trying to wrap her head around what had just happened. Then she noticed the others finishing up and realized she must have missed Raun calling an end to training.

She was about to force out an apology when Grid came toward them, tossing his blond hair so that the victory beads clinked at the end of their string. He was expecting to earn a sixth during the next tournament, which wasn't far off. He asked Skerri if she had any plans.

Hirka left them to it so she wouldn't have to hear him being rebuffed again. She went into the armory and leaned the staff against the wall. Then she toweled herself off and put her woollen tunic on. She didn't bother taking off the leather straps across her chest. The Seer was expecting her. She'd have to change later.

She put on her cloak and pulled up her hood, then pulled the sleeves of her tunic over the arm cuffs so they wouldn't be as noticeable. She'd started with the lightweight ones but quickly switched to a heavier pair. They went almost all the way up to her elbows. They were part of her now. She only took them off when she was sleeping. She liked wearing them. They made her forearms look like they were made of iron. Possible to scratch but not destroy.

She threw her bag over her shoulder and picked up the box containing Naiell's heart. It was still cold. Insulated with mightglass that would have been worth about twenty horses, had they had any use for them.

Then she walked up the tunnel to the street and headed toward the sea. Alone. Another thing that had changed. She refused to have an escort. She hadn't even needed to make a point of it. She'd just said no.

The box started to feel heavier as she approached. The heart had been shown to many people now, but it still made her sick to see people look at it. It did something to them. Turned them into animals. Their lips pulled back, exposing their canines, as if they were looking at something spoiled. Particularly those old enough to have fought in the war. Those who remembered.

But the Seer had said he wanted to see it, and if that was what it took, she was willing to go along with it. She was willing to do more than he knew.

Willing to let them kill one another?

She knocked on the iron door which time and the sea had covered in rust. It struck her that she'd never seen anyone else here, even though he was a seer. A kind of healer, like her. But then again, Umpiri never admitted to needing help.

He'd lit two lamps in the corridor. For her benefit, she assumed. Or maybe to make more of an occasion of it, since she was bringing him the heart.

The cave itself was darker. There was no fire in the grate. A small amount of daylight filtered in through a crack in the door to the sea room. Even the sea seemed subdued. Expectant.

Hirka felt her way over to the table, put the box down, and slipped through the door. The Seer was standing out by the edge. Hunched with his hood up, as if he were trying to protect himself from the dripstones hanging from the ceiling.

"Bring the bowl," he said.

She looked around. There was a three-legged stool in the corner with a bowl on it. She picked it up and carried it over to him. Its contents were unmistakably red and viscous.

"Drink, then we'll sss . . . see how long it takes for it to come back up."

She tried to hide her disgust. "What's the point of drinking it if it'll come back up?"

"Doing it every day until it *doesn't.*"

Hirka didn't ask how many days he expected it to take. Chances were she wouldn't like the answer. "What happens when it doesn't come back up?"

"Then—"

She lifted the bowl to her lips.

"Is that cloak dear to you?" His question said more than enough about what she could expect. She put the bowl on the floor and took her cloak off, pulling up one of her tunic sleeves in the process.

"Arm cuffs?" He asked in a way that told her he had an eyebrow raised. If he had eyebrows. She couldn't remember seeing any.

She shrugged. "You said Naiell was strong. And that was why he could sling the Might without breaking his arms. If it helps, I'll wear arm cuffs." She lifted the bowl again.

"Ah, sss . . . so that's what you're doing . . ." It sounded like he didn't believe her. "I thought you were punishing yourself. But I can promise you, you don't need arm cuffs to do that."

She pretended not to hear, even though the words were true enough to be troubling. She rested the bowl against her lips, trying to block out the smell. Then she drank. Quickly, so she wouldn't have to taste it. Her stomach churned. She doubled over, dropping the bowl on the floor and moving closer to the edge. The blood forced its way back up, pouring out of her as quickly as she'd drunk. A red stream that turned to spray before it reached the sea far below. The Seer grabbed her so she wouldn't fall.

The taste was intense, flooding her with dirty steel. She rested her hands on her thighs. Her elbows were unsteady. Weak.

He picked up the bowl. "As I said, you don't need arm cuffs, because you'll punish yoursss . . . self more than enough without them."

Hirka breathed shallowly until the nausea passed. Her chest and nose stung. Her lips quivered.

This is more than blood.

She straightened up again. Slowly and experimentally. She felt like she'd failed, like it had happened too quickly. But he said nothing. Just limped back toward the door. Hirka picked up her cloak and followed him into the darkness. She fumbled her way over to the table and pushed the box toward him. He hesitated, stopping a few steps away.

She looked around. "Can we light a lamp or some—"

"No!" There was something panicked about the interruption. "No, it—it's not necessary," he said, calmer now. He padded over to the table and rested a black and long-fingered hand on the lid. His thumb pointed backward, disappearing over the edge of the box.

Raven talons.

"Can I keep it until tomorrow?"

Hirka shook her head. The House of Hod guarded the box like a treasure. She couldn't leave it here.

"No . . ." he said quietly. "I thought not."

He doesn't want to be seen . . .

The Seer opened the lid. Hirka folded her arms across her chest and braced herself for the usual sound of pleasure. So far it had come without exception, as if the lid itself were sighing. And the Seer had more reason to hate Naiell than anyone else she'd met. A thousand years as an abomination, trapped in a terrible existence between man and raven, all because Naiell had extinguished the Might in one short, fateful moment.

No sound came. No words. She studied his bent form. A darker black against the black room. He bowed his head. His shoulders started to shake. His body sank, as if his knees were giving out.

Hirka slipped around the table and caught him, guiding him down onto the bench. He whined like he'd lost his breath.

Then she realized he was crying.

Hirka tried to push the box away, but his hand was locked around it. Clamped in place. She lifted her iron-weighted arm and put a hand on his back, only to give a start. His shoulder blades were knotted under his robe. Worse than she'd thought. They stuck up like . . .

Like torn-off wings.

She snatched her hand back, scared to show pity. She'd promised both of them that she'd never do that. But when she thought about how his body must look . . .

Hirka sat down next to him on the bench. Outlines of skulls, eggs, and dead animals emerged on the table in front of her. "You must have hated him more than anyone," she said, turning a small egg in her hand.

He shook his head under his hood. "No," he whispered hoarsely. "I loved him."

The egg cracked between her fingers. There was nothing inside it. An empty shell.

"I loved him," the Seer repeated. "Loved him more than . . ." He was clearly unable to find anything to compare it to. "I loved him."

"But . . ." Hirka tried to find the words, but he interrupted.

"Sss . . . spare me. I know what you're going to sss . . . say. I don't need you to tell me that he sss . . . sentenced us all to an eternity without the Might. I was there. I know he betrayed us."

"Us?! What about *you*? You've lived like . . ." She searched in vain for words to describe him. "Like this! In pain. A life under a robe because he stole the Might. He destroyed you!"

The Seer pulled the box closer. "Oh, he destroyed me long before the war," he replied. The warmth in his voice was at odds with his words. "He destroyed me, but it wasn't his fault. Had he known I was about to be ravenborn, he'd have waited. But he couldn't have known."

Hirka could feel his words softening her. No one here had said anything good about Naiell. No one had talked about him with love. He was nothing more than an object of hate.

The Seer took a deep, ragged breath, taking in the smell of the man he'd loved. His head quivered as if he were struggling to hold himself together. He closed the box again.

"How did he die?"

Rime.

Hirka felt her jaw tense. She knew there was no point lying. "The man you loved was killed by—"

"By the man *you* love."

Hirka glanced at him. "I was going to say steel. Killed by steel."

The Seer snorted. "Now you sss . . . smell of lust and lies." He pushed the box away. "Tell me about Naiell instead. What did you think of him?"

Hirka hesitated. Naiell had betrayed her as well. When it had come down to it, he had shown her who he was. He had threatened her life in the burned-out church to get Graal to send him back to Ym. But that wasn't how she liked to remember him. She remembered everything that had happened before then. The little things. Hirka smiled.

"He thought he was a god. He'd take his clothes off at the first opportunity. And he could sink his claws into a chicken and make it disappear in the blink of an eye."

The Seer rasped out a laugh. "Hungry and strong. Always."

"And he could sleep in the strangest places," she continued. "On rafters, and in the car, and—"

"Car?" The Seer repeated the strange word.

Hirka felt her smile falter. The creature next to her was thousands of years old, but she had experienced things he could never dream of. The sum of all she had seen swelled in her body, threatening to tear her apart. The certainty that worlds would die if she didn't succeed suddenly became very real again.

"You wouldn't believe me if I explained." Hirka got up. "I'll be back tomorrow." She put on her cloak and picked up the box.

"Hirka . . ."

She turned toward him again. His head drooped as if he'd lost his courage. "Keep a disss . . . stance from them. Don't dig. Don't ask. Don't let them destroy you. And they don't need to know what has been sss . . . said here today."

"It's your secret to share," Hirka replied. "Not mine."

She walked toward the corridor and noticed that the staff she'd given him was leaning against a different wall than before. As though he'd used it.

THE FALLEN

Hirka waited until it was dark, then went out onto the balcony and lowered herself down onto the road below. It was easy without the arm cuffs. She'd left them on the bed. Anything could happen where she was going. The last thing she needed was heavier arms.

Fog seeped down from the ice above her, sinking to the bottom of the crater like silent waterfalls, drawing a dreamlike veil over the houses on the far side. The gleam of lanterns shone through, making the abyss seem even bigger. There was something tragic about the center of the city being a void. A hole left by the Might.

The sight of it drained her of courage. Could anything fill such an abyss? Who did she think she was, interfering in things beyond her comprehension?

Start with the small things.

That was her plan for the evening. Build an army. A teeny-tiny thing. She'd have it out of the way in an hour. She'd have laughed, had blindcraft not been coursing through her body. Raven blood chilled her own, so it was like frost running through her veins. It warped her sense of reality. Like she might wake up in her own bed if everything went to Slokna. If only it were that simple.

She followed the road in a gradual curve around the wall of the crater. Past houses with mightglass windows and imposing doors carved with mythical creatures. Though for all she knew, they could be real in this world.

She could see people inside in some places. Hired warriors keeping an eye on her as she passed. The guard had become more conspicuous, increasing in line with the riots. Even the leading houses seemed to understand what such a period of unrest could mean. They did their best to hide it, but they were marked by their fear. By the certainty that war could change the game, even for them. Had they known what she was up to, she'd have been raven fodder before daybreak.

The road turned into one of the crevices that led away from the crater. The deepest street in the city stretched ahead of her as far as she could see. She crossed the nearest bridge. They were everywhere, crossing the divide at various heights. Some were rendered practically invisible by the fog that was sinking to the bottom, far below her. The weather seemed to sense that she had no business being south of the crater. But that was where she had to go.

It was the same road they'd taken her along when she first arrived. The way to the growing caves and to Kolail's. The last place she ought to be on her own—but the best place to find allies.

Back then they'd walked along the bottom of the crevice, the most direct route, but with the riots in mind, she decided to stay higher up. Taking the uppermost route, one that passed just beneath the glacier. It was more tortuous, but it felt safer.

The road hugged the rock wall, occasionally meandering in and out of it, through tunnels beneath dwellings. She recognized the sloping bridge near Kolail's and continued a little farther.

But the farther south she got, the worse the bridges became. Hirka stopped in front of one that had been repaired in the middle using rope that looked like it needed repairing itself. It was only a few steps over to the other side, but she had too much to do to chance death. In any case, it was time to head down to the bottom.

The steps were close by. Hirka kept her staff at the ready and felt her way along the wall. The steps zigzagged their way down through the fog, to the street at the bottom of the crevice.

There were more people here. Enough to make her uneasy. A few rushed past with their faces hidden by hoods. Others walked in groups, having loud, drunken discussions. She tried not to look up. Everyone in Ginnungad knew who she was, even here. Perhaps even more so here, seeing as she seemed to be the symbol of everything they had reason to hate. Dreyri's great hope. Proof they would always reign supreme.

The tavern appeared in the darkness, just as she remembered it from the night she'd arrived. Hirka stopped.

The cliff face towered above her, overshadowing the entrance. Windows and doors climbed upward in the fog, so haphazard that it looked like someone had just chucked them there. Rainwater had run down crooked window ledges and collected at the ends as glittering needles of ice.

Two men walked past and disappeared under the moldering eaves. She heard a door screech on its hinges and slam behind them. There was no sign outside. Not even a teardrop to indicate that fallen were served there. There was probably no need, considering it was largely fallen and houseless living here.

But she knew she was in the right place. This was where she'd seen Kolail nod to the man with a wolf on a leash, and Kolail had smelled of wet dog the night she'd patched him up. She'd bet her staff he was a regular here. Meaning chances were good that other rioters hung out in the same place.

The flaws in her plan suddenly became clearer. As the new darling of the leading houses, what would stop these deadborn from quietly doing away with her? The fallen had already killed and had nothing more to lose . . . What was it Oni had said?

If you bring more than two men who have nothing to lose, then you've only yourself to blame if something goes wrong.

Hirka heard footsteps behind her and tightened her grip on the staff. A skinny fellow walked past and approached the darkened entrance. A low growl stopped him. Hirka gave a start. The wolf launched itself out of the shadows, tugging at its chain as it snapped at the new arrival. The man cursed and sped off in the opposite direction.

The wolf met her gaze, its eyes gray orbs in the darkness. It stared at her for a moment, then retreated into the shadows beneath the eaves. Hirka stepped closer. It didn't move. It hadn't stirred when the two men had gone in earlier, either. What was it trained to sniff out? Drugs? Opa? What would he smell on her?

Human blood and raven blood . . .

The wolf's ears pricked up when she passed, but it didn't growl. Hirka went in through the red door. It slammed behind her. She followed a winding staircase down into a cellar that was divided into booths—small rooms within the main room. Tendrils of smoke escaped through carvings in the partitions. Hanging lamps shone down on tables that were just heavy stone tablets with broken corners. They seemed out of place alongside the beautiful carvings. Hirka got the feeling the tables and the partitions had to have come from different places or different times.

The back wall was decorated with a mural in mother-of-pearl. It depicted a loving couple. Fragile and emotive. Another relic from another time.

There were a handful of Umpiri in each booth. Some of them were drinking. Others smoked long pipes. At least three of them had knives in their belts and teardrops in their foreheads. Men who had nothing more to lose. Not even carrying a weapon could send them farther down the ladder.

Hirka took a breath and summoned her courage. Found a seat at the back, where the bar met the wall. She could sit there without having anyone behind her. She leaned the staff against the wall and rested her arms on the counter. It was too high for her, making it painfully obvious that she was smaller than those who normally sat there. It drew glances from the people in the booths.

She fought off the urge to leave. Reminded herself that the worst of Ginnungad could be the salvation of Ym. In any case, there were clearly people who were worse still. They had a wolf outside to weed them out. She chose to cling to that as a good sign.

Hirka opened her coin purse and pulled out a pound. A British pound. She stared at the coin she'd brought all the way from York. Through the raven rings to this place. Dreysíl. Worlds collided in her hand, and she was the only one who could see it.

Her head grew heavy as she remembered. Father Brody with his I-need-a-wee smile. Stefan who saw death at every turn. He'd have laughed at her now. Come out with one of his bad jokes.

A child of Odin walked into a bar . . .

She remembered Jay and her little sister, who died in the church. In another world that was doomed and mightless.

That one and how many others?

The doubt she had been racked by all evening disappeared. She knew what she had to do. But first she needed something to drink. She dropped the pound coin in her purse and grabbed a different one. One she could use here. It was too much, but she wanted to know what kind of man the guy behind the counter was. Father whispered from Slokna.

Good to know in a new place.

Hirka slid the coin toward him. "I'd like something to drink—is this enough?"

The man behind the counter was organizing plants in drawers. Tobacco, she guessed. He didn't look up, but she'd seen him sneak a glance at her.

"What would you like?" he asked, voice slightly strained.

"Not fermented milk."

He was easy on the eye, but like all Umpiri, in a somewhat scary way. Narrow face, high cheekbones. His black hair was tied at the base of his skull, with a string decorated with animal teeth. He put a glass containing some brown substance in front of her. Hirka took a sip and had to force herself not to grimace.

"What is it?" she asked.

"Not fermented milk."

He left two small coins next to her glass and went back to sorting his plants. Long, stiff blades in various shades of green. He glanced at the door when the wolf started barking again, but nobody came in. Hirka looked around. People spoke in hushed tones in the booths. She saw one of them press two fingers to her throat and whisper to her neighbor.

Dreyri. Blood of the first.

They'd seen her eyes. Seen who she was.

"Are you sure you're in the right place?" the man behind the bar asked, still not looking at her.

Hirka forced a smile. "You know who I am, don't you?"

He nodded, but said no more.

Hirka drained her glass and pushed it away. "You don't like me being here," she said, emboldened by the warmth in her chest.

He paused for a beat before returning to his work. "All are welcome here." She knew that he'd intentionally misunderstood her.

It had gone quiet around them. Hirka continued, a little louder so everyone would hear. "I don't mean here, I mean *here*—in Ginnungad. You want the Might as much as everyone else, but at what cost? Everything staying the way it's always been? You on the bottom, and them on the top . . ."

She heard the door slam. Someone had left. Someone who didn't want to get mixed up in what was happening. She couldn't blame them.

A couple of the patrons did their best to avoid looking at her. The rest stared openly. One of them got up and stood at the other end of the bar, the teardrop gleaming in his forehead.

"Them? Aren't you one of them?"

Hirka wrapped her feet around the stool so she wouldn't give in to the urge to run. "I belong to no one. Unlike you lot, who are basically property." It wasn't entirely true, but she needed a reaction. And a reaction is what she got.

He moved closer. His eyes had black outlines that made him look like a lynx. A blind lynx. The light from the lamps danced across his bald head.

"Do you think we're idiots?"

One of the others from his booth got up. "Skolm . . ."

Hirka didn't give him a chance to interrupt. "Yes, you are idiots. For the first time in a thousand years, you can actually change something. But it won't happen. You're more interested in drinking. And by the time the war is over, it will be too late."

Skolm bared his canines. "It's never too late—"

The man who had stood up grabbed him by the arm. "Skolm, you're talking to *them*!"

Simple words that opened a chasm between them. They had no reason to trust her. She was Dreyri. Someone who slept behind mightglass. Who doled out teardrops. What had she expected?

More people had stepped out of the booths. Some headed for the exit, while others gathered around. Desperation rose inside her. She stood up.

"I'm not here to trick anyone! I don't speak for Dreyri. Or for the houses. They don't know I'm here. Had they known, they'd have hired one of you to dispose of me, so who's taking the bigger risk here? *You* have something on *me*, not the other way around."

Skolm growled. The door crashed open and Kolail entered. The relief she felt was almost embarrassing. He came down the stairs, forced his way past the others, and dragged her toward the exit.

"What do you think you're doing?!"

"I'm telling it like it is!" She raised her voice. They had to hear. Everyone had to hear. "This is the only chance you've got! You can win this fight!"

Kolail tightened his grip on her arm. "Many of these people have lost everything. They know better than to defy Dreyri. *I* know better than to defy Dreyri."

Hirka laughed coolly. "Fear? You're afraid of them?" She tore her arm free. "Then you've just proved them right. There *is* a difference between you and them. None of them would hesitate. So by all means, just sit there," she spat, knowing how much it would irk them.

She went to get her staff as she spoke. "Or keep throwing bottles in the streets. As if *that* will change anything."

Kolail growled, like the wolf. "Don't you realize that you're worse than them now? You came here because you think we're all the same. Fallen are fallen. Houseless are houseless. We probably all think the same, want the same, right? What makes you think everything's so bloody simple? No, nobody here trusts the houses. Or you. But they don't trust each other, either."

"And that's exactly what's holding you down," she answered. But she felt her cheeks flush in embarrassment. He was right. She'd tarred them all with the same brush. Made too many assumptions. But that didn't change anything. She walked halfway up the stairs. Turned and nodded at the man behind the counter. "You can start with him. Him you can trust."

She continued up the stairs and went out into the cold. Stopped outside the door. The wolf looked at her. His tail started wagging as he approached her. He let her scratch him behind the ears while she waited for Kolail to come after her. She knew he would.

The door opened and Kolail emerged. He looked at her like a father would a disobedient child. Dejected and furious.

"You know I'm right, Kolail. It might seem mad, but it's the only chance you've got. I want to help you."

"Help us? You want to pit us against each other to save your own people!"

The wolf growled at him. Hirka pulled him a safe distance away. "I *have* no people, Kolail! I'm speaking for the ravens, for the trees, for the water we drink, and the earth we till. The only side I'm on is the Might's. But you have something else to fight for."

"You? Who are you calling *you*? That lot?" He pointed at the door. "A handful of world-weary men in a tavern?"

Hirka smiled. "A handful of men is enough to spread the word. In a few days there won't be a single fallen or houseless who hasn't heard about this. So what are you going to do, Kolail?"

He laughed, the sheepskin on his shoulder shaking. "Me? You want me to be part of this? You want *me* to join them?"

"No," Hirka answered. "I want you to lead them."

She turned and started to leave. He shouted after her.

"How stupid do you think I am?! As if there aren't enough things to risk life and limb for!"

Hirka shrugged. "Rabbits die."

"You don't even know what that means!"

"No, but I expect you'll tell me one day."

FREE TOWN

Rime caught up with the procession half a day's march from Ravnhov. He got an update from Marrow, who told him the reason they were taking so long was because Kolkagga had needed to hunt for almost thirty people who weren't used to providing for themselves. The Council families were dirty and exhausted, clearly suffering from the fatigue that comes with knowing the journey is almost at an end. Apparently none of them could possibly survive another night under the open sky.

Jarladin and Sigra were putting on brave faces, but each in their own way. It was like the wilderness had sharpened them. Stripped away what was unnecessary until they were more honed versions of themselves. Jarladin was leaning on his calm disposition. He was a big, sturdy ox who could withstand almost anything. Sigra was running on pure spite. Her angular features were grim and focused. She kicked obstacles out of the way and pulled stumbling children back to their feet without a word.

The atmosphere grew increasingly tense the closer they came to Ravnhov. The conversations quieter. How would they be received? It would have to go well. Anything else was unthinkable. Yes, Ravnhov and Mannfalla were old enemies, but they were on the run. Surely no one would turn their back on people on the run? Ymlings who had lost everything they owned?

Rime knew Eirik well enough to know he wouldn't kill anyone, but he wasn't as sure about the rest of the townspeople, so he'd sent Marrow ahead as a scout. It was ironic that Sigra Kleiv was now depending on the people of Ravnhov being nothing like she'd always made them out to be—defiant and foolhardy wild men.

The wind had picked up, throwing pine cones and needles along the narrow path that wound its way between the trees and up the slope. Marrow appeared up ahead. He jerked his head and held up three fingers. Rime nodded. Ravnhov had sent people to meet them.

He rounded a bend and spotted them up on the ridge. Ynge and two women he hadn't met before. All wearing leather armor and carrying bows on their backs. Hair whipping in the wind. They nodded but didn't say a word. Then they turned and led them onward. Rime guessed that Eirik had sent his most diplomatic warriors, which in this case also meant the quietest.

The path joined up with a bigger road, and soon the town wall came into view. A seemingly random collection of rocks of various sizes, with a heavy wooden gate. It opened as they approached. Men stood atop the wall, sneering at Sigra and Jarladin. They brought their hands to their foreheads in a greeting Rime doubted was particularly polite.

Inside the walls, the town was unrecognizable. Open spaces had become camps. Every alley had acquired a makeshift roof with a curtain. Even the stables were being used to shelter people. Clearly the rumor of changes in the Council and a restless army had driven half of Foggard here. Probably far more people than last time. It had come as a shock when Mannfalla and Ravnhov had clashed on the battlefield almost a year ago. It hadn't happened in anyone's lifetime, but now they'd seen war. Now they believed. Now they were afraid.

But that didn't stop them from being curious. They flocked together along the roadside. Stood in the gutters and gaped at the procession of Council folk. Ynge slowed down and waited for Rime. "Tein's never been good at keeping his mouth shut," he mumbled, not sounding that apologetic. On the contrary, the twitching of his lips suggested he was enjoying himself.

It was going to be an interesting afternoon.

People lined the road all the way up to the chieftain's household. Old and young, women and men. Some had abandoned their work and still had flour in their hair or dirt on their hands. A blacksmith stood in a leather apron, holding his hammer. Rime could see people running ahead of them and into the buildings to announce they were coming. Mannfalla was coming. The Council had fled to Ravnhov.

Few of them said anything. Some sneered and folded their arms over their chests. A couple others whooped and whistled, though it didn't sound like their hearts were really in it. Rime had a feeling that when it came down to it, it was frightening for them to see Mannfalla's unravelling.

Jarladin did his best to appear unaffected, chatting with his family as they walked the final stretch, pretending not to notice. Sigra lifted her chin and tensed her jaw. The shame and humiliation were hard for her to bear. Rime couldn't help but be impressed that she'd defied Darkdaggar despite everything. She must have known what it would mean, but all the same, she'd done what she thought was right. Maybe he had more to learn from Sigra than he'd once thought.

They crossed the yellow bridge over the ravine, approaching the chieftain's household. Blue flags with golden crowns fluttered in the wind. The courtyard was teeming with people. They came from homes and storehouses, from stalls and henhouses. Eirik came to meet them with Tein close on his heels. Tein was clearly delighted at the turn of events.

Rime held out a hand to Eirik. The chieftain snorted and pulled him close, like a son, patting him on the back. Then he pushed him back again, gazing at him with twinkling blue eyes surrounded by a gray-streaked haystack of hair.

"So . . ." Eirik said, turning his gaze on Sigra. He signaled to servants in blue, who started relieving the visitors of bags, bundles, and raven cages. Now that they'd arrived, they looked more like refugees than ever. Tired and grubby, with windswept hair. Some visibly anxious. Rime heard Sylja whisper to a servant girl that she didn't really have anything to do with the Council. That she was from Elveroa. From Foggard. It sounded desperate, all things considered.

Eirik took a step closer. "We're a bit short on space . . ."

The only response came from the wind whistling between the branches of the big spruce in the yard where Rime had once fought Tein. Rime met Tein's gaze. He clearly hadn't forgotten.

Sigra nodded at Eirik, trying to scrape together a dignity she'd lost the moment she walked through the gate. If Sigra had had her way, there wouldn't have been a Ravnhov to run to. A fact that clearly wasn't lost on her, or anyone else who was present.

The councillor let her gaze sweep the yard. Then it faltered for a moment. Rime knew why. Ramoja's dark face had appeared in the crowd. She'd gotten safely out of Mannfalla, but he doubted Sigra had expected to find her here.

Eirik shrugged his sloped shoulders. "We've made room for you in the boathouse. I assume you know where that is?"

Sigra looked at him. "I've never been here before."

Chuckles rippled through the crowd. "Enough!" Eirik shouted. "Leave us." People reluctantly withdrew, throwing long glances as they went.

Eirik walked over to Sigra and put a huge hand on her shoulder. "First time, huh? Then let me explain. You follow the path up behind the great hall and keep right. Then you'll come to a boat-shaped building. The same building where you sent Kolkagga to kill me. Does that jog your memory?"

Sigra's gaze faltered. She was a strong, thickset woman, but now

291

she'd had her feet knocked out from under her by words alone. By Eirik's mere presence. Rime watched them, transfixed. The chieftain and the councillor who still bore the sign of the Seer on her forehead. If anyone had told Rime a year ago that this day would come, he'd have laughed.

Sigra was speechless. Jarladin came to her rescue.

"We all have mistakes to answer for, Eirik. I'm Jarladin An-Sarin." He held out a hand. Eirik took it.

"So, Jarladin . . . When the Council decided to take me out, what did you say? Were you for or against?"

"Against," Jarladin replied. "But as far as I can see, that's irrelevant now."

Eirik nodded. He looked at Sigra. "And you? Sigra Kleiv. For or against, hm?"

Sigra lifted her chin again. "For. And were circumstances different, I'd do it again."

Eirik hummed into his beard. It might have been a grumble. It might have been a chuckle. It was hard to tell.

"Well, Sigra . . . You're as discerning as a doorknob. But at least you're not a coward or a liar. Welcome to Ravnhov."

Unngonna swept across the yard with keys jingling at her waist and her hair scraped into a bun. She puffed her way over to them. "No one's going to bed before they've bathed. Come on!" She ushered both children and adults away.

Rime and Eirik stood watching them. Eirik tugged at his beard. "What do you think? Too much?"

Rime smiled and shook his head. "Just what I would have done."

Eirik laughed and patted him on the shoulder. Then his gaze turned solemn again. Encumbered by Rime's loss. A thousand dead Kolkagga that neither of them mentioned.

Rime lowered his gaze. "Have you secured the provisions against sabotage?"

Eirik nodded. "As best we can without building walls around the fields."

"And the jarls? Have you talked to them?"

"Some are with us, but not all."

"Good . . ." Rime looked away again. It was good that they had allies. Good that they could build a new army. But deep down he felt cold. Who was he building an army for? Himself? Ravnhov?

Or Graal?

The wind tore at the spruce, making the branches shake. Then the ravens came home. A shrieking blackness blanketing the sky.

THE FROST GARDEN

Jór kept stopping, as if he wanted Hirka next to him, but she felt more comfortable walking behind him. She could have blamed it on all the servants flanking them, but that wouldn't even have been half the truth.

Her fear had been roused as soon as the invitation arrived. The House of Hod wanted her to pay them a visit, and apparently it was urgent. Why? Hirka hadn't been able to think of a single reason that boded well.

She'd wanted to decline, but Raun and Uhere had made it clear that wasn't an option. So Jór had come to collect her, on foot this time, and with every step they drew closer to the house. It was like a small city in itself, situated just inside the hollowed-out crater wall.

Jór was impatient. Tense. She knew something was wrong, despite how charming he was being. Had he seen her with the fallen? Had someone blabbed?

Over and over again she thought about her visit to the tavern near the south gate. Who'd been there? Anyone who might have snitched on her? Had she passed anyone on the way?

They can't hurt me. They need me.

For once she found comfort in being a symbol. But there were limits, she knew that. Symbol or not, if they knew what she'd done, no one could save her. She'd end up in tiny pieces in a bucket. Scattered on Crier's Rock for the ravens to eat. Not exactly the raven-birth she'd hoped for . . .

Jór continued ahead at a brisk pace. The wind toyed with his corn-yellow hair. His long jacket billowed around his thighs, like a black sail. It was tight at his sides, accentuating his narrow waist. His arms were bare.

They followed a tunnel that curved into the crater wall and emerged inside the rock—in a cave big enough that half of Eisvaldr could have fit inside.

They approached the House of Hod from the back. Hirka felt ill. She blamed it on the raven blood. That morning was the first time she'd been able to drink it without bringing it back up. It was a start, the Seer had said before giving her more. It was disgusting. Excruciating. Frightening. But it wasn't for nothing. She had a job to do, so if Jór thought she'd just lie down and die, he'd have to think again.

"What is it that's so urgent?" Her voice was almost lost in the cave.

He was waiting for her again. "It's gotten warmer, don't you think?" His answer was just an elegant way of avoiding the question. He glanced at the servants flanking them. "We've received a shipment of tea from Ferenval. I think you'll enjoy it."

His hand brushed hers. A signal, she guessed. She didn't ask anything more.

Heavy iron doors opened as they approached, as if someone had been waiting for them. They went in together and the doors closed behind them. The sound sent a shudder through her. She was trapped in the House of Hod.

Jór dismissed the servants and continued along a black corridor. It was lit up by lamps on either side. Living lamps, she realized. The same type of birds she'd received as a gift. They flitted around in the cages and gave off a silvery glow. It was heartrending to see so many of them.

Jór hurried ahead, as if it were a matter of life and death. The sound of his footsteps on the stone floor bounced off the walls. She darted after him. The corridor led into a bright and chilly room. A wonderful winter garden.

Jór stopped. "I call him Kurly," he said, nodding at a wall of ice. Hirka stared at the glistening surface. It was sweating, as if tired of keeping the secret inside. An animal. A spiral-shaped animal, bigger than her. Frozen in a distant past. Tentacles snaked toward them through an opening, as if trying to grab them. An illusion. The animal hadn't moved in gods only knew how long. Size notwithstanding, it was impossible not to see the similarities between it and the spiral-shaped stones she had in her purse. One a gift from Hlosnian, and the other a gift from a raven.

Different worlds. Same shape.

Hirka continued to stare. She felt like an ant by comparison. She held her hand to the ice. "Kurly . . ."

"Because he's curly . . . Get it?" Jór raised a hand to signal to someone out of Hirka's eyeline. Probably servants standing in the gallery above them. Then he went over to a seating area by a tall window overlooking the crater. He pulled out a chair and looked at her.

He wanted to sit down. So it was serious.

Hirka went over to him. Leaned her staff against the wall and sat down. Both the table and the chairs were made of wrought iron in a webbed pattern.

A servant in a long tunic came in with a tray and put it on the table. A pot and two bowl-shaped cups. Then he disappeared as quickly as he'd come.

Jór filled one of the cups and handed it to her.

Hirka took it. "Tea?"

He nodded and smiled, exposing his canines. But he was unable to hide his apprehension. Hirka warmed her hands on the cup.

Tea. He'd invited her to drink tea. And to show her one of the most beautiful places she'd ever seen. She'd thought he was going to threaten her. Hurt her. He was a deadborn. His muscles were stronger and more defined than any ymling's. His eyes were white and his canines pronounced, but she was the monster here. She was the one planning to pit blindling against blindling. She was the one drinking raven blood to the point of vomiting. Charged with an undertaking that was simply too much for her.

She felt her embarrassment rising. She sipped her tea to force it back down. Listened to the rumbling of the ice. Jór looked at her.

"Did you hear what the war cabinet decided yesterday?" he asked.

Hirka swallowed both the tea and her annoyance that he had brought her here to talk about war. It felt like sacrilege. Bloodthirst had no place here. She didn't answer.

"We'll pass through the gateways on the first day of autumn."

Hirka squeezed her cup. Tried to count the days on her fingers without being too obvious. She came to forty-three. Forty-three days. Far too few. In less than six weeks, nothing would ever be the same again. Jór continued talking. A monologue that wasn't getting through to her. All she could think about was who would live and who would die in forty-three days.

Then one word did make it through. She looked at him.

"What was that?"

Jór refilled her cup. "They want to wait for the ninth house," he repeated.

"No. Before that."

"Nifel? They'll start the migration in twelve days."

Hirka felt her lip quiver. She tried to smile. "My umǫni is still a little wobbly," she apologized.

They'd launch the invasion from the ruined city of Nifel. Of course. That was where she'd come through, and as far as she knew, there were no other working stone circles in Dreysíl. But twelve days . . .

She'd have to hurry. How would she convince the fallen to rise up in only twelve days?

Jór got up, seemingly already bored of sitting down. He stretched like a cat and laced his claws around the back of his neck. Unmoved by what he'd said. Unaware of the knot that had formed in her stomach. Or did he know? Was that why they were there? So he could see how she'd react? There had to be a reason.

Then he crouched down in front of her. His black jacket spread across the floor behind him.

"The House of Hod is powerful, Hirka. The most powerful of all." He lowered his head but continued to look up at her. His smile told her that he believed every word he was saying. A new unease gnawed at her. Where was he going with this?

He continued. "But that doesn't mean other houses won't exploit the coming war. Attempts to shift the balance of power are not inconceivable, and the houses that have been promoted most recently are most vulnerable. Houses like Modrasme's. But you have to remember there are other ways to strengthen both our houses."

"What ways?" Her voice was thick. She was afraid she already knew the answer.

"A union."

The knot in her stomach sank like a stone. All the talk of how many days they had left. This visit. She understood.

"You and me. Before the war . . ." she whispered, staring at the man crouched before her. He gave her a dazzling smile, as if she'd just been offered an extraordinary gift. A gift no one in this world would turn down.

"I know what you're thinking," he said. "You're wondering what the balance of power would be in such a union."

Hirka huffed out a laugh. He had no idea what she was thinking. But he continued talking like he did. "You won't need to leave your family. We envisage a complete unification of the houses. You, Raun, Uhere, Modrasme, Vana . . . Everyone, Hirka. The House of Hod and the House of Modrasme, but under Graal's name. We like *the House of Hod and Graal*. We thought you might, too."

"We? How many people are asking for my hand?"

Jór laughed. His laugh was warmer than most Umpiri. Less animalistic. He stood up, and she was suddenly aware of just how tall he was. How broad his shoulders were. What would happen if she said no? He wasn't in love with her, so he wouldn't be hurt. Or angry. But what would the House of Hod do? This wasn't a choice he'd made on his own.

Jór pulled her to her feet. "Just me, but I'm amazed that I'm the first."

Hirka wanted to feel flattered, but she knew all too well what she was in the eyes of Umpiri. This had nothing to do with her. The war would change many things, and they wanted to secure the position of their house. Get closer to Graal and the feat he'd accomplished: producing an heir in exile.

"Let's go to the fights together tomorrow," he said, gazing at her. "Would you like that?"

A question. The first one he'd asked, she realized. Everything else had been more of a speech than an inquiry.

Jór frowned, sensing her uncertainty. "I wouldn't have asked if I didn't care for you," he said. Hirka didn't know whether to laugh or to cry. Was this a declaration of love? Was that passion in his eyes?

She thought back to the red pulsating room in York where she'd kissed Rime. His lips against hers. The hunger. The feeling of slipping into a madness she'd never known before. And now she was supposed to marry someone else? For simplicity's sake? For the stability they imagined she could offer a house?

She was ready to burst with all the secrets she couldn't reveal. She couldn't tell Jór he'd asked for the hand of someone who'd already betrayed him. Someone who wanted to divide his people and let them kill each other on the battlefields of Mannfalla.

For the sake of everyone. For the Might.

Hirka averted her gaze. Looked at Kurly, frozen in the ice. Long since dead. Long since free of thoughts. If only they could swap places.

Suddenly something occurred to her. Time. Umpiri had more than enough of it. So why this haste? This unease? There was more to this than a thirst for power.

She looked at Jór. "Why now?"

Jór lowered his gaze. "Come with me," he said.

She did as he asked. Followed him up a set of stairs and along yet another corridor. There was a tall red door at the far end. Hirka could hear servants whispering, but she couldn't see them. There were too many passages and alcoves to keep track of.

Jór knocked on the red door. "It's me. Hirka's here." Then he opened it and stood there for a moment, as if he couldn't bring himself to go in. He motioned for Hirka to enter. "She wants to talk to you," he said, his voice faltering.

Hirka went in.

It was a bedroom of pure gold. Golden tiles covered almost every surface. Ceiling, floor, and walls. The effect was so intense it was almost nauseating. A swinging bed hung at the end of the room. That too was gold, and considerably bigger than her own.

Hirka walked along the only wall with windows. Curved might-glass with a view of the roughly hewn cave. Hod stood with her back to Hirka, looking out.

"They say you're a seer. That you heal," Hod said without turning.

Hirka felt like she was on shaky ground. "That's what I do where I'm from."

"Are you good at it?"

It was a question that could only come from someone who had everything. Someone used to getting whatever she needed. It was also an impossible question to answer.

Hirka looked up at the ceiling, as if the right words might be hanging there. "Some live, some die. That will never change. Is there anything I can . . ." She swallowed the word *help*. "Is there anything you want me to do?"

Hod turned. "I want you to do something about this."

Hirka looked at her. No wounds. No marks. And she stood tall, seemingly in no pain. Wearing a green dress that emphasized just how healthy she was.

"What's the matter?"

"Look at me!"

Hirka scanned her narrow face. She had strange features. Her eyes were more sharply angled than any ymling would deem natural, but it was impossible to call her anything but beautiful. She certainly didn't look sick. In fact, she looked healthier than most blindlings. Perhaps it was just the way the light was reflecting off the golden walls and making her skin glow.

Hirka moved closer. There was something she couldn't put her finger on. Hod seemed older than before. She had lines around her eyes and on her neck. Not exactly normal for blindlings, but nothing Hirka hadn't seen before. Still, she had a sneaking suspicion that that was exactly the problem. Hod was aging.

Hirka ran through all the rules in her head. What should she say? She couldn't exactly confirm that the woman had aged.

"I suppose that's . . . natural?" she tried.

Hod came right up to her. Pointed at her own face. "This? You call this natural? It's a disease! A plague! You have to do something!"

"Do something? It's age. Everyone gets old . . ."

Hod's eyes turned inky black. "Not us! Not Dreyri!"

Hirka took a step back. "But . . . not even Dreyri can live forever, can you?"

Hod slumped into a chair. She suddenly seemed small. Her arms thin. As if they too were diminishing.

"None of our healers have a cure," she said quietly. "And you don't either, it seems. I'll be gone before winter."

Hirka shut her eyes. Remembered what she'd learned from Oni. Once Umpiri started to age, death came quickly. That was one of the reasons she hadn't seen a single old person since she'd arrived. The woman standing before her had probably been around longer than Mannfalla, and now she had only months remaining. The House of Hod would lose its namesake.

That was why they wanted to unite the houses. And why they were rushing into the war. False and trivial matters. But Hod's despair was sincere and heartfelt.

Hirka crouched down in front of her. Searched for the words. "When I first heard how old Umpiri could get, I thought death would have to come as a relief. But everything I've seen since I came here makes me realize how wrong I was. The longer you live, the more you cling to life. Living longer than everything else has made you feel omnipotent. Like you have the right to shape. To rule. Control everything you see. But this is the one thing nobody can control, Hod. Not even Dreyri."

Hod's eyes were shining like black glass, making them look fragile. "Leave me," she said, pointing at the door.

Hirka got up to leave. She'd helped so many people in her life, but even where she hadn't been able to help, she'd seldom felt so powerless. Fortunately she was done with compassion. She'd never again allow the suffering of others to hold her back.

She retreated a few steps before turning away from Hod.

"Jór thinks it's because of the unrest," Hod said behind her. "That it's become too much. That age has come for me because of you. Graal's daughter. Naiell's heart. The open gateways . . ."

Hirka headed for the door. "Death doesn't need a reason. There's nothing you could have done differently." She turned to look at Hod. "Rabbits die." And finally she understood what it meant.

Hod looked up at her. "Rabbits?"

Hirka smiled wistfully. "Don't ask."

She opened the door and went out. Paused. She poked her head back inside. "You ought to celebrate, Hod. There are so many things that could have killed you before you got a single wrinkle. Accidents, illness, enemies . . . Getting old means you're stronger than all of them."

She closed the door and left.

Jór scuttled over. "Can you help her?"

Hirka sighed. "No," she answered. "Only she can do that."

AN ENEMY'S ADVICE

Hirka sat on a bench in the corner and listened to the soundscape of agitation. Skerri snapped at the servants about clothes laid out in the wrong place. Uhere scolded Vana and her boyfriend, Moinus, because they weren't ready yet. Raun paced back and forth by the window, doing a poor job of hiding his nerves. Modrasme herself sat like a ghost amid a pile of animal pelts and cushions, a study in low expectations.

Hirka didn't know what to expect. She'd only seen the fights from a distance. Some sort of brutal festival? In any case, she found herself hoping to see Skerri on the receiving end of a blow she wouldn't soon forget.

Floating lanterns had started to fall outside. They were being thrown from streets and windows. Hundreds of them. Flickering lights sinking down into the darkness, only to disappear at the bottom of the crater.

Vana and Moinus went out onto the balcony. Lit a lantern and let it sail down as they kissed. Hirka averted her gaze. Would she ever be able to kiss a deadborn? Surely their canines got in the way?

Jór's proposal had dredged up feelings she'd thought she'd put behind her. A fear of the unknown. A need to keep her distance from Umpiri, even her own family. She'd spent the past day remembering old stories she'd grown up with. Everything people had said about the blind. It made her feel ashamed and angry. She herself had been hunted for being what she was. Shouldn't she, of all people, see things more clearly? See past teeth and claws?

She probably wouldn't have any choice. In only a few days, the first groups would set out for Nifel. For the raven ring. And there was nothing she could do to stop them. The House of Hod would push to unite the houses as soon as possible.

Times like these were the worst. When her rage simmered down, and she realized how flimsy the straws she was clutching at were. The scant hope that all the death to come wouldn't be in vain. That it would give the Might enough sustenance to create new channels. And to achieve that, she would have to be ravenborn in Ym. Learn to bind.

Her, the girl who had nothing more than constant nausea and the taste of blood in her mouth. It was sheer madness.

That was why she needed to come up with alternatives. What she would do if she failed. But the alternatives were slipping away from her, too. Everything seemed to indicate that the beak would be the death of Rime—if he and every last ymling didn't fall on the battlefield first, that was.

Neither the fallen nor the houseless would help her. No one would rush to her aid and give her reason to hope that Ym would be able to defend itself. On the contrary, she'd probably made bad worse. The streets had been quiet as Slokna since she'd made a fool of herself in the tavern. She'd probably put an end to what little insurrection there had been. She'd made them skeptical. Scared them into submission. And sentenced Ym to death. In a few centuries, the deadborn would scare their children with stories of the tailed ones who'd once walked among them.

No!

Hirka got up and left the others. She went out into the corridor and stopped outside Urd's door. What was it he'd said?

You need to use people to survive in a place like this.

Hirka unbolted the door and went in.

Urd was standing with his back to her, watching the lanterns falling outside his window. Soft points of light in black night. He turned to look at her and his shoulders relaxed, presumably because she wasn't Skerri. He gestured to the bench. An invitation to sit. She stayed standing.

"You're a monster," she said.

His face betrayed no reaction. She continued. "You're a liar. A murderer. You manipulate people into doing what you want. Use them to your own ends."

A twitch of his lips hinted at a smile, but it disappeared too quickly for her to be sure. He sat down on the bench. "So you need my help?" he asked hoarsely. Hirka didn't reply. The admission would have been too painful.

The scar on his throat stood out in the dark. Pale and shaped like a half moon. He seemed to weigh his words before speaking again.

"Hirka, I'm living at your mercy here. Solely because you want it that way. I owe you my life. If there's something you need, tell me."

Hirka hesitated for a moment. But he had no reason to lie, and everything to gain from helping her. She took a step closer.

"I need to convince someone to fight for me."

"Mhm . . ." Urd crossed one leg over the other. It made his black robe look even more like a sack. Visual confirmation of how important it had been for Umpiri to humiliate him.

He patted the space next to him on the bench. "Please." He was so polite about it that she'd have bitten him, had she been blessed with blindling canines. Instead, she sat down.

Urd looked her over. "It's unbelievable," he said.

"What is?"

"That you're the same girl."

Hirka's eyes narrowed, as if to warn him she wasn't easily fooled. She knew who he was.

"Who do you want to fight for you?" he asked.

"You don't need to know that."

He raised an eyebrow and nodded, as if to say that was fair enough. "Would they be risking anything in doing so?"

Hirka hesitated. "Yes . . . but they'd also be risking something if they didn't."

"Ah! So they have something to gain from helping you. Is that what you're saying?"

"It could give them everything. Or leave them with nothing."

It was true. The same applied to her, and it made her feel vulnerable. Sharing something that meant so much, with *him* . . . It felt unnatural. Abhorrent. But Urd wasn't the same anymore, either. Neither of them were.

Urd stared out the window. The lanterns were reflected in his eyes. Eyes like her own. The only other pair in this world. He dragged his hands over his face and slumped slightly, as if suddenly tired.

"If you'd asked me a year ago, I'd have told you to do what I did. I'd have asked you to find out what they're hiding. What they want. *Who* they want. Everything you could use to make them your allies. But that would make you like *me*, wouldn't it? And right now it seems the gods prefer your way of doing things. Not mine."

Hirka measured his words but found nothing false in them. He meant what he was saying. He'd lost so much of himself that he didn't even believe in his way of doing things anymore.

"So you can't help me?"

He straightened up again. "Well, you seem to have a talent for getting people to fight for you, so no, I doubt I can, incredible as that sounds. But I will say one thing: a promise holds a lot more weight if you prove you can keep it."

That sounded right. Clever, even. But it was impossible. Hirka bit her lip. "What if it can't be done?"

He looked away, amusement playing at the corners of his mouth as he enjoyed some private joke. "Most things can be done. If not entirely, then in part. Give them a taste of what they want. Just a morsel. Enough that they'll follow you to get more."

He scratched the scar on his forehead. "You know, all you need to do is give people space to show who they are."

Hirka looked up. The lanterns outside were now accompanied by shouts that echoed along the curved walls of the crater.

Give them space to show who they are.

It was genius. The words turned to action in her mind. A plan. Risky. Difficult. An awful lot of pieces would have to fall into place. But it was possible. And it was all she had.

Hope blossomed in her chest, spreading until her fingers tingled. She smiled widely. Felt the corners of her mouth ache, as if it had been far too long.

She squeezed the back of his neck. "You're a genius," she said. "You're a . . ." She tried to remember the word Stefan used to use. "You're a bastard!"

The sudden warmth seemed to disconcert him. He gave her an awkward smile, but mostly he just looked anxious.

Her name boomed along the corridor. Skerri was calling her. It was time to go. She would spend the evening watching grown men and women bash their staffs together. And all in the company of Jór. A deadborn who didn't love her but nevertheless wanted to be her husband.

She got up to leave.

"Hirka . . ." Urd lifted his chin, as if trying to salvage his dignity. "What will become of me? When this war starts?"

She'd thought about that. Often. Urd was like the caged birds. The living lamps. She couldn't let him go without risking his life. But she couldn't keep him, either. He would have to be part of the plan.

"Urd, I'm going home in a few days. To Ym. Would you like to come?"

His eyes widened. He stared at her as if it were a cruel joke.

"Isn't that what you want?" she asked.

He took a deep breath, then exhaled as if he hadn't breathed properly in a long time. "Right now I can't think of anything I want apart from calm. To be left in peace."

Hirka looked at him. "Well then, Urd Vanfarinn, it seems we finally understand each other."

ONE OF THEM

Hirka walked as tall as she could next to Jór. Most of the House of Hod was with them: his older sister, Ganei, and her husband, along with someone Hirka thought was their daughter. It was hard to keep track of families where nobody looked much older than anyone else.

Hod was conspicuous by her absence, and Hirka guessed she would be for some time. Perhaps until she was no more.

They were surrounded by servants. Hirka was conscious of the two walking closest to her. Fallen with teardrops in their foreheads. Insurance, in case it became necessary to take a life.

Let those who've done it before do it again.

She hadn't seen these two before, but they kept throwing sidelong glances at her. Was it because of who she was, or had word spread? Would they turn and tell Jór that he was walking side by side with a traitor? Someone who'd tried to incite insurrection?

Her body tensed. It was hard to shake off such thoughts. But she had to try. It was going to be a long night.

The fights were important to everyone but her. To Umpiri, they were a celebration of all the good that was to come. And a way of gauging the strength of the newly promoted families. To her, they were an unwelcome delay. A waste of time when she had none to lose. Her conversation with Urd had made it very clear what she had to do. Certainty bred urgency.

People moved in packs along the roads that circled down into the crater. She'd never been all the way to the bottom before. The crater was narrower here. So much so that she could see the people on the other side, packed into recesses and onto benches and ledges. All depending on which spot they'd paid for.

The House of Hod had a spot reserved. The first of a series of balcony-like structures that were carved into the crater wall. Hirka followed Jór inside. She was about to sit on a bench but stopped herself. The benches were for the servants, of course. She was Dreyri. Dreyri stood.

She looked up. She could see Crier's Rock jutting out far above. She'd stood there when they'd presented her. Feeling like she was being swallowed. Like she was staring up a throat that opened far, far above, where the northern lights danced across the sky, hinting at a vastness and truth she would never reach. She was trapped here, among small things. Ridiculous things. People who were about to pummel each other with staffs.

She looked down and was surprised to see that the bottom of the crater was filled with water. But perhaps that wasn't so strange considering the sea wasn't far away. In the middle of the water there was a platform. Asymmetrical, as if it had formed naturally. But its surface was level and flat, connected to the crater walls by several rope bridges.

Three rings were marked out on the platform. There was a man wheeling a cart around on it, picking up lanterns, some of them still burning. He stomped them out, then threw them in the cart. There was something touching about how he didn't just chuck them straight in the water.

A group of battle-ready Umpiri appeared on one of the rope bridges, and the crowd started to shout. The lantern collector picked up the pace, scooping up the last few and disappearing across a rope bridge just below her.

Jór leaned toward her. "My money's on Grid. He's been unbeatable these last few months." His voice revealed neither the sorrow nor the fear she knew he felt for his mother. But that was what Dreyri did best. Hid their feelings.

Hirka spotted Grid's fair hair on the platform. He had his staff resting across his shoulders. Relaxed. Full of confidence. Not far from him was Raun, with his bloodred hair in a knot. He was there purely as a trainer. Skerri was there, too, surrounded by women and men who were all sizing her up.

A shout echoed through the crater and the fighting commenced. Two in each ring, going at it tooth and nail. Staffs colliding in a morbid rhythm. Grid had no sooner knocked out his first opponent than a new one was sent in. He too was knocked back, driven out of the ring by a kick to the chest that Hirka could hear from where she was. She felt ill.

And this is what Ym will have to go up against?

She looked away. Straight into Kolail's eyes.

He was standing in the crowd a little way below them, pretending he hadn't seen her. She had to talk to him!

"I'll be right back," she said to Jór and left the balcony space before he had a chance to ask. An insult, she remembered far too late. Not only had she not asked for permission, she'd turned her back on him. She hesitated. Should she go back? No, this was more important. She had to hope he'd cut her some slack under the circumstances.

Slack . . . Does that sound like Umpiri?

Hirka pushed her way through the shouting crowd. Sweat smelled like sweat, no matter what world you were in. She found Kolail and dragged him away. He tore himself free but reluctantly followed her. She found a little breathing space under some steps that climbed the crater wall. Everyone else was pushing forward to get as close to the action as possible.

Kolail shook his head. His gray hair hung in his eyes. "Really? Here? You think this is a good place to talk?"

Hirka glanced around. "The more noise, the less anyone will hear," she answered. "What have they been saying?"

He barked out a laugh. "If you were just planning on making my life a nightmare, you might as well have not bothered saving it."

Hirka made no attempt to hide her irritation. "It's never too late . . . What have they been saying?"

He looked at her. "What *haven't* they been saying? That would be easier to answer. I haven't had a moment's peace since you decided to start lighting random fires! They're saying you're a traitor. A trap. A savior. The only thing they can agree on is the fact that they don't agree. What did you expect?"

Hirka smiled. "Exactly that."

"They won't go to war for you, Hirka. They won't turn against their own just so you can save a few ymlings."

"You mean you're afraid?"

Black flooded his gaze. He tugged at his jacket. "I mean we have everything to lose and nothing to gain."

She leaned closer, a fire burning in her eyes. "What if I were to give you victory in advance, and then you can choose what you want to do?"

Kolail frowned warily. She continued before he could interrupt. "I can take you to the Might. To Ym. And I can do it before they set off, Kolail. Do you understand what I'm saying? You don't need to promise you'll fight. You don't need to risk anything at all. All you need to do is get through the gateways and enjoy yourselves. And then when the rest come, you can do what you want. Fight for them, fight for yourselves, or run off into the woods. It's up to you."

He rubbed his chin. He was tempted. She could almost smell it. He saw a new possibility, just as she had done. She drove the point home. "It can be done, but it has to happen before the first group leaves for Nifel. We won't get any of you through the gateways if the city is full of people. Time is running out."

He hesitated. "They'll never let you leave."

"Leave that to me," she answered, sounding more convinced than she felt.

He growled like a wolf. "You're planning to kill us all!"

"I'm planning to let you kill *each other*!"

The truth came so easily. Unleashed by a simmering rage. She took a deep breath.

"Listen, Kolail . . . Do we have the same aims, you and I? No, not by a long shot. You want to be rid of the teardrops in your foreheads and bring down the system that put them there. I want to heal the Might. This way, we both have a chance at success."

He glanced around, afraid someone might see them together.

"You're pitting Umpiri against Umpiri, brother against brother. You'd have us all die to save your own people. To strengthen the Might. To get what *you* want."

She crossed her arms, assuming that would be confirmation enough.

He stared at her. "And they say you're not Dreyri . . ."

"Well, rabbits die," she answered. "And I know what that means now."

Hirka caught a movement out of the corner of her eye. Jór. Her blood ran cold. Time felt like it was standing still. He couldn't see them like this. Couldn't suspect trouble. Hirka struck Kolail with the flat of her hand. He stumbled back. Grabbed his cheek.

"When I tell you to do something, you do it," she said. "You don't ask questions, Keskolail."

His lips twitched. Then he backed away and disappeared up the steps. Jór watched him go. Hirka rested her hand on his arm. "Sorry, Jór. I asked him to get me something to drink, but he has difficulty understanding the simplest of things."

Jór laughed. "He's not stupid; he's just stubborn. He's always taken more liberties than most fallen, but perhaps that's not so strange."

"Oh? How so?" Hirka tried to hide just how curious she was.

Jór leaned toward her, as if they'd always shared secrets. "He was made one of the fallen during the war, it's said. For killing a man who set fire to a tent. Keskolail saved Skerri's skin, and he's had ideas above his station ever since."

Hirka glanced back at Kolail, but he was long gone. So he hadn't been lying the night she'd pulled glass out of him. He'd been in a daze, but he'd spoken the truth. He was fallen because he'd saved the wrong person.

And she's never forgiven him.

Hirka shut her eyes. The sound of staffs and shouts grew until it felt like it was coming from inside her. Strange and animalistic. She expected to feel a fire in her chest. Anger at such cruel injustice. But she felt nothing.

Finally she'd grown accustomed to things here. Finally she'd stopped letting them shock her. It was a victory that smacked of defeat.

THE AGREEMENT

Rime walked along the bottom of the ravine. The air was close and the vegetation lush, though the night drained it of color. The ravens sat huddled in the trees, dark shadows puffing out their feathers. Every now and then they took flight to find a new perch. He had a feeling he was the one making them uneasy. Then again, he made everyone uneasy these days.

He approached the cliff edge where the ravine opened onto Blindból, sat down on a rock, and took out the bottle. It was black in his palm. In the darkness it looked like someone had chopped his fingers off. Maybe that wasn't far from the truth.

His life revolved around a bottle of blood. Around appeasing a dead beak. It was sick. Perverse. He hated it. And he hated that he had only himself to blame.

The urge came, as it always did, to pour the blood out onto the ground. Dispose of it. Rid himself of the option of responding. Then the choice would no longer be his when Graal called on him. But what would it cost? More than pain. More than death. Graal was his only link to Hirka. Severing it would be abandoning her to an unknown fate. To Graal's dubious mercy.

Then there was the fact that Ravnhov and Kolkagga needed him. At least as long as he was on their side. As long as Graal *let* him . . .

No. He had to keep his composure. Maintain an illusion of

control. And he had to know exactly how painful it could get. Better now than later.

Rime drew on the Might and dripped blood onto his tongue. It soothed his throat, giving a momentary sense of satisfaction, as if the beak were rewarding him for his compliance. He'd heard that opa did the same. Drugs that drove men to abuse. How much of himself would he lose?

The beak came to life in his throat.

"I've been thinking about you, Rime. Are we friends again?" His voice sounded genuine and warm. Devoid of sarcasm. Strange coming from the man who had Rime's life in his hands.

Rime suppressed a laugh. "Well, we're certainly not lovers."

A wave of sadness washed over him. A fleeting emotion that wasn't his own.

"I'd planned to contact you soon, in any case," Graal said. He was back in control. Exerting his cool dominance. "Mannfalla has sent a few hundred men north, and I'd hoped you might be able to shine a little light on the situation. Where are they going?"

Rime hesitated. He knew about the troops, and chances were it was part of a deal with Meredir Beig. The eleven kingdoms were buying and selling friends like animal pelts these days. He assumed Graal had long since come to the same conclusion. This was a test.

"If I knew where they were going, I wouldn't be sitting here gabbing to you," Rime replied. He steeled himself through a charged silence.

"Why?" Graal eventually asked. "Why would you lie about something so inconsequential? Do we not have the same aim? Both you and I want to weaken Darkdaggar's hold."

"If we both have the same aim, what makes you think I'm lying?" Rime stared into the darkness as if Graal were sitting in front of him.

"Because you're not asking!" The outburst tore at Rime's throat. "If you didn't know, you'd ask. How many men? When did they leave Mannfalla? Your lack of interest can only mean you already know, so why would you—"

He cut himself off. He had said too much. Rime felt Graal's anger turn to wonderment. Then, most dangerous of all, to understanding.

"You're training yourself . . ." he whispered. "You're building up your tolerance. Your resistance to the pain."

Rime picked up a stick from the ground, knowing he would need something to bite down on. Knowing the suffering was coming. He squeezed his eyes shut.

Come on. Come on.

It came, slicing through him like steel. The beak pushed against the inside of his throat with such force that it pitched him forward. Sent icy jolts through his head. All thoughts of biting down abandoned him. All thoughts of resistance. Rime buried his face in the moss. Inched along on his elbows. Swallowed blood. He reached the cliff edge and stared down into the abyss. The fall that might save him.

His body suddenly went numb. The pain stopped, leaving a sweet, sweet emptiness. His arms and legs refused to cooperate. Then the realization hit him, adding to the torment. The beak wouldn't let him die. It could smell how tempted he was, and it was stopping him. Panic made his heart race. It pounded against the ground under him.

Rime screamed soundlessly into the earth. Tasting soil. Tasting blood. He ran out of air.

Then his freedom was returned to him. He could move. He flipped over onto his back, swords digging into his spine. He lay there, panting, staring up at the top of the ravine. A gash in the night sky.

He'd thought he understood what taking the beak meant. What being a slave would be like. But it was only now that he grasped the scope of it, and the truth threatened to suffocate him. A true slave couldn't escape.

The beak was no longer moving. But he could feel Graal. Feel his sorrow, like a boulder on his chest. The deadborn whispered his name.

"Rime . . ."

Rime pushed himself up onto all fours. Spat. The beak felt like it was squirming. Begging for more blood.

"Drink. Please. It'll make it better."

The words were a perverse plea. Rime didn't reply. Didn't move. He could hear someone coming.

"Rime, you needed to know . . . I wouldn't—"

"I'm not alone," Rime said. His voice was rough. Damaged. He was surprised it worked at all.

Graal hesitated. Slowly and reluctantly his presence faded. And then he was gone.

Rime forced himself to his feet. Looked up at the figure standing between the trees and aiming an arrow at him.

Tein.

His shirt was barely able to contain his arms. "You should know I'm better with a bow than I am with a sword."

Rime chuckled. It felt like he had sand in his throat. "Let's hope so."

The chieftain's son stepped out of the shadows. His bow creaked like he'd been given an excuse to loose the arrow. Rime found himself hoping he'd try. Maybe he'd let him succeed this time.

"Who were you talking to, Rime?" His lips twitched. He clearly knew the answer wouldn't be good.

"If you're going to shoot me, shoot me."

Tein tensed the bow. "You think I'm bluffing?"

"I think you'll miss."

Rime watched him, waiting for the subtle movement that would reveal he'd released the bowstring. It didn't come. Rime opened his arms wide and walked toward him with his chest exposed. "Do you want me to put down the swords so you know—"

"Who were you talking to?"

Rime was close now. "You want to. I know you want to. It doesn't matter who I—"

"Answer me!" Tein backed away and lost his balance. The arrow slipped, plunging into the ground with a thunk. Rime threw himself at Tein, pushed him face-first against the rock wall, and locked his arm behind his back.

"If you'd shut up for a moment you'd get your answers, Tein."

Tein dropped his bow and tried to get free. He was strong but lacked technique and stamina. He was already breathing heavily. Rime snarled in his ear. "I'll tell you who I talk to, and once you've understood, all your dreams will come true. I need your help. Do you hear me?"

Tein growled into the rock. "To do what?"

"To kill me."

Tein stopped struggling. Rime let him go. "Can we talk like adults now?"

The chieftain's son turned. His black hair was plastered to his forehead. "You *want* me to kill you?"

Rime leaned against the rock, suddenly exhausted. He sank to the ground. "I have a beak in my throat."

The words ran out of him like poison. He felt cleaner the moment they left his mouth. He leaned his head back against the cool rock. "A raven beak. It's dead, yet alive. Blindcraft, Tein. That's what I talk to."

Tein sank down next to him. "Like Vanfarinn had? The councillor?"

Rime nodded. "Same beak. And it makes me a slave. A tool."

320

Tein met his gaze. His anger had given way to disgust and distrust. "A slave to who?"

"To Graal."

For a moment the chieftain's son looked confused. Then the name clicked and he seemed to remember. Rime didn't know how much Eirik had told him, but it was clearly enough. A raven gave a disgruntled caw nearby. A chorus of support rippled through the ravine, and then it was quiet again.

Tein tore up chunks of the heather between his feet. "Darkest Slokna . . ."

"Something like that . . ." Rime dragged his hands over his face. "Listen, I don't know what will happen, or whether that bastard will seize control of me. But the day he does, I'll need help. Understand? I'll need someone to end me. I'm asking you because—"

"Because you can't ask my father. He'd never do it. He'd sooner shoot *me* than you." Tein smiled in a failed attempt to hide his bitterness. Rime looked at him. Eirik's son. Eirik, who had time and energy for everyone. The beloved chieftain of Ravnhov. Maybe that was the price to pay for being responsible for so many people—forgetting those who were closest to you.

"Tein—"

"You don't even need to try, Rime. You're all he wants. You're all *anyone* wants. Including her . . ." His voice grew thick, as if forcing down his own bile.

"That's why I'm asking you," Rime said. "Not only are you strong enough to do it, you might even enjoy it."

Tein laughed, but it was a joyless sound.

Rime held out his hand. "So you'll stop me when the time comes? Do we have an agreement?"

Tein gripped his hand. It was as warm as his was cold.

"We have an agreement."

THE THIRST

Hirka sat up and the bed started to swing. Something had woken her, but she didn't know what. A feeling. A need. Her stomach clenched, but not out of nausea. She was thirsty. Unbelievably thirsty.

She grabbed her throat. Drink. She had to have something to drink.

She hopped down from the bed and went into the bathroom. Water from the glacier trickled down the groove in the stone wall and collected in a hollow. She drank. It didn't help, so she drank more. Ice-cold water eased the spasms, but not her thirst. She wiped her mouth and noticed the veins in her forearm were swollen, like they were on the outside of her skin. Was she still sleeping? Was this a nightmare?

I've had this dream before.

In the pits in Eisvaldr. When they'd imprisoned her. She'd woken up with swollen veins then, just like now. Fear rose inside her, but it was nothing compared to her thirst. She bared her teeth at her own reflection. Urd was right. She wasn't the same. She was pale. Her hair had grown longer and wilder. Red contrasting with white. She could see muscles in her arms, sculpted by staffs and cuffs. And the fact that she hadn't eaten a single proper meal since she'd come here.

Her mouth was as dry as sand. She tasted blood. She needed to taste blood.

No sooner had the thought come than her veins settled. As if the realization alone were a promise.

Thirsty. So, so thirsty.

Hirka pulled on her clothes. Grabbed her staff and went out onto the balcony. Jumped down to the street below. It was so early that it was still dark. Not even the ravens were awake. She raced off toward the Seer's house. The closer she got, the worse her thirst became, as if its source were her very heart. A yearning that sucked up every drop in her body. Made her tongue swell. Her pulse race.

She took all the shortcuts. Across bridges and along alleyways. Cut corners as she ran down toward the sound of a raging sea. Black cliffs towered above her on both sides, glistening with meltwater. She could see waves. The sight made the thirst unbearable. She ran faster. Slipped on some sand that had been washed up the street by the sea but carried on. Up the steps. She tore open the rusted door.

"Seer!" She shouted as she raced along the corridor and into the cave. It was empty. Maybe he was still asleep, but she couldn't wait until he saw fit to rise.

Hirka rummaged through jars and bowls on the shelves. She could hear herself breathing. She sounded like an animal. A jar crashed to the floor. Shattered. No matter.

Where is it?!

"Is this what you're looking for?"

Hirka turned toward the Seer. Grabbed the bottle he was holding and drank. The tension let go. Everything let go. She sank onto the bench but continued to drink until there wasn't a drop left. She let go of the bottle and it rolled across the table. The Seer picked it up and sat down across from her.

Her heart was pounding in her ears. Too quickly to count the beats. She shut her eyes. Waited until she'd caught her breath before looking at the creature on the other side of the table. His face was exposed in all its appalling detail. The gaping red hole. Half mouth, half beak. Eyes stared at her from the wrong places, like they'd melted and been displaced. Loose skin hung under his chin.

Yet still, she was the animal. It was the same feeling she'd had with Jór. She was surrounded by monsters, but there were none worse than her. She ran her tongue over her teeth. Sucked down any blood trapped between them.

"What's happening to me?" Her voice was hoarse.

The Seer met her gaze. "Do you feel ill?" he asked.

Hirka shook her head.

"If I had more, would you drink it?"

She nodded.

He laughed. A gasping that landed somewhere between a cackle and a screech. Hirka leaned over the table. "It's been a tough year," she seethed. "What little patience I once had has left me, so I'll only ask *one* more time: what's happening to me?"

The crinkling around his beady black eyes was the only thing that hinted at a smile. "Raven has accepted you. You, a basss . . . stard. Half menskr, half Dreyri."

Hirka looked at him. All her questions wanted out at once. Formed one big glob. She could no longer pick them apart. She seized on one that was important enough to detach itself from the others.

"I can be ravenborn? If I can get to Ym, right? To the Might?"

He sighed, his lungs whistling. "It sss. . . seems impossible, but you have the ravens' blessing. And you are strong. Whether that means you'll ever be able to bind . . . There's no knowing."

"I know. If I can just get there."

"And if you find the beak, you have to ask for a favor. Ask if it is willing to help you, despite you not knowing the raven's name. And if you'll be able to survive the transformation. There are many *ifs* in your future, Hirka."

She hated what he was saying, because she'd had those exact same thoughts. He was right. There were many uncertainties, and they were inextricably linked. It was all or nothing. She could even end up like him. Spend the rest of her life in agony. Hidden under a robe, sequestered from the rest of the world. But hadn't it always been that way? Hadn't she always been hidden? Lived in secret?

She gave a bestial smile. "What's the worst that could happen?"

"I don't know. You're the first of your kind."

She'd hoped he'd say something else. Anything was better than not knowing.

Still, she had to try. Perhaps she'd never be ravenborn or learn to bind. Perhaps the Might was so damaged it would never be the same again. But if she could just get the fallen to follow her . . . and get the beak out of Rime . . . at least then she'd have given Ym a chance at survival.

The Seer went over to the hearth, aided by the staff she'd given him. He pushed some dry moss in between the firewood and lit it. The fire caught straight away.

"Do you realize what this means?" he asked. "You have less blood of the first than anyone here, but still the ravens have blessed you. You're going to change everything."

Hirka looked at him. "If I survive long enough to make it to Ym."

"Why wouldn't you? Worry instead about what will happen *after* you get there."

"After, it's up to me. Up to the Might. That I can deal with. It's worse here. Here my own family tries to bury me alive! Here I'm put on display as proof of Graal's superiority, when in truth they despise me. Mixed blood. Menskr. You said so yourself!"

He leaned his staff against the table and sat down opposite her. "Bury you?"

325

Hirka scrubbed a hand across her face. "When I came here and told you I wanted to be ravenborn . . . you never asked what had happened. Skerri had happened. She's out of her mind. Sometimes she sees me as someone who can elevate her house. Other times she sees the daughter of a lover who no longer wants her."

He rested a hand on her arm. His black claws sprawled across her skin, making it look like she had been cut into little pieces. "Why didn't you mention this before? You can't let her hurt you! Not now! You are . . . You . . ."

Hirka studied his birdlike face. His concern seemed genuine. It was so unexpected that she regretted telling him.

"It's out of my control, Seer. But if something happens to me before the war, now you know it's her."

He closed his eyes. Cocked his head, as if listening for something. All she could hear was the sea crashing into the cliff outside. He tightened his grip on her arm. Opened his eyes and looked at her.

"Your family has a dangerous secret," he said. His gaze had grown solemn. As if he'd made a difficult decision.

Hirka had heard similar before. The House of Modrasme had far too many dark corners. Places she'd been deftly steered clear of.

The room seemed to shrink around her. The walls closed in, as if listening. She didn't move, afraid he'd stop talking.

His arms dropped into his lap. "I'm alive because I've never shared this secret with anyone. But it might keep you alive, if you use it right."

"Why tell me now? Don't tell me you care all of a sudden . . ."

He stared at the floor. Had she hurt him? No, it was something else. Shame. Suddenly she understood.

"You didn't believe in me," she whispered. "Until now. You never thought I'd get the ravens' blessing. Or be ravenborn. But *now* you believe. *Now* you care."

He thinks I can heal him . . .

His head twitched, like a bird shaking off the rain. He leaned over the table. His deformed back made it look like he was kneeling in front of her. "Hirka . . . They weren't brothers."

"Who? Who weren't br—" Her question fizzled out.

Graal and Naiell.

She stared at him. He nodded eagerly, as if to coax out her understanding. "Graal is the true sss . . . son of Raun and Uhere. They are your family, Hirka. But Naiell . . ."

"How can you . . .? Why would . . .?"

He pressed a black claw to her lips. "Listen, child. Raun and Uhere had a son. This was a long time ago, as far back as the war and twice that again. A house with high sss . . . status. But in Dreysíl, nothing is high enough."

He instinctively glanced around, but his gaze was still steely and determined.

"Uhere fell gravely ill, and they kept it sss . . . secret, as best they could. Rumors were rife. Threatened their position. Until Uhere came forward with another son. Brothers. And only a hundred years separated them. Legends, they became. Celebrated. Loved. Idolized. The House of Modrasme was elevated to the Council. That was how they made their name. Their legacy."

His unnaturally sloped forehead creased into a frown. "We might never have gone to Ym had it not been for the furor that grew around those two. But it was never right. I know. I tended to Uhere when she was ill. And she was never pregnant, I can promise you that. Where Naiell came from, I have no idea. But he sss . . . smelled like them. Raun and Uhere knew that I knew, but they never said anything. They came to see me often, bearing gifts, as many did. They had Naiell with them every time. If his sss . . . smell could deceive me, then it could deceive everyone. And it did. Deception or miracle, he had Modrasme's blood. No one could question that. But they kept coming. Year after year. And sss . . . so I saw him grow up. Into a god of a man."

The Seer hesitated. Hirka hardly dared breathe.

"I loved him. More than he loved me, but I could live with that. You're centuries too young to know what I'm talking about, but that's how it was. Sometimes the longing is sss . . . so strong you take what you can get."

His words conjured the image of Rime. Beautiful. Unrestrained. Raw. Her exact opposite. Nevertheless, her soul. He'd done things he considered necessary but that she considered horrific. With the best of intentions, he'd trampled over everything she believed in. Still she loved him. Loved him and longed for him. Condemned, dreamed, and raged. But nothing would change the fact that she would do anything for him. And she was being forced to prove it.

"That's how it was," the Seer continued. "Right up until I told him the truth, during the war. Do you understand what that would mean for your family? Somebody finding out?"

Hirka nodded, even though she didn't completely understand. But they'd be punished, that much was clear. Perhaps even get teardrops in their foreheads, all of them.

Fragments came together in her head. The traitor Naiell. Why had he turned his back on them all? To be a god in Ym, Graal had said. To rule over people, Rime had said. But what if he'd acted out of anger, after being lied to his entire life?

She remembered him. His long black hair. His vanity. His screeching laughter. A lump formed in her throat. She reminded herself of how he'd tortured Graal. And how he'd threatened her. He was anything but holy.

No one is holy.

Hirka got up. "There may come a time when I have to tell them that I know. You realize that?"

"I undersss . . . stand."

"They'll know who told me."

The Seer rose, a little steadier than before, she thought. "Kill a seer? No one would court such ill fortune before a war." His eyes crinkled, indicating a smile his face would never be able to form. "In any case, they cannot hurt either of us. The sss . . . seal has been broken. I've taken precautions. The truth will come out if anything should befall me. So now we're the sss . . . same, you and I. We live or die by the sss . . . same secret."

There was sadness in his words. But for her there was hope. A weapon. Now she had a sharp edge she could use if they tried to stop her from leaving.

Hirka held out her hand. The Seer took it. Black fingers curled around hers. Rough as raven talons. A handshake. A thank you. If nothing else, she knew he was on her side now. He'd been afraid to hope. Now he believed. Now he was willing to take a chance. She prayed he wouldn't be the only one.

She left him. Opened the rusty door and went out. She could smell the sea. She could smell change. Nothing was as she'd thought. And Naiell was dead, so she'd never learn the whole truth.

She set off on the long journey back, to a house that was built on a lie.

STOLEN

"It's out of the question," Uhere said. She was mumbling around the hairpin in her mouth, but the message was clear enough. It occurred to Hirka that this was the first argument she'd had with her family. And it would only get worse.

"It's not a request," Hirka replied. "I'm going. I have to go."

Uhere twisted her hair back and pinned it in place. Once again it came loose, as her hair wasn't quite long enough. But she wouldn't give up. Probably because the pin was a gift from the House of Delnare, the third. It dripped with beads in the house's yellow colors, and everyone who saw it would know where it had come from.

Her hair came loose again. She turned to Hirka with an exasperated look, as if she were the reason it wouldn't stay put.

Raun put his glass on a shelf and came over. He was dressed to impress. His shoulder, elbow, and forearm were decorated with gleaming steel. Something between armor and adornment. Just enough for him to look the part.

He helped Uhere with her hair, lovingly gathering it between his fingers. "When we're in Ym, you can spend as much time learning to use the Might as you like," he said. "You'll have all the time in the world then. But until then, we need you here. What do you think Jór would say if you disappeared just before the march to Nifel?"

Hirka looked at him. She hadn't told anyone about Jór's proposal. Yet somehow he knew. She was starting to realize that she and Jór were probably those least involved in the plan to unite the houses.

"Why would Jór have anything to say about it?" she asked, feigning naivete.

Raun and Uhere looked at each other in the mirror. She made her case as quickly as she could while they were still on the defensive.

"You might not see any reason to let me go, but it's important to me! I can't go to war without knowing whether the Seer has helped me, whether I can master the Might. And there's no reason not to. There's no risk! Of course Skerri, paranoid as she is, thinks I'll take off and never come back. She thinks I want to warn friends in Mannfalla, but I don't have any friends left! In any case, she'll be able to stop me if I try, because she'll have to come with me. She's the one with the raven. And if you really think her incapable of keeping me in line, send another twenty! Send as many as you like. It makes no difference to me. I only need a couple of days, and I won't even have to leave the stone circle. After all, it's underground! How much trouble can I cause underground? No one in Ym will know I was there."

Raun let go of Uhere's hair. This time, it stayed put. "Graal would say the same as us, Hirka. There's no reason for you to go. I'm sorry."

Hirka swallowed a growl. She'd hoped she wouldn't have to use the secret. It would come across as a threat, but what choice did she have? She had to get home before everything went to Slokna. Find Rime and get the beak out of him so he would be free to fight. And if Kolail convinced the fallen, Rime might even have something to fight *with*.

She looked at Raun. "Can I talk to you alone?"

Uhere's eyes narrowed in the mirror. Her necklace was coiled tightly around her neck in several loops. "What did I tell you? You're too lenient with her." She was talking to Raun but didn't take her eyes off Hirka.

Raun put a hand on Hirka's back. "It won't change anything for—"

"Now," Hirka said.

She turned her back on him and left the room. It broke all the rules of etiquette, but she didn't care anymore. War would come and worlds would fall. Caring who she could or couldn't turn her back on was absurd.

Raun followed her into her room. He closed the door behind him. Maybe he'd finally realized that this was important to her. Or maybe he just wanted to make sure Uhere wouldn't hear. Then he could pretend he'd been strict with her.

"Sit, Raun."

Hirka had meant it in a nice way, but of course asking Umpiri to sit was tantamount to telling them to brace themselves for terrible news. For something that might knock the ground out from under them—and that was saying something.

He hesitated but did as she asked. She sat down next to him on the bench by the window.

"Does Graal know they weren't brothers?"

Raun's eyes turned jet black. He seemed to stop breathing. Hirka suppressed the urge to pull away from him.

"You would ruin us?" Doubt made his voice quaver.

"Never," she replied. It was the most unpalatable combination of truth and lie she had ever served anyone.

Raun slumped, the steel around his arm clinking. His pointless armor. His reaction wasn't at all what she'd expected. It was genuine. And physical. She went to put her hand on his back but stopped herself.

"I'll kill him," he growled.

"I guessed," Hirka lied. "But his reaction confirmed it, just as yours does now. He did nothing wrong. But if you touch him, no good will come of it. You know that. You've always known that."

Tremors in Raun's red beard revealed he was shaking. Something that had happened long, long ago still had power over his body.

She'd always imagined that time would take the edge off of everything painful and difficult. But maybe that wasn't how it worked with secrets. Maybe they just got worse the longer they simmered. And this one had been simmering for almost three thousand years.

"It wasn't what you think," Raun said. "It was never planned. No one went out looking for a child. That would have been madness."

He leaned on his elbows like his body was too heavy to hold up. "It was so long ago . . . We lived in Nifel back then. Uhere got sick and I thought I might lose her. I thought old age had found her and she only had months to live. But she had no wrinkles. No gray hairs. All she had was a fever."

He dragged his hands over his face. "The Seer was powerless to help but said there might be something that could. Silvercorn seeds. But silvercorn was almost impossible to get hold of. Of all the ravens we sent, only one came back with a yes. From a peddler here in Ginnungad. For a higher price, he agreed to send a man to meet me halfway."

Raun cleared his throat. A warning that the worst was still to come.

"I was attacked along the way. Stopped. There were three of them. None of them survived. I pursued the last of them across a bog and drowned him in the mud with my own two hands. He was Dreyri."

Hirka tipped her head back and closed her eyes. Realization dawned. Raun had killed one of his own. Had anyone found out, he'd have been made one of the fallen. Had a teardrop embedded in his forehead. He'd have struggled to buy things, had to make a living from odd jobs, and ended up throwing bottles in the street.

"I climbed out of the bog. Watched him sink. It could have been over, there and then. But then I saw something move out of the corner of my eye. Someone had seen me. A woman. I took chase. Heard crying, but not hers. She was carrying a child. Even so, she ran toward the edge of a cliff. She was Dreyri, too, and would sooner have jumped to her death with her child than let anyone kill them. I grabbed her without knowing what I planned to do. Was I trying to save her, or was I making sure she could never tell anyone what she'd seen? I don't know. Not even now."

He reached out as if to show her what he'd done. "I grabbed her, and she stumbled. We both fell. She squeezed the child until it stopped screaming. Maybe she just wanted to make sure I didn't kill it. I don't know. But I broke her arm. Got the child away from her. She kicked. Fought like a bear. I dug my claws into her and dulled her senses until she stopped moving. It was only then that I noticed it. The smell of the child. So familiar that he could have been my own. I . . . I sat there with my arms around him, the First know how long. By the time I got up again, nothing in the world could have taken him from me. He was mine."

Raun looked at her. "I don't know how much of you is menskr, and how much is Dreyri, but the smell of family . . . Our own blood . . . Never before and never again have I heard anything like it. Maybe there was something wrong with him from the start. Something that meant he didn't smell like his parents. Maybe that's why they lived out there, or maybe they'd stolen him themselves, I don't know. But I took him. I did. I snapped her neck and put her in the bog, too. But I took the child. You might think it was to elevate my own house, but it wasn't! It wasn't . . ."

Hirka nodded. She felt unwell. Not because of what he'd done, but because of what she'd done. Because she'd used such a tragedy to coerce him. Who was she? What had she become?

"I hid him from the peddler. Got the silvercorn seeds and went home. When I put him in Uhere's arms, I knew I'd done the right thing. She didn't let go of him for days, but the illness let go of her. With no further help. And that became our story. Admitting she'd been unwell was less painful when we could say it was because of the child. Because she'd been pregnant. It blessed us more than I could have dreamed."

He looked at her with tired eyes. "Until he turned his back on us."

Hirka didn't reply. Chances were that Raun had no idea why Naiell had turned his back on them. He didn't know that the Seer had told Naiell the truth. And he didn't need to know. That would only make things even more difficult for the Seer. And it might prove too much for Raun to bear, knowing his actions were the reason for his son's betrayal.

Raun. Her father's father. But even he could only bear so much.

"So who knows?" she asked.

He gave a deep sigh. "No one else was supposed to know. It was supposed to stay between me and Uhere. But the Seer had tended to her, so of course he realized. But he had the most to gain from keeping the secret. He would never have gained the status he has now if we hadn't gone to him as often as we did."

"Graal knows," Hirka said. "Or he wouldn't have been so scared of what the Seer might tell me. But what about Skerri?"

"I don't know. Something happened during the war. I know they argued, the three of them. It's not impossible that . . . I don't know."

Hirka put a hand on his back.

"Raun, I'm going to Ym. Soon. I'll take people you trust. I won't stay on the other side for more than a couple of days, and I won't try to contact anyone. Do you understand? Talk to Skerri and Graal if you must. Find an explanation for the House of Hod. Whatever works. Tell them I've gone to Nifel to prepare. Tell them I'm meeting you there in about eight days. You have nothing to fear from me."

The lie left a rotten taste in her mouth. It was like the words belonged to someone else. Like they were changing her. Raun had everything to fear. She was like Naiell. She would betray them all. Let them clash on the battlefield. Let them fight and maybe even die.

Raun gave a meek nod and looked at her. "No one has ever realized they weren't brothers. No one. So how did you guess?"

Hirka scrambled for a reason. A good explanation. She smiled. "I can't smell things the way you can. I couldn't use my senses to connect them. All I saw were the differences. They were like night and day."

Raun stared into thin air. "The son I stole tortured the son I had . . ."

Hirka didn't comment, even though she knew both sons had suffered equally. And now, because of them, worlds would suffer.

NO WAY BACK

They were approaching Nifel. The journey had seemed shorter than when she first arrived. Maybe because the weather was milder now. Or because they were using the roads instead of trudging through the snow in places no one ought to tread. But it was probably mostly because she knew what to expect. The cold and the snow came as no surprise, and neither did the lack of breaks or proper food.

She was better prepared this time. She had an extra waterskin. Dried fish and seaweed cakes in her bag. She knew she wouldn't freeze or starve. But that was all she knew. Everything else was so uncertain that she'd spent a needless amount of time agonizing over the little things. The things she could control.

Skerri plowed ahead of her, straight-backed in the snowy weather that had everyone else hunched over. Hungl and Tyla brought up the rear. They were pulling a sled piled so high it was taller than they were. Blankets, lanterns, oil, cups . . . The first unofficial transport to Nifel, the broken city.

Urd was their strangest cargo. He sat on the sled for most of the journey because he was too slow for Skerri. After almost a year of imprisonment, he was poorly equipped for the merciless conditions. But Hirka had said she needed him. That he was crucial for her learning to bind the Might. She had shared as little as possible of his story and avoided telling them he'd used the Might to kill. Instead she'd focused on how he'd experimented and learned using Umpiri

337

blood. So there he sat, between the trunks, bundled in a blanket. Pale and tentatively calm.

They had no fallen with them. No one had been able to get hold of Kolail when they were leaving. Hirka chose to take that as a good sign. He would be in Nifel. He would turn up. He had to.

She'd only just managed to talk to him. A stolen moment at the arena where she'd told him to gather those with the guts to follow her, because it was now or never. But they'd have to keep off the roads and travel in small groups, not all at the same time. Had he understood her? Had he drunk too much? No one being able to get hold of him could just as easily mean he was passed out in a gutter somewhere . . .

Hirka threw stolen glances up at the mountains. Were the fallen and houseless in the shadows? Were they forging their way onward like her, battling ice and snow? Or had they set out ahead of them?

She'd been given eight days or so. Skerri thought six would be enough for what she wouldn't stop calling Hirka's idiocy. An ego-centric project born of delusion. And that was when she was in a good mood. What would she have said had she known her true intentions?

The details pounded her thoughts like hail. Tormenting her. What if no one came? What if Kolail wasn't there? What if no one was able to overpower Skerri? She was bersarkí. A ring warrior. Hungl and Tyla weren't exactly weaklings, either.

Hirka had made it clear that no one should die, but how else could they be neutralized? Then there was Damayanti, on the other side. What if she wasn't alone? And what if Graal tried to contact the dancer or Skerri before the agreed time had passed? Without getting an answer?

He would take his revenge through Rime. She had to get the beak out before Graal realized Hirka had betrayed him. It was as simple as that. And utterly impossible.

Hirka tightened her grip on her staff. At times it was the only thing that held her up. It had become a part of her. She felt naked without it. And it stopped her from wandering off the road.

Though *road* was a generous name for what was nothing more than a long depression in the snow. Now and then she glimpsed piles of stones, half frozen in the ice. Road markers. Or perhaps ruins. Who knew what the snow was hiding.

They walked between what looked like jagged ice floes jutting up out of the snow. When they came out on the other side, she could see Nifel. A labyrinth of black stone, abandoned in the middle of an icy wilderness. Large parts of the ruins were buried in the snow. All that revealed the scope of the city were the circular depressions spreading through the snow like ripples. The hall with the stone circle was easy to spot. It towered over the surrounding structures.

She'd been here before, when they'd come to collect her, but now it didn't look like anyone had visited in generations. No tracks in the snow. No lanterns. And no fallen.

They toiled along the final stretch. The hall loomed over them, as if to warn them against going in. As if it knew it might collapse at any moment. Hirka had to remind herself that it had been standing for at least a thousand years.

It was calmer inside, though the wind still howled through the holes in the wall. Ice poured out of archways on multiple levels, just as she remembered. The stone circle stood in the center of the vast room. Snowdrifts had formed around it. Hirka could almost picture herself as she must have been the day she'd come through the stones. What she'd expected. What had greeted her. It was like remembering a child.

What it would have been like back then to be greeted by herself as she was now? What would she have made of herself? Of someone who was planning to let people bleed?

Hirka shook off the thought. It was too painful.

Skerri stopped in the shadow of the closest stones. "Hungl, you take that side. Tyla, you take the other. Check which rooms are most habitable."

Tyla stretched her arms back, joints creaking. "Are there rooms around the hall? Behind the ice?"

"This is Maknamorr," Skerri replied dryly, as if that ought to mean something to them. "There are more than enough rooms here. Mostly in the cellars. There should be space for a couple of hundred houses."

Maknamorr.

The word sounded familiar, but Hirka couldn't place it.

Skerri set her staff aside, plunging it into the snow. She waited until the others had disappeared before heading over to the sled. Urd shrank away from her, unable to hide his fear. Skerri grabbed him by the throat. His eyes widened, staring at Hirka as if she'd betrayed him.

"Wait!" Hirka ran toward them.

Urd keeled over in the sled, one hand hanging over the edge. Skerri had knocked him out.

"Did you think I'd let that animal see how this works?" Skerri wiped her hand on Urd's blanket. Her lip curled in disgust. She took the raven quiver off her back.

No! Not yet!

Panic gripped Hirka. There was still time. They might still come. "Shouldn't we make camp first?" she asked anxiously.

Skerri snorted. "Unlike you, I don't think we have time to waste. The sooner the better."

She crouched down and opened the lid. Then she clenched her fist, sinking one of her claws into her hand. Blood dripped down onto the raven cadaver. Hirka stared at her black lips, hoping she might see what she whispered. The name of Damayanti's beak. But as far as Hirka could tell, she didn't whisper anything. Maybe it didn't even need to be said.

A moment later, the dancer spoke. It was the silkiest voice Hirka had heard in a long time. Warm and deep.

"Skerri? I wasn't expecting you until tomorrow morning."

"We made good time," Skerri replied. "How quickly can you be in position?"

A short pause. "Soon. I'll leave at once."

Skerri closed the lid and got up. She put her hands on her hips and surveyed the hall. She seemed so much bigger now. Stronger. For a moment Hirka was relieved they were alone. No Kolail. No fallen. Relieved they wouldn't have to attack her.

But then she remembered what that would mean. No support for Ym. And no chance of running off on the other side. No Rime. She was alone.

Skerri narrowed her eyes at her. "I know what you're thinking. You can fool the others, but not me."

Hirka's heart leaped into her throat. She didn't dare reply.

"You're not one of us," Skerri said. "You never have been. And you think you can run, but you're wrong."

"Is that what you would do? Run?" Hirka forced a cold smile onto her face. Skerri bared her teeth and took a step toward her. Behind her, snow was now being sucked between two stones, as if caught in a draft. Hirka nodded at them. "Damayanti's in position."

"As are we."

Hirka jumped. That was Kolail's voice.

He came marching over a snowdrift, and he wasn't alone. Hirka counted six. Then she saw more coming from the other side. They'd come! They'd been waiting in the rooms around the hall.

Skerri was surrounded in an instant. Hirka hardly dared breathe. The gateway was open, and they had no time to lose. They couldn't have Skerri warning Damayanti, either. Hirka threw herself forward, grabbed the raven quiver, and backed away.

For a moment Skerri was stunned by her own incredulity. She grabbed her staff, but then she hesitated. She wasn't scared. Rage contorted her features. Raw, unabashed rage. But she hesitated because she was thinking. Hirka could almost see her assessing the situation. Deciding what was more important. Fighting until her last breath, or warning Graal.

The gateways! There's only one way out.

It was as if the thought struck them both at the same time. Skerri took off toward the stones. Toward the snow being sucked through. Hirka took a deep breath and screamed.

"KOLAIL!"

The arrow was already in the air. It plunged into Skerri's back. She dropped to her knees and fell forward into the snow. The sight was a distortion of Hirka's memory. She had once stood by the stones and heard Skerri shout. Seen a man fall. Now she was the one shouting, and Skerri was the one who had fallen. But the archer was the same.

Kolail stopped next to Skerri. She was trying to prop herself up on one arm, but he sank his claws into her neck and held her firm until she stopped struggling. He met Hirka's gaze and nodded, as if to assure her that Skerri would be fine. Hirka didn't have time to check. Only *one* thing mattered now: securing the raven ring.

She couldn't bind, so it would have to be one of the others. Someone had to go through so they wouldn't need Damayanti to awaken the gateways again.

Hirka waved her hands frantically at Kolail. "Go!"

Kolail understood. He waved two of the others with him. Together they ran between the stones and disappeared. Hirka closed her eyes, hoping Damayanti was alone, hoping she wouldn't resist, hoping she wouldn't have time to contact Graal . . .

Time stood still.

Please, please . . .

Kolail reappeared. He leaned against the closest stone, out of breath. Nauseous, too, she guessed, if he were anything like her. He looked up and gave her a dopey smile. Like he was drunk.

The Might. He's felt the Might.

Hirka wasn't sure whether to laugh or cry. The gateways were secured. Skerri and the others were out cold. They had no time to lose. There was no telling when Graal might try to contact Skerri or Damayanti. They were probably safe for a day or two, but he wouldn't leave it any later than when she was supposed to be back. He wouldn't get an answer. He would realize something was wrong. That gave them five days at most. Five measly days. It was ridiculous considering everything that had to happen in that time.

Hirka stared at the snow being pulled between the stones like sand through an hourglass.

"Wait! Let me see." Hirka grabbed the man who was about to lift Skerri out of the snow. She hung limp over his arm. Her black cloak had been pulled taut around her neck by the arrow that was now lodged at an angle over her shoulder blades. Deep, but not fatal. Hirka drew her knife and cut the cloak free.

"Have the others been taken care of?" Hirka gripped the shaft of the arrow.

"Kolail's checking now," the man replied. She remembered him from the tavern. Bald with black circles around his eyes, like a lynx. The one who hadn't been afraid to challenge her.

"You're Skolm, right?"

He nodded. Hirka yanked the arrow out. Blood trickled out until the wound foamed white and started to close.

"I'm glad you're here, Skolm. There aren't many of us, but anything's better than nothing." She wasn't sure she'd managed to hide her disappointment. A handful of fallen wouldn't make much of a difference in a war.

Skolm laughed. A booming laugh that reminded her of Eirik of Ravnhov.

Soon. I'll see them again soon.

He threw Skerri over his shoulders as if she were his kill and walked toward the stones, where Kolail had just reappeared.

"Graal's heir thinks we're it," he said as they passed each other. Then he disappeared between the stones.

Kolail snorted. He stuck two fingers in his mouth and whistled. The sound rent the air of the hall. Hirka could see something moving in the shadows. Someone whistled outside as well. She looked over at the collapsed wall. It was hard to see anything. The sky had darkened. It looked like a flock of wild sheep was coming toward them across the snow drifts. Then she realized it was people. Lots of people. They kept coming, streaming in through broken walls. They emerged from the shadows. From the rooms. They stared down at her from the levels above.

Hirka dropped her knife. Heard it hit the floor beneath the snow.

"What did you expect?" Kolail asked. "The first thing you saw when you arrived here was our thirst for the Might. Glimau died for it. And now you've told them you can take them to it, as free women and men."

Hirka picked up her knife. She went to slide it into her shoe, but then attached it to her belt instead. She stared at the horde surrounding them. She pressed her lips together so she wouldn't cry. She didn't know whether her eyes were stinging out of relief or fear. Probably both. The war felt closer than ever, and she was no longer alone. But what expectations did they have? What did they think would happen?

What have I done?

She swallowed the lump in her throat. "How many are there?"

Kolail shrugged. "Dunno. Haven't counted."

Hirka suspected he couldn't count that many people. She looked up at him. "What did you tell them?"

"The same thing you told me. First you'll take them to Ym and the Might. Then it's up to them."

Hirka felt a coldness spread through her chest. It was all too vague. There would be chaos the moment they reached the other side. But it was too late to go back now. She'd set something in motion, and she had to see it through.

Skolm came back through the stones. He'd left Skerri in Ym with Hungl, Tyla, and Urd. He met her gaze and let one knee dip slightly. An acknowledgment. Because she'd kept her promise. Skolm had felt the Might.

"Is Damayanti still in one piece?" she asked.

He nodded. "They've all been subdued and tied up. The ymling, too. We've left Brilik, Brey, and Vinrid to watch them. Do we need to move them somewhere else?"

"No, nobody knows about the cave beneath the stones. It's safe there. Did you tell them Damayanti needs proper food?"

"Yes, they know. She eats like you do. But she'll have to make do with what we've brought."

"And no one can bind after we've left. That's important. They understand that?"

"They understand," he replied. "They're trustworthy. If any of the captives try anything, they'll be knocked out again."

Hirka nodded. Fallen and houseless encircled her. She hated crowds. She'd avoided people her entire life. Feared them. *People mean danger*, Father had said. She was still afraid, but of completely different things. Now she was afraid she'd promised too much. Afraid she'd started something that would end in a bloodbath.

Those who were closest stopped a couple of paces away, but there were still more coming. She craned her neck but couldn't see where they ended. They threw hungry looks at the stones behind her.

"Listen!" she shouted, surprised by the strength of her voice. "There are a lot of you. Too many for us to hope Ginnungad won't notice you're gone. That means there's no way back anymore."

"We didn't come just to turn back," said one of those closest to her. Shouts of support spread among them. Those with staffs thumped them against the floor, making holes in the snow. She'd have found their unrestrained joy touching had all their lives not been at stake.

"You didn't come just to die, either!" she shouted. She had to repeat herself before they would simmer down. "You didn't come to die. When we pass between the stones here, we'll come out beneath Mannfalla. Out of sight. And it has to stay that way. There are a lot of us, but nowhere near enough to take Mannfalla alone. I'm telling you this because you'll soon taste the Might again. And I've seen Umpiri on the Might before. You'll be intoxicated. You'll think you're invincible. But you cannot give into your urges. That would be suicide. Do you understand? We need to get out of Mannfalla. Unseen. Once we've done that, you can choose. You're free men. Free women. You can disappear into the forests, or up into the mountains. Live in hiding until age takes you."

Hirka watched as they crossed their arms over their chests. Skeptical, as she'd hoped. That would make the alternative seem better.

"Or you can follow me to Ravnhov. Fight alongside those who can give you what you want more than anything: a victory over the houses. Over Dreyri. And over Mannfalla."

She'd expected them to ask who would be fighting at their side, but they didn't. Maybe it didn't occur to them that she was talking about ymlings. Or maybe they understood but needed time to get used to the idea.

"And after?" a woman farther back asked.

The question was unexpected, making Hirka's shoulders drop like she was still wearing arm cuffs.

After . . . After the war. After someone had emerged victorious. Either Ravnhov and the fallen. Or Dreyri. Or Darkdaggar. After a bloodbath horrific enough to give her what she thought she needed to spread the Might to where it belonged. With everyone.

And after?

She surveyed them.

"There is no after," she replied.

The reaction surprised her as much as the question. A jubilant roar rang through the hall until she feared it would collapse. Kolail leaned toward her. "What did I tell you? You're like us. You're Umpiri."

Hirka shouldered her bag and picked up her staff. Then she turned her back on them and walked between the stones. The emptiness enveloped her. The ground disappeared from under her feet. Dropped her in an eternity of nothingness.

Then the stones appeared in the darkness and she was stumbling out into the cave beneath Mannfalla. Dizzy, but not nauseous.

It was dark. A lone torch was wedged in a crack in the wall, doing its best to illuminate far too large a space. The three blindlings were leaning against the wall. A woman and two men. Their eyes were hooded with pleasure. She could feel them binding. Feel the Might powering the stones. Energy that was supposed to power worlds. Her body responded with thirst. The blood vessels in her arms dilated. She wanted to touch it. Shape it. But it wouldn't be held. She was unearthed, just as she'd always been.

Five figures lay unconscious on the ground, hands and feet tightly bound. Skerri, Hungl, and Tyla were slumped in a row along the wall. Damayanti and Urd were in a corner. Urd she'd take with her, but the others would have to stay. No one could find out what she'd done, or how many people she had with her. Kolail had chosen three reliable fallen to stay behind and watch Skerri and the others until she returned.

What if I never return?

The raven quiver stood by the wall. Hirka hesitated. Should she take it with her? She needed one of the first ravens to ask. A beak that could help her become ravenborn. She'd planned to ask Rime's, but what if she couldn't get it out?

The thought made her feel sick. She'd had the same thought before, and it always hurt. But now it was unbearable. Now she was here, in Ym. Rime couldn't die now that he was within reach.

She looked at the raven quiver. Something told her Skerri's raven wouldn't be inclined to help her, so she left it where it was.

The next group of blindlings emerged from between the stones. Hirka could hear them breathing in the dark. Sighing as they felt the Might. Those who were too young to have fought in the war had never felt it before. It made some of them laugh. Others gasped. They were like children taking their first steps.

She asked Skolm to carry Urd, waited for Kolail, then led them onward in silence, squeezing between rock walls and into what Damayanti had told her were tunnels beneath the old city walls.

The close, dank darkness made her uneasy. Brought back the feeling of being buried alive.

She heard whispering behind her.

"Kolail, tell them to be quiet."

He did as she asked. The message was passed back, and to her surprise, they fell silent. She guessed they were willing to do almost anything to keep the Might they'd just sampled. Even listen to her.

They came to an opening in the wall. Hirka walked past it. That had to be the one Damayanti used. Meaning they were out of Eisvaldr and down by the river. A bit farther, and they'd be able to emerge well beyond the city gates.

After a while, the tunnel ended. It had been sloping upward and she had a feeling they were now aboveground.

"Here," she whispered to Kolail.

He bound the Might and shoved his claws between the stones of the wall. She heard a crackling that reminded her of melting tallow. The air grew warmer and suddenly smelled of burning hair. She met his gaze in the darkness.

"What are you looking at? I'm no mightslinger. If you want precision, go back and get someone else."

He was clearly embarrassed, but precision had been the last thing on her mind. All she could do was stare.

He started to pry the stone loose. It was long, so she helped him pull it out. She peered out through the hole. It was almost as dark outside. They were to the east of the city, as she'd thought. Near the hills where the tea plants grew. Safely out of reach.

The blindlings murmured impatiently in the dark. She helped Kolail make the hole bigger so they could get out. He paused, looking at a small rock in his hand. She could just make out the melted edges.

"What's that?" she whispered.

"Mightglass," he replied. "This could buy me a new place to live."

Hirka smiled. "Not anymore. Now you have the Might and can make as much glass as you want." She crawled out through the gap in the wall, then stuck her head back in again. "Last one out takes care of the hole."

Kolail passed the message back.

Then she started to walk. Umpiri crawled out of the wall behind her. She could hear them following her up the hill. Hirka didn't turn until she reached the top. They still weren't all out. They were like ants walking in a long line. Hundreds of them. Thousands. Silent in the night.

She could see the lights of Mannfalla beyond the city gates. Lanterns along the streets. The wall separating Eisvaldr from the rest of the city. She'd thought she'd never see the city again. She'd left it as a child of Odin. As the rot. What was she now? Half human. Dreyri. Full of raven blood, leading a horde of deadborn who intended to raze the city to the ground.

She couldn't help but look toward the riverbank and the place where the teahouse ought to have been. But both the teahouse and Lindri were no more. Darkdaggar had destroyed what little she cared about. Lindri and Kolkagga.

She looked up at Eisvaldr. One day deadborn would swarm the walls like insects. An unstoppable army. And she would let them.

DANCE

Ym . . .

Being exhausted had never felt better. They'd walked all day, through a thousand lush shades of green. Between spruce trees standing so close together that their branches intertwined. Over streams trickling down rocky slopes. And best of all, they'd walked in the warmth of summer. Summer as it was meant to be. Summer that was more than just less ice.

Hirka settled in between the roots of an old oak, leaning back against rough bark. The branches twisted and turned above her, bending and diving back toward the ground. The roots meandered past her, plunging down into damp, black, fertile earth before spreading farther across the mossy forest floor, which was thick and springy as a carpet. The ferns had just started unfurling.

She took in the smell as if for the first time. A rich, earthy smell so dear to her that she could have cried. It filled her. Spoke to her. It *was* her.

The sun was setting, bathing the forest in a dim bluish-green light. It was almost like being underwater. Small moths fluttered around a rotten tree stump covered in moss. She could hear the wind playing in the leaves above. Humming. Murmuring. Rustling.

And the sound of a thousand blindlings howling as they ran naked among the trees.

Hirka rested her head against the tree, smiling lazily.

She had finally let them celebrate. Let them bask in the Might now that they were far away from Mannfalla. Far away from people. It was strange to watch. They howled like wolves. Pranced like calves in the spring. Grown women and men. Some of them thousands of years old. The Might put a spring in their step. Sent them gamboling around. Pale bodies darted past. Strong and beautiful. Disappeared, and reappeared elsewhere. It was a game the likes of which she'd never seen. A celebration of nature. Of life. Of oneself.

Some of them had settled down again and were sitting in a group nearby, chatting. Urd had been wandering around, too. She'd been keeping an eye on him. Keen to see what he would do.

Kolail was coming her way, naked as the day he was born. She wondered whether she should explain to him that he couldn't walk around like that. That it wasn't what people did here. But she couldn't think of a single good reason why he shouldn't. It ultimately came down to shame, and no Umpiri would understand that. It was a completely foreign concept to them.

He stopped in front of her. Pale scars crossed his arms. One ran across his stomach. Maybe they were from the war. Wounds bad enough to have left marks. His gray hair was tangled at the back and unintentionally decorated with moss.

He ran a hand over it. Glanced at the others. "I've asked them to build a fire," he said, somewhat sheepishly. Like he'd neglected a responsibility. "And to catch something to eat."

Hirka set her bag down between her feet and opened it. "I can catch my own rabbits, Kolail." She smiled. Not that she planned on catching anything at all. This was too precious. A rare moment of happiness before the end. Before the war. Before she had to make the man she loved think he was going to die.

Think about something else!

"So what is this 'rabbits die' thing?" she asked, even though she was sure by now that she understood.

352

Kolail crouched down next to her and rested his arms on his knees. He looked like he'd been born out here. As much a part of the wilderness as the tree she was leaning against. He gave her a gummy smile, like he was still trying to get the hang of it.

"It started with him," he said, nodding at one of the men. The one with the black ponytail who'd been behind the counter in the tavern. "He came out with an old saying one night. 'The last rabbits to change their coats are the first to die,' he said. Because they get whiter in the winter, you know? And if they change too late, it's easier for predators to see them."

He stooped, leaning closer. "Of course, Skolm said it was nonsense. That a new coat was no guarantee against predators. So we started to argue. In the end we agreed that some rabbits are caught because they don't change their coats and others are caught *in spite of* changing their coats. You can't know what will happen. Understand?"

Hirka nodded. "That's what I thought."

He snorted. "You don't have a clue, do you?"

She dug a cake out of her bag. "I know it doesn't matter what you do. You can do everything right and still die. I mean, look at you. You've been changing coats all your life, thinking it would protect you. But it's only made things worse. Rabbits die. Regardless. You might as well do what's in your nature to do. Lucky for the rest of us you realized in time."

"Heh," he said, sounding surprised. She didn't know whether it was because she understood or because he hadn't thought about it that way. Probably the latter.

He looked around. Suddenly alert. Sensing something missing.

"Where is he? You know, what's-his-name . . ." He snapped his fingers, trying to remember.

"Urd? He's gone," Hirka said, taking a bite of the cake. "I saw him slope off a little while ago. I doubt he's coming back."

Kolail got up. "Should I go and find him?"

"No. Let him run. I expected him to. He'll buy his way back onto the Council with what I've told him."

"You're letting him escape so he can stab us in the back?"

Hirka took another bite of the cake and forced it down before putting the rest back in her bag. They tasted just as foul here as they did in Dreysíl.

"I told him Umpiri will come from the south," she continued. "From a stone circle in Bokesj."

Kolail scratched his head. "But that . . . that's not right."

"No."

Hirka rolled out her blanket between the roots. She would sleep here tonight. A wild bear couldn't dissuade her. Kolail stayed where he was, afraid to ask. She took pity on him and explained.

"If the Council believes him, they'll send troops south. If they don't believe him, at least they'll be less likely to realize the danger is coming from within. We benefit either way. And the stories he could tell them of Dreysíl will really shake their confidence. Scare them witless, I'd think."

"Ah! So . . . why don't you sound pleased?"

Hirka shrugged, as if she didn't know. In truth, she'd been nursing a hope that Urd had changed. But he hadn't. She'd followed his advice. Given him space to show who he was.

Kolail sat down next to her on the blanket. She tried to take no notice of his nakedness, but he didn't make it easy. The Might played in him, making him somehow bigger and wilder. The smell of him warmed her cheeks.

"You should always assume people will disappoint you," he said, as if talking to a child.

She turned to look at him. "Is that what I should have done with you?"

"Especially with me!"

Hirka studied him. The teardrop in his forehead was supposed to say it all. Was that what had created the divide between what he was and what he thought he was? Had it colored his view of himself?

She pulled up her knees and hugged them. "Why did you come, Kolail?"

He plucked at the moss, hesitating for a moment before answering. "Because you drank from me." He sighed, and she assumed he'd seen her confusion. "You drank," he said again. "On the way to Ginnungad, when you were thirsty. You drank from my claws."

"So? I was thirsty."

"That's what I mean. And you weren't afraid to show it. I was one of the fallen, and you showed me your weakness. Like we were equals. You touched me."

Hirka hid a smile. "You mean like this?" She poked him in the ribs. He rolled his white eyes. She pressed her finger to his throat. "Or like this?"

"Hey!" He swatted at her.

She leaned forward and shoved her finger in his ear. "Like this?"

He grabbed her arm and forced it behind her back. His playful gaze suddenly grew anxious. As if he were remembering who she was. He let go.

Hirka crawled around to face him. Put a hand on his cheek. "You never need to be afraid of me, Kolail. I don't touch you *like* we're equals. I touch you because we *are* equals. Do you understand?"

He looked at her as if she had fallen from the sky. Then he closed his eyes and laughed. "You're going to tear the world apart," he said.

It sounded like he was genuinely looking forward to it.

BLINDRING

Rime crawled up toward the crest of the hill, trying to find a better vantage point. It was chilly. Not a sound could be heard. He poked his head up over the heath and peered down at the camp. The tents appeared pale in the early dawn. They flapped in the wind, like the pages of a book. There were at least eighty of them, pitched close together. Sandwiched between the river and the rocky slope.

"There's too many of them," Tein whispered behind him.

"There's as many as we expected," Rime replied. "Four hundred at most, probably only three."

"But they're—"

Rime held up a hand to silence him. Tein made far too much of a racket for missions like this, but Rime could no longer refuse him. Not without him pitching a fit and threatening to blab.

A man emerged from one of the tents, nearly tripping over the ropes as he made his way over to the river to take a piss.

"Thanks, I've seen enough." Tein pulled back. Rime grabbed him by the shoulder.

"Not yet."

He studied the camp. Armor drying on posts under makeshift roofs. A couple of firepits. Only a few horses.

Rime slipped back through the heath until it was safe to stand again. Tein followed close on his heels. Then they started running though dead woods. Little had grown here since the volcano had awoken on Bromfjell. The trees were white and bare. Like it was still winter. Nothing was as it should be anymore.

Things improved when they reached the spruce woods, under a whispering canopy of green needles. The terrain angled upward and flattened out near the mountain. Ravnhov's tents were dark and difficult to spot. There were also fewer of them.

"What should we tell him?" Tein asked.

"The truth."

"That there's too many of them." It didn't sound like a question.

"That's up to your father to decide."

"Great. We're all dead men."

Rime didn't answer. He nodded at Ynge, who was standing guard, and walked between the tents until he spotted Eirik. It wasn't difficult considering the chieftain was the same height as the tents. His undershirt glowed in the semi-darkness. He was turning a birchbark cup in his hand, as if reluctant to sample its contents. His beard had grown so much that he'd had to tie it.

Rime approached him. "We found them."

The chieftain met his gaze. "And?"

"There's too many of them," Tein said.

Eirik took a sip from the cup and scowled. "How many?"

"Around eighty tents," Rime answered. "Probably fewer than three hundred men. Clothes out to dry after yesterday's rain. No indication of proper meals. Wet and hungry, if we're lucky."

Tein stepped between them. "What's the point? Let them leave. They're not headed for Ravnhov!"

Rime looked at him. "The fight is coming regardless. It's either now or later, and it will only be worse later. They're on their way to Meredir. Do you want him to have more men he can use to trap us between him and Mannfalla?"

Tein's lips thinned, and he looked away. The camp was waking up around them. Crotchety women and men in undergarments puttered into the undergrowth to relieve themselves. Eirik poured the contents of his cup into the heath. "What do you think, Rime?"

"I think we're fewer but stronger. Not many of them have full armor, and even fewer have horses. They won't be expecting a fight, since they're here as a gift to Meredir. To buy his allegiance. Nothing more. They're hemmed in between the river and a slope. We have the element of surprise. But we'll have to act quickly. They . . . They're going to realize a couple of scouts are missing. It's now or never."

Eirik chewed it over. Spat in the grass. "So it begins."

They ran through the woods. Between tall spruces. A steady rhythm of feet on the ground. Rime motioned to Kolkagga and they veered west. The others continued straight ahead. Smoke was rising beyond the hill. Men eating. Soon to be dying.

It used to be so simple. His heart pounding in his chest. Ice running through his veins. Fear and frenzy, but it had always been for the Seer. For something bigger than him. What was it now? What had it become? Revenge? Survival?

He bound the Might. His feet found fresh impetus. Strength and determination. The Might lied to him, telling him he'd always have more to draw upon. It soaked into his muscles. Reinforced his conviction and wore away his fear.

The ridge leaned over the camp like a cliff. Rime launched himself over the edge. Out of the corner of his eye he saw the others follow. A deluge of Kolkagga. The Might caught him and he hit the ground running. Drew his swords. Men were shouting, racing between the tents, some only in undershirts. They fumbled for swords. Tripped over ropes.

Startled horses whinnied and struggled to break free. Rime swept out into the river. It was wide but shallow, barely reaching his knees.

Water surged around his feet, as if trying to evade him. A man stood on the far shore, fumbling with a bow that he never managed to draw. Rime sliced open his chest. Raced onward, without looking back. Without thinking. Without feeling.

Coldness was all there was. Single-minded coldness.

He swung his steel into a body in front of him. The man sank to his knees. Rime sensed someone else approaching from behind. He crouched down and thrust one of his swords back. A maneuver he'd done hundreds of times.

Banahogg.

A gurgling told him that his aim had been true. More came. They were slow. Scared. Enraged. And many.

See it through. Soon. Victory will soon come.

Rime spotted horsemen in the crowd. They were struggling to get their mounts under control. A lean-to collapsed. Someone stumbled out of a nearby tent. A young man, almost paralyzed by fear. He clutched his sword in front of him with both hands. Raised it over his head. Exposed his chest.

Rime felt despair break through the cold. Who trained these men? Who was responsible for them dying so quickly and so needlessly?

The man swung, putting all his weight into it. Lost his balance and tumbled forward. Rime slipped around him and plunged a sword into his neck. He had to wrench it out again. The tent was sprayed with red.

Ormskira.

A maneuver he'd gotten wrong last time. Against Svarteld.

Someone shouted his name. He turned. Men were storming toward him. One in chain mail, two in leather. He raced to meet them. Their eyes widened as they realized what he was. A black shadow.

Already dead.

One of them hesitated, condemning the others to die first. Rime felt something hit him in the side. Blunt. Harmless. He drew on the

Might. Heard his heart in his ears. Racing. Pounding. He lunged toward them, planted his feet, and jumped. Spun. Crossed his swords as he hit the ground.

Blindring.

One of them collapsed. The other fell to his knees. Screamed. Gasped for air and screamed again. Like an animal. Drawn-out. He was dying, but it wasn't a scream of fear or pain. He was screaming like he was trying to say something. Something important. Rime struggled to remember the Seer's words. *Strength . . .* What else had he said, the Seer he had killed?

He had killed.

No doubt. Doubt means death!

He spun around to face the third man, who'd gained support. More men. More shouting. Gleaming steel. Rattling armor.

Then they stopped. Froze mid-movement, as if petrified. They gaped at Rime. At something behind him. Then they started running. Not toward him. Away from him. Something was wrong. The Might had grown more demanding. Different, somehow.

Rime turned.

Blindlings. Deadborn. Fighting their way through the camp with only their fists.

"NÁBYRN!"

The word spread across the battlefield like wildfire. Frantic warriors jumped into the river. Pushing against the current on all fours. Rime saw one of them fall. Disappear farther down, where it narrowed.

Rime sensed someone coming. Prepared to strike. Paused. It was Eirik and Tein. Tein's arms were shaking. Eirik had blood in his beard. "They're not attacking us!" he shouted. "Why aren't they attacking us?!" His question betrayed his bewilderment.

Rime looked around. The dead lay staring in the heath, as if fear alone had killed them. Ravens had already found the bodies in the river. They perched on bobbing heads and pecked at them with their beaks.

Men were gathering by the shore. Rime waved for Eirik and Tein to follow. Not everyone he saw was from Ravnhov. A few bore the sign of the Seer. Enemies. Men they'd just been trying to kill. Now they thronged together, friends and enemies, as if they needed one another just to stand. They gaped. Soundlessly. At a forest of blindlings.

Dressed like savages. Eyes white. Claws stained red.

Rime felt the bile rise in his throat. How many were there? Hundreds? What would they do?

A man sprinted across the river. His panicked splashing sounded almost comical in the otherwise complete silence. No one else moved.

The forest of blindlings parted, making way for someone advancing through their midst. A woman. She was wearing wide trousers and a tunic that exposed her stomach. Her hair was red as blood and for a moment Rime thought he was dead. That he was lying in Slokna, dreaming.

Hirka . . .

His feet suddenly felt weak. She came toward them. Planted her staff in the ground and stopped. Rime noticed the blood on his hands. His swords. He hated her seeing him like this. Her being here. In the wrong place, at the wrong time. This was him at his worst. This was the part of him that she hated. The part that meant she would never be his.

There was a coldness in her eyes that cut right through him. What had they done to her? She was different. Yet still painfully beautiful. She was Hirka. His chest tightened.

"Hirka?" Eirik's shaky voice was full of wonder. The chieftain took a step closer. "Is that you, girl?"

Hirka looked at Eirik. Her gaze grew warmer. She smiled sadly. Rested her head on the staff. "Eirik . . . I hear you need men."

TIES

The great hall was packed. The air thrummed with an unlikely mix of excitement and exhaustion. Joy and sorrow. Half of Ravnhov was crowded around Hirka.

Rime was sitting at the top of the stairs leading up to the gallery. He went to tuck his tail out of the way before remembering he no longer had one. That happened sometimes. His body still thought it was there.

He watched her.

She was standing next to one of the big fireplaces, surrounded by people. Tein was sticking to her like glue. Grinning at people like he'd carried her there himself. Jarladin embraced her as if she'd come back from Slokna, drowning her in his arms. Hlosnian was making his way through the crowd as well, pale red tunic sweeping through the room. The stone whisperer reached Hirka. Pinched her cheeks. Murmured something Rime couldn't hear for all the noise.

Ynge and one of the blue-clad servants were trying in vain to stop more people from coming in. They thronged together, craning their necks, desperate to see her—whether they knew her or not.

People loved her. People and deadborn . . . and probably menskr, too. She was loved in three worlds. And those who had never met her came because of the rumors of the red-haired girl who had led nábyrn to Ravnhov.

Questions rained down on her. Many ripe with fear. People wanted to know whether the town was besieged. Whether the blind had come from Mannfalla. How many were dead. And whether they should stay within the walls while deadborn made camp up by the ice.

Eirik finally lost his patience. He climbed up onto a table. Sloped of shoulder, weighed down by leather, and so large that it was a wonder the wood supported him. He bellowed that everyone would have their questions answered, but not until the soldiers had had a chance to wash the blood out of their damned beards.

People filed reluctantly out of the hall. Ynge closed the door once they were all out, and then leaned against it to be on the safe side. The soldiers started to take off their armor and shoes. The servants picked them up, wrinkling their noses as they took them away. A powerful odor filled the room. Smelly feet, sweat, and worse still.

Everyone's exhaustion was suddenly plain to see. Tein leaned against the fireplace, his grin no longer as convincing. Ynge slid down onto the floor by the door. Others settled against the heavy wooden pillars that ran in two rows through the hall and threw long shadows across the floor.

Kolkagga remained standing in the gallery—with the exception of Marrow, who sat down on the stairs with Rime.

Servants came in with tankards of ale and bowls of porridge. All chatter ceased.

Eirik studied Hirka as he ate. "Have they had anything to eat? Your lot?"

She shook her head. "They don't eat like us. They use . . ." She glanced down at her fingers. "They can find sustenance anywhere."

Tein replied with his mouth full of porridge. "Are we to feed them now, too? Is that how it's going to be? Are they to build houses and live up by the glacier? Is that the plan? Deadborn guests?"

For once, Rime could understand the outburst. The circumstances were far from usual. It was difficult to imagine this ending well.

"Umpiri," Hirka replied. "They call themselves Umpiri, not deadborn. They've lived more years than you can count and have a much bigger vocabulary. Not to mention they just saved your skin, Tein." She swallowed a mouthful of porridge as an uncertain chuckle rippled through the room. Tein's cheeks turned red, but to his credit, his grin didn't falter.

"Did they sell you a spine, too? Oh, that I can't wait to see!" He leaned toward her.

"Careful what you wish for, Tein."

"Yeah, because careful sounds like me, doesn't it?" The chieftain's son elbowed her playfully in the side. Her laugh was genuine yet burdened by things Rime knew she'd never share with him. He tensed his jaw as the sound gnawed its way into his chest. If only he were the kind of person who could make her laugh. Make her happy. Make her feel safe.

The kind of person she wanted.

Not someone doomed to disappoint her. To pull her into the darkness. Time and time again.

But that was how it had always been . . .

He'd come to Elveroa a son of the Council. Prim and proper. Tightly wound. She had coaxed him loose. Together they'd wreaked havoc. Climbed, swum, and run. She was free. And at times she'd made him believe he could be, too. They had been friends and rivals, battling for points to determine who was bravest.

Until Rime had gone through the Rite. Until the expectations of what he was to become had driven him to Kolkagga. Would he have done the same today, knowing it would only push her away?

Her eyes met his, giving him a jolt. The room seemed to shrink. His lips twitched. They remembered. Remembered meeting hers.

Could she see what he was thinking? Could she see that he wanted the whole hall to go to Slokna so he could have her to himself? The longing was eating him up inside. Stronger than ever, now that she was within reach.

She turned to Eirik again. Kept talking like she hadn't lit any fires. Rime looked down at his hands. His pulse raced under his skin.

He realized he hadn't heard a word of what was being said while she was looking at him.

"And you're sure of this?" Eirik asked.

"Sure as Slokna. They'll be here on the first day of what they call autumn. And there's a lot of them."

"There'll be even more of them when your lot up there stab us in the back," Tein said.

She gave him a look, and he had sense enough to lower his gaze.

"The world isn't as simple as you think, Tein. Aren't you fighting Mannfalla? Haven't you just killed ymlings? If *we* fight against our own, why wouldn't Umpiri? My lot have already severed ties with their world. They're called fallen. Houseless."

"Are they poor people?" asked one of the soldiers whose name Rime didn't know. He was leaning against a pillar and had only removed his shoes, too exhausted to manage the rest.

"In a way. More like outlaws."

Tein pushed his empty porridge bowl away. "Great . . . Murderers."

"Like you and me." Hirka reached for a tankard. "Eirik, you can't let yourself be caught between enemies. Mannfalla from the south and Meredir from the east? It's no good. Ravnhov might not be easy to capture, but it's a death trap if the enemy has enough time and bodies to throw at it. And they do. March on Mannfalla at the same time as Umpiri. You move in on Darkdaggar from the outside while I move in on him from the inside."

Her words surprised Rime. He was suddenly overcome with sadness. She was talking like a councillor. Strategic words about a world

365

she despised. War and death. And now she'd been forced into it. Forced to confront the distance between what she'd become and what she believed. It was a vile thought.

Eirik studied her for a moment. "So you're not staying, then?"

Hirka shook her head. "I can't. I have other plans."

Silence settled like a blanket over the room. Rime closed his eyes. A hand patted him on the back. Marrow. Rime glanced at him, but the black shadow took his hand back and kept eating, not looking at him. Rime suddenly felt naked. Tricked into showing something he hadn't meant to.

Hirka looked around. She seemed to realize everyone was waiting for her to continue. She cleared her throat. "The Might," she said. More cautious now. "I intend to heal the Might."

"What's wrong with the Might?" Ynge asked from his spot by the door.

"It no longer flows between the worlds," she replied. Rime could see a terrifying conviction in her eyes. One reminiscent of an augur in mid flow.

"It's pooled in Ym. Weakened, in a way. You must have heard that. That it's not what it used to be? That it's growing weaker and weaker? I don't think Ym can survive without it. No other world, either. It's only a matter of time. A hundred years. A thousand. I don't know."

She took a deep breath. "In any case, if it can be healed, it has to be during the war. Because nothing—"

"—feeds the Might like death," Eirik supplied. "My father used to say that."

She met Rime's gaze again. This time sharing his despair. Frustrated over everything she couldn't say. No one here would understand what they'd seen together. The human world. The Seer. Graal. The Might.

Or maybe he'd read her wrong. Maybe she was just remembering everything he'd done wrong.

Yes. See me. See everything I've done.

He wanted to hear her say the words. Hear her list every single misdeed he'd ever committed. Every misstep. Every single death. He wanted her to lay into him. For Svarteld. For Naiell. For Kolkagga. He wanted to taste the pain of her condemnation. Absolute. Irreconcilable. Cold. At the very least it would confirm he could make her feel *something*.

His heart was pounding in his chest. Adding to his suffering. Rime tore his eyes away from her. Got up and went into the gallery. Scared of his own thoughts. His own need.

Someone started wailing outside. Fists pounded against the doors. Ynge leaped to his feet, drew the bolt, and cracked one of them open. Vetle squeezed in. The boy plowed through the soldiers, upsetting a porridge bowl on the floor. Oblivious, he kept going. A young man with the mind of a child.

"Hirka!"

Hirka set her tankard down and opened her arms. They collided in a heartfelt embrace.

"You stink!" Vetle shouted. "You all stink!"

Tein stretched like a cat and folded his arms behind his head. Probably to show off the size of his arms. "Just as well it's bath time, then, right?" He nudged Hirka again. "It's been a while since we last bathed together. Feel free to join me if you—"

"Feel free to drop it, Tein." Her smile took the sting out of her words. "I need to check on the blind and make sure they're settled."

Tein snorted. "Of all the things I never thought I'd hear . . ."

"Even blindlings need rest, Tein."

"I meant someone not wanting to bathe with me. Unheard of." He winked and reached out to her. He was interrupted by a knock at the door. A man stuck his head in. Gray-haired with a teardrop in his forehead. Eyes like egg whites. A deadborn. The one she called Kolail. Every single ymling stopped what they were doing. Gaped.

The blindling looked embarrassed. "Hirka?"

She excused herself and left the hall. Her departure prompted several others to take their leave. It was time to make their way to the bathhouse. The taverns. Home.

A few men stayed behind. Those who hadn't managed to eat. Or laugh. Those who'd seen things they'd never forget. Those who'd perhaps fed the ravens for the first time. Those who were too shaken to pretend they still had hope. They sat in silence along the walls, not even looking at each other.

Rime had seen a lot in the past few years. More than any of them. But he felt just as dazed. He stared out of a small window overlooking the mountain behind the great hall. There she went. Walking up the path ahead of a deadborn.

Her hair hung in long, red tangles that brushed her back. Her tunic looked like it was strapped to her. A strange garment, but still so utterly her.

Rime turned away. Leaned against the wall and closed his eyes.

NAKED

Hirka climbed up the rock and sat down. She ran her fingers through her long hair. Too long, really. It fell to the middle of her back and was always getting tangled. So she'd stopped trying. Just started tying sections of it off. Bundling them together where necessary.

She let her hair dry on its own. It was gusty up here, the wind measuring its strength against the wall of ice behind her, only to be thrown back in waves. A never-ending battle of the elements. Autumn was on its way.

Ravnhov lay below, telling its beautiful lies. The chieftain's household with its great hall bid her welcome. The spruce in the yard whispered that she was finally home. That this was where she belonged. The wooded raven ravine that crossed the plateau . . . It remembered her. Reminded her that she'd stood there with Rime and looked out over Blindból. All the houses with their pointed turf roofs, hugging the slopes, getting closer together to form the town. Stalls. Inns. She could see The Raven's Brood from here. Where she'd pulled her knife out of the thigh of a man whose name she no longer remembered. It was so long ago. Back when she was the rot, and the blind were the monsters.

They were allies now. Family. And she'd turned the world upside down by leading them here. Hundreds of them. She glanced behind her to see them settling in along the wall of the glacier. They were pitching makeshift tents of staffs and animal hides. Skolm was farther down, past the rocky ground, lying in the heath with his eyes closed.

She heard footsteps. Kolail appeared next to her, leaned against the rock, and took a sip from a tankard. She was surprised he'd found one. Most were drinking from bottles or bowls now that Ravnhov was full to bursting.

He looked at her, the wind tugging at his steely hair. His lips drew back into a smile. She had to hand it to him—he'd gotten much better at it.

"You smell better than them," he said, jerking his head in the direction of the others.

"I've had a bath. You should try it sometime."

"Takes more than a bath to get the fallen clean." He took another swig.

Hirka looked at him. He'd done away with the sheepskin, which made him look lighter. Stand taller. He'd done away with a lot. His people and his home. He'd thrown caution to the wind and embraced a new fate. Left. Followed her. Made her proud.

"Come here," she said.

She took his tankard and put it down on the rock. She pulled him closer. Scooched to the edge until she had his shoulders between her knees. She lifted his chin. He looked scared. He tried to back away, but she squeezed her legs to hold him in place. "Stand still!"

She drew her knife and brought it to his forehead. Strangely, that set him at ease. She wedged the tip right in under the teardrop. Looked him in the eyes. A storm of black and white, like he didn't know what to feel. She asked the question without saying a word.

Are you ready?

He gave an almost imperceptible nod. Hirka struck the blade of the knife. The teardrop came loose and stuck to the steel. Blood welled forth and trickled down his nose. The wound closed before her very eyes. She leaned forward and kissed his forehead. "You're in Ym now," she said. "We don't have fallen here, Kolail."

She placed the teardrop in his hand and wrapped his claws around it. His eyes were black and shining, like fireglass. Like the night sky. And it was quiet. Too quiet, she realized.

She looked up and saw that they were no longer alone. Umpiri had gathered around them. Houseless made room for the fallen as they pushed their way forward. A sea of teardrops. She knew what they wanted, but it wasn't right. This wasn't about her. She sheathed her knife.

"You left Dreysíl on your own. You can free yourselves on your own."

That was all they needed to hear.

Knives were drawn. Weapons she hadn't noticed before. Hidden in shoes, under their clothes. The myth that Umpiri feared nothing was long dead. Teardrops were removed. Some did it themselves. Some helped one another. A festival of blood for free folk.

Kolail looked up at her. "I'm going to give you a name, woman. When I find one good enough." He said it in ymish, as if he were trying to practice.

Hirka smiled. "Names don't stick to me. I've had a lot. Tailless, child of Odin, the rot, girl, Red, Sulni . . ."

"Sulni . . ." He tested the word. "That's perfect."

Hirka frowned. That was what Naiell had called her. Mayfly. "Why?" she asked, even though she wasn't sure she wanted to know.

"If you don't get it, then you haven't seen one. Sulni is a kind of . . ." He searched for the word. "Butterfly? It makes patterns on stone. Out of the strangest little things. It can carry hundreds of times its own weight. And its wings . . ." Kolail stroked her hair. Hesitantly, as if trying to restrain himself. "Well, it's the most beautiful creature in all of Dreysíl."

Hirka felt her throat tighten. She clutched her chest in an attempt to dull the ache inside her, but she was powerless to stop it.

Sulni. Strong. Beautiful.

She'd thought it was an insult. Proof of how little she meant to Naiell. She needed to keep believing that. Needed to believe he hadn't cared about her. How else was she supposed to live with his death?

She felt ill. She'd just bathed, but her hands were sticky with blood. From Kolail's forehead. Naiell's heart. A hundred soldiers from Mannfalla. Mickey in York. Blood from all worlds.

Suddenly she was in Kolail's arms. Had she fallen? He lifted her down off the rock and led her away from the others. "You need rest," he said, and she understood what that meant coming from Umpiri.

"You think you know what she needs?"

Rime.

He stood on the path ahead of them. His hair was white again, no longer caked with blood. He stood ready to draw his swords. Always ready to draw his swords.

Kolail crouched, equally ready to pounce. Hirka put a hand on his chest. "Leave us, Kolail. I'm not in any danger." He growled but withdrew. Rime watched him for a moment before meeting her gaze.

"What is he? A bodyguard? A pet?"

She grabbed him and dragged him along the side of the glacier until they were some distance off. That didn't stop white gazes from following them.

"Look at them!" Rime said. "People are terrified. No one wants to fight alongside deadborn!"

"They're Umpiri, and they can hear every word you're saying!"

"From there?"

"Yes, from there."

His gaze swept over the blindlings, who stood a good distance away, doing a poor job of concealing their interest. She could see how he was sizing them up. How he feared them. And it was no wonder. They were quick. Strong. With hearing like wolves.

Rime shook his head. "They'll kill us all."

She wanted to tell him off, but she couldn't be entirely sure he was wrong.

Kolail watched them over the rim of his tankard as he drank. She tried to imagine how his narrow white gaze must have appeared to Rime. To anyone who hadn't lived with them. Could she blame them for being terrified? For believing the arrival of the deadborn signaled their doom?

Rime clenched his fists. "We're going to lose allies, Hirka. No one will understand . . . this." He pointed at them.

"They don't need to understand. It is what it is."

"And what's that? Dancing with monsters?"

"I'm one of them!"

The sound of her voice bouncing off the wall of ice gave her a start. Kolail looked ready to come running if she needed him. A monster, ready to save her from another monster.

Hopeless. Had this ever been anything other than hopeless?

Hirka signaled for Rime to follow her. She slipped gratefully through a crevasse in the glacier. Away from prying eyes. The shimmering walls seemed familiar. She'd been here before. Seen something terrible.

Hirka continued through the crevasse, which led to a hollow in the ice. Protruding from one wall was a frozen surface. A table of snow. That was where he'd lain. The first blindling she'd ever set eyes on. The light coming through the ice had made his skin look blue. A gaping wound had stretched across his body.

She didn't know who had killed him. It could have been Eirik. It could have been someone else. But there she'd stood, what felt like a lifetime ago, face-to-face with the existence of blindlings. Finally she'd known the truth. Until that moment, she'd been ignorant.

Hirka placed her hands on the frozen surface where he'd lain. There was something awful about how it looked like he'd never been there. He might have been a friend of Skerri's. Maybe even family. No one should have to vanish without a trace.

Faces pushed their way through her thoughts. Father, in his wheeled chair. Lindri. Svarteld. What remained of them? Their tracks ought to have been so deep that no one could erase them. She heard herself laugh, and she didn't like the sound of it.

"Hirka?"

Rime had followed her. She turned to face him. The shadow who had killed Naiell. Grief sliced through her. She so needed him to understand that he was as much a monster as the blind.

"They weren't brothers, Rime. Graal and Naiell. That may not be important to you, but it means everything to Umpiri. The brothers were a lie. My family's house was built on a lie. Naiell found out, and he knew that his life was over. That it would all come out one day. And I guess he didn't want to wait for the repercussions. So he betrayed them and came here. That was how it started. The war. Perhaps he only did what he felt he had to. And for that you killed him. Without knowing. Without knowing him."

Rime tensed his jaw and looked away. He didn't answer. He would never feel he had to answer for death. She knew that. He was what he was.

She looked at his throat. The scar was no longer visible. She was suddenly very aware of the weight of the knife on her hip. He was close. It would be so easy. Just one small step. One stab. The rest was up to fate, and to those gods who might exist.

If she could only hold on to her hate for a little longer.

"You really think he was the Seer?" Rime asked. "You think he'd have followed you, the way this lot follow you? But what do you

374

think will happen afterward? If this ever ends, what do you picture happening? Think about it! Are they going to stay here? Do you think ymlings can share the world with deadborn?!"

Hirka could hear her teeth grinding. "Before I'm done, all peoples will share all worlds. The Might will be owned by everyone."

He blinked, as if he couldn't believe what he was hearing. "No matter the cost? You hate me for the lives I've taken, but you're planning the biggest bloodbath the world will ever have seen!"

Hirka lowered her eyes. He doubted her. She couldn't blame him, not even for that. She moved her hand closer to the knife. Glanced at the swords strapped to his back and tried not to think about how ridiculously easy it would be for him to disarm her.

"You don't think twice about sending men to Slokna," she said bitterly. "So can you explain something for me? If you knew that Graal was willing to go to such lengths . . . If you knew that he'd use us against each other to win his war, why didn't you kill him? Why was the man costing us the most allowed to live?"

Her hand shook next to the sheath. She couldn't control it.

Rime took a step closer. Eyes narrowed in anger. "Because he's your father, and he wasn't threatening us."

Hirka threw up her hands up in frustration. "So? You've killed for far less! Naiell because he *might* pose a threat. Svarteld because he challenged you. And gods know how many you've killed for a seer who had long since abandoned Eisvaldr, so why couldn't you kill the one person you really should have killed?! The one who's the reason—"

"Because you wouldn't have wanted me to!"

His voice bounced off the ice. His top lip twitched, pulling into an unrecognizable shape, and she hated it. She could have drawn his lips blindfolded, but now they were strange. He was more of an animal than any blindling she'd seen. Pale, with hair like snow.

His rage turned to confusion, as if he hadn't realized he'd been shouting. Then his stony face cracked. He slumped back against the wall. Stood there panting, as if he were wounded.

"Because you wouldn't have wanted me to," he repeated in a hoarse whisper. "Because it wouldn't have been right. But nothing is right anymore. You think I've killed a lot of people, but you have no idea . . . Kolkagga would still be alive had it not been for me." His voice was gravelly. As if he were dying. He looked up. Pale-gray wolf eyes. Exhausted. Haunted. They tore her up inside. They were unveiled. They saw her. And they implored her to see him.

Hirka felt the shaking in her hand spread upward. Even her jaw was quivering. He couldn't do this to her. Not now. He had to be cold. A murderer. Someone she could hate. Not an open wound. But it was too late. Every muscle in her body knew it was too late. Her hand dropped. He would die for Graal. Because she couldn't do what had to be done.

Pull a knife? On Rime?

No. Never.

"We burned them," he said. "It took days." He started to slide to the ground. Hirka pressed her arm against his chest, pinning him against the wall so he wouldn't fall. Never fall.

"Who are you, Rime?" She grabbed the leather straps that crossed his chest. Shook them. "Who are you, Rime? Say it!" She wanted him to remember. More than anything. Say who he was.

He leaned forward. Pressed his lips to her temple. "I am Rime An-Elderin. And if I am anything else at all, I am yours."

Hirka sobbed into his chest. His words bored into her. Something inside her broke. Something that had contained her longing from the moment she'd set eyes on him. Now it flowed through her blood unimpeded. She couldn't hide it. There was nowhere for it to hide. She was powerless. Naked. Exposed.

The feeling sent a shiver surging through her. Intoxicating and terrifying. What if she wanted him more than he wanted her?

She lifted her head and looked at him.

His eyes were burning with desire. They told her everything she needed to know. Hirka wrapped her hands around his neck and pulled him toward her. His lips found hers. A trembling touch. Then he awoke.

She kissed him like a woman starved, but it wasn't enough. It would never be enough. She had to have more of him.

He buried his hand in her hair. Pressed her against him. One warm hand against her head, another against her back. Hirka knew what was going to happen. What had to happen. There wasn't a force in the world that could stop her. Her longing had been building for too long.

The smell of him was intoxicating. She pressed herself against him to erase any and all distance between them. His leather armor creaked—a sound so utterly him that she could have cried. She fumbled with the clasps on his armor. Tore at them until they loosened and his swords fell.

He gasped and pushed her back. His gaze flickered, as if searching for something in hers. What? What was he waiting for?

"Are you . . . It's . . ." He swallowed.

Hirka looked at him. What was he afraid of? Her getting cold? She'd lived in ice for as long as she could remember.

"You forgive me?" he whispered.

"No," she answered. "When I forgive you, you'll know." She pulled him toward her again. His kiss grew harder. More demanding. He'd understood. Finally understood. He pulled at her tunic and she helped him get it over her head. Found his belt. And a heat swelling against her hand.

He gasped for air, making her lips tingle. The Might hit her like a tempest. She didn't know whether he'd meant to bind, but it didn't matter. The Might was here. It opened her. Opened him. His hands were burning against her back. Against her skin. They tore at the straps around her waist. His body was solid against hers. Solid and alive.

The heat from the Might made the ice sweat. Drip from the ceiling and rain down on his chest.

It was strong. Wild. Dangerous.

He slipped around her. Pressed her up against the ice. Met her gaze. Raw. Naked. There was nothing between them. He grabbed the back of her thighs. She wrapped her legs around his hips and pulled him toward her. Into her. They were one. She and Rime.

He whispered her name.

Where once there had been nothing, now there was everything. An exploding warmth. A sweet, intense pain. He thrust into her. Forced gasps out of her lungs. Hard. Rhythmic. The Might picked them apart. Pieced them back together as one. In waves. All her blood rushed to her sex. She tightened around him. Trembled. Was shaken from within.

Rime stifled a scream against her neck.

She welcomed a warmth that threatened to burn her from within. She was trapped between hot and cold. Her legs grew weak, but he had her. Held her.

His name bounced around inside her head.

Rime. Rime. Rime . . .

They sank slowly to the ground, bodies no longer able to hold them up. They lay on their backs, breath mingling in the cold air.

He pulled himself up onto his elbow. Leaned over her. She looked into his eyes as he eased her tunic underneath her so she wouldn't stick to the ice. A touching but pointless gesture considering what they'd just done.

His eyes roved greedily over her body as if he'd never see her again. He ran a hand over her breast. Cocked his head. Hirka studied his face. Took in every detail. His chin. His sculpted lips. Warm and red now.

This. This one moment. Now time could stop. Now worlds could fall.

His smile twisted in pain. He grabbed his throat.

Hirka closed her eyes. Certainty sank into her. Pierced her like steel. It was over. It was too late. The time they'd been given was up. Graal hadn't been able to contact Damayanti or Skerri, and now he knew that he'd been played for a fool.

Rime felt for his clothes. For the blood Hirka knew he needed to answer Graal. Oblivious to the fact he was about to pay the price for her treachery.

She sat up. "Lie down. I'll find it." She pushed him down onto the ice. The ground was cold now that the Might had released them. Hirka pretended to search for the vial of blood in his pockets while she fought back tears. Her hair stood on end. She slid the knife from its sheath without a sound.

He coughed. "Hirka . . ."

She had to hurry. She kneeled down next to him. Held her hand to his belly. Then she thrust the knife in. He howled. Arched against the ice. She held him down so she could pull the knife back out. The wound belched blood.

She dropped the knife. Her body was numb. Cold. She didn't think she'd ever be able to move again. Rime dragged himself back on his elbows, tracking blood with him. Black in the light from the ice. He slumped against the wall. She'd expected retaliation. He was Kolkagga. His swords were within reach.

A part of her had hoped he'd go for them.

He looked at her. The shock was gone. The horror had made way for something else. An incomprehensible peace.

"I . . ." He groaned. "I'd thought I'd have to do it myself. Take the power from . . . from Graal. But . . ." He cleared his throat. Grimaced in pain. "If you wanted me dead, all you had to do was ask."

Hirka swallowed a sob. It got stuck in her throat and seemed to grow. Until her head felt like it might explode. She felt his warmth dripping down her thighs. She stared at his throat. In the Seer's name, why was nothing happening? Where was the beak? Did he really think he couldn't die?

He is Kolkagga.

"I dipped the knife in bloodweed," she said, not recognizing her own voice. It was like someone else was speaking. "It will all be over soon."

The fear returned to his eyes. He started coughing so violently that he fell onto all fours. He put his hand on the wall as if to pull himself up, but he didn't have a chance to.

He vomited.

It was the most beautiful sound she'd ever heard. The sound of salvation. And choking. Hirka threw herself at him. Thumped his back with her fists. He vomited again.

The beak forced its way out. Dropped onto the ice. Thick blood dripped from his lips.

Hirka pushed him onto his back. No time to lose. She held his tunic to the wound. Strapped it in place with his belt. Rime stared at her with glassy eyes. She found the knife again. Clamped her hand around the blade and pulled. She barely noticed the pain, dulled as it was by her heart pounding in her mouth. She felt everything. She felt nothing.

She lifted his tunic and dripped blood onto his wound. Blood of the first. Blood of raven. It would make it heal faster. All she could do was hope she'd stuck him where she'd meant to.

"There was no poison, Rime. You're going to be fine." She wasn't sure he could hear her.

She picked up the beak. Squeezed it in her bleeding hand. She could no longer contain her sobs. So violent it felt like they were being wrenched from her very core.

Just a little longer. She had to hold on just a little longer. "I don't know what your name was," she gasped in umǫni. "But I'm calling you Kuro. After my first raven. After my heart. Take me. Make me one of you."

The beak neither answered nor moved.

Then she heard the shrieks. The ravens soaring over the ice. Flying home to Ravnhov for the night.

The beak writhed in her hand. She gave a start. Dropped it.

Pain.

Her body started to contract and convulse. She thought she heard her name. Rime shouting. But she no longer had a name. She was nothing more than fear and anguish.

Her blood vessels became blue serpents enveloping her arms. She heard a sound and knew it was her skin tearing, but she was afraid to look. Her bones started to contract. Her neck was wrenched to one side. The space changed. Pulsed red. She curled up into a ball and cried.

Her body was torn to pieces. Every part of her crumpled. Every part of her cried. Then she spread her wings. All their wings. She was raven. She was a flock. She exploded in black and flew out of the crevasse.

Born of ice.

RAVENBORN

I am. Who am I?

Uncertainty. A wonder that ought not be. Where did it come from?

We are raven.

Raven flew over green spruces. High and low. Some dropping down, others rising up. A river sparkled down below. Waves silver. Raven wanted to take it along, but river was too big. River did what it wanted. It had no beginning. No end. River was for all, not just for raven, raven reluctantly accepted.

Who am I?

We are raven! Stop asking.

The wind was like water between her feathers. Not nothing, but a mass. Strong in some places. Weak in others. The wind wasn't emptiness. Raven knew that. Where did this wonder come from? This compulsion to marvel? Who didn't know what the wind was? raven wondered. But then she remembered it wasn't important. She was neither hungry nor cold, and there was no danger here. She was raven.

The nests of the wingless rose up from the ground. Raven flew higher. They weren't to be trusted, the wingless. They didn't look far enough ahead to know that river had no beginning. Or end. That nothing did. Raven wanted to rest, but fear pushed her onward.

Fear? What did she have to fear? She was raven.

Who are you?

I'm Hirka!

Panic ripped through her. All the way out to the end of her tail. The tips of her wings. Her heart felt too small. Her body too tight. She plummeted toward the ground. Dropped like a stone. Spread her wings. They were swept backward.

We don't fight the wind!

We? What we? Hirka gasped for breath. Her, or someone else? She was raven. She let raven take over. Raven had to fly. She couldn't. Raven took back control. Raven understood the wind. The treetops. The sea. The sand. Nothing was where it was supposed to be. She was seeing too much. Her thoughts were torn to shreds. Fragmented. Scattered in every direction. She was raven.

Where are we?

We are everywhere.

She squinted into the wind. Everything felt wrong. And right. So very right. She'd climbed all her life. Trees and roofs. But never like this. Never as raven.

Of course we have. We are raven.

Raven who are. Raven who were. Raven who always will be.

The thoughts came like drips from eternity. Truths and lies. Connections. Like falling rain. Stone and blood. Earth and fire. The wingless had a name for this.

The wingless have a name for everything.

Raven understood. Raven spoke all languages. From all times. Because everything came from the same place. Everything was one.

The Might.

Hirka could feel it. Knew she shouldn't be able to feel it. Did she deserve it? She couldn't shake the feeling she'd done too much wrong.

We all have.

But it shouldn't have been possible for Hirka to be here. She'd been a child of Odin. The rot. Deadborn. She was unearthed. She wasn't welcome anywhere. In any world.

You're welcome here.

Raven landed on a pile of charred planks amid the ruins of a cabin overlooking the sea. The Hovel. The wingless had plunged a sword into the ground. Father's sword. Thorrald's sword. Ashy and gray on one side. Washed clean by the sea and the rain on the other.

A headboard lay on the ground. Fire hadn't been able to consume it. Wings were carved into it, stretching out from the center. Father's work.

My bed.

Does it make you sad?

Raven asked indifferently. Neither warm nor cold. It just asked. A wheel stuck out from under a pile of rocks. Ash had settled in the broken spokes.

Yes.

Raven spread its wings and circled the skies above Elveroa. Something on the riverbank caught their attention. Something that didn't belong there. Something pale between the rocks. Raven landed on one and pecked at whatever it was. It was something the wingless had made. A wooden horse. A toy.

Jomar. Do we want it? Do we want to take it with us?

No. Some things are lost forever.

Raven flew away from the sea. She put her grief behind her. The notion of living or dying. She put aside her shame and fear. She was raven. She was one of the first.

The landscape rushed past beneath her. It rose up as mountains. Tall, thin mountains with rivers of mist between them.

Blindból.

Kolkagga, who no longer were. Svarteld. Lindri. A white city rose up beyond the mountains. Eisvaldr. The Seer's city. My city. Our city. Mannfalla.

Darkdaggar...

Hatred and fury ripped through raven. Wind tore at their wings until she thought they might break. She fell. Plummeted in a spiral of pain. Bones splintered. Raven screamed. Raven died. Hirka was frozen in free fall. Crumpled. She fought her way out of a strange body in an explosion of blood and bone. Then she slammed into the cobblestones. Blind, broken, and naked.

She tried to move her hands. They listened. She hadn't thought they would. She dug her fingers between the stones. Found earth. Pulled herself forward. The Might pulsed through her. She blinked. Could see again. See that her arm was bent in the wrong place. She considered binding, but there was no need to. The Might was already there. Interwoven with and inseparable from her. They were one.

Hirka squeezed one of the cobblestones. It cracked under her hand. She got up and realized she wasn't alone.

People stood staring around her. Strangers. No one she knew. But she knew the city. She was near the river, at the end of Mannfalla. Where the houses leaned toward each other and the streets smelled of fish. No one said anything. They just stood there, stunned. A woman pulled a boy closer to her, keeping an arm over his chest so he wouldn't run away.

A dead raven fell down between her and the onlookers. It smacked into the ground like a bundle of wet clothes. Black and bloody. Then came another. And another. Dead birds rained from the sky. Hundreds of them. People backed away. No one screamed. She found that strange. The rain didn't stop until the street was black with bodies.

A thickset man pulled off his tunic. Held it out to her. Hesitantly. Without a word. She took it and put it on. It fell almost to her knees.

She smiled at him. He gave her a cautious nod in return.

The boy tore himself out of his mother's grip. "You're bleeding."

Are we bleeding? No. We're alive. We're raven.

A hundred voices in her head. A hundred thoughts. She was legion. Hirka rolled up the sleeves of the tunic. The Might looked black in her veins. Her skin was sticky with raven blood. She brought a hand to her broken arm. Forced the bone back into place. Saw where it was supposed to go without knowing how. Bone fused with bone. The Might saw. The Might knew.

"We're not dead," she said to the boy.

They'd been wrong. They'd all been wrong. They'd said she could never become one with the Might. Only Umpiri could. Dreyri. Those who had pure blood, blood of the first. But she'd seen the spiral stones in three worlds. Three different worlds. What was old was old for all of them.

There was no such thing as pure blood. There was only a beginning, and in the beginning, everything was one. Interwoven.

Like her. Everything had begun like her.

FREE

Rime blinked the fog out of his eyes. Tried to get up but was pushed firmly down again.

"Not yet," a deep voice said. A gray-haired deadborn was crouched down next to him. Rime knew him, but the name escaped him.

Light filtered in between animal skins. A primitive tent. So he was still in Ravnhov. In the blindling camp.

I'm alive . . .

He grabbed his throat without thinking. Felt pain, but nothing more.

"Here."

The deadborn tossed a beak onto his chest. Rime picked it up and held it to the light. Solid. Wretched but harmless. It was dead. As a beak should be. Only the blood in its grooves revealed that it had lived inside him. Made demands on him.

He was free.

Still . . . Something niggled at him. Something he ought to remember.

He'd loved her. By the gods, how he'd loved her. His body quickened at the memory. Hot and intense. He discreetly pulled the wool blanket up over his midriff. The blindling moved a hand to his forehead, thinking his flush was due to fever.

Rime remembered. Graal had called on him. She'd cried. Stuck her knife in him. And then . . .

"She was . . . Her body . . ." He didn't have the words to describe what he'd seen. None that anyone would believe or understand. "She was pressed together. Into . . ."

"Into a raven. We know." The blindling handed him a tankard of water. "We saw them come. She isn't dead, if that's what you're thinking."

Rime drank. The blindling eyed him dubiously, with eyes like wet snow. Bright. Glassy. Intense. He took the tankard from Rime and set it down. "You're alive because she loves you, and for no other reason. So tell me, why did she stab you? Did you hurt her?"

Rime leaned back, against what he thought was a pillow. Then he noticed it was green. Her bag. It made him smile.

"Never. I would never hurt her. We were . . . We . . ."

"You don't need to tell me what you were doing, ymling. I could smell it from here. Why did she stab you?"

Rime hesitated. He didn't know why. He could only guess.

"Because I had this." He tossed the beak to the ground. "It's a raven beak. It can—"

"I know what it is. I'm old enough to have fought in the war."

Rime started to laugh. His stomach twinged. He lifted his head to look, but there were no signs of damage. He lay back down.

"She stabbed me because I was useless. A slave to Graal, and a weapon he could use. Against her. Against everyone. She did the only thing that was right. She did what was necessary."

Svarteld would have been proud.

"I thought that, too," the blindling answered. "But it's rare to see such a fortunate stab wound. She has a pretty good idea where everything is in there, doesn't she?"

Rime pulled himself up onto his elbows. It was surprisingly easy. The deadborn was right. Hirka knew. Had she wanted him dead, he would be. Rime glanced at the beak.

"You're saying she freed me?"

The blindling shrugged. "She freed us all."

Rime sat up. Rolled his neck from side to side and was rewarded with a satisfying crack.

Free.

He'd been fettered since he took the beak. Lived with the constant knowledge that he was doomed. That Graal would be able to use him. Manipulate him. Coerce him. Or kill him, if all else failed.

Not anymore. Never again.

Rime took a deep breath. It flowed freely into his lungs. Filled his chest. He was freer than he'd ever been. Untethered. And more of a man.

He loved her. More than life itself.

Rime got up. The blindling looked at him as if he'd expected him to fall.

Rime looked down at his hands. Opened them. Closed them. He felt strong. Blessed. Deadly. Freedom pumped through his veins, invigorating him. A promise of everything he could now do.

He was Kolkagga. What remained of the black shadows. Svarteld's legacy. He wasn't dead. He was alive.

Rime held out a hand to the blindling. He got up and looked at it as if he weren't quite sure what he was supposed to do with it. But he gripped it anyway.

"I'm Rime."

"I'm Kolail," the blindling answered, baring his canines in what Rime realized was an attempt at a smile.

"I saw you on the battlefield, Rime. You give as good as you get."

Rime looked at him. Savored the coldness of his own smile. "You haven't seen anything yet."

DREYRI

Hirka put her audience behind her and continued down the Catgut. They would talk about what they'd seen. The red-haired girl who had fallen from the sky and lived. Who was wandering the streets of Mannfalla in nothing but a baggy tunic. It would reach the ears of the Council. And Darkdaggar.

She knew she ought to hurry, but she was having a hard time convincing herself of the urgency of anything. There was too much going on in the world around her. She was seeing everything for the first time.

She could smell the Might. Strong in some places. Weaker elsewhere. A network, like roots in the ground. She walked until the streets were no longer cobbled. Until the houses grew more dilapidated and leaned against one another. Then she knew she was in the right place.

She squeezed between two houses, into an alleyway that smelled of decay. A low stack of wood leaned against the old city wall. She moved the logs, exposing the stones.

They were gray and worn, flecked with yellow moss. They'd been there since time immemorial, but still they seemed fragile. Like she could see through them. Into them. They were so insubstantial that all she needed to do was . . .

Hirka raised her hand and hadn't even gotten as far as pressing it to the wall before the stone started running. Sweating. She dug her fingers into it. Drew it out in ribbons, like red-hot clay. The Might thickened around her fingers. It was the only thing stopping them from burning. Or *were* they burning? She wasn't sure. It was just pain. Pain was something she understood.

She thrummed with pure, raw energy. Stone dripped from her fingers. A fluid and impossible heat. Like the heat from Rime between her thighs. She looked down. Streaks of raven blood had dried on her legs. Part of her knew nothing would ever be the same again. That what she was doing didn't belong in her reality. Stone slinger. Stone whisperer. She was like Hlosnian, but without the need for tools. Blindcraft. Mightcraft.

What would she be capable of when it was truly strong?

We have blood of the first.

We can shape.

Hirka pushed in what remained of the stones. They were long and heavy. Then she crawled into the wall. Once inside, she stuck her arm back out and restacked as many of the logs as possible. Then she put the stones back, too. Covering her tracks as best she could.

It got darker, but it was more of a feeling than reality. She could see just as well as before. The passage sloped down, narrow between the walls, and she followed it until she recognized where she was. The crack leading to the cave appeared before her. She continued through it. She wasn't scared of confined spaces anymore. She'd been earthborn. And ravenborn.

She came out in the cave where the stones hung from the ceiling in an enormous circle. A mirror image of the raven ring on the surface.

The three guards leaped to their feet. They didn't want to be seen sitting down. Umpiri were Umpiri, fallen or not.

The others were sitting or lying along the wall. Hands and feet bound. Someone had gagged Skerri, and it wasn't difficult to guess why.

Skerri spotted her. Struggled to her knees. It was the best she could do, tethered as she was. Her eyes flooded black. She stared at Hirka. Then her fury faded. Became something else. Confusion. Fear. She didn't dare move.

The guards stared, too. One of them pointed. Brey, if she remembered correctly. "Your eyes," he said. "They're like ours."

Hirka understood his words. Understood that they ought to mean something, but she couldn't bring herself to do anything except shrug. "Yet still we see."

We see. We see everything. Everywhere.

We see wingless. Broken stone. Channels in the earth.

Hirka clamped her hands around her head. Breathed deeply until the voices of raven became a whisper she could ignore. She couldn't be everywhere. She had to be here. Now. So much depended on her.

Damayanti stirred and dragged herself up until she was sitting against the wall, peering into the darkness.

Hirka looked at the guards. "Are there more torches?" Brey nodded and went over to the bags. Hirka crouched down next to Damayanti. The torch ignited, forming a ring of light around them. Pitifully small in the space. A star in a dark sky.

Damayanti blinked. Recognized Hirka. The relief in her eyes was almost touching.

Hirka held out her hand. Brey put a knife in it without comment. An astute man. Hirka cut the ropes. Damayanti let out a sob and rubbed her wrists.

"Thanks for waiting," Hirka said, as if she'd had any choice in the matter. "I've done what I came to do."

Damayanti met Hirka's gaze and jumped as if she'd seen a ghost. But she managed to recover her dignity. "He won't like this," she said thickly. Several days underground had left her with a blocked nose.

"No," Hirka replied. "He won't. Has he tried to contact you?"

Damayanti nodded, face stricken. How painful had it been, not to be able to answer him? Hirka spotted red claw marks across her clavicle and glanced at the three fallen. The woman called Vinrid crossed her arms over her chest. "She started screaming. I didn't have a choice."

Hirka put a hand on Damayanti's shoulder. She was cold. "Forgive me. I wouldn't have kept you here unless I had to."

Damayanti rubbed her nose. She even managed to make that look graceful. "I hope it was worth it," she said. "Your father's not the forgiving kind."

Hirka chuckled. "That's the understatement of the century. But he betrayed me first. *You* betrayed me first."

Hungl and Tyla shifted where they lay. Listening. Gauging the situation. Unsure as to what was going on.

Hirka got up and went over to Skerri.

"She tried to draw on the Might," Vinrid said. "We had to knock her out a few times. And she wouldn't shut up."

Hirka loosened the gag. Skerri didn't waste time.

"I don't care what you've done. You've lost either way!" Her voice echoed around the cave. "They'll have gathered in Nifel by now. All of them. Every single Umpiri in Dreysíl is on the other side of these stones, and there's nothing you can do to stop them! Nothing!"

Hirka couldn't believe she'd missed her voice. Her angry screeching. Her black lips. Maybe it was because they couldn't hurt her anymore.

"I'm not planning on stopping them, Skerri. I came here to lead them, remember?"

Skerri snarled. "Lead them? You're a traitor! I've always known you were a traitor. Like Naiell. You're only bringing more shame on the family." She leaned away from Hirka, demonstrating her distance and disgust.

Hirka leaned closer. "Ah, but you're forgetting something important, Skerri. Naiell wasn't family."

Skerri froze, pulse visibly pounding in her throat. She glanced around involuntarily, fearing what the others might have gleaned.

"You've nothing to fear, Skerri. It'll stay a secret." Hirka brought her knife to the ropes but then paused. "Unless you're planning on causing trouble and doing something really stupid. Like trying to bury me alive, say."

Skerri was torn between anger and confusion. "What are you expecting me to do?"

"What you've waited a thousand years to do. Start a war."

"So why have we been tied up here for the first know how many days?! What was the point if you didn't want to stop us?"

Hirka cut the ropes. Skerri leaped to her feet straight away, quick to conceal how unsteady she was.

"That's just it, Skerri. You didn't understand. You've thirsted for the Might but never made any attempt to understand it. All you thought about was blood and death. Tearing everything apart with your claws. I don't have claws. But now I have raven."

She gave the knife back to Brey. "Get Hungl and Tyla on their feet. We're leaving." Brey did as he was told. Hirka held out a hand to Damayanti. Helped her up.

"Damayanti, you're a free woman again. As free as you can be with that beak. The next time he asks you to open the gateways for us will be the last."

Hirka let the Might fill the room. Fill her. It vibrated between the stones, making a ringing sound Hirka was pretty sure no one else could hear. Stonesong.

"Wait . . ." Damayanti touched her arm. "Have you . . . Is Rime alive? Have you seen him?"

Hirka looked at her. The treacherously beautiful dancer who had tricked Rime into taking the beak. The woman who was to blame for Hirka having to stick him with her knife. She'd made him Graal's slave. And before Rime, it had been Urd.

Damayanti was an extension of Graal in a world he couldn't reach. And here she stood, her eyes filled with love for someone she'd used and betrayed.

Skerri snorted at Damayanti. "Is he alive? Gweni, can't you smell it? Her thighs reek of him!"

Damayanti stepped back, lifting her chin in a failed attempt to look unruffled.

Hirka suppressed a smile. Picked up the raven quiver and gave it to Skerri. "This belongs to you." Then she walked between the stones.

The empty space wasn't like before. The silence was fuller. And it no longer made her feel sick. A few steps into nothingness and she came out between the towering stone monoliths of the hall. Maknamorr, Skerri had called it. And now she remembered where she'd heard the word before. Something Naiell had said.

The things you don't know could fill Maknamorr, Sulni.

He'd been right.

The hall was packed. People elbowed their way forward and surrounded the raven ring. They must have noticed it was awake. Seen the snowflakes being drawn in.

The room was a hive of activity. The largest of the snowdrifts had been cleared. Cartloads of furniture, chests, and clothes had been stacked everywhere.

People whispered. Still full of the Might, she could hear fragments of conversations from all over the hall. Between people looking down from the galleries above. Between servants. And between the Dreyri standing closest, as if to prevent anyone from pushing their way into the stone circle.

They're talking about us. They recognize us.

They know we're raven. They remember us.

The voices inside her mixed with the voices outside.

Her. Graal's daughter. Half-blood. Vanished. Fled.

She was balanced on a sword-edge. They were speculating, and they had every reason to. People had noticed the absence of the houseless. The fallen. No one knew how many, or whether it had anything to do with her. Unless someone had talked.

Either way, she was being sized up. Who was she? Friend or foe? Savior or traitor?

Hirka heard Skerri and the others come through. She glanced back and saw her bare footprints leading away from the stone circle.

"Hirka?"

Raun broke away from the crowd. He stopped in front of her. Her lips quivered, making it difficult to smile. She was painfully aware of how she looked. Raun's expression shifted between tenderness and anger. Revealing he hadn't been sure he'd ever see her again.

She would never be able to explain. All she could do was keep herself alive until this was over. Until the war was over. And then they'd have to follow her. Believe in her. Then they would no longer be able to doubt her loyalty or power.

"It's done," she said. "I'm Dreyri. I'm ravenborn."

She knew they could all see that it was true. She had eyes like them. A murmur went through the hall. Hirka lifted her hand to Raun's cheek. Felt every single bristle of his red beard. His eyes widened. He gripped her arm with both hands, as if afraid she might let go. She felt him draw on the Might. Drink it from her, making her blood itch.

Then he looked at Skerri. Eyes black with fury.

"You would have buried her alive . . ."

Skerri froze. Hirka held up a hand in the hope of calming her. Where was the Seer? It had to have come from him. Days had passed, more than planned, and he had feared for her life. Feared what Skerri had done, and gone to Raun with the secret. But she couldn't see him in the crowd.

Hirka let go of Raun. "Now is not the time," she said and kept walking. The Might had started to wane. She moved slowly past people, letting them touch her skin. Letting them draw out what remained. People pushed to get closer. Some more determined than others. Hirka could smell the danger. They were kindling, primed to ignite. Some started to shout from the back of the hall.

Time was running out.

Hirka spotted Jór. He was standing next to a mountain of furniture and chests with his hand on a small mica box. The red serpent slithered across his chest. He looked at her in awe. Gave her a tentative nod.

Jór . . . I let you down.

She'd let the House of Hod down. Ruined the plan to unite the houses. But that had always been their plan. Not hers. She walked over to him and picked up the box. Jór didn't stop her. He leaned toward her and whispered in her ear.

"You've never been more beautiful."

Hirka gave him a mournful smile. "You're only saying that because you've never seen more of yourself in me."

She started to climb. Ascended the mountain of dressers, cabinets, and chests. At the top, she opened the box. Naiell's heart lay in the ice. It smelled stronger than before. So strong that it was like she could smell his very essence, what made him different from Graal, Raun, and Modrasme. What made him a lie.

The voices inside grew more eager.

It is him. We remember.

He is one of us. Bring him.

A memory pushed its way to the fore. Hirka saw herself. After Father had died. She'd gone in to see him while he was lying on his workbench. Cut part of him away and given it to Kuro. Let him fly with the ravens, like the Council families did. Like Umpiri did.

She lifted the heart up. The hall fell silent. All of Ginnungad. All of Dreysíl. Gathered in Nifel. In a ruined city. Brought together by a memory of the Might. By their thirst for revenge. By her.

Kuro. Heart.

She held the heart in both hands and sank her teeth into it, tearing chunks loose. Cold, tough flesh filled her mouth. It tasted of steel and earth. Rotten and wet.

He is one of us. Bring him.

Naiell's heart slowly thawed in her hands, becoming wetter as she ate. She wiped blood from her lips with the back of her hand. Swallowed. And swallowed. Became one with the man they had hated for a thousand years. But she knew they shared something. They had both been born into a lie. And they'd both done what they had to because of it.

Hirka licked her fingers. She was raven. Scavenger. Dreyri.

She scanned the crowd.

"I AM THE MIGHT!" she shouted, her voice so strong she didn't recognize it. Carried by the power of what they longed for more than anything.

"I AM HIRKA! DAUGHTER OF GRAAL, SON OF RAUN OF THE HOUSE OF MODRASME! I AM RAVENBORN! I AM THE FIRST!"

No one shouted. She'd expected them to cheer. Bash their staffs against the floor. But they said nothing. She could hear faint thumps. Not from staffs, but from knees hitting the ground. They were kneeling. One by one. Like a wave through the hall. Like Mannfalla had done for Rime. But people in Mannfalla had always kneeled. Umpiri didn't kneel. Not for anyone.

Only for us. Only for the Might.

Only for the first ravenborn in a thousand years.

Even those standing outside kneeled as they peered in through holes in the walls. Through open doors. Pale and lightly clothed for the snow. A sea of milky white eyes. A sea of deadborn.

Then she saw him. He was standing not too far away from Raun, hunched by the wall. Almost invisible in his black robe and the hood that covered his head.

He had to feel the Might. Had to lay his hands on her before it disappeared. She jumped down and walked through disorderly rows of kneeling nábyrn. Stopped in front of him and gripped his hand. He curled his fingers around hers, black claws digging into her skin.

He stepped close to her. Leaned his head against her chest. Breathed in her scent. His lungs whistled, deformed as they likely were.

"We did it, Seer . . ." she whispered.

His head rubbed against her throat as if he were nodding.

"North, sss . . . south, east, and west . . . The ravens sss . . . say you were there. In every direction. How many ravens were you?"

Hirka intertwined her fingers with his.

"All of them, Seer. I was all of them."

She whispered her thanks to him, for going to Raun with his concerns. For fearing for her. Then she went over to her family.

They were down on one knee, looking up at her with a hunger that was terrifying. They knew she could have destroyed them. Could have told everyone the truth about Graal and Naiell. But what good would it have done?

Instead, she'd given them everything they'd dreamed of.

Until they realize I'm like him.

Skerri stared at the floor, shoulders hunched, painfully aware that Hirka's words could ruin her. She'd buried one of her own. Would they make her one of the fallen? Give her a steel teardrop? Or just make her houseless?

Whatever happened, it would have to wait. There were more important things to consider.

"Get up, Skerri," Hirka said. "It's time we talked to my father."

THAT NIGHT

Hirka had found a room at the top of the hall. Half the roof had collapsed, taking large sections of the wall with it, which meant she could see the rest of the city far below. Nifel wasn't a city in the truest sense of the word. It was a ghost of a city. A circular maze of ruins that only just managed to make itself seen in all the snow.

Maknamorr was its center. The hall around the stone circle. The closer you got, the taller the buildings. Black stone colossi, riddled with rooms. Twisted into impossible shapes using the Might. Three spires billowed upward as if giants had squeezed them between their fingers. One of them had been too narrow in the middle to survive the loss of the Might. It had snapped. Calved like an iceberg. Sacrificed part of itself to survive another winter.

Hirka had done the same. Sacrificed so much of herself that she didn't know if she'd ever be the same. She'd changed shape. Yet she would have to give more still. Perhaps even her life. And even then the survival of the Might was far from guaranteed.

She leaned against the window ledge. Felt a stabbing pain and tore her hand back. The window was long gone. Jagged bits of glass stuck up like rotting teeth. Blood ran down her thumb. For a moment she expected the wound to heal itself, but the Might had run out of her. Left her empty. As it had done during the Rite, back when Rime had tried to give her enough of it to see her through.

It hadn't worked out that way.

But what if he had managed? What if Sylja hadn't trodden on her so that she ended up last? What if the Ravenbearer hadn't taken so long? What if she'd made it through her own rite without incident?

She could have passed as an ymling. Urd wouldn't have hunted her. Many who were now dead would still be alive. Svarteld, Lindri, Ilume . . . The Council wouldn't have fallen. Rime wouldn't have become Ravenbearer.

He'd still be Kolkagga. But would he be hers? Would their love have found a way regardless?

Crones' talk.

Father whispered from Slokna. But the longing that usually came in its wake failed to materialize. She used to wish that he'd lived. That he could see all the things she'd seen. Not anymore. She was glad Father couldn't see her, and everything she was willing to sacrifice. She would heal, but to heal she had to destroy.

Hirka pressed the cut against her tongue. Stopped the bleeding.

She heard footsteps outside. Turned toward the doorway, though the door was long gone. Rusted hinges were all that remained. Skerri came in. Two fallen remained in the corridor outside, presumably charged with keeping an eye on her until the question of blame could be settled. One of them briefly met Hirka's gaze, long enough for her to realize that he hadn't chosen to be there. He was among those who would have followed her had they only heard the rumor sooner.

Skerri put the raven quiver on the table, a solid stone slab that no one had bothered to take with them when the city had fallen. It was the only piece of furniture in the room, so Hirka climbed up and sat on it.

Skerri moistened her black lips, as if she wanted to say something but couldn't find the words.

"I thought you'd betrayed us," she said at last. "That would have been . . . natural. Under the circumstances. But you came back. And you've done what you set out to do. Without telling anyone about . . ."

She glanced at the door and lowered her voice. "About the brothers."

Hirka wanted to ask if she was trying to say sorry, but realized she hadn't learned the word for sorry in umoni. Presumably because there wasn't one. She nodded instead.

"If I were . . . If you choose to . . ." Skerri struggled to find her way. Hirka decided to help. Put an end to her suffering.

"I consider you family, Skerri. We are tied by blood and lies. If one of us falls, we all fall. I know of many who would be happy to see a teardrop in your forehead, but I don't count myself among them. Anyway, Kesskerri doesn't have a very good ring to it."

Skerri looked away. Rubbed the back of her neck. The beads in her hair clacked together in a nervous melody. Hirka changed the subject before Skerri felt the need to thank her. That would probably finish her off.

"They want to unite the houses, through me and Jór. That's not going to happen." She smiled at Skerri. "I don't suppose you want him?"

Skerri immediately turned up her nose. "No, may the first preserve me!" She seemed to realize what she'd said and tried to backtrack. "Not that there's anything wrong with him. He's strong, and from the House of Hod. Not unattractive, either, but . . ."

"But he's not Graal?"

Skerri moved her hand to the raven quiver, a telling reflex. "You've chosen the ymling, haven't you? Could you imagine anyone else taking his place? Maybe we're not so different."

Hirka looked at her, astonished. In Skerri's world, this had to be straying into sentimentality. An admission and a compliment. And under the circumstances, it also meant the door had opened a crack. The way to the truth about Naiell, if Hirka played her cards right.

Snowflakes danced in through the hole in the wall. Drifted toward the ground, then changed their minds and danced back out. As if they had a will of their own and weren't slaves to the wind. Hirka caught one in her hand. It tried to escape, but melted against her skin.

"I was in the human world for what felt like an eternity," Hirka started. "It wasn't even a year, but it felt like an ocean of time. They surround themselves with noise. Light. Bury their dead in the ground. Let them lie there and rot. Sometimes I missed Ym so much that I couldn't breathe."

Skerri's features softened. Pride in one's home was something she could understand.

"I wasn't able to see what was good about their world," Hirka continued. "And with every day that passed, Ym got a little better in my memory. A little lusher. A little more beautiful. It became an unhealthy longing. In the end I almost forgot that Ym had hunted me. Despised and tormented me. It's strange how time can wear away the ugliest of things. The flaws."

Skerri stared out through the broken roof. Distant, as if she were trying to remember.

"Skerri . . . You know my father better than I ever will. But I spent enough time with him to know he is not the man you've made him out to be in your mind. A thousand years is a long time. Even for Umpiri. He has an almost irresistible charm. Mood swings, sure . . . yet still this . . . alluring calm. I met a lot of people who'd been close to him, only to lose him. There were so many of them that they had a name. They called themselves the forgotten."

Skerri quirked an eyebrow. "You think I'm pining? That everything I do is about *him*?" The very idea seemed to shake her. "This isn't about him. I let go of Graal centuries ago! Don't think I haven't had to fight for my place in a good house, because I have."

Hirka hid a smile. "But you don't want Jór from the leading house?"

Skerri bit her lip as if she regretted every word she'd said.

Hirka had to steer the conversation in a different direction. She wouldn't get anywhere with Skerri as long as she felt like she was being attacked.

"I don't know your reasons, Skerri, but the end result is the same. Graal has controlled your life for so many years . . . How many others have you rejected? How many chances at happiness? Just look at Grid! How long has he been mooning after you? A hundred years? Two hundred? Do you think his victories in the ring are for his own sake? He does it for you!"

Skerri gave a start, like she'd just woken up. Hirka went in for the final blow. "Graal turned his back on you long ago. You don't need to protect him anymore. And you don't need to worry about anyone making you houseless. I told you, you're family, for as long as you want."

For as long as we live, anyway . . .

Skerri looked down. Hirka cocked her head, trying to maintain eye contact. "I know they weren't brothers. But I have to know why Naiell turned his back on everyone. And I know you can tell me. What happened?"

Skerri shut her eyes, as if searching for the strength to continue. She took a deep breath.

"He was furious," she said. "Furious beyond belief. I heard him screaming at Graal just as I was about to go in, so I stayed outside. Watched their shadows on the tent wall."

She cleared her throat. Hirka gave Skerri all the time she needed. It was a story she must have promised she'd never tell.

"It was in a camp north of Ravnhov. I heard what he said. That they weren't really brothers. It was . . . I was in shock. If anyone had heard them, it would have changed everything. Not just for the family, but for the war. They were like gods, those brothers . . . Sent by the first."

Skerri leaned against the table, like her arms were all that was holding her up. "Naiell had just found out. He flew into a rage. Said Graal must have known all along—but he hadn't. Graal had no idea! They were brothers, anyone could smell that. Graal wanted him gone. Told him to leave the family. Leave everything. One brother disappearing was better than anyone finding out. It was . . ." She sighed. "It got ugly. Of course. They were threatening to kill each other. I went in and told them to lower their voices. Tried to make them see that they could lose everything, both of them."

Skerri took a breath and straightened up. "That night, someone tried to kill us. Graal and me. In the most cowardly way imaginable. It was supposed to look like an accident. A fire. And he didn't even have the guts to do it himself! He used a friend. But it didn't go as planned. No sooner had he thrown the oil lamp than he was felled by an arrow through the neck."

Hirka closed her eyes for a moment, piecing together the bits of the story she knew in her head. The burns on Skerri's hips. Jór's story about Kolail and the burning tent. An unfortunate chain of events, leading to tragedy.

She looked at Skerri again. "Kolail . . . Kolail was the one who stopped him?"

Skerri nodded. "People woke up and saw what he'd done, so there was no saving him. He got the teardrop in his forehead. And Naiell . . . Well, he disappeared, and we all know what happened next."

Hirka felt heavy. Weighed down by all the years that had passed. A thousand of them. An incident such a long, long time ago, yet still it shaped the world. A stolen child. An argument. One night.

Hirka stifled a laugh. "I assume it's occurred to you that if Graal hadn't hounded him, he might never have betrayed you. This treachery you've rallied around for a millennium . . . It was your own doing."

Skerri didn't answer.

405

"Graal would still be here, or in Ym. The Might would freely through the gateways. And I would never have been born. The Council would never have been formed, and Eirik of Ravnhov would be king. Or you would have won the war and wiped out every single ymling. We'll never know."

Skerri wrapped her arms around herself. For the first time, she looked cold. "Raun thinks I don't know . . ." Her words held a silent plea.

"Maybe. Maybe not. We'll never know," Hirka answered. "Not until you both realize you need to have a chat. About everything."

Relief washed over Skerri's features.

Hirka nodded at the raven. "Can you call Graal for me?"

Skerri clenched her fist and let a red bead of blood fall on the raven cadaver. They waited in silence until the bird creaked to life.

"Let me talk to him alone," Hirka said.

Skerri nodded. Then she backed out of the room, as you did for someone in a higher house. She stopped in the doorway. Raised an eyebrow. "Grid?"

Hirka fought back a smile. "It's a shame, really. Knowing him, he'll make sure he's right in the thick of battle, so I guess it doesn't matter."

Skerri disappeared out the door. Hirka thought she could hear her pace quicken as she made her way down the corridor.

A FATHER'S CHOICE

Hirka sat in the middle of the table so that she could see out through the hole in the wall, its dismal, irregular shape framing the sky. Broken stone lay strewn across the floor. In the corner, dry grass stuck up from an abandoned bird's nest.

She crossed her legs and rested her arms on her knees. The raven cadaver opened its beak.

"What have you done, Hirka?"

His voice was deep and calm, but it had a rough edge. He knew something was wrong.

"I've done what I said I'd do. I've found the Might. Though I expect Damayanti's already told you that."

A short pause. Hirka could almost hear him thinking. Would he rage about how Damayanti had been held captive for days? Would he ask about Rime? They both knew something was different. That the relationship between them was no longer the same. But the consequence of that depended on him.

The raven lifted its chin. "That's . . . impressive. I'm proud of you, blood of my blood. You're the first ravenborn in Dreysíl in a thousand years. I knew you could do it."

Hirka gave a cold smile. "You know nothing yet. Father."

He hesitated for a moment. Sensitive to the nuances in her voice, as always. "Are we enemies now, Hirka?"

"Now? We were enemies from the moment you let Rime take the

beak. It doesn't matter that he did it voluntarily. You chose to use him, and that made us enemies. And now we've become something far worse, Father. We've become equals."

"Hirka . . ."

She continued before he could. "I've freed him, Graal. You might think him dead, but that's not why you haven't been able to get ahold of him. He's a free man. That means neither he nor I need to listen to you anymore."

"You think you can stop this war?" A touch of arrogance had crept into his voice. Born of fear, she guessed. The sudden loss of control.

Snowflakes landed on her thighs. They lay there without melting. She was cold like them. A stone figure on a table. She felt like she'd always been there.

She pushed her hair back. The ties were stiff with raven blood.

"That's what you think, all of you," she replied hoarsely. "That I want to prevent a bloodbath. Stop the fighting. But after three thousand years, you ought to know better. No one has the power to stop wrath. People are always going to hate. Destroy. They're always going to want more. Look at us, Father. We live from one day to the next, like animals. Shit in our own nests and kill each other for glass beads. Blindlings, menskr, ymlings . . . We're all the same. The first would be ashamed. No gods can bridle us. So no, I'm not going to stop any war. People will bleed and die whatever I do. And they'll do it unknowingly, not realizing they're killing something much bigger. Something we never had the right to destroy. *That* is what I will prevent."

The raven creaked but remained silent.

"I promised you the Might, and now I'll tell you how I intend to make good on that promise, Graal. We will go into Mannfalla. Nowhere else. No one will continue into the other kingdoms. No one will attack ordinary people. You'll soon learn that Umpiri are missing an army of fallen and houseless. They're in Ravnhov. I took them there. And they're going to march on Mannfalla to meet the Council's army outside the walls at the same time as we cross into Ym. That's what's going to happen. Dreyri will hold a war council soon, and then you'll have two options, Father. You can support me and the only hope you have of feeling the Might again. Or you can defy me and die without it."

Hirka tapped her knuckles soundlessly against her knee as she waited for an answer. Graal wanted to reign supreme. He wanted Ym. As revenge for what he felt Naiell had stolen from him. But was his thirst for revenge stronger than his thirst for the Might? And did he think she had what it took to heal it?

Graal could still coerce her if he wanted to. His silence suggested he was thinking about it. He could threaten the people she'd met in England. Stefan. Father Brody. Rime wasn't the only person he could use against her.

But if he really considered himself her father . . . If he had any feelings for her whatsoever, he wouldn't. So much hinged on the next words he spoke.

"Had I not been your father, Hirka, I might have asked you to consider the priest and Stefan . . ."

Hirka suddenly had a bitter taste in her mouth. It was an empty threat. Pathetic. Testing the waters. But all the same, it disappointed her. She'd given him a chance, and now he was forcing her to threaten him in return. Forcing her to be like him. To throw his words back at him.

"Had I not been your daughter, I might have asked you to consider how you weren't brothers, you and Naiell. How that made you drive him away. I might have asked you to consider how you made him into a traitor."

The silence that followed seemed to stretch on forever. The sky had grown darker. Her hands were blue in the light. She knew she'd won. She knew the secret that could bring down his house. It was his turn to be a slave.

The raven stared at her. A dead bird in a dead room.

"Hirka, I never wanted to threaten Rime, you have to know that." The words came quickly. A belated attempt at damage control. "Not him and not you, Hirka. If you think I'd have hurt him, you're—"

"The damage is already done. It can never be undone. You had a chance. You could have trusted me. Trusted I'd do what I said I'd do, but you used him, Father. Used us. There's nothing to discuss. So, when I tell the war council what's going to happen, can I count on your unconditional support?"

"Blood of my blood, I will always support you."

Hirka felt her shoulders relax. The worst part was over.

"Hirka?" He sounded pained. Vulnerable. "No matter how this ends, you must know that you mean more to me than anything else. More than this war. More than my house. We have much to discuss, and discuss it we will. I know you'll understand one day. Forgive me one day."

Hirka got up and jumped down from the table.

"I don't think any of us will live that long, Father."

WARHEART

The sky was a dark sea rolling over her. Endless and suffocating. Hirka took the pass to the outskirts of Nifel. She'd hoped to see mountains or hills, something that would give her a sense of attachment, but the sky was never-ending—and it seemed to be looming closer and closer.

Every step she took was an exercise in keeping it at bay. An exercise in pushing the sky away. She didn't deserve to be ground into the dirt.

This isn't my fault.

Heavy clouds rumbled in protest, and they were right, of course. She was as much to blame as anyone else.

Nifel had come back to life in only a few days. The snow had given way to Umpiri. Crumbling towers and icy halls had become home to thousands of white-eyed deadborn. The eldest—those who still remembered—held forth, waxing lyrical to those who had never seen the city before.

They argued over the best rooms. Over dusty bottles of undrinkable wine they'd found in the cellars. And over who would do what. It was a world at a crossroads. A people headed to war.

Hirka had seen the beginnings of war before. In Ravnhov. This was different. No one was preparing for death. No one was forging weapons or sharpening swords. There wasn't a shield to be seen, not even among the remaining houseless and fallen. The armor wasn't made for protection, it was made to flaunt what Umpiri valued above all: themselves.

Hirka sat down on what she thought was a wall, but then she spotted the curve of a window frame by her feet. The rest was buried under the snow.

She unfolded her linen handkerchief and took a bite of cake. Ate slowly. A ritual older than the ruins she was sitting on, but which was frowned upon here. She forced herself to ignore the nausea. Closed her eyes. Heard ravens screech like they knew they'd soon be able to gorge themselves.

And what would *she* do while others fed the ravens on the battlefields?

Find a balance between saving lives and taking them. Make sure as few as possible died, but enough to satisfy the Might.

How did I get here?

It felt like her body belonged to someone else. She'd lost touch with it. She knew she was in there somewhere, but she had to be kept under. In the background. Her heart couldn't take what was happening. She had to be Dreyri, for just a bit longer. The war council was waiting for her.

And then?

One hour at a time.

She stared down into her lap. She hadn't even eaten half the cake. She wrapped it up and shoved it in her pocket. Got up and walked back into the city. Into the hall where the stones reached for the ceiling like pillars propping up eternity. Dead, now that no one was binding on the other side.

The floor was bare. Snow and time had taken their toll on the tiles. Transformed them into a mottled sea-green landscape. Like the swell of turbulent waters.

She found the steps up. The old council chamber hung from the ceiling like an enormous lamp. Black with yellow windows all the way around. Some of them were cracked or broken. It was strikingly similar to the Seer's tower in Mannfalla, right down to the slender bridge. Yet more evidence of how Naiell had tried to build a new home in Ym.

Hirka crossed the bridge but stopped outside the door. It was ajar. The others were already inside. The Council. Representatives of the nine leading houses. And those who couldn't be excluded for other reasons. Skerri, who had the raven. The Seer, now that they had seen the first ravenborn since time immemorial.

Hod's voice carried over everyone else's. "She's young, Graal. How can we expect discipline from someone who is yet to see even a quarter of a century? I'm not questioning anyone's intentions. I could say the same about my son. The young ones don't know. And what little they know, they've forgotten. That's the problem."

Hirka entered the room. Silence fell. Unnecessary confirmation of who they were talking about.

She looked at Hod. "The problem isn't that we've forgotten. The problem is that you still remember."

Hod lifted her chin. Her skin seemed slacker than the last time they'd met. Age was well and truly upon her. But it was good to see she was no longer hiding in a golden room. It would do Umpiri good to see age. Face their decline.

All the chairs were taken, so she climbed up to sit on the table. At the end, right next to the raven cadaver.

She continued before anyone could protest. "You remember far too much. You remember old injustices from epochs gone by as if they happened yesterday. You despise an entire race for a loss that was actually your fault. *Yours!* Not theirs. You talk about revenge even though not a soul in Ym was alive back then. The oldest ymling you could find wouldn't be much more than a hundred years old."

"You think we don't know that?" Hod cocked her head condescendingly.

"You certainly behave like you don't know," Hirka replied. "What's more important? The Might or Ym? If you had to choose?"

"Can someone get her a chair?" Tyr sighed, prompting laughter around the table.

Hirka remained impassive. Cold. She'd broken so many rules she might as well continue, because clearly more was needed. She stood up on the table. "I don't have claws, Tyr. Or teeth like yours. But I've seen three worlds. I've seen more in under twenty years than you have in two thousand, and only a fool would refuse to listen to me."

"Hirka . . ." Graal's voice came gently from the raven. She ignored him.

She walked down the middle of the table. "Since I arrived here you've marveled at my weaknesses as if they were foreign to you. Because if there's one thing you're really good at, it's hiding your own."

She crouched down in front of Tyr. "You would never reveal your weaknesses. Few things scare you more than your own inadequacy. Me? I'm open about my shortcomings. I don't fear my weaknesses. How strong do you think that makes me? How superior, for daring to say I'm weak? Do you still think I need a chair, Tyr?"

Tyr gaped at her. A savage with black hair bound with iron rings, brought to heel. She stared at him. Forced herself not to blink, because she knew he saw eyes like his own. Not those of an ymling. He knew what she'd accomplished. He also knew that they needed her. Even if only in the hope of uniting the houses.

"I am Hirka, daughter of Graal, son of Raun of the House of Modrasme. But more importantly: I'm ravenborn. And I'm telling you I can give you the Might again. Not in Ym. Not in exile. But here."

She thumped her chest with her fist. "Here! Nifel can be as it once was. Ginnungad, too. But we have to do it my way. The way the ravens say it should be done."

The Seer stepped forward. He and Skerri had no place on the Council and had been banished to a corner.

"You've sss . . . spoken to them?"

Hirka got up again. "I *am* them."

She went back to the other end of the table. "You're missing a few hundred fallen and houseless. They're in Ym, and you'll meet them there, in the battle against the Council's army. They'll be coming from outside, and we'll be coming from inside."

Hod put her hands on the table. The skin around her knuckles was wrinkled. "You've come up with a strategy without us?"

"No, a strategy would mean that those who have left were on your side, Hod, but they're not anymore. The fallen have risen up. None of us know what the outcome of that might be, but it's useful either way. Mannfalla will have to fight on two fronts."

A fair-haired man leaned over the table. A mightglass arrowhead hung from a chain around his neck.

"Can someone explain to me how this *isn't* treason?"

Hirka looked at him. Scoured her memory. "It's Fled, right? From the second house?"

She hadn't meant to affront him, but he clearly wasn't used to anyone asking who he was.

"Well, Fled," she said. "You can call it treason if you're torn apart by one of your own, but until then, no one's betrayed you." Hirka gave him a lopsided smile. "Unless you think they actually pose a threat. Unless you're . . . scared? Hm? No, I thought not."

Hirka sat down on the table again, next to the raven. "If nothing else, at least those who've gone ahead will ensure the war isn't boring."

Their laughter would have chilled her to the core had she not already been cold as could be.

Hirka held out a hand to the man sitting closest to her. A man holding scrolls. He looked confused for a moment, but then he handed her one. Hirka rolled the map of Mannfalla out onto the table.

"*Now* we can talk strategy."

ANIMALS IN THE WALLS

They were built like gods. Terrible and beautiful. Sharply defined muscles wound around pale bodies. Leather straps crossed broad chests. Mythical beasts and talons of steel curved over strong shoulders.

Umpiri. Made to dominate. Proud and bold. Had Hirka not convinced them otherwise, they'd have been naked as the day they were born. An overbearing tactic intended to shock and conquer. Undoubtedly effective, but Hirka needed them to be seen as people, not wild animals. In spite of all the war and death.

They stood in orderly rows around the stones, in groups of a hundred per commander. They were an army unlike any other. Nothing suggested they feared attack. They bore no shields. No armor or chainmail. A few fallen and houseless were armed with bows and knives, but otherwise there wasn't a weapon in sight. Just a sea of teeth and claws.

In Ravnhov, the young and the elderly had stood outside their homes. Some sobbing, some silent. Here, no one would stay behind. Everyone would fight. And the youngest in Dreysíl was Hirka herself.

They talked in low voices. A buzz throughout the hall. But every eye was fixed on the raven ring, which threw long dark shadows in the dying light.

A shimmering revealed that Skerri was binding on the other side. Hirka took a couple of steps forward. They all looked at her.

Raun. Uhere. Jór. Hod. Hirka wondered whether she ought to say something, but decided against it.

She nodded, then walked between the stones.

She was drawn in by a force that was impossible to fight. It was as if the stones remembered and grew stronger every time. Less emptiness, more . . . something. She only needed to take a couple more steps before she was through.

Skerri and Damayanti stood before her. She heard the first Umpiri stumble through behind her. She turned toward them. Brought a finger to her lips to remind them to be quiet. But that didn't stop the noise. The same sounds as she'd heard from the fallen. Gasps as they found the Might. Deep breaths. Muffled laughter from those who hadn't truly believed.

Skerri hissed at them to keep rank. She looked at Hirka and pointed at the dark crack in the rock. "Lead the way."

Hirka walked past Damayanti. The dancer whispered behind her. "So this is how it ends?"

Hirka glanced over her shoulder. "How did you think it would end, Damayanti? Happily?"

She continued along the tunnel and into the old city walls. Into a pitch darkness that ought to have made it impossible to orient herself, but her eyes weren't the same anymore. She could make out the contours of the wall now. Rats scurrying along the ground. Pieces of wood. And a rusted gauntlet that she realized had to have been there since the last war.

It's too late now.

The tunnel forked and she went right. Another group would go left. They would fill the walls, like rats. Shoulder to shoulder they walked. Until she reached the end. The air suggested that this part of the wall was above ground.

Hirka turned to those behind. She couldn't make out any faces, only sense them. Hear breathing. Beads clinking.

Skerri's hair.

A mumbling that sounded like Raun. "The end," she whispered. He seemed to nod. Hirka put her staff aside. One she'd borrowed. She'd left her own in Ravnhov. Along with everything else she owned.

She leaned against the wall and took a sip from her waterskin. Closed her eyes and bound the Might. She could feel the others doing the same. A charged darkness as they waited.

She tried to think clearly but gave up. A chaos of feelings warred within her. Fear. Anger. Despair. Everything that could go wrong, and everything that had already gone wrong.

I'm standing in the walls with deadborn.

The Might revealed all. The creaking of leather. The smell of sweat. Trapped dust. It almost smelled like tobacco. The air grew thicker and thicker. Made humid by their breath.

What if Ravnhov didn't come? What if the battle never began?

A sound. Faint at first. Then louder. Like crackling.

"What's that?" Jór's voice. A barely audible whisper. "Is it burning?"

Hirka smiled in the darkness. "No. It's raining."

THE PROPHECY

Time stood still. It was as if it no longer applied to them. They'd been swallowed whole. Lived on within the dark entrails of Mannfalla, ready to cut their way out.

If Ravnhov didn't come and nothing happened, they'd return to the stone circle. That was the agreement. But Hirka was starting to realize that would be impossible. There was too much at stake. The pressure had been building for too long, and there were limits to the power she had over Umpiri.

They were impatient, these animals in the wall. The silence was superficial. Composed of sighs. Scratching. Mumbling. People shifting restlessly.

Outside, rain pounded the wall. A child started to cry. The Might carried the sound through stone. It bored into her. Loud, unabashed crying. The way only a child could.

Hirka put her hands to the wall. Gripped a stone that crumbled beneath her fingers. Her throat tightened. She fought to regain her composure. To remember the big picture. What was a crying child compared to a dying world? To multiple dying worlds? Many had to die so more could live. That was why she was here. That was why.

I'm not afraid.

A lie she'd told herself countless times. But she'd never understood how big the lie could get. She'd never needed to fear for anyone other than herself. Her own life. Now she feared for every-one. No one could afford to see her fail.

Skerri whispered beside her. "They're not coming."

"They're on their way," Hirka said.

"How—"

Hirka shushed her. "Listen . . ."

Skerri listened. "I don't hear anything."

"Exactly."

No shouting or singing in the streets. No hooves on the cobble-stones. No music from the taverns. The city was as quiet as Slokna. Shuttered. Terrified. Mannfalla was holding its breath.

She heard a shout in the distance. Cocked her head. Listened. Another one. Then there was a pealing from the bell tower. The sound carried down into the city. A resounding alarm. People came running outside. The heavy footfall of guardsmen.

It's started.

Her heartbeat slowed. Almost reluctant. As if it were trying to lull her to sleep. To convince her she could stay here in the dark. Forget the war. Forget the Might. Just hide in the walls while the world raged outside. Because that was what it would do. Rage.

Ravnhov. Blindból. The blind.

Skerri shifted impatiently. Hirka put a hand on her arm. Waited until it was quiet again. Until every single guardsman in Mannfalla had run to Eisvaldr, at the end of the city.

"It's time," she said.

Her words were passed back. Metal clanked as Umpiri readied themselves. Hands slapped together as they wished each other luck, or said a final farewell, just in case. Even deadborn could never know.

Hirka bound the Might. No one could see it, but still it saturated the air around her. Making it almost sticky. She drew it into her fingers. It was darker than before. Deeper. She made a fist. Punched the wall.

Her hand didn't even touch the stones, but all the same they ruptured. The sound rent the darkness. Rumbled. Crackled. Then it was quiet. Hirka raised both hands to the wall, but it no longer felt like a wall. Stone wasn't stone. It was less solid than that. Composed of tiny parts that barely held together. That could be moved.

She flung her arms wide.

The stones exploded in a wall of sand. Billions of specks of dust were suspended in the air before her, as if for a brief moment they weren't sure what to do. Then they crashed to the ground, leaving a jagged hole in the wall.

The wall groaned. She heard stones falling farther behind her. Dust filled the confined space.

Hirka put her arm over her face to shield herself. Grabbed her staff and stepped out between two stooping houses, into a dark and rainy evening. Umpiri streamed out behind her. Pushed her onward.

She continued along the alleyway and out onto the street. A man poked his head out of a hatch nearby. Scared but vigilant. He spotted Hirka. "You can't be out there, girl! They're coming! We have room if you—"

Hirka looked up at him. His eyes grew wide as they took in the line of Umpiri emerging from the alleyway. He didn't move. He didn't even try to close the shutters. He stared as if spellbound.

Hirka continued between the houses until she reached the Catgut. She looked over her shoulder. Skerri, Raun, Hod, and Tyr were right behind her. Then came the rest. Four abreast. In a seemingly endless column. A pale serpent moving through the streets. Glistening in the rain.

She hadn't expected it to be like this. She'd expected chaos. Screaming. Panic. But those few who dared to poke their heads out just stood watching. Silent. As if turned to stone.

A plump man stood on his doorstep nailing a plank of wood over a shutterless window. A flimsy defense if, against all odds,

Mannfalla's army were to fail. He stared at her. At the parade of deadborn. Hammer frozen in the air. Mouth open. Two nails fell and clattered against the step. Then he pressed himself back against the wall. Into the shadows.

Hirka passed a small square full of boarded-up stalls. She remembered the place well. This was where she'd once tried to blend in with the crowd. With a dead man's tail strapped to her body. An old woman had stood on a box and shrieked about the child of Odin. Shouted to a terrified audience. Hirka remembered every word.

The child of Odin comes first. Mark my words! The blind are her slaves! And with her she brings all the ashes of Slokna.

It had seemed like madness back then.

The lanterns along the road had burned out. No one had bothered to light them again, even though night was drawing in. Not even in the merchant district.

But the lanterns along the wall still burned.

It loomed before her at the end of the street. A pale and lonely giant. There were no guardsmen there. Not even farther along. The danger was coming from outside—or so they all thought.

Hirka passed through one of the archways. Through the wall separating Mannfalla from Eisvaldr. Poor from rich. People from the Council. A wall that had been built to stop the blind.

She'd walked here before. So terribly alone. Now she could hear thousands of heavy footsteps behind her.

A guardsman with his sword drawn ran across the square just ahead of her. Steel-plated shoes rang against the cobblestones. He spotted her. Spotted the army following her. Hirka hoped he'd run away, but it was as if all sense drained out of him. He slowed down. Stopped. His sword sang against the ground. He didn't shout. Showed no intention of attacking. All he did was take off his helmet. He hugged it to his chest, like a bowl. The rain pattered into it.

Hirka continued past him. No one touched him. Umpiri knew her rules. Only attack when attacked. Never before.

The dreadful sounds of battle reached her, growing louder and louder. The sky over Blindból blazed orange. Hirka tested the Might. Felt for signs of it growing stronger but found none. It was as always. Eternal and patient.

It's too early.

She held her arms out and pointed to either side of her. Umpiri split up behind her and ran. To the outer walls. To the fighting. To death.

A small group followed her toward the heart of Mannfalla: the new Council Chamber. She could see it from where they were. Part of the complex of white buildings. The bridge stuck out like a broken tongue, right above the stone circle.

Not that the stone circle was visible anymore. A wall had been erected around it. As if bricks would be able to stop the blind when not even the walls of the Rite Hall had been able to keep her and Rime out.

It looked so pathetic out there. Built without any clue that the gateways were still open, just below ground.

An arrow whizzed to the ground in front of her. It pinged off the cobblestones and clattered to the ground, lifeless. She looked up. The archer was on a landing halfway up the steps leading to the Council Chamber. His gaze faltered, as if he couldn't quite believe he'd actually fired. Hirka smiled at him.

So they've spotted us. Finally.

More joined him. Soon the steps were teeming with guardsmen. They spread out along walls and newly built towers.

Hirka raised her staff and raced up the steps before they had a chance to compose themselves. She heard a roar, then realized it was her own. It merged with the chorus of howls from the deadborn.

The guardsman who had fired collapsed before she reached him.

No one had touched him. It was as if fear had simply snuffed him out. Then the others arrived. Umpiri charged past her up the steps. People screamed above her. Below her.

A guardsman in red armor stood tall on the rampart of one of the towers. He stared at her. Then his knees gave out, and he dropped like a stone. Lay there motionless, his arm bent at a nauseating angle.

Hirka felt like she was in a dream. Like she saw without seeing. Thought without thinking. It was madness, all of it.

She reached one of the guardsmen. Slammed her staff into his stomach. He stared at her as if he hadn't expected her to do anything. Then he slumped against the wall and vomited.

More arrived. Some ran away, too. The clever ones. Maybe some of them would survive the night. Hirka drew on the Might and raced up the steps. She saw Skerri ahead of her. A storm of black braids and claws. A guardsman tumbled off the rampart, but he hadn't even hit the ground before Skerri sliced open his chest. Hirka wanted to scream but suddenly found herself face-to-face with a red-clad giant of a man.

He raised his sword. She raised her staff. Swung with all she had in her. She struck him in the head, leaving a sickening dent in his helmet. He stumbled back and ended up facedown on the wet steps.

Hirka reached the top. Gasped for breath. Leaned on her staff as she looked around. Fought down the panic. Someone approached her from behind. She drew her knife and swept it behind her. Raun grabbed her arm. Her Raun. Red Raun. Not a guardsman.

She looked around. They were standing where the rampart was wider, like a balcony. Right by the broken bridge. Raun nodded at pale-blue double doors. The Council Chamber . . .

Hirka started to run. Skerri and Tyr had already torn open the doors and made it inside. Hirka followed them into the hall. Two guardsmen lay on the floor bleeding. A councillor was lying in a heap, eyes closed. There was something shocking about seeing her like that, crumpled against a golden wall beautifully decorated with twelve family trees. Hirka couldn't remember having seen this woman before, but she had the sign of the Seer on her forehead. From what she'd heard, this had to be Telja Vanfarinn. A distant relative of Urd.

Two other councillors were slumped over the table, facedown. Subdued but not dead, if Umpiri had done as instructed.

The table . . .

Hirka rested her hands on the round stone slab. It looked smaller than she remembered. The family names were engraved in gold around the edge. Cracks in the surface revealed that it had been repaired. Altered. The Council had tried to keep things together to the very end. She had to give them that.

But where was Darkdaggar? Where were the others? Only three of them had been accounted for.

A chest lay overturned on the floor. Papers were strewn everywhere. Nearby was a lamp, overturned but still burning. Hirka picked it up and set it down on the ledge of one of the tall windows. Judging by the state of the room, the Council had been in the process of absconding. She couldn't blame them if that was the case, caught as they were between deadborn and Ravnhov. None of them could have seen what was coming.

"Is this it?" Skerri held out her arms demonstratively. "Is this the heart of Mannfalla?"

Hirka nodded. "Mannfalla is ours. Enjoy it while you can."

Skerri screeched with laughter.

Hirka looked at the two councillors at the table. One of them was Leivlugn Taid. Nearly a hundred years old, the one who Jarladin had called *confused*. Not much to be had there. She tipped back the head of the other one. Still alive. His eyelids were drooping, but he was fighting to keep them open. His hair was graying at the temples, and he was missing a few teeth. Tyrme Jekense, if she were to guess.

"Where are they?" Hirka asked. "Where are the others? Where are Urd and Darkdaggar?" Just saying their names made her gorge rise.

The councillor's eyes rolled back as his body went limp.

She let go of him. Opened the doors to the bridge. The sound of battle drew closer. Shouts of rage. Shouts of fear. Shields absorbing blows. She closed the doors again. Didn't want to see. Didn't want to hear. Didn't want to think about those fighting for their lives out there. Rime. Jarladin. Eirik. Tein.

Her chest felt like it was burning. The Might flowed through her, unchanged. It was still too early.

Raun shook the blood off his claws. "Who are we missing?"

Hirka ran through the names Jarladin had given her. Eir and Noldhe were dead. Miane Fell was in the pits, if she was still alive. Telja, Tyrme, and Leivlugn were here.

"Saulhe Jakinnin is missing, but his family is wealthy. My guess is he was the first to run. Other than him, we're missing Urd, Freid Vangard, and Darkdaggar."

Urd was what he was. She was done with him. But Darkdaggar . . . Hirka clenched her teeth. He'd cost her far too much. Lindri. Svarteld. Kolkagga. And he'd almost cost her Rime, too. It scared her how badly she wanted to confront him.

Raun dispatched a group of Umpiri to continue through the corridors. Hirka doubted they'd find the councillors there. She looked out the window. Where would be the most strategic place to wage a war from, if not here? Where would Darkdaggar go if he . . .

Her gaze fell on the building they'd thrown up around the stone circle. A circular gray wall with an uneven roof, rather modest next to Eisvaldr's mighty walls. Dangerously close to the fighting.

Still . . . Darkdaggar and Urd would have gone somewhere with a way out. And when the end of the world came, there was only one way out.

She smiled. "I know where they are."

FORGIVEN

Red-clad guardsmen swarmed up the slope.

Kolail scratched his chin. "We could always try going over the ridge and coming around from the inside," he mused, like he was talking about the weather.

Rime looked at the deadborn crouched down next to him. If he was scared, he hid it well.

"Too late. They've seen us. We have to face them."

Kolail nodded. Rain dripped from his gray hair. He raised a hand and signaled. The others emerged from the trees behind them. Deadborn and Kolkagga, side-by-side.

Kolail got up. He bared one canine in a lopsided smile. "Well, we both knew death might come for us tonight."

Rime drew his swords. "It might. But it'll come for *him* first." He glanced at the building concealing the stone circle. A curved and crude wall, built in haste. An insult to the Rite Hall that had once stood there.

The stone circle was Darkdaggar's only way out if he intended to save his skin. The councillor had met Damayanti, so he probably knew he needed blindling blood to use the gateways. And even if she hadn't given him any, there was plenty to be had now.

The wall wasn't far away. It was just a matter of getting across the frenzy of the battlefield.

"So all we need to do is survive long enough to get over there?" Kolail elbowed him in the side like an old friend.

Rime smiled back. "Over there . . ."

Then he was running down the hill with a throng of men at his heels. Black-clad and half naked in an unlikely alliance, thundering across wet grass.

Rime collided with the Might and the first guardsman at the same time. His sword sang against his breastplate. It didn't do the man any harm, but he lost his balance on the slope, armor too heavy. He tipped over backward and rolled a short way. Another man jumped over him, coming to meet Rime with a touching conviction. Heavy. Slow. Old.

Rime knocked the man's helmet off. Noticed he had crow's feet around his terrified eyes as the life left them. Then came the others. A wave of red and black. Weighed down by their own protection. Rime danced between them. He didn't care how he took them down. He didn't have time to die or kill. Not until he'd seen the councillor draw his last breath.

And not until I've seen her.

The wound tore at his side. Where she'd stabbed him to free him from the beak. From Graal. She was in Eisvaldr. Somewhere behind the walls. Only a few more dead men and he'd be able to thank her.

Rime whirled around. Cut the tail off a guardsman he'd already killed. The man simply hadn't had time to fall. Hot blood spurted into Rime's face, running down his chin with the rain.

The Might let him hear what he needed to hear. Muffled the sound of screams and steel. The night smelled of blood, fire, and spoiled crops.

He saw Kolail charge past out of the corner of his eye. His claws ripped across a throat. He was fast and unrestrained. Taking men down before they knew what had hit them. A guardsman struggled back to his feet. He'd lost his helmet. He lifted his sword tentatively, like he wasn't sure he could. He staggered but got it up over his shoulder. Kolail had moved on and had his back to him.

Rime threw a knife, all too aware that he only had one shot. It hit its mark. Kolail turned. The guardsman fell to his knees in front of him, more out of shock than anything else. The knife was embedded in his temple. His face bathed in red.

Rime met the deadborn's gaze, and in that moment, he knew he would never again doubt that nábyrn had the same feelings as ymlings.

Kolail nodded at him. A pale man wrought of steel. A wall of fire licked the night sky behind him. The smell of burning pitch clung to his nostrils. Some of the guardsmen started running. Men who knew where things were headed. They ran up toward the ridge. Stumbled and crawled onward.

You could prepare people for war. For swords. Spears. Armor. Fire. You could prepare them for pain and loss. But nothing could prepare anyone for their first encounter with claws and teeth.

Rime fought his way through the sea of guardsmen until it felt like that was all the world had to offer. Red. He saw red. Tasted red. His pulse raced in his ears. Wild and elevated by the Might. Thundering into a rhythm in his head. Words.

Madness. Madness. Madness.

He spotted Jarladin. The ox was surrounded by deadborn. Some were fighting alongside him. Others against him. It was no longer possible to tell who was who. Rime felt his body scream for air. His chest exploded. He gasped for breath.

This has to end. It has to end now.

The crowd thinned. They were through the worst of the fighting. He signaled to the others to follow him and ran toward the city walls. It ought to have been suicide, but there wasn't a single archer left. The blind had put an end to them all. Hirka had kept her promise.

Mannfalla has fallen.

Rime ran along the city wall. His arm ached from a wound he hadn't noticed before. The wall swung inward toward the city, making way for an open area where the Rite Hall had once stood.

Where the stone circle stood now, hidden within the round, gray structure. Maybe it was supposed to prevent nábyrn from using the gateways. A pathetic and futile effort.

There was only one opening to be seen. Rime knew it was risky, but he couldn't hesitate or stop to make a plan. At any moment, the Council could realize the battle was lost. That Mannfalla was overflowing with blindlings. And then they would choose the easiest way out. They would leave the city and the people to save their own skins. Rime knew that for a fact.

He ran inside. Felled two guardsmen as his eyes adjusted to the dark. The stones stood like pale monoliths, almost flush with the curved walls. Two lifeless figures lay on the floor. Councillors. Freid and Saulhe. It seemed that cooperation had broken down in the end.

Darkdaggar stood in the center of the circle, half hidden by a chest. As if he'd planned to drag it with him to gods knew where.

More guardsmen charged Rime. He ducked under a battle-ax. Yelled for Kolail but got no response. The guardsmen advanced on him. He raised his swords to cut his way through. He was surrounded now. Bloodshed was inevitable.

Then the floor dropped out from under him.

He fell. His head hit stone. Pain shot through his body. He landed on his knees. Unable to see anything other than fog. He blinked frantically. Felt the dizziness come.

No.

All other words escaped him. That was all he had. Just *no*.

He staggered to his feet, only to find he was standing up to his neck in a pit next to one of the stones. Staring at someone's feet.

Darkdaggar was standing at the edge with a knife in his hand. A ridiculously small knife. Ceremonial, not for fighting. Rime laughed, but the pain lancing through his head stopped him.

"We started digging, you see." The councillor gave him a vacant look. "It turns out these stones go much deeper than you'd expect. But I think you knew that."

Rime heard someone shout his name. Kolail. Guardsmen running. Steel against steel outside.

Darkdaggar backed away from the pit. Barked an order at the guardsmen. Rime seized the opportunity, throwing his swords over the edge and pulling himself up. He felt sick. Dizzy. He reached for his swords again, but then there was a blow to his back. The impact stunned him, leaving him on his knees. He tipped his head back and stared into the face of one of the guardsmen. A sword hung over him. Ready to strike.

Rime realized he knew him. He was twalif. The lowest rank in the army. Commander of twelve. This man had hauled a dying man back from Lake Stilla when the army had been returning from Ravnhov. Rime smiled.

"It's you," he mumbled.

The man suddenly recognized him. Gaped. And hesitated. Clearly remembering that Rime had been the Ravenbearer the last time they saw each other. Everything felt interminably slow. Interminably quiet.

There was a snap. A resounding crack. A series of them. It was coming from the walls. Moving around them in a circle. Darkdaggar swore and shouted. Sent guardsmen out to investigate. Rime heard them collide with Kolail and Kolkagga outside.

Then the walls exploded. The Might hit him like an almighty gust of wind. The twalif dropped his sword and stumbled back. Rime looked up. The wall hadn't fallen. It hung around them like an enormous ring of gray sand.

He was dead. He had to be. He was in Slokna dreaming about being in the middle of a sandstorm. It whirled around the raven ring. A living wall outside the stones. He glanced down at his chest, half expecting to see a sword thrust through his body, but he was still whole.

Then the sand slammed into the ground. The wall was gone, like it had never been there at all. The stone circle was surrounded by gray dust. It was beaten back by the rain. Drawn into wet earth.

I'm dreaming.

But the Might was real. And mingling with something familiar. A smell. A sensation. A certainty.

Her.

Deadborn gathered around the stones. And there she stood. Outside the circle. Rime stopped drawing on the Might. Stopped binding. Knew that was the only way to get her closer without her disappearing through the gateways. She came toward him. Dressed like them. Like a deadborn. Her chest was strapped in leather, like someone had just wound strips of it around her. Feathers and animal teeth hung from her skirt. Her thighs were bare. As were her arms. Eyes white. Blind.

She was here. She was real.

Rime tried to get up, but his legs wouldn't cooperate. He fumbled for his swords.

Darkdaggar stood rooted to the spot. Gaping at the deadborn. Defeat was clear to him now. His face contorted in anger. He started running toward Rime.

Rime clambered to his feet and lifted his swords. The councillor was coming at him with his knife. Bloodlust. As if this one act was all the world needed. As if it would save him.

Madness. Enough death.

Rime could see Hirka out the corner of his eye. She'd seen him kill, far too many times. He was done. Enough was enough. He threw his swords aside. They clattered to the floor. The same floor Svarteld had died on.

Then he sank to his knees. Unable to stand anymore.

Darkdaggar only hesitated for a moment. Hirka came up behind him. Hit him across the back of the knees with her staff. Darkdaggar fell forward, shrieking as his knees hit the floor.

Hirka gripped her staff in both hands and hooked it around the squirming councillor's neck. Rime could see her gathering her strength. Then she twisted. Using her entire body. Darkdaggar's neck broke with a slow crack. The squirming stopped.

Hirka let him go. He crumpled like a sack, ending up on his stomach, head twisted at an impossible angle.

Rime stared at her. She was terrifying. Eyes white as snow. Blazing with the Might. Strange. Ravenous with hate. He knew she had reason to hate, as much as he did. For Kolkagga. For Lindri.

But this was Hirka. This was the girl who despised him for killing. He saw her now and saw himself. He saw all the people he'd ever killed.

His blood ran cold as he understood. This was how she'd seen him. As he saw her now. Dangerous. Uncompromising. A wild animal.

Hirka met his gaze. Her red hair hung in wet ropes down her chest. The rain drummed against the floor.

"I forgive you," she said, voice rough.

Then she threw down her staff and walked away.

FLOW

Hirka could hear Rime following her up the steps. He shouted her name, but she kept climbing. Nothing he said would change anything.

She made it up to the balcony and headed for the Council Chamber. A group of Umpiri were standing around outside. They gave her a questioning look. She jerked her head in Rime's direction. "He's with me. Where's Skerri?"

One of them nodded toward the battlefield. "Where else?"

Hirka threw open the doors and entered the Council Chamber. The room had become a grandstand from which to observe the war raging outside. A victory nest. Deadborn were clustered around the windows. Laughing and shouting. Someone had discovered the wine cellar, judging by the bottles and the smell. The three councillors were still in the same place. Still out cold.

"What are they doing here?" she asked.

Fled, from the second house, turned to her. "No one knows what to do with them."

"I told you to throw them in the pits!"

Fled set his bottle down on the window ledge. Three others came over, and together they hauled away what remained of the Council.

Hirka sat down. She clasped her hands around the back of her neck and put her feet up on the table, over Darkdaggar's name. Judging by the scarred stone, his name had been removed at some point.

On the opposite side she saw Rime's family name. An-Elderin. She pointed. "Take a seat. It looks like you've still got one."

Rime stepped into the room. "What are you doing, Hirka?" He sounded weary. Confused.

She didn't look at him. Stared at the gilded name. "Strange that they kept the table, isn't it? After the coup. But I suppose they had other things to worry about . . ."

Rime leaned over the table. "You can stop them, Hirka. No one knows who they're fighting anymore. Deadborn against deadborn, ymling against ymling. The Council has fallen. It's over now. Tell them."

Hirka could smell how dangerous he was to her. How he could ruin everything she had fought for, and that couldn't happen. She looked at him.

"Not yet."

He looked utterly bewildered. "Not yet?! You've taken the city. What more do you need?"

Two deadborn glanced at them curiously. Hirka got up. Couldn't be near him anymore. He didn't understand. Never would. She'd flown with the ravens. She'd seen everything.

"I'd have thought you'd be pleased," she said. "This is necessary. This has to happen to heal old wounds. Old injustices."

"By creating new ones?"

His voice was hoarse. It chafed at her. Got under her skin.

He doesn't understand. We have to go.

We have to change. We have to leave him.

Hirka opened the door and went out onto the bridge. No one had fixed it after the fall of the Rite Hall. That was the problem with people. All people, from all worlds. They didn't fix things. They just destroyed.

Night had fallen. Bringing wind. Heavier rain.

Rime followed her.

"Have you seen what's going on out there?" he asked. "I don't know what they've done to you, but this isn't the answer! I know who you are, Hirka, and this isn't you."

Hirka felt weak. Torn. But she couldn't give in. Not yet.

"The Might . . ." she whispered. "I'm waiting for the Might. Nothing feeds the Might like death."

He stepped closer. Pointed in the direction of the fighting. Toward Blindból. "Look around you! If that was true, you'd have enough to tear down mountains!"

He's right . . .

Doubt hit her. Sliced into her chest. She took a deep breath to force it out. She couldn't have it. There was no room for doubt. Everything depended on this and this alone, on death feeding the Might. Enough to heal it. Many had to die, so everyone could live.

"It's like you've always said, Rime. We're already dead."

He stared at her. Wolf eyes in the rain. He clenched his fists, as if to grip his swords tighter, but they were sheathed on his back. His expression suggested he was thinking about drawing them.

He ran toward her. Hirka was so ripe with the Might that she could have avoided him if she'd wanted to. But she let him come. Wanted him to come.

He collided with her. Dragged her down. They fell. She saw the end of the bridge getting smaller above them. Carved serpents gaping down at her, their tongues dripping with rain. Rime was heavy and wet. Pressed against her. They plunged toward the ground. She drew on more of the Might and saw that it was hurting him. She was too strong. But she could either break their fall or die.

They slammed into the ground as one. Him on top of her. The air was trapped in her lungs. He locked his arms around her. His white hair clung to her cheek. Blood trickled out of the corner of his mouth.

"This ends here," he whispered. "Now."

She looked up at him. Rime. Ridiculously beautiful Rime. His narrow gray eyes, which she'd always drowned in. His sculpted lips. His high cheekbones. Rime, who had lost so much. Just like her. Was it loss that had brought them together? Made them one? The longing grew painful inside her.

"Rime . . . This ends when I've healed the Might. Don't you understand? It belongs with everyone. Peace cannot last while some have it and others don't. But I can fix it. I know I can. But first I have to be like you. You've taught me that sometimes you have to make sacrifices."

His gaze faltered. His eyes lost their coldness. His pupils dilated, as if trying to contain the despair. His head drooped.

"I never wanted you to be like me. I needed you to be *you*. And the whole world needs you to be you. I'm . . . poison to you. I've destroyed you."

He pulled himself up onto his knees. A grimace of pain cut across his face. He rose unsteadily to his feet.

Hirka felt cold and naked without him. Without the weight of him. She pushed herself up onto her elbows. Spotted a dead man nearby. A guardsman in red. Eyes staring into Slokna. Oddly, he had a smile on his lips, as if his last thought had been of something good.

No!

Hirka fought back tears. Dragged herself to her feet. Looked around. The sight of Blindból made her stomach lurch. Eisvaldr's gardens were no longer beautiful. They were a battlefield. As they had been a thousand years earlier. Men colliding in a seething mass. They moved slowly. Unsteadily. Tongues of fire sputtering in the rain.

She looked down at her hands. They were shaking. The Might remained unchanged. It hadn't exploded from all the death and given her the power to save worlds. What had she been thinking? Had she really believed it would?

Tears forced their way out. She couldn't contain them anymore. "Enough," she whispered. But no one could hear her. She stumbled toward Rime. Past an overturned cart. She could see something moving underneath. Gleaming eyes in the dark. A cat. Of all things, in a place like this. At a time like this.

Hirka held out her hand. The animal hissed. Retreated farther under the cart. The Might melded with the animal's heartbeat. It was much too fast. Hirka could taste the fear. The certainty that she was an enemy. Her. The girl who always kept her eyes on the path so she wouldn't step on ants.

The Might surged through her and revealed everything she'd done wrong. Picked her apart. It fed on her despair. Her grief. But she didn't want it anymore. She couldn't bear to look at herself.

Hirka heard herself scream. She clawed at her chest, but the Might forced its way through her veins. Rupturing her from within.

She became one with the animal. She became one with Rime. With his deepest darkness. One with the fighters. The more she struggled against the Might, the stronger it got.

She stumbled forward. She was an animal, terrified in the dark, hiding under a cart. She was a man with a gaping wound in his thigh, awaiting certain death. Ax met shield and she was forced to the ground by a bearded giant. She could see her own ribs. She fell forward. She was a boy who had lied about his age in order to fight. A woman spitting blood and wishing she'd never left Ravnhov. She was a mother of three children in an overcrowded boat, fleeing the city. She was a man who could no longer walk. Looming over her was a deadborn, eyes glowing white in the darkness. She'd never been so scared. She couldn't move. She was all of them. Felt all of them.

The Might pressed in on her from every direction. Pressed her into a lump. A mass ready to explode. And she understood.

The Might had never wanted blood. It didn't feed on death. It fed on the emotions of the dying. Friend or foe. All were one. No one out there was hurting anyone else. They were only hurting themselves. Every blow was suicide.

She buckled. Screamed. Dug her fingers into the earth. Tore them back out. The earth came with them. Black soil and shattered stone rained upward. Pulled her to her feet. Lifted her off the ground. Her arms quaked such that she feared they might break. Stone and earth came together. Whipped around her like ink. Buried alive.

Everything suddenly went quiet. She was held aloft by the Might. At the center of a black whirlwind. Ravenborn. Stone whisperer. Child of Odin. She was everything she had been, and everything she would be. She was the Might. Blood from every world.

We are the first.

The ravens fought to get out. Out of her mind. Out of her body. She was tiny, tiny pieces of everything that had lived. She stretched her legs until she touched the ground again. Gathered all the strength she had. She was pulsating. She was one big heart. Pounding. Grieving. Self-sacrificing.

Hirka slammed her fists into the ground.

Whirling black stone followed. Broke through. Twisted its way under the ground. Under houses. Under running men. Thunder boomed from deep, deep down, and she knew where she had to go. She'd seen this. Seen the map in a book. Seen how the rings were connected. She'd seen the Might as raven. Knew where it was strong. Where it was weak.

New channels formed. The ground writhed beneath the dead. She needed more! More stone. More earth. She had to feed the flow. She fumbled her way forward in the dark. In her thoughts. Found the wall. The one separating those who had everything from those who had nothing. She could hear it falling. A deluge of stone that mixed with screams. It was absorbed into the earth.

She closed her eyes. The channels grew. Met the emptiness. The all-consuming emptiness between worlds. The force surging through her arms died. As if nothing existed. Then she hit solid ground again and felt it tearing at her shoulders.

Her thoughts grew dull. Vague. She realized she was losing consciousness.

She clung to the ground. It ruptured and disappeared out from under her.

Then she heard the ravens screeching. Tens of thousands of them. They forced their way out of her. Took the Might and disappeared.

The last thing she saw was a memory. Graal's broken bowl, repaired with gold. Like tiny cracks in glass. More beautiful for having been destroyed.

SCORHILL

Graal closed the box containing the raven cadaver. There was nothing more he could do. The war had forced Damayanti into hiding. She wasn't alone and was no longer able to talk to him. The day of reckoning had come—and he couldn't lift a finger.

The landscape of Scorhill lay gray around him. Bathed in typical English drizzle, so light that it couldn't be felt. Not until you were soaked through. It forced the mist to crawl along the ground. To wind around the stones, which stuck up like rotten teeth. He didn't know what he was doing here. He had no reason to be here. His scorched blood meant he would never be able to use the gateways.

Had he succumbed to sentimentality? Was this an urge to be close to what was happening? At best, it was an illusion. The war was underway. Somewhere, a world was being rocked to its core, but here there wasn't a sound to be heard. Just the odd mournful cry from a bird. The stones stood as they always had, isolated in the hills. So old and overgrown with moss that they made the silhouette of his helicopter look fake. Like a film prop.

He gave a deep sigh. Rested his forehead against the cold stone. A thousand years . . . What had he done wrong? What had he done right?

He'd had *her*. Blood of his blood. Hirka.

She'd kept her word. Gone into Mannfalla with Umpiri. The

outcome remained to be seen, but on the other side of this stone, they were dying for her. Because she wanted to feed the Might.

He laughed. Was laughing to yourself a sign of encroaching madness?

Everything he'd done to get here . . . Everything he'd made *her* do. Plans that had taken centuries to orchestrate, and now she'd supplanted him. It was her they followed, not him. He was still a prisoner. An exile in the human world.

What if Damayanti was killed? What if Skerri was killed? What if this was the end? No contact with anyone on the other side. No ravens. Just dead gateways . . .

The thought burrowed inside him, forcing out a scream. Surely another sign of madness. Or was it a natural defense against the pain? Against the torment of not being able to see the outcome of a war he'd waited generations for?

The worst thing was he wasn't sure he cared anymore. Naiell was dead. Hirka had restored his house to its position on the Council. Given them back their honor. All that was missing was the Might.

His plan had been to give them Ym. Hers was something completely different. She thought she could give the Might back to Dreysíl. To everyone.

Was that why he was here? Had he started to hope?

It was an unsettling thought. He wasn't someone who hoped. He was someone who acted. He shaped the circumstances until the outcome was favorable, sometimes so meticulously that it took generations.

This was a bad day.

Graal fastened the top button of his coat. There was an autumn chill in the air. He had to get back. There was nothing for him here. He turned his back on the stone circle and headed toward the helicopter. Then he took one last look. The mist was being pulled between the stones.

A vacuum.

He dropped the raven box. Ran back down toward the circle. Maybe she was coming to him. Maybe Hirka was on her way. Or maybe someone else . . .

Graal rested a hand on the stone. Waited.

Then he felt something.

Something.

A prickling in his blood.

Nobody came. Nothing happened. But his blood . . . His heart swelled in his breast. Started pounding. Sluggishly, like it suddenly had more blood to deal with.

It came. Hit him like a tidal wave. Poured into his veins and forced him to his knees.

Graal dug his claws into the yellow heath. Down into the earth. And it came to him. For the first time in a thousand years. What they'd taken from him. What he'd been fighting for. What he'd thought he'd never again feel.

It was here with him.

The Might.

The Might was here.

It grew, forcing him open. He let it in. He drank. Fell on all fours. Crawled forward. Buried his nose in the heath. Smelled earth. Mold. Bark. Dirt. He drank. He was going to die. He was going to bind himself to death.

Someone was watching him.

Graal looked up. A raven. It was sitting over him on a low stone. Like a grave ornament. It cocked its head. Blinked.

Graal pulled himself to his knees. There was something accusatory in the bird's gaze. Or mocking. He crawled toward the stone. Sat with his back to it while he caught his breath. The knees of his suit were filthy.

The raven took flight and soared across the moors.

Graal bound the Might again. It exposed him. Laid him bare. Picked him apart and let him see himself. It was the most wonderful and terrifying thing he'd seen in a thousand years.

Graal rested his elbows on his knees and wept.

ONE LAST POINT

Rime got up. A silence had settled over the battlefield. It felt wrong. Perverse. As if it were trivializing the chaos they had experienced.

"Rime?"

Rime recognized the distinctive pronunciation of his name. The sharp *r* and an almost silent *e*. He turned to see Kolail. The deadborn sat hunched over on the ground. A cat rubbed against his leg, but he didn't seem to have the strength to move. They looked at each other, but neither of them said a word. What was there to say?

Deadborn sat in clusters around the stone circle. Exhausted. Silent. Stunned by what she had done. It was as if she had sapped them of the will to stand. Rime bound the Might to make sure it was still there. It had been gone for a moment. It had been like taking a breath and finding there was no air. It hadn't hurt him, but there could be no doubt that it had hit the blindlings hard.

What about her? What has it done to her?

"Hirka?"

No answer. Rime picked his way across the battlefield. He couldn't stop himself from looking at the faces of those who had fallen. He had to look. Had to know who he'd lost. Some of them stared back with dead eyes. He turned them onto their fronts so the ravens wouldn't peck them out.

He saw others doing the same. A man in red and black armor

staggered between the bodies a little way off. Rime met his gaze. Recognized him. He'd raised his sword to him not long ago. An eternity ago. Then. Not now.

Now they looked at each other before going on their way. What was the difference between then and now? Could men ever learn to live in this now? In a silence like this, without first bleeding? And who was he to ask that question? Him, who'd never done anything but give the earth blood.

He felt empty. Like an abyss that couldn't really process anything meaningful. Apart from her.

"HIRKA?!"

It had stopped raining. The wind tugged at dead men's hair. Tricking him into thinking they might still be alive. But anyone still alive had fled. Or was trying to. Dragging the wounded up the hillsides to give them room to breathe and die in peace.

They can be saved. More can be saved.

Nábyrn and ymlings kept their distance from each other, not knowing that the blood of one could ease the suffering of the other. Not knowing anything about each other. Kneeling just ahead of Rime was a blindling he remembered from Ravnhov. One on their side, though he wasn't sure what that meant anymore. He was pale, even for a blindling, like he'd lost a lot of blood. But he had no visible wounds.

The earth had ruptured. From Eisvaldr into Blindból. Rime followed the fissure through the battlefield. It was breathing dust, like a living thing. A creature from a bad dream. For a moment he thought it was screaming, then he realized the cries were coming from a woman.

A deadborn was wedged in where the fissure was narrowest. Her lips were black. She stopped shouting when she saw him. Just stared up at him with colorless eyes. He hadn't seen her in Ravnhov. That had to make her the enemy.

446

Rime crouched down and offered her a hand. She gripped it, and he helped her up.

There was something scary about her. Not just that she was a tall, strong deadborn. Not just the black lips. She leaned toward him. Sniffed him like an animal. Smiled crookedly.

"So you're the one," she said in ymish.

Rime didn't answer. He turned and continued searching.

"HIRKA?!"

And then he spotted her. Her red hair stirred his blood, as if it had been standing still inside him. She was lying on a stone slab that was wedged between the walls of the fissure. She forced her eyes open. Blinked. They were tired, but they were hers. Her own wonderfully green eyes. Not those of a deadborn. She closed them again, as if she didn't have the strength to look at him.

"One point to you if you pull me up," she said.

Rime leaned over the edge. "I thought we'd stopped that game?"

"Then just come here."

She said it as though he wasn't already moving toward her.

Rime slipped down onto the stone and sat next to her. She lay there with her eyes closed. Dressed like a deadborn, with shoes that looked like bandages. They wound all the way up her lower legs, soaking up blood from open cuts above her knees. Her hair was fanned out like a halo over the stone.

He hated the world for what it had put her through. Hated being a part of what had destroyed her.

But she was here. She was alive. And she'd done what she'd set out to do.

And me? What have I done?

Something tightened in his chest. Suddenly all the expectations he'd grown up with came back to him. The demands for his future. Who he'd be. Leader. Assassin. Soldier. He'd defied Ilume. Defied Svarteld. The Council. But he hadn't really chosen a different path than any of them. Not like her. He'd chosen death. And seen more of it than he could bear.

She sat up and looked at him. Through him. She stroked a thumb across his cheek. He didn't realize he'd been crying. She pressed her hand against his chest. Forced him onto his back and lay next to him. She closed her eyes again and he assumed he was supposed to do the same. He couldn't. There was too much to see behind closed eyes. Betrayal. Far too much betrayal. Everything that had lived had betrayed.

He saw something move out of the corner of his eye. Rime looked up.

Tein . . .

The chieftain's son stopped at the edge, bow tensed. He seemed to be intact apart from a red gash across his thigh. But his eyes told a different story. He looked confused, as if he hadn't known who he would find. Friend or foe. Then recognition struck. But he didn't lower his bow.

Rime understood. They'd once made an agreement. Before he was free of the beak. A promise Tein longed to keep. It would be so easy. A single arrow. No witnesses. Rime would be dead before Hirka could even open her eyes.

Tein looked at him with a wounded expression. Looked at Hirka. Rime felt no fear. Not even anger. He was done. He was ready.

The chieftain's son lowered his bow. The pain on his face was fleeting, becoming a forlorn emptiness. Then he stepped back and was gone.

Rime stared up at the gray sky. Wind blew sand over the edge, like small swarms of insects.

RUINED

Hirka walked from cot to cot, tending to the wounded. She'd tried to keep Umpiri and ymlings separate, but Eisvaldr was bursting at the seams and people had to take what they were given.

In several places they lay side by side. Tailed and tailless. With and without claws. There wasn't a bed to be had, which was probably for the best, because if there had been, she'd have fallen into it and never woken up again.

The studded door stood open, letting fresh air into the pits. Even Eisvaldr's prisons had been made into infirmaries. Holding areas for a bizarre combination of dying and lawless. But what was the difference between them, when it came down to it? Some were in the pits for killing. Others were being nursed back to health for doing the same. The only difference was the time and place of their misdeed.

Justice was like stone. Everyone thought it was solid. Eternal and constant. But she'd seen something else. It was more like grains of sand barely managing to stick together. Volatile and changeable, under the right circumstances.

Hirka looked around. She hadn't thought she'd ever set foot here again. Her gaze was drawn involuntarily to one of the grates in the floor. Down there was where she'd lain after the Rite. Down there was where she'd fashioned a knife from a splinter of wood. Poor defense against the man who'd wanted to rape her. He was dead. Killed by Urd, who had taken her away from there.

Urd . . .

Jarladin and Sigra had interrogated the imprisoned councillors, but none of them knew anything about Urd. Even Telja Vanfarinn believed he'd lost his life on Bromfjell, long ago.

Hirka had been sure he would betray her. But he'd just run off. Perhaps through the stone circle. Only the gods could know. But it didn't matter. She'd let go of him now.

Nothing was as it had been. Urd was no threat. The Council no longer existed. The world had been turned on its head.

She felt dizzy. Leaned on the edge of one of the bunks that had been put together by volunteers. Shelves with space for people on three levels. The man before her grunted, eyes squeezed shut. Hirka lifted his bandage. The wound hadn't improved since the previous day. She pulled the stopper out of the bottle and dripped blood down into the wound. He grabbed her arm. His grip was astonishingly strong for a dying man.

He stared at her with feverish eyes. "If that's blindling blood, get it away from me! It's filth and I won't have it!"

Hirka pushed his arm back down. "Tough, you're getting it. Then you might live to moan about it later."

He loosened his grip. "Where are they?"

"Most of them have gone back home," she replied, neglecting to tell him there was a blindling in the cot above his. She also neglected to tell him they could come and go as they pleased now that the Might had found its way to Dreysíl.

His head dropped back onto the pillow. A shimmering silk number embroidered with golden thread. She'd rarely seen anything more out of place. But they needed pillows, and the city was full of Council families and rich merchants who now wanted to be considered allies. Some of them had given generously from their own homes. Others had even opened their doors to the homeless and wounded.

"They were fighting . . ." The man cleared his throat and tried again. "They were fighting each other. Some of them."

Hirka smiled. "What's your name?"

The question seemed to confuse him for a moment. "Runar. My name is Runar."

"Well, Runar . . ." She rested a hand on his forehead. "Some of *us* were also fighting each other."

He croaked out a laugh. Almost inaudible. "So . . . how many died?"

Hirka covered his wound again. "We've paid the price. I don't want to know what it was."

Runar closed his eyes. She wondered whether he knew who she was. That she was the one who had brought the blind here. That he might die because of her.

Again came the suffocating weight of what she'd done. A feeling that threatened to press her into a small, hard lump. The decisions she'd made on behalf of so many others. And with what right?

She stared down at the floor. It seemed to move. Buckets, cloths, and items of clothing swam together.

"When did you last sss . . . sleep?"

Hirka turned toward the voice. The Seer was standing in the light from the doorway. Hunched and swathed in black, his hood covering his face. She tried to pull herself together but knew she hadn't managed.

"Soon I'll have more than enough time to sleep," she said, and walked over to the stool where she'd left her linen bundle of herbs. She rolled it up and shoved it in her bag, grateful that someone had brought it from Ravnhov.

She'd been avoiding him, and she was sure he knew that. He hobbled over to her. Put a hand on her shoulder and led her toward the exit.

Hirka pointed at the healers in the next room. "But . . . look at them. They won't wash their hands if I don't—"

"I think the guild will sss . . . survive an hour without you."

Reluctantly, Hirka followed him outside. He pulled her down onto a bench overlooking the gardens. Or what was left of them.

Hedges had been trampled over. Trees stood bare and blackened by soot. Straps, gauntlets, and broken shields created sinister silhouettes. And farther away on the outskirts of Blindból, smoke rose from the pyres. But she was responsible for the worst of the damage. A fissure that split the landscape in two. It ran between the city walls and had reduced parts of Eisvaldr to rubble. And she knew that if she looked up, the wall would be gone. The one that had towered between Mannfalla and Eisvaldr. Always. Now they were one and the same city.

They were still sweeping sand from the streets. People would argue about what had become of the stone until the end of time.

"So . . . tomorrow?" he asked tentatively. Mere preamble. Really he wanted something very different. And she hated it. Hated circling the inevitable.

"Yes. They're coming from all over," she replied. "People from Brekka, people who didn't choose sides. Now they want to be included. Now the power is to be divided up." She wasn't able to hide her bitterness.

They sat in silence for a while.

"You have to talk about it," he said finally.

Hirka leaned her head against the rock wall. "What's there to say?" She closed her eyes. Had to rest, just for a moment. "I let it happen. Everything you see here, I let it happen. For no reason."

"For no reason? You've given us the Might."

"But no one needed to die for it! No one! What everyone says isn't true. Death doesn't feed the Might. It's something else. Seeing . . ." She searched for the right words. "Seeing connections. Seeing others. Feeling them, as if they were me. Pain, grief, joy, or fear. That was what saved us, not death. Don't you get it?"

The Seer ran a knotted hand over his hood, revealing the outline of his ruined face. The beaklike protrusion. A forehead that sloped too far back. Half raven. The man who had loved Naiell.

Hirka leaned against him. Rested her forehead against his shoulder. "Naiell must have done the same," she said. "He must have felt the same pain. He must have felt all of them. He couldn't have done what he did without feeling them. He . . . his heart wasn't all bad."

"I've always known that," the Seer replied.

Hirka felt leaden. She wasn't sure she'd be able to get up again. So tired. But it wasn't over yet. She still had one thing left to do. It would hurt, but it had to be said. She'd put it off long enough. Her eyes started to sting.

"I can't help you," she whispered, gripping the bench. "I can bind, and the Might can show me how things fit together. I can see you. See bone and blood. But you're not made of things that can be pulled apart. You're not a broken bone. You're . . ." She swallowed the lump in her throat. Felt her lips fail her and twist into a grimace. "You're a knot. You'd die if I tried."

His robe fluttered in the wind. Dark and crumpled, like a dead leaf.

"I've always known that, too," he said.

She suppressed a sob. A sound she knew would only get worse. Much worse. Exhaustion caught up with her. He put an arm around her shoulders. Pulled her close. Her face rested against jutting ribs. Unnatural. Deformed. Painful.

"You can't heal everything, Hirka. And not everything that is mended becomes more beautiful for it. Sometimes things are just ruined. That's all."

She started to cry. The sobs came in spasms. He hugged her. Caressed her tear-stained cheek with black claws.

"Hirka . . . Daughter of Graal, sss . . . son of Raun of the House of Modrasme. You have given far too much of yourself to the world."

THE RAVEN RING

Hirka crawled out onto the ruined bridge. Got down on her stomach and peered over the edge. She wasn't alone. The carvings of serpents and dragons kept her company. Mythical creatures, worn by the elements. One of them flicking its long tongue in the direction of the stone circle.

They were gathering there. Far too many women and men, all of whom believed they deserved a share of the power. Or, at the very least, that they deserved to have a say when the power was divided up. Before the day was done, some would have more, while others would have none.

They were to be called the Raven Ring, provided they could find enough common ground to be anything at all. Rime had suggested the name. With the demise of the Council, no one would accept anything new with the same name. The purge had to be complete.

Hirka bound the Might. She needed to know their thinking before meeting them. Senses honed by the Might, she could see and hear things that would normally be too distant. Through space, and perhaps also time. Sometimes she'd get impressions of past events. And of events she believed were still to come.

The fighting had taken its toll on the floor inside the circle. A large section, where Darkdaggar had ordered excavation work, was covered with wooden boards. Had he been trying to tear down the gateways? An impossible task, of course, as the stones reached farther down than they did up. A lot of the tiles were missing or broken. The motifs were faded, almost impossible to interpret. But people probably weren't that different. Especially the ones standing below.

Their words intermingled with rustling leaves from the few surviving trees.

Eirik was there representing Ravnhov. He still had a line of congealed blood on his nose where it had been broken.

A man of similar stature was standing next to him. Varg Kallskaret, representing Ulvheim. Hirka had never met him, but she felt like she already knew him. She'd been on the roof in Ravnhov, listening in as his son explained his father's absence. How he'd gotten into a fight with a mountain bear and broken his leg in three places. The memory made her cling to the edge of the bridge, her body suddenly remembering her fall from the roof.

Conspicuous by their absence were the former Council families. Many had wanted to throw Darkdaggar's wife in the pits, but Hirka had put her foot down. She and her daughters had lost enough. Because of Hirka. His family had been the farthest thing from her mind when she killed him. Was that why he'd waited to run through the stones? Had he died because he was waiting for his loved ones? She knew she'd carry that uncertainty and pain with her forever.

Jarladin was there. Hirka had barely seen him since the fighting. Sigra Kleiv, too. Miane Fell had been chucked in the pits by Darkdaggar, for treason. She was free now, and also present. Others Hirka knew by name only.

None of them would ever have believed they'd end up standing together with blindlings, but they were. Hod was there, representing Dreysíl. Umpiri. Kolail was there for the fallen. Those who had fought against their own. There was no doubt as to what Hod thought of that. Rime had been wise enough to place them on opposite sides of the circle of women and men.

Rime . . .

He stood between Eirik and Kolail. Both were taller and broader than him, not to mention considerably older, but in her eyes, Rime still stood out the most. He was so handsome. His white hair was tied back. His brown leather armor crossed his chest, but he carried no swords. None of them did.

It struck her that she'd forgotten to pay attention to what they were saying. The tone had become sharper. Sigra Kleiv wanted to tear down the gateways, and that was all it took to start an argument.

Hirka decided it was probably best to put in an appearance before things deteriorated. She bound the Might and eased herself down from the bridge. Not just for the rush it would give, but also so they would see what she was capable of. She had to make the most of that.

The Might gave her a soft landing. She entered the circle and stood next to Kolail. All eyes were on her. The conversation had died.

"The gateways stay," she said.

Surprisingly, there was no immediate reaction. Sigra was the first to break the silence.

"Because *you* say so? Who are you representing here?"

Hirka lifted her chin. "I'm here for the Might. I'm here for the earth and everything that grows in it. I'm here for the life that can't speak for itself the way you can, Sigra. And if that's not good enough for you, then I'm here as a child of Odin. For the time being, I'm here for menskr."

Jarladin took the floor. "She's opened the gateways, Sigra. Her role here is indisputable."

Sigra threw her hands up. "Exactly! She's opened them to seers . . . to gods know where! Do I have to remind you that she did this on her own, without consulting anyone else? We have deadbo—"

Hod's lips curled into a devilish grin. A striking contrast to her otherwise irreproachable elegance.

Jarladin rested his hand on Sigra's arm. "Umpiri. They're called Umpiri."

Sigra crossed her arms. "Call them whatever you like, but apparently they can now come and go as they please! And who knows what else is out there? It could be anything, and work on a new wall hasn't even started, as far as I can see. And we've sent them the Might without any thought as to what it could be used for. We've shared it indiscriminately, with creatures we don't know."

Hirka stepped forward. "You're right, Sigra. There are many stones in this circle, and we have no idea who's on the other side of them. But they'll come. Sooner or later. The question is *how* you want them to come. Grateful that we've shared the Might with them, or determined to take it by force? We're still burning the dead because the Might was here and nowhere else. It needs to be free."

Varg from Ulvheim growled. "Baah! No matter the wretched creatures that come through here, we can handle it." The way he spoke reminded her of Father.

Hirka smiled. "I don't doubt you can handle wretches, Varg. But can you handle blessings? Both good and bad could come of it."

Silence descended as each and every one of them glanced at the stones.

"So what do we do now?" asked Veila of Brott. Hirka also remembered her from the meeting in Ravnhov.

Hirka shrugged. "We wait."

Hod seized the opportunity to comment on what was clearly the biggest thorn in her side. She narrowed her eyes at Kolail. "If this is a gathering of representatives, I'd like to know why Umpiri have two."

Rime answered her. "Kolail is not here for your world. He's here for Umpiri in Ym."

457

His words unleashed a barrage of questions. The thought of blindlings settling permanently in Ym was clearly something they'd need time to get used to.

Hod laughed bitterly. "Do you mean to say they're going to *stay* here? That you would harbor traitors?"

Sigra stepped forward, breaking the circle. "Traitors who fought *with* us, against you? That doesn't make them traitors in my eyes."

"Whatever happens, who would take them in?" Veila cast her eyes heavenward.

Objections swept around the circle like wildfire. Hirka glanced at Kolail, who was staring at the ground. It wasn't just his fate they were arguing about. He was responsible for a lot of people now. And it was a responsibility she'd bestowed on him.

"We will!" Eirik shouted. "We will take them in. Ravnhov has already welcomed them."

Hirka felt a warmth spread through her chest. Grateful for the words he spoke, which had the power to silence the others.

She seized the opportunity. Stepped into the center of the circle and looked around. Looked at all of them.

"I know this seems unimaginable. Impossible, to some of you. You see enemies. Strangers. But what you're doing here now is bigger than any of us. We are the first in the Raven Ring. We are the first to converse across worlds. I've been to other worlds, and good things can come from them. Beauty. Healing. Knowledge. And we will share what we have. And if you're having trouble accepting Umpiri and ymlings living side by side, I guarantee it's going to get worse. Soon humans will come, too. And one day the Might will reach everyone. All worlds will stand here, together."

Sigra snorted. "Who's going to find them?" she asked. "Just who is going to arrange this miracle?"

Hirka closed her eyes for a moment. Summoned the courage to tell the truth, even though she'd hadn't had a chance to talk to Rime.

"Me," she answered. "I am."

She glanced at Rime. Knew he grasped the significance of what she'd said. That she wasn't planning to stay. If he'd reacted at all, he hid it well.

Hirka stepped back.

"Well," Rime said, with forced calm. "Now can we work out how the people in the regions are going to choose their representatives?"

The question unleashed a frenzy that Hirka couldn't bear to watch. She turned and left. They could carry on without her. Anyway, it wasn't up to her how Ym was to be governed. She didn't belong here anymore. She wasn't the same. Nor would she ever be.

THE GATEWAYS

The first stall reopened a mere two days after the battle. A baker in the square, right next to where the wall had stood. People stared and walked on past. Some hurled abuse. Threw horseshit at his door. But the baker didn't let that stop him. He had a sourdough to feed. And ovens to keep hot.

The next day, all the stalls were open.

Hirka walked from one to the next, along narrow alleyways. Joy and sorrow warred around her. Those who had lost someone were silent, and those who had survived celebrated. Life went inexorably on.

Counters were piled high. Hirka haggled for herbs she could do without, though less tenaciously for those she really needed. Ylir root was a must. For the humans. It might have been too late for Allegra's husband, but he wasn't the only one suffering from memory loss.

Vetle walked ahead of her. He grabbed her every time he spotted something she had to see. Ramoja had already refused to buy him several things. Like a pendant of a small wooden horse. That had triggered a bout of tears.

Ramoja strolled along beside her, telling her what people were talking about in Ravnhov. There were few surprises. People were people. Some would always believe, others would always doubt, whether in gods or those in power.

Hirka shifted her bag into a better position. It was stuffed like a sausage. Full of things to take with her on her journey.

She stopped next to a stall loaded with trinkets. Scarves with golden threads lay on the counter. Big piles of bangles. Necklaces hung from the low ceiling. Ravens. Seer amulets. Good luck charms. One of them drew her closer. A round silver coin with a child's face stamped on one side. The child the Seer had said would live. The child everyone had waited for.

Rime An-Elderin.

Her heart clenched. Her skin started to prickle. She ran her thumb over the charm. Rime was distant in so many ways. And yet not. She'd been as close to him as it was possible to be. The man behind the counter beamed at her. He had thick golden rings in one ear.

She was struck by a sudden need to say that she knew Rime. An inexplicable urge to explain she'd been with him.

Lain with him.

The thought made her flush. She let go of the charm and continued on.

"He'll bring you luck!" the man called after her. Hirka suppressed a bitter laugh.

The sun was sinking down behind the mountains, bathing the streets in red and orange. Vetle ran over to a bricked-up pool in the middle of a small square, scaring the birds. Ramoja went to keep an eye on him. Hirka sat down on a bench against a wall. She opened her bag and pulled out the book. Black with a soft cover. She started to flip through it. Page after page of circles. Nothing else. Circles with lines coming out of them. Maps of worlds. Perhaps more than she'd ever be able to visit. How many of them could she even survive in?

She heard Vetle laugh as the smell of spiced bread wafted past. Little things that felt far too big to leave behind. If it hurt that much to leave laughter and bread, how would she leave the big things?

Hirka put the book back in her bag before finding the other one. A smaller book bound in brown leather with a compass on the front. She opened it. Swallowed when she saw the pain in her own words. How little she'd understood when she first came to the human world. The language. The noises. The cars . . .

But she'd learned. Her drawings became increasingly confident as she flipped through the pages. As did her words. Pictures and postcards were tucked between the pages. Things she'd cut out. A painting of a tree. A picture of Venice. Drawings of plants. On the last page she'd drawn a circle broken by lines of varying lengths. Like a mended bowl.

More beautiful for being destroyed.

But that wasn't the case with her. She was broken. She'd lost too much. She'd done things that kept her awake at night. Things she'd sworn never to do. She'd taken lives. Sacrificed so many people for something bigger. And been so wrong.

She couldn't stay here.

Even the ravens had said as much. She belonged to all worlds. Her home wasn't with Umpiri, humans, or ymlings. Her home was on the road. As it always had been. With Father, in a red wagon. That was home. Drawing and writing about plants in all the worlds she could. Finding connections. Learning.

Hirka tore out a page and started to write. A breeze played with one corner.

Ramoja sat down next to her.

Hirka folded the letter. "Will you see him tonight?" she asked, trying to sound casual.

"I'm seeing Eirik, and I expect Rime won't be far away."

Hirka gave her the letter. "Can you give him this?"

Ramoja looked at her. She clearly wanted to ask, but didn't. Much to Hirka's relief.

"Did you hear he's been copying books?"

Hirka shook her head.

"They say there have been books hidden in the library for generations. Books about the blind, and about the brothers. Even books in the blindling tongue!"

Umǫni. They call it umǫni.

But she said nothing.

Ramoja leaned back, legs crossed. The golden beads on the hems of her trousers rattled. "Do you know what Eirik said? He said Rime's been determined to get them out. To write a new history and this time make sure it's true. Of course, Eirik asked whether he really thought he could write a truer history than those before him. Do you know what Rime said to that? He said no, but at least it would teach people to read more than one history."

Hirka smiled through the pain.

Vetle came running over. He lifted up a pendant. A small wooden horse on a black leather strap.

Ramoja clutched her chest. "Did you steal that?!"

"I was given it!" Vetle said, affronted.

Ramoja raised an eyebrow, a dubious expression on her dark face.

"The man gave it me." Vetle pointed. He looked confused for a moment. Looked at his mother again. "He was just there. He gave it me."

Ramoja sighed but still helped him put it on. Hirka looked up. A prickling feeling made her draw on the Might. She let her gaze sweep over men and women. Then she spotted a familiar face.

Urd . . .

He met her gaze across the square. A hood hid the ugly scar from the mark of the Council. He nodded at her. For a moment she was at a loss. Like she couldn't decide how she felt.

Ramoja would never forgive or understand. But she didn't need to know.

Hirka nodded back at him.

Urd gave her a cautious smile. Then he pulled the hood farther down over his face and disappeared into the crowd.

Hirka went out onto the cliff and looked out over the battlefield. It was shrouded in darkness, belying peace. No red spatters in the grass. No scorch marks. Only night-blue countryside rolling toward the mountains of Blindból.

They seemed more dangerous than she remembered. Like losing Kolkagga had made them wilder. Like the Council's assassins had been all that could tame them. But they were dead now. Almost all of them.

Don't count the dead.

She turned toward the city. White roofs and towers stuck up from Eisvaldr. In the rock diagonally below her were the pits. She'd stood here before. With Rime. The memory was so clear it could have happened only yesterday. The look he'd given her when she'd sent him to get her bag . . . like she'd lost her mind.

Tonight she could have gotten it herself, had it not already been on her back. She was the same, but she was different. Whole, but still broken.

She tightened the strap over her chest so the bag would sit better. Reached instinctively for her staff before remembering she'd tossed it away after killing Darkdaggar. The feeling she was missing something was intense, but it was about so much more than just the staff.

Hirka bound the Might and threw herself into the night. Landed softly on a nearby dome. Ran onward along the bridges, the same route she and Rime had taken the night they'd broken into the Seer's tower. Then up the tower with the steps on the outside, pulling herself onto the roof, just like he'd done.

It had seemed incredible back then. Divine, even, to a girl who had never been able to bind. Now the ravens had given her the gift. The Might coursed through her blood. Made her strong and supple, like Rime. Heightened her senses. Let her see how things slotted together. A blessing and a curse. Sometimes she needed to feel that things were solid. Roofs, for example.

She took off her bag and sat down on the edge. It was just wide enough that she could have her legs out in front of her and lean against the dome. It was curved and cold against her back. From here, they had flung themselves at the Rite Hall. The big red dome. Mother's bosom. All that remained of it now was the stone circle far below.

She'd always longed for solitude. Climbed up onto roofs and into trees, always to get away from people. To be alone with the sound of leaves. The whisper of the wind. Now she wanted anything but.

The solitude up here was intense. So all-consuming that she felt stupid for thinking he would come.

But at least this time she'd done everything right. She hadn't tried to leave without telling him, like last time. She'd been honest. Told him what she needed to do. Tried to explain why. There was nothing else to be done. They had always belonged to two different worlds.

Lanterns burned in Mannfalla. Hundreds of them. Fewer farther down, in the poorer areas. There were some things she would never be able to change. But she would never stop trying. Her gaze followed the river, to the place where the teahouse ought to have been. And Lindri. Hunched old Lindri. With scores of crow's feet around his eyes. For the first time, her grief was numb. No longer a claw around her heart, like it had been with everyone she'd lost. Was numbness the price you had to pay to survive?

Something tugged at the Might. A feeling she knew heart-wrenchingly well.

Rime . . .

He was close.

Her heart started to pound in her chest as if mocking all thoughts of numbness. She felt shaken. Straightened her clothes for some reason she refused to think about.

She opened herself up to more of the Might. Smelled him. Felt him. She got up. Rime pulled himself up onto the roof, so easily it was like he'd never done anything else. Then he stood looking at her. The wind played in his white hair. The pendant hung around his neck. An oval shell. With the marks that had always connected them. His swords stuck up from behind his back. He was Kolkagga. Black-clad. Dangerous. Beautiful.

She searched for words. "I . . . I wanted to tell you I'm sorry about how . . . how everything turned out. That I . . ."

He came toward her. Took her face in both hands and kissed her. She stumbled back against the dome. It made her body arch in all the right places. He pressed himself against her. The closer he got, the harder her heart had to work. It was pumping blood through two bodies, not just one.

She laced her fingers through his. They were strong and warmed by the Might. He let his lips rest against her, and she could feel him smiling. He lifted his head and met her gaze. His wolf eyes shone with pure love. For her. She could have cried at the certainty of it. Loving Rime. Being loved by Rime.

"You want to leave me?" he asked huskily.

"No. I just want to leave."

His breath warmed her cheek. "Then we'll leave together."

She put her hand against his chest. Against straps. Fastenings. And bumps that revealed where he kept his throwing knives. "You want to leave Eisvaldr to . . ."

"Yes."

"While they're arguing about who's—"

"Yes."

466

"But you have nothing else, you know nothing else. I can't ask you—"

He kissed her again. Her lips grew against his. Swollen. Needy. Everything else ceased to exist. She dug her nails into his neck. Blood surged through her body. Converging in a hot knot. They tipped over onto their sides. She tore herself free to breathe.

"We're going to fall," she murmured hazily against his chin.

He smiled. It was the most beautiful and self-satisfied smile she'd ever seen. "We fell a long time ago, Hirka."

He picked up her bag and pulled her with him over the edge. Emboldened by and brimming with the Might. With lust for life. They fell. He rolled them over so he hit the ground first. In the center of the stone circle. She landed in his arms. They hugged her waist as if made for that purpose.

"So where are we going?" he asked.

It was the most wonderful question anyone had ever asked her. Hirka felt her eyes shine with joy. She looked at the floor. At the huge picture made up of small tiles. Faded. Damaged. Bloodstained. She reluctantly let go of him and walked around to look. Found a motif that appealed. A sleeping dragon.

Why not?

"Here?"

He grabbed her hand. They looked at each other. Broken. Whole. Ymling and half blindling. Assassin and healer. Never had the unknown felt less terrifying. She let the Might swell. Then they took a deep breath and started to run.

The space between worlds enveloped them.

ACKNOWLEDGMENTS

First and foremost, thanks to all my amazing superfans and ambassadors. All of you who couldn't shut up about *The Raven Rings*, and who have helped me on this adventure. Those of you who read, recommend, mention, and share. Those who cosplay, draw, sew, knit, create, compose, and tattoo. Those who've read the books multiple times and practically throw them at anyone who hasn't. Those who've nominated me for the Booksellers' Prize and the Book Bloggers' Prize two years in a row . . . I have no effing words. You've made the past few years the best of my life, something I'm afraid I'll never be able to repay you for. Thank you so, so much.

To the "Fantastic Four," my excellent author friends and those responsible for the most irresponsible chat history on Facebook: thank you from the bottom of my heart, dear Tone Almhjell (*The Twistrose Key*), Tonje Tornes (the Kire series), and Torbjørn Øverland Amundsen (*Bian Shen*). And to fanboy-in-chief and budding author Tom-Erik Fure. It's easy to forget to say thank you to people you talk to every day :)

Writing is one thing, but working in the wings are an incredible number of people who make this possible. Thank you to everyone at Gyldendal Norsk Forlag, who support me every day, especially my dear editor, Espen Dahl, and my retired editor, Marianne Koch Knudsen, who still works on the series. And of course to my rock at the publishing house, Eva C. Thesen.

A huge thank you to my wonderful agents, Lena Stjernström and Lotta Jämtsved Millberg, with Grand Agency in Sweden, who make sure that *The Raven Rings* can be read in more and more languages. And a heartfelt thank you to my publishers and translators abroad, a group of talented and devoted people who've jumped right in at the deep end, bringing the series to new readers in new countries.

The audiobooks have received a lot of praise, thanks to narrator Erich Kruse Nielsen, who continues to be exceptionally dedicated. The same can be said about my unsurpassed language guru, Alexander K. Lykke, who developed umǫni, the language of the deadborn.

I'd also like to thank Mats Strandberg and Sara Bergmark Elfgren, the lovely and generous authors of the *Engelsfors* trilogy, whom I've been fortunate enough to meet on a couple of occasions, always returning home happier and wiser. The same goes for the marvelous Lise Myhre, creator of *Nemi*. A unique and fascinating woman.

At the time of writing, I've had two fantastic launch parties. Those sorts of things don't happen by themselves. Thank you so much to every single person who's taken part, especially those who helped me with the arrangements: Frederik Kolderup and Jørgen Ljøstad of Non Dos; Jon Marius Slette, the inked chef; Anders Braathen, the hipsta chef; Ragni Hansen, who bakes the cakes; and photographer Kine Bakke, who immortalized the party for *The Rot*.

Party aside, thanks to Frank Cornelissen for the wine, Valrhona for the chocolate, and my eternal gratitude to my coffee dealers: Camillo Bastrup and Mean Bean in Kristiansand, places that really ought to charge me rent, and Supreme Roastworks, Fuglen, and Java in Oslo <3

As usual, thanks to Mom, family, and friends. Especially those I've promised to call or have coffee with, but haven't managed. And to my friend Rune Karolius, who I've now had coffee with after a ridiculous number of years, though the last time still feels like yesterday.

And last but not least: to my beloved Kim, who has given me food, wine, and love, and who has pointed me into the light and taken me for regular walks. I couldn't have done this without you.

GLOSSARY

HOUSE OF HOD

Hod   head of the house

Tyr   husband of Hod

Jór   son of Hod

HOUSE OF MODRASME

Modrasme   head of the house; grandmother of Graal

Raun   father of Graal

Uhere   mother of Graal

Graal   Hirka's father; exiled to the human world

Naiell   brother of Graal; killed by Rime

Vana   the youngest of the house

Skerri   member of the house; Graal's contact in Dreysíl

Hungl   servant to the House of Modrasme

Oni   servant to the House of Modrasme; tutor to Hirka

Skilborr   servant to the House of Modrasme

Tyla   servant to the House of Modrasme

THE FALLEN

Kolail   a disgraced warrior whose fate becomes entwined with Hirka's

Glimau

Skolm

OTHER DREYRI

Grid	friend to the House of Modrasme
the Seer	a wise and revered Dreyri

PLACES IN DREYSÍL

Criers' Rock	a crag from which pronouncements are made
Ginnungad	the first city of Dreysíl
Maknamorr	a hall in Nifel with a stone circle
Nifel	an abandoned city

CHARACTERS IN YM

Damayanti	a dancer; Graal's contact in Ym
Eirik Viljarsón	chieftain of Ravnhov
Hlosnian	a stone carver and stone whisperer
Ilume An-Elderin	Rime's grandmother; a deceased councillor
Kunte	servant to Darkdaggar
Kuro	a raven
Lindri	a teahouse owner
Meredir Beig	jarl of Urmunai
Ramoja	a ravener
Sylja Glimmeråsen	a girl from Elveroa
Tein	son of Eirik of Ravnhov
Urd Vanfarinn	a former councillor
Vetle	Ramoja's son

KOLKAGGA

Svarteld	former master
Orja	new master
Jeme	
Launhug	
Marrow	

COUNCILLORS OF YM

Rime An-Elderin	Sigra Kleiv
Jarladin An-Sarin	Eir Kobb
Garm Darkdaggar	Noldhe Saurpassarid
Miane Fell	Leivlugn Taid
Saulhe Jakinnin	Telja Vanfarinn
Tyrme Jekense	Freid Vangard

PLACES IN YM

the Alldjup	a gorge with the River Stryfe running through it
Blindból	a forbidden mountain range, where Kolkagga have their camps
Bromfjell	a mountain near Ravnhov with a stone circle
the Catgut	a main street in Mannfalla
Eisvaldr	a walled city within Mannfalla; the home of the Council
Elveroa	a small village where Hirka and Rime spent some of their childhoods
Mannfalla	the biggest city in Ym
Ravnhov	an independent settlement in the region of Foggard
the Rite Hall	a large ceremonial hall built around an old stone circle where the Rite occurred each year

CONCEPTS

binding	the act of using or drawing upon the Might
blindcraft	the feared and forbidden way in which the blind use the Might
child of Odin	someone from the human world, born without a tail, who cannot bind the Might; synonymous with embling, menskr, and the rot [derogatory]
the Council	the twelve individuals who interpret the word of the Seer and govern all of Ym

Dreyri	high-born Umpiri belonging to the named houses
Kolkagga	the Council's assassins
the Might	a powerful current of energy that can be drawn upon for strength
mightslinger	one who is able to use the Might to manipulate the physical world
raven rings	ancient stone circles through which, by binding the Might, people can move from one world to another
the Rite	a coming-of-age ceremony during which young people were given the Seer's blessing and protection
Slokna	where the dead go to rest
Umpiri	an ancient people from the land of Dreysíl; synonymous with nábyrn, deadborn, and the blind [all derogatory]
umǫni	language of the Umpiri
ymlings	people from the land of Ym

UMǪNI: THE LANGUAGE OF THE FIRST

Headwords unless otherwise noted are:

For nouns nom. sing., for verbs present infinitive (see Abbreviations below glossary). Nouns are listed with grammatical gender after the headword (m., f., or n.). Verbs are listed with inflectional class (v1, v2, or v3).

Entry	Explanation
bersarkí m.	stick fighter, one who fights in a ring with a staff
dósem v3	to be, copular verb; to exist
dreyri m.	one of the true First
esse acc. 2sing.	acc. sing. of *iss*
gweni m.	she (animal), female creature who is not *umpír*
iss 2sing.	you (implying that the object is of lower social status); cf. *esse*
iss ghené woykhail	you have betrayed us
-kes-	abbreviation of *kwessar*, prefixed to the name as a kind of designation
koy interj. indec.	see! (corresponds to Latin *ecce*!, English *lo*!)
koyem v1	to sense, to perceive with the senses
kroyo loc. sing.	where (referring to place): locative singular of *krai*
kűru m.	heart
kwainsair n.	cruel imprisonment; prison cell, prison
kwessar m.	fallen, of the fallen, one who is of the lowest social rank, casteless
kwo adv.	also, and, in addition

óz 1sing.	I
ozá 1sing.	I (implying that the speaker is of higher social status)
ozá kwo kwessere dósem	I am also one of the fallen
ǫni m.	tongue
pír m.	(Umpiri) blood
sekhes f.	suffering
sekhþainari m.	self-flagellator, one who wallows in (one's own) pain, woe-wallower
sulni m.	mayfly, small harmless insect
umkhadari m.	brother (formal)
umǫni m.	the Language, the Tongue, Umpiri's only tongue
umpír m.	one who is of the blood
wai det.	my
wári m	the Might
wokhem v3	betray, fail

Abbreviations

1/2/3	first/second/third person
acc.	accusative
adv.	adverb
det.	determiner
f.	feminine
ind.	indeclinable
interj.	interjection
loc.	locative
m.	masculine
n.	neuter
nom.	nominative
pl.	plural
sing.	singular
v1–v3	verb, inflectional class 1–3

The language of the blind was developed in collaboration with linguist Alexander K. Lykke.

Siri Pettersen made her sensational debut in 2013 with the Norwegian publication of *Odin's Child*, the first book in The Raven Rings trilogy, which has earned numerous awards and nominations at home and abroad. Siri has a background as a designer and comics creator. Her roots are in Finnsnes and Trondheim, but she now lives in Oslo, where you're likely to find her in a coffee shop. According to fellow writers, her superpower is "mega motivation"—the ability to inspire other creative souls. Visit her at SiriPettersen.com, or follow her on Twitter or Instagram @SiriPettersen.

Siân Mackie is a translator of Scandinavian literature into English. They were born in Scotland and have an MA in Scandinavian Studies and an MSc in Literary Translation as a Creative Practice from the University of Edinburgh. They have translated a wide range of works, from young adult and children's literature—including Ingunn Thon's *A Postcard to Ollis*, which was nominated for the 2021 Carnegie Medal—to thrillers and nonfiction. They live in Southampton on the south coast of England.

Paul Russell Garrett translates from Norwegian and Danish, with drama holding a particular interest for him. He has translated a dozen plays and has a further ten published translations to his name, including Lars Mytting's *The Sixteen Trees of the Somme*, long-listed for the International Dublin Literary Award, and a pair of novels by Christina Hesselholdt, *Companions* and *Vivian*. Originally from Vancouver, Paul is based in east London.

Siân and Paul have previously collaborated on a translation *of A Doll's House* by Henrik Ibsen, which was commissioned by Foreign Affairs theater company and performed in 2015 in east London. They hope their shared passion for bringing Norwegian literature to English-speaking audiences will continue in future collaborations.

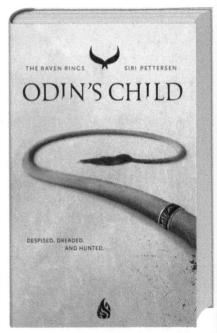